The
BATTLE
of the
CRATER

The
BATTLE
of the
CRATER

A NOVEL
OF THE
CIVIL WAR

NEWT GINGRICH,
WILLIAM R. FORSTCHEN
and ALBERT S. HANSER,
CONTRIBUTING EDITOR

THOMAS DUNNE BOOKS.
ST. MARTIN'S PRESS ✿ NEW YORK

THOMAS DUNNE BOOKS.
An imprint of St. Martin's Press.

THE BATTLE OF THE CRATER. Copyright © 2011 by Newt Gingrich and William R. Forstchen. All rights reserved. Printed in the United States of America. For information, address St. Martin's Press, 175 Fifth Avenue, New York, N.Y. 10010.

Illustrations on pages 13, 34, 79, 118, 120, 170, 297, 300, and 358 by Evalee Gertz.
Illustrations on pages 54, 65, 83, 135, 191, 234, and 254–55 courtesy of Applewood Books.
Illustration of President Lincoln on page 36 courtesy of the Library of Congress, Prints and Photographs Division, LC-DIG-pga-03412.
Illustration of Robert E. Lee on p. 282 courtesy of the Library of Congress, Prints and Photographs Division, LC-USZC2-2408.

www.thomasdunnebooks.com
www.stmartins.com

Library of Congress Cataloging-in-Publication Data

Gingrich, Newt.
    The battle of the crater : a novel / Newt Gingrich and William R. Forstchen.—1st ed.
        p. cm.
    ISBN 978-0-312-60710-4
    1. Petersburg Crater, Battle of, Va., 1864—Fiction.   I. Forstchen, William R.   II. Title.
    PS3557.I4945B38 2011
    813'.54—dc23

                                    2011026677

First Edition: November 2011

10   9   8   7   6   5   4   3   2   1

In memory of the men of the 4th Division,
IX Corps,
Army of the Potomac,
who on July 30, 1864, gave the "last full measure of devotion."

ACKNOWLEDGMENTS

When my coauthor, Bill Forstchen, and I first met early in 1994, I was Minority Whip, laying out the first stages of the "Contract with America" that would help propel my party to its first majority in the House of Representatives in nearly fifty years, and Bill was spending the summer in Washington D.C., working on his doctoral dissertation at the National Archives and the Library of Congress. He was breaking new ground in historical research with a first-of-its-kind study of a Civil War regiment of African American troops, the 28th United States Colored Troops (USCT) recruited out of Indiana. On more than one evening, he'd walk up from the National Archives to Capitol Hill, where over sandwiches we would talk about our projects. I found his topic fascinating even then, and a seed was planted that nearly two decades later became this novel.

We have written nine books together since then, but this one is unique and close to the heart for both of us. The role of the USCTs in winning the Civil War and preserving the Union is little known today. Few are aware that at the end of the war one out of every five men wearing Union blue was of African descent. Nearly two hundred African American regiments were mobilized for the field, with tens of thousands more blacks serving in the navy, which had been an integrated force ever since the American Revolution. The USCTs were the direct ancestors of the famed Buffalo Soldiers and the Tuskegee Airmen until full integration in all branches of service was finally achieved during the Truman administration. Bill's deep involvement in the study of this topic led him to write a young adult's novel on the 28th USCT, *We Look Like Men of War*, a decade ago. When, last year, we were approached by our publisher to write another book on the Civil War, the topic of the USCTs, and in particular their misdeployment in their largest single combat engagement, the Battle of the Crater, was our obvious first choice.

There are so many to thank for making this work possible. Two acknowledgments date back twenty years to Bill's dissertation committee, headed by his beloved mentor Professor Gunther Rothenberg, a famed military historian and the head of Bill's graduate program, Professor Gordon Mork. Long before heading to D.C. to wrap up his research among the pension records of "his" regiment, Bill found invaluable help with the teams at the Indiana State Archives, the Indiana Historical Society, and those working in the Indiana War Memorial, truly one of the finest of state military memorials, located in Indianapolis and its attached library and archive. The only surviving flag of the 28th USCT is located there and Bill speaks with deep emotion about the experience of actually being able to see it.

Personnel associated with the Petersburg National Battlefield Park have been most gracious and eager to see this work move forward, and, as will be explained in the postscript of this book, they are delighted to work with us to fulfill a long-held dream of ours to see a monument placed on the site of the Crater in memory of the thousands of men of the USCTs who fought on that field. As far as we have been able to find out, not a single battlefield monument to any USCT regiment exists on ground they fought for. We hope to rectify this long-overdue honor and acknowledgment.

Any book is a team effort involving the work of many more than just those names listed on the cover. As always we wish to extend our thanks to Pete Wolverton and Tom Dunne for their suggestion to write this book and their support of it. Anne Bensson, Pete's assistant, is a real gem, as are the copyeditor, Sui Mon Wu, the proofreader, Ted O'Keefe, and the production editor, David Stanford Burr. Additionally, we want to thank Ruth Chambers for identifying our talented illustrator, Evalee Gertz, and her gracious agent, Shelley Pina.

Within our own "teams" of course a thank-you to our agent Kathy Lubbers and our advisers Randy Evans and Stefan Passantino; the talented members of Gingrich Communications and Gingrich Productions, including: Catherine Butterworth, Joe DeSantis, Sylvia Garcia, Anna Haberlein, Vince Haley, Jorge Hurtado, Bess Kelly, Christina Maruna, Crissy Mas, Alicia Melvin, Kate Pietkiewicz, Michelle Selesky, Liz Wood, Ross Worthington, and interns Kathryn Erb, Justin Lafferty, and Lindsay Meyers.

We would be remiss if we did not thank the American Enterprise Institute and the very capable Caitlin Laverdiere, Brady Cassis, and AEI interns: Ellery Kauvar, Adam Minchew, Alex Hilliker, and Danielle Fezouati.

A special thank-you goes to Albert S. Hanser for his ongoing participation, partnership, and friendship in this and previous novels.

And, as always, thank you to our spouses and families for their patience when the next chapter "calls" and other things have to be put on hold "for just a few minutes longer—!" Thank you, Callista Gingrich, Krys Hanser, and Bill's daughter, Meghan, for your continued love and support throughout.

In closing we must offer a special acknowledgment to Major Garland White. Born a slave, he was the personal servant of Senator Robert Toombs (D-GA) at his Washington residence before the war. Escaping to freedom in Canada, White taught himself to read and write (a study of his letters between 1861–1865 revels a brilliant intellect always striving forward). He helped with the organization and mobilization of the famed 54th Massachusetts, the regiment immortalized in that wonderful film *Glory*, and was offered the rank of sergeant major, the highest position a "man of color" could hold at that time, but felt his duty was to press forward with helping to mobilize yet more regiments in the Midwest. The key figure in bringing the 28th USCT to life, he became its sergeant major and served gallantly with the regiment in every campaign. He was one of the first eleven men of African descent to be commissioned as chaplains/majors. For thirty years after the war he was a passionate activist for equal rights, fair treatment of "colored" veterans, and the fulfillment of the promises of the Thirteenth, Fourteenth, and Fifteenth

Amendments. He died in obscurity and poverty sometime in the 1890s in Washington, his burial site unknown to us.

We close this acknowledgment with a salute to this gallant man. Shortly after the war he wrote: "The historian's pen cannot fail to locate us somewhere among the good and great, who have fought and bled upon the altar of their country."

We pray that this work is a fulfillment of Major Garland White (28th USCT) and his dream and that the 28th's sacrifice shall be forever honored.

Thank you, Major White, and thanks to all those who served with you on that terrible day of July 30, 1864.

The
BATTLE
of the
CRATER

Siege of Petersburg
Actions June 30, 1864

0 _____ 2 km
0 _____ 2 miles

COLD HARBOR, VIRGINIA

JUNE 3, 1864

FRONT LINE OF THE SECOND CORPS,

ARMY OF THE POTOMAC

4:50 A.M.

✳✳✳✳✳✳✳✳✳✳✳✳✳✳✳✳✳✳✳✳✳✳✳✳✳✳

"TEN MINUTES TO GO, BOYS!"

James Reilly, artist and illustrator for *Harper's Weekly*, looked over his shoulder at the colonel, who was holding his pocket watch up in the pale light before dawn; the man's hands were shaking.

"Will someone tell that old bastard to shut the hell up?" a sergeant whispered.

"You go tell him, Patterson," another sergeant groaned.

"He's rattling the men."

"Oh, shut the hell up. We're all rattled," a young lieutenant sighed. "Now see to your men."

Reilly, having just reached the forward trench through a "covered way"—a communications trench from headquarters back in the secondary line—was confused as to which brigade and regiment he had fallen in with. Dawn was rapidly approaching and the dark shadows of huddled men, packed shoulder to shoulder inside the forward trench, were now being illuminated as they waited out the last minutes.

"Which regiment are you?" James asked the lieutenant.

"71st Pennsylvania. Why?"

"I'm looking for the 88th New York."

"Down the line a bit. I think next brigade on our left. Why you asking?"

"My brother's with them. Wanted to see him."

"You'll never get there in time. Who are you?"

"Just an illustrator with *Harper's Weekly.*"

Like many of his profession traveling with this hard-fighting army, he had adopted their garb: a now battered, faded shell jacket he had not changed out of or washed since the beginning of the campaign twenty-eight days ago, when the army had crossed the Rapidan, filled with high hopes. In the dark he was often mistaken for a soldier. It allowed him to blend in without notice, but at times it caused problems with some officious types demanding identification.

His black, wide-brimmed slouch hat had lost all semblance of shape, one side of it clipped off by a Rebel bullet when he had incautiously decided to peek up over the lip of a trench at Spotsylvania. His shirt beneath the shell jacket was a dingy gray and beginning to rot off his body. He had lost his pack during the Wilderness when the forest caught fire, driving him and the regiment he was sketching back in a hasty retreat. A correspondent with the *New York Herald* had taken pity on him and given him an oversized haversack, a writing board, some pencils, and a sheaf of papers.

"Illustrator?" the lieutenant muttered, stepping back slightly, looking at him appraisingly.

"Nine minutes, boys."

James nodded to the lieutenant, ignoring the colonel's nervous timekeeping. There was a time when such an introduction would have elicited delight, a demand to have a sketch made for the papers, or at least something to send back home to the folks.

Not this morning.

He half-expected the man to request a quick sketch. There was silence for a moment.

"Can I have a sheet of paper?"

James hesitated but could not refuse the appeal, though his supply was running short. He nodded, tore a sheet off his pad, and handed it to the lieutenant.

"Sergeant Patterson, I got some more paper."

The sergeant came over as the lieutenant took the oversized sheet, folded it into four sections, and tore it up, handing three to the sergeant, who grunted a thanks.

"Can I borrow your sketch board and a pencil for a moment?"

James handed them to the lieutenant, who then leaned against the wall of the trench and began to scribble something.

"Eight minutes, boys, eight minutes."

"Someone tell him to shut the hell up," came a whispered retort.

Finished writing, the lieutenant handed the board back.

James leaned over the lieutenant's shoulder to see what he had written.

Lieutenant Andrew McCloskey
25 Exchange St., Philadelphia
71st PA
Wife: Ellen. Son: Eli, 4 years old

"You got a pin, sir?"

James, unsure what was going on, could only shake his head.

"I got some primer wire, lieutenant," a young drummer boy offered, holding up a sliver of brass from an artillery primer. The lieutenant nodded a thanks, handed the piece of paper to the drummer, and squatted down. Laughing nervously, he admonished the boy not to stab him in the back as the youth pinned the slip of paper to the back of the lieutenant's jacket.

James stood silent, as the light continued to rise around them. He saw that all the men were doing the same with slips of paper, envelopes, or any scrap they could find.

The lieutenant thanked the boy, putting a firm hand on his shoulder.

"Remember, Billy, you stay here. Promise me, you stay here."

"No, sir," the boy's voice began to break.

"You stay here."

"I ain't no coward. I'm goin'."

"That is an order, son."

The boy began to cry.

"My God," James whispered, "what in hell is going on here?"

The lieutenant looked up at him.

"You know, don't you? You know what is over there."

He looked at the lip of the trench but was not fool enough to stick his head up for a quick glance. The sun was rising behind them; a head sticking up, silhouetted against the dawn sky, would be the last futile gesture he'd ever make. He had not survived three years of this war by making futile gestures and long ago had abandoned any shows of bravado. His job was to sketch the fight, which was easy enough to do once it was over . . . that, and to report privately to an old friend the truth of what he saw.

"They know we're coming. You could hear them digging all last night, laying out dead falls. One of my boys crept up to their line and said the trenches are layered three deep over there."

"I heard that, as well."

"Where?"

"I was back at headquarters."

"Six minutes, lads."

"Do those damn fools know?" the lieutenant pressed.

"Yes, they know."

"Damn them! Damn them!"

He did not bother to reply. Why tell them the truth now? He had a "friend," a contact with General Hancock's headquarters, well lubricated with an extra bottle of whiskey whenever James could find one. He had received the inside word. All corps commanders had said the attack was impossible. Two days ago the way to Richmond was wide open. Only six miles away, they were so close that with the westerly breeze yesterday evening he could hear the church bells.

But that was two days ago. Old Bobbie Lee had rushed in troops to block the way, and they had heard the Rebs had been digging ever since. Yesterday morning it just might have worked, but no firm plan had yet been laid. The assault by the entire army, a full-out frontal assault, had been postponed for twenty-four hours, to but a little more than five minutes from now.

"They say the plan will work."

Men around the two snorted derisively.

"We got twenty-five days left to our enlistments," the lieutenant hissed. "We served three years and only got twenty-five days left. They used to pull you off the line for your last month, but not now. Not now. We've been in every fight since the Peninsula. We was at Antietam, we charged at Fredericksburg, we held the center at Gettysburg. And this is what they do to us now? In our last twenty-five days?"

His voice was edged with hysteria, nearly breaking. A gray-bearded sergeant put a hand on the lieutenant's shoulder, and he braced himself.

"Now this."

"Five minutes."

"I don't give a damn if he is the colonel," the lieutenant hissed. "I'm ready to shut his damn mouth."

"Leave off him," the old sergeant whispered. "You know he ain't been right since the Wilderness."

James looked over at the sergeant.

"We lost half the regiment, including his youngest boy. The oldest was killed the year before at Gettysburg. He ain't been the same since, God bless him.

"Hey, it's Father Hagan, boys," the sergeant announced, nodding to the communications trench that James had crawled out of minutes before.

The priest was wearing an officer's jacket, unbuttoned, revealing his collar beneath and a crucifix resting on his breast.

"How are you, my lads?" his Irish brogue rang forth and for James, who was a son of Ireland as well, it was soothing to hear.

No one spoke.

"Boys, I am giving you all general absolution. Before I do so now, lads, empty those whiskey bottles," and he tried to force a laugh. "No devil's drink in your pockets when you go in."

A few laughed nervously in reply, and some men began drawing out bottles. The priest forced a good-natured smile as they passed the bottles around, draining the last of the contents and then throwing them out of the trench to shatter.

"Four minutes, me boys, four minutes."

Father Hagan looked back at the colonel, who was visibly trembling, and sighed.

"Now kneel, boys, and be quick."

Nearly all did so. It was a moment that James could not etch on paper but he knew would be etched into his soul. He went down on his knees and joined them, even though he would not be going into the maelstrom. The rising light of dawn arched the sky overhead with shimmering streaks of red and gold, tracing over the wisps of fog and smoke that hung in the still morning air.

"Ego te absólvo a peccátis tuis in nómine Patris, et Filii, et Spíritus Sancti."

As he whispered the prayer, Father Hagan repeatedly made the sign of the cross; nearly all the others were doing the same. Some of the men leaned forward, picking up a pinch of earth and putting it into their mouths, an all-so-ancient gesture and acknowledgment that from dust we have come and to dust we must return.

Finished with the absolution, the priest gazed upon them.

"God be with you, boys, and those who fall, tonight you shall sup in Paradise."

Usually such words from a chaplain would elicit a chuckle, an invite for the priest to go along with them, but all knew his post was with the surgeon. His duty was to help there; to comfort the dying that were dragged back to face the blade and the saw, to offer final words of comfort and blessing as life slipped away.

There was no joking this morning, only a nervous silence.

"I must get to the rest of the regiment, boys," the chaplain said, his voice nearly breaking. "God be with you."

He edged his way through the crowd and pressed on down the

trench. James could hear him. "Kneel, boys, and let me give you general absolution. God bless you, my brave lads."

"Two minutes! Fix bayonets and form up!"

There were sighs of relief from some, the tension nearly at an end. The hiss of bayonets being drawn and locked into place over the muzzles of rifles was audible above the soldiers' rustling. Some were praying out loud. A man backed away from the forward edge of the trench, sobbing. There was no problem with the sergeant; he was ignored. Several leaned forward and vomited. A man cursed as he was splattered and then turned to offer a bracing arm to his terrified friend.

The colonel, still holding his watch, started to push down the line. James caught a glimpse of the man's face—ashen, lips trembling. His anger toward the unnerved colonel was gone, replaced with pity. The man's nerves were shot: one charge too many, one death too many, had at last consumed him.

Some of the men had rosary beads out, muttering Hail Marys; others were stoic, silent. The lieutenant was up by his side.

"Keep Billy here," and he nodded back to the drummer boy, who sat slumped over against the back of the trench, crying.

James nodded.

There was a distant cry and seconds later the hum of bullets was overheard. Fifty-eight-caliber minié balls began to snap overhead. The Rebs knew what was coming. He could picture them less than two hundred yards away, rifle barrels resting on the lip of their trenches, hammers cocked. The more excitable began to lay down fire and a Rebel yell began to swell up—a taunting challenge.

"One minute. Uncase the colors! And God be with you, boys!"

The colonel—sword drawn, a foot resting on a short trench ladder, hand poised on the top rung—was still holding his watch. Behind him, the regimental flag-bearers pulled the coverings off their tattered colors—the National Flag and the dark blue flag of New York. Emblazoned on them were the names of past glory, from Fair Oaks to Gettysburg. They had not bothered to note the half-dozen fights of the past month; there was no time to do so . . . and no desire. For no one had yet determined if the battles had been victories, defeats, or just senseless bloodlettings with no winners or losers. James looked at the flags as they were held up high. Within seconds the silken folds were struck a dozen times, tattering them into barely recognizable shreds.

What caught James's eye, what he could not tear his gaze away from now that they were poised and ready, were the slips of paper pinned to the men's backs, every single one of them. Men who had braved the cornfield of Antietam, had swept forward at Fredericksburg, had covered the retreat at Chancellorsville, and already, as the stuff of legends, had stood against Pickett's Charge. This was now their Pickett's Charge, but they would not go forward with a cheer and a deep belief in victory, as did the boys of Virginia and North Carolina on that sunlit field in Pennsylvania a year ago. Three years had taught them much. It had taught them that this morning they would die.

Cannon fire, a battery firing to the east, back at the secondary line, was followed seconds later by the roar of a hundred more guns up and down the Union line. There would be no preparatory bombardment. The single massed salvo was the signal to begin the charge for miles along the entire front. There was a time when such charges had a purpose and a hope, when this war had been fought out in the open, volley lines facing volley lines. But a battle had not been fought like that since Gettysburg.

Perhaps Gettysburg had indeed been the last battle of a different age. It was now a war of digging, of trenches, revetments, moats, and deadfalls. Give the enemy two days, and they would construct two or three lines of trenches in depth. No artillery could dislodge that, and in reality no charge or bayonet could dislodge it, either, if the men behind the barricades held their nerve. Facing them were the veterans of the Army of Northern Virginia. They had nerve aplenty.

It seemed that only the high command in their tents behind the line still believed in the bayonet. But the men around James had lived the last year of warfare and knew far better about the new reality.

"71st! Charge, boys, charge!"

The colonel, his voice strangled, mounted the ladder. Before his foot even reached the top rung he was already pitching over backward, forehead shattered, his agony ended.

"Charge!"

Some went up the ladders, others vaulted up onto the lip of the trench.

The lieutenant looked back at James.

"Draw the truth, artist. Draw the truth!"

He went up the ladder.

A thunderous roar erupted. The sky overhead came alive with bullets clipping the air overhead, along with canister rounds hissing, mingled with the horrid sound of bullets striking flesh. Men were collapsing, falling back into the trench, or tumbling back to the earth like insects caught in a burst of flame. Men were screaming; a sergeant reaching out to pull the lieutenant up doubled over, collapsing; the lieutenant, letting go of the sergeant's grasp, held high his own sword.

"Come on, boys! Come on!" The charge swept forward.

James had to look even though he already knew what he would see. But he had to tell his friend the truth, what he had actually seen. Swallowing hard, he mounted the ladder, climbing halfway out of the trench, crouching low. The lip of the trench was a writhing mass of dead and wounded. The charge was going forward; no lines, just a mass of men. In the dawn light, their ragged blue uniforms looked black with shades of dark brown and gray. And on each back was a piece of paper. He focused on a man for an instant, the paper fluttering—blown off as a bullet exploded out of his back, the man collapsing. They were not falling by ones and twos—they were collapsing by the dozens with each step of the advance. They were falling all up and down the line as far as he could see, until the vast stage was concealed by morning mist and smoke. The charge was going forward.

No cheers. This sound was different, sending a shiver of anger through him. The men were not cheering, some were braying like sheep. They were going forward as ordered but now voicing a final contempt for those who had ordered this . . . brave men, three-year veterans of the Union Army of the Potomac *baa*-ing like sheep even as they charged.

The original flag-bearers for the regiment were down. Others picked up the colors, advanced a few paces, and then collapsed as well.

The charge was barely fifty yards from the trenches and already disintegrating. The Rebel lines were concealed in roiling clouds of yellow-gray smoke, illuminated with hundreds of flashes of light. There was a continuous roar punctuated by blasts of artillery from their reserve line, which was higher up and a hundred yards back.

And then it was over. The lieutenant holding the national colors went down on his knees, struggling to hold the flag aloft. He was hit several more times and fell; the flag lay in the dust. There was no one left to pick it up.

Hundreds were down on the field, not a single man still standing. Some had gone to ground and by ones and twos, crouched low, tried to run back toward their trench. A burst of fire and they, too, collapsed.

To his right came a flare of thunder; another regiment, come up from the reserve trench, was trying to go forward. The Rebels to James's front shifted their aim, pouring enfilading fire into the flank of the charge. It broke apart in a matter of seconds, the survivors turning about, diving back into the trench for protection.

Fire slackened. A Rebel yell erupted but somehow it was muted, no roar of triumph like he had heard when they swept the field at Chancellorsville and Second Manassas.

"For Christ's sake!" came a cry. "This is murder! For Christ's sake you damn Yankees, go back. Go back!"

Not everyone felt the same compassion. Those with colder hearts gunned down wounded soldiers who stood and tried to hobble back. Three years of war had left an indelible hole in such things as chivalry and pity for far too many.

A bullet slapped close to James's face, and he realized that for some time he had been crouching atop the lip of the trench. A plume of dirt snapped up by his bent knee. He tumbled over, falling back into the trench, landing on the body of man who had been hit in the chest, driving out the last gasp of air from the bloody corpse.

Young Billy stood, looking up at the lip of the trench, sobbing, while trying to take hold of the ladder with the hope of going up.

"I'm not a coward, I'm not a coward," he babbled. James grabbed hold of him, pulling him back. The boy was shaking like a leaf. He pushed him back and set him against the opposite wall.

"You are not a coward, son. The wounded need your help."

The boy looked at him wide-eyed. The front of his trousers were soaked. In his terror he had wet himself.

The boy saw him gaze down, realized his humiliation, and, collapsing, he curled up and continued to sob.

"I absolve you in the name of the Father . . ."

He turned away from Billy. Father Hagan was making his way up the trench, kneeling by each of the fallen, bending low to kiss a forehead, making the sign of the cross, crawling a few feet to the next man to do the same . . . and the same yet again.

"Merciful God, what have we done?"

James looked up. It was General Horace Porter, trusted friend and adjutant of General Ulysses Grant. Emerging from the communications trench he stood in silence, obviously overwhelmed.

James stood, the general coming toward him, shuffling as if stricken.

"My God, what have we done?"

"You've killed an army, that's what you've done," James hissed.

Porter focused on him for a moment; there was a flash of recognition for the artist from *Harper's Weekly*.

"I told Grant, I told him and Meade . . ." and then his voice trailed off.

He knew Porter to be a good man, one who would stay loyal to his general.

"I told him . . ." and again his voice dropped.

"Told him what?"

Porter stood silent.

He sighed and lowered his head.

"This war will go on forever," and his voice was choked.

"No," James sighed. "We will lose if it goes on like this; then it will end."

He started back toward the trench leading to the rear, but a column of men were emerging, heads bent low, blocking his way.

"What is this?" James cried.

"The next wave," was all Porter could say.

"May God forgive you." It was Father Hagan, glaring at Porter, eyes cold.

"Yes, Father. May he forgive us all."

The last of the regiment, another veteran unit—colors of the 12th New Jersey as tattered as those of the 23rd New York—emerged from the communications trench, filing to their right, away from James. On the back of each was pinned a slip of paper: FRANK SMITH, 43 BROAD ST., NEWARK NEW JERSEY, 12TH NEW JERSEY, MOTHER: RACHEL; CHARLES ANDREWS, NO FAMILY BURY ME WITH MY COMRADES . . .

A procession of the walking dead.

James forced himself to remember one of the two reasons he was there that day. Lifting up his sketch board and using a blunt pencil— the one the now-dead lieutenant had handed back—he drew a few quick lines. Jotting down notes and a numbered code he and other artists at the front used to indicate where to put the enemy line, how many men were in the charge, where to put the colors . . . all to be turned into rigid steel engravings, churned out by his employers in New York; rigid steel engravings, of rigid men, in lockstep, going forward to yet another victory. The engravers, turning out a dozen etchings a week for the public, could never possibly capture the impossible contours of the dead or the hollow eyes of a priest—and besides, the paper was anti-Catholic and did not show priests favorably. It could not capture the urine-stained drummer boy, curled up, sobbing, nor would it ever show a general in shocked grief, or a colonel who had lost his nerve and yet still tried to lead. In his newspaper, generals were wise and heroic; colonels poised with swords raised.

And how—how could he ever capture the image frozen into his heart forever? That field just over the lip of the trench. The hundreds of bodies, each with a slip of paper pinned to his back ... PATRICK CALLAHAN, 44 PEARL ST., NEW YORK CITY, 23RD REG'T. WIFE: KATHY, FOUR CHILDREN ... QUENTIN O'NEAL ... ROBERT THOMPSON ... So many names. The first stirring of morning breeze was setting the slips of paper fluttering.

How could he ever name them all?

But there was someone he could tell it to. The other reason he

was here, which no one but his friend knew. The communications trench to the rear was clear now, except for the walking wounded who filled its shadowy darkness; walking, some crawling, men helping each other. He turned back and grabbed the drummer boy.

"Come along, son. You can help this man like the brave lad you are."

Stifling back his sobs, the boy put his arm around a man who was hobbling on one foot, his left leg a mangled wreck below the knee.

"God bless ya, laddie."

In the half-light of the covered trench he continued to sketch even as he walked, turning a page, drawing quick outlines of the boy and the wounded soldier leaning on him: the boy crying, the wounded man murmuring words of comfort even as he left a trail of blood with each step.

How could *Harper's* capture in its engravings the blood—the blood that was in drips, trails, and pools within the trench? The body of a man who had collapsed and was dead, face down in the trampled earth? TIM KINDRAID . . . 21 EXCHANGE ST., PORTLAND, 17TH MAINE, . . . MOTHER: ELIZABETH, FATHER: WILLIAM.

Gunfire rose up again. A second wave going in, and in less than a minute, dropped off. He hoped the men had refused to go, or had just made a sham of it for a moment to please those in the rear and then ducked back down.

Most of the veterans had learned that game by now. Their generals might urge, but they knew the reality far better. After the annihilation of the first wave, no man with any sense of battle would go into that killing ground, no matter who ordered it. This army was fought out.

James reached the end of the communications trench, six hundred yards behind the line, out in the open. Shots could reach this range and reserve regiments were down on the ground. With bayonets, canteen halves, the occasional small pick or shovel, they were already digging in.

He caught a glimpse of them. Hancock, commander of the Second Corps, still limping from the wound that had nearly killed him at Gettysburg, was pacing back and forth, head lowered. Was the man crying?

Grant, and Meade by his side, both with field glasses raised, and staff around them. In an outer circle, there were correspondents and the usual hangers-on.

"What was it like up there?"

It was his friend Jenkins with the *New York Herald.*

"Why ask me? Go up yourself and take a damn good look," James snapped.

Jenkins shook his head.

"They won't let us. Provost guards have been ordered to stop us. It looks bad, James. They said we'd be in Richmond by noon and the war over."

His voice trailed off, and he gazed toward the smoke-shrouded front.

James actually laughed derisively.

Jenkins motioned to his sketch board and he offered it over.

"How bad was it?"

James could not reply, as he was afraid he'd break.

"What's this?" asked Jenkins, pointing at a sketch at the corner. "Who is 'Lieutenant' . . ." he hesitated, trying to read the hurried print, "'McCloskey'?"

James snatched the sketch board back.

"He's dead. They're all dead."

Jenkins said nothing as he reached into his breast pocket and pulled out a flask, unscrewing the cap and offering it over.

James took a long, grateful drink.

"Thanks," he whispered.

"Looks like they've made some decision," Jenkins said, nodding back to Grant and Meade, who had lowered their glasses, staff around them mounting up, hurrying off with orders.

"I better go see what's up," Jenkins replied.

"Don't bother."

"Why?"

"I can tell you already."

"Tell me what."

"We've lost the battle. Richmond will hold, and come November Lincoln will be defeated, and we will lose the war."

Jenkins stood silent, and uncorking the flask, he drained the rest of it off.

"Coming with me?"

James shook his head and flinched slightly as battery after battery along the secondary line opened fire again.

He started to walk away.

"You heading back to New York to report? If so, would you carry a dispatch for me? Word is that headquarters is blocking us from filing reports from here."

"No, Washington," replied James.

"Why there?"

"A friend. I'm going to see a friend, that's all."

"Who?"

"Just a friend. Be careful out there, Jenkins. Don't stop a bullet, it's bad press when a reporter gets killed."

Jenkins forced a smile and turned away as James walked off.

The sun was up, a red ball of glaring heat. In a few hours the bodies on the field would begin to swell, and by evening the cloying smell would carpet the battlefield, as it did all battlefields of this war, of any war. By the following morning, the uniforms they wore would burst at the seams, the pieces of paper pinned to their backs forgotten. When a truce was finally called, burial details would go forward with their faces covered with rags drenched in coal oil to block the stench. They would dig long trenches, no more than a foot or two deep, and then dump the bodies in and cover them over.

James would leave it behind for now. By tomorrow night he would be at the Willard Hotel in Washington, across the street from the White House, where his friend Abraham Lincoln now lived and was waiting for his confidential report . . . his friend who would want the truth about what happened here at Cold Harbor, Virginia, on this morning of June 3, 1864.

CHAPTER ONE

ARLINGTON, VIRGINIA
JUNE 6, 1864
THE ESTATE OF GENERAL ROBERT E. LEE
DAWN

✳✳✳✳✳✳✳✳✳✳✳✳✳✳✳✳✳✳✳✳✳✳✳✳✳

"HERE THEY COME, PARSON."

Sergeant Major Garland White, 28th United States Colored Troops, turned from his labors and looked to where Jeremiah Smith, a private from Company A, was pointing north to the road leading down from the "Iron Bridge" across the Potomac.

It had been raining most of the night, a slow steady drenching downpour out of the east. It had done little to drop the temperature and now added to the misery of the men of the 28th who had been out toiling by lantern light since midnight. The Potomac was concealed beneath coiling fog and mists rising up from the river, shrouding the capital city on the opposite shore.

The first of a long line of ambulances, emerging out of the mists, was drawn by two mules, ghostlike in the morning light, followed by another and another, mud splashing up from the hooves of the mules and the wheels of the wagons.

"Back to it, Jeremiah. I want it dug straight."

"Ain't no difference, parson, we be filling it back up shortly."

He put a fatherly hand on Jeremiah's shoulder, guiding him back to the hole, seven feet by three and supposedly six feet deep.

"It's not parson, it's sergeant major now," Garland said. "Do as you are ordered; back down there you go."

Jeremiah looked at him sullenly, as Garland released his hold on Jeremiah and reached down to lend a hand to Private Thompson, who had finished his half hour stint in the hole.

"Come on, Willie, take a quick break, there's hot coffee under the tarp." He helped the private, covered head to foot in warm clinging mud, out of the ground and pointed to where the regimental cooks had ten-gallon vats of the brew waiting.

"Thank ya, Reverend . . . I mean, Sergeant Major, sir."

"I'm a sergeant major, not a sir, save that for . . . the officers." He almost said, "your boss man," but caught himself.

Taking Willie's shovel, he handed it to Jeremiah and helped him slip down into the hole.

"Hurry it up, men," Garland announced, stepping back, his voice carrying to the rest of the regiment. "They're almost here, and I want this done right and proper now."

"Sergeant Major, damn it, it's like trying to shovel out the Wabash River."

Garland turned, struggling to control his anger as he gazed down at Corporal Turner in the next hole over. He bent over at the waist, fixing the corporal with an icy gaze.

"Corporal Turner," he hissed, voice pitched low, remembering it was not proper to reprimand another noncommissioned officer in front of the men, or the officers for that matter. "I will not tolerate profanity in my presence. Next, I will not tolerate profanity on this ground, which is consecrated and . . ."

He hesitated.

"Damn it, I will not tolerate beefing from someone who is supposed to lead. If you don't like that, Corporal, you can climb out of there right now, take off those two stripes, and I'll find someone else to wear them."

He gazed down at the mud-drenched corporal.

"Do I make myself clear, Corporal, or is it Private?"

"Yes, Sergeant Major."

"You can stay down there and keep digging until I tell you different."

Turner said nothing, though the next shovelful up, containing more water than muddy earth, landed within inches of Garland's feet.

Garland turned away and noticed that young Lieutenant James Grant was looking his way. The lieutenant gave a nod of approval and turned away, going back under the tarpaulin where the officers of the regiment had gathered while the men labored.

Grant had wanted to "dig in" with the rest of the men of his company. As the detail started their labors in the pouring rain, however, Garland heard Colonel Charles Russell, commander of their regiment, restraining Grant, saying that this was an enlisted man's job, besides, the lieutenant had to keep his uniform relatively unspoiled for the brief ceremony which would commence in a few minutes. Grant was a good man, a three-year veteran of the war, who at heart still acted as if he were a sergeant. He led by example and Garland deeply respected him for that, even though he was not much more than a lad of twenty.

He left Turner's hole, and continued down the long line—a long line of seventy-one graves.

Seventy-one graves for seventy-one men—men who had died the previous day in the dozen military hospitals that ringed the city of Washington. Seventy-one graves for men wounded in the grueling campaign, which had started exactly one month ago today, on May 6th. Seventy-one graves for men transported back across rutted roads and aboard hospital ships from the Wilderness, Spotsylvania, the North Anna, and according to the newspaper reports, a new battlefield just six miles short of Richmond at a place called Cold Harbor. Graves for men who had survived all that, only to die in Washington and now be buried here.

Garland's regiment had come to this city from Indianapolis at the beginning of May. Five months of training had prepared them for combat, for battles that every last man of them longed for, a chance to prove themselves, a chance to show that they were of the same blood as their comrades with the 54th Massachusetts. They wanted to show that they were as worthy of the honor of serving as any other citizen, white or black, and that they were therefore worthy of the rights of freemen.

Across the cold months of drills during their winter of recruitment and mobilization back in Indiana, Garland had joined their ranks as the "parson," but had soon earned the coveted chevrons of a sergeant major, the highest rank a colored man could hold in this army. In their nightly prayer services, he had dwelled again and again on Psalm 91, calling it the soldier's psalm, and entreated his men to memorize it to prepare themselves for the battles to come. He had promised them battle, and they were eager for it, as ready as any regiment had ever been.

On the day they arrived in Washington, he had still promised it. They detrained and marched down Pennsylvania Avenue to the cheers of the colored in the city and many of the white folks as well.

And then they had been marched here, to this place called Arlington, the plantation once owned by General Lee. Muskets had been stacked, they had been handed shovels, and told to dig—not fortifications, but graves.

He had cajoled them, told them that to do this fittingly was an honor while they waited for the call to join the army on the front lines. That was a month ago—a long month of a dreadful routine. Each evening a telegram would be sent over, informing the colored troops of this and of two other regiments stationed here how many graves were to be dug during the night, in preparation for the funeral train of mule-drawn ambulances that would arrive at dawn.

The digging was done during the night so that this grisly task and the horrific numbers could at least in some way be concealed. That had been obvious to all of them. Bring the dead out quietly; put them in the ground quietly. The number this morning was typical, not as bad as the week after the Wilderness, when the daily number had been a hundred or more. Tonight was seventy-one graves, a typical night for those who died in Washington, and only one regiment, his regiment, had drawn the detail. Only the good Lord knew how many were being buried up on the front lines.

There were rumors afloat that three days ago, up in front of Richmond, it had numbered in the thousands.

Once the graves were filled and covered over, the men would be paraded back to their barracks. First, clean the mud-drenched uniforms, then breakfast. Most of the men of Garland's regiment had been freemen living around Indianapolis when the regiment was mobilized last December and were used to hard labor. As for those who had escaped from bondage, the labor was typical of any day in slavery, but a breakfast of fried salt pork, grits, fresh bread or hardtack, and coffee, *real* coffee—not the slave brew of chickory and various roots—was an absolute luxury. But for men who had trained for and had expected war, morale was at rock bottom.

After breakfast they would be allowed six hours of sleep, then fall out for inspection, and a few hours drill. Then the next telegram would arrive, reporting how many graves were to be dug that night. Muskets would be exchanged for shovels and picks, and then they would march down to what had once been the front lawn of Robert E. Lee's family home.

The rain came down in a steady, warm flow; not at all refreshing. Rivulets of muddy water were pouring off the piled-up earth by each grave, following the laws of gravity, and thus flowing over the lips of the graves and cascading onto the drenched kepis, upturned collars, and backs of the laboring men.

Their regimental commander, Colonel Russell, stood with the other officers; he was silent beneath a vast tarpaulin, sagging with the weight of wet canvas. Occasionally one of the company commanders would step out to walk down the line, offering a few words of encouragement, and then retreat back to cover.

Fog had concealed the ambulances, but Garland knew they were drawing closer. They only had minutes left to complete their tasks, and the moment he dreaded came as General Meigs, commander of the garrison of Washington, emerged out of the coiling mist. He was coming down from General Lee's mansion, followed by several of his staff. The men behind him sat hunched over in their saddles with hat brims pulled low against the easterly breeze, which carried the lashing rain.

Meigs slowed as he weaved his way past the mounds of hundreds of graves that had been dug over the previous month. The raw earth, turned to rivers of mud, was running off the mounds. The older graves were already starting to sink in, and the bodies concealed below returning to the earth. All was mud, and in the damp, fog-shrouded world, a dank unsettling musty smell hung in the air.

Meigs reached the end of the row which had been dug during the night. Colonel Russell, coming out to meet him, followed by the other officers of the 28th, saluted and waited for this morning's criticism.

"The line doesn't look straight to me, Colonel Russell," Meigs announced, voice high-pitched with a nasally twang.

"Sir, I personally supervised the laying out and alignment for seventy-one graves as ordered."

Meigs sniffed. It was the same complaint every morning.

He slowly rode down the line. Garland quickly scanned his men. Those actually down in the graves, still digging, were excused from coming to attention and saluting; besides, it was a rather macabre, even absurd sight to see a man standing chin deep in a grave saluting a general riding by on a horse. However, those above ground did as expected, and Garland nodded inwardly. They were acting like soldiers even when drenched and covered in mud.

Meigs said nothing as their own colonel walked beside him, and that bothered Garland. Russell was a good man: fair, even respectful of the men in his charge, proud of them and eager to show what they could do with a rifle rather than a shovel. Yet it was always the same. Meigs reached the end of the row and turned to look back.

"I tell you, Russell, the line is not straight, and I will not stand for that again. And the graves, can't your damn darkies dig a proper six-foot grave?"

Of course none of the enlisted men spoke. They had borne worse insults nearly every day of their lives.

"Sir, it has been raining steady, nearly a downpour all night. My men know their responsibility here and respect it. At this moment, we need buckets more than we need shovels," he paused. "Sir."

Meigs gazed down coldly.

"I will accept no excuses, Colonel."

"I am offering none, sir."

Even as the two officers confronted each other, shovels continued to rise and fall rhythmically, a few of the men whispering shanties and work songs as they labored.

Meigs gazed coldly at Russell and then to the fog-shrouded road. The ambulances were again visible, now only a few hundred yards away.

"This job will have to be sufficient, though I do not approve of it," Meigs announced. "Order your men to get ready."

Russell offered a salute as Meigs rode over to the drooping tarpaulin to dismount and escape the rain.

"Sergeant Major White!"

Garland, standing a respectful distance to one side during the confrontation, double-timed over with mud splashing, came to attention, and saluted.

"Order the men out of the graves and prepare for burial detail."

"Yes, sir."

Garland turned and shouted the order.

The sight which confronted him in the gray light of early dawn chilled him. Men—his men—his comrades, were crawling up out of the ground, covered head to toe in mud. They looked to his faithful eyes and soul as if the graves had just burst asunder on the Day of Judgment, the saved and the damned answering the call of the last trumpet to arise.

He quickly unbuttoned his uniform and wiped his dirt-encrusted hands on his vest, which was somewhat clean. He then reached into his breast pocket to pull out a fresh pair of white linen gloves. They were wet but unstained.

The men began to form up, a detail of four or five by each grave; men putting on their four-button dark-blue uniform jackets, helping each other to wipe off some of the mud. It was a futile gesture.

Well drilled, one man from each grave detail fetched a couple of fifteen-foot lengths of rope and fell back into formation.

The first of the ambulances turned off the river road and up the muddy track to the lower field of Arlington. The lead mules were struggling with their burden, slipping in the mud; the driver, snapping a whip, cursed them soundly.

As the first wagon came to a stop down at the end of the line of graves, Garland went down to meet it. The driver sat motionless, head bent over, cupping his hands as he struck a match to light the stub of a cigar, not bothering to help unload.

The details from the first four graves went to the back of the ambulance, dropping the tailgate open.

Four rough-hewn pine coffins and four simple crosses lay within, each cross stenciled with a name, date of birth, the year 1864, and a regimental number.

The coffins were not stamped with names. The graves would have to be nameless, and that deeply troubled Garland. At most of the hospital morgues, someone would pencil the dead man's name on the lid of the rough-hewn coffin. Some, like this load, did not. Four nameless coffins, four crosses that did bear names. In this assembly line of death, once the coffins we carried out of the morgues, the overworked orderlies and drivers usually just tossed the coffins on, and then piled the crosses atop them, to rattle off in the long nighttime drive out beyond the city. It was always done at night; the authorities did not want people to see this daily ritual, especially over this last month with its tide of death.

"Show some respect, boys," Garland sighed. "Try and match the crosses up as best you can. Corporal Turner, you can read. See if there's any markings on the coffins."

The second ambulance pulled up, then the third and the fourth. Garland went to each, motioning over his exhausted diggers to pull out the coffins and carry them the last few feet. There was no ceremony. Mud-splattered men, slipping and sliding, rough-made coffins. He had heard a contractor got $1.25 for each one; rope handles tacked onto the coffins cost 15 cents extra, so that had been stopped. The men struggled to hold on to their burdens as they placed them beside the open muddy graves.

The team lugging a coffin from the fourth ambulance slipped, dropping its burden, and the tacked-down lid broke open. A couple of the men gasped, recoiling at the face peering out at them. Garland rushed over to help them lift it back up, ruining another pair of expensive gloves as he did so. He was joined by Lieutenant Grant, who offered soothing words to one of the bearers who began to sob, saying a dead man had looked into his eyes.

He heard a muffled curse from where the officers waited. It was General Meigs commenting on the "superstitions of these men of yours, Russell."

One by one the coffins were placed beside their graves. The first ambulance driver, his charges removed, cracked his whip without a word and started back across the field. Garland worked his way down the row of ambulances, whispering calming words of encouragement, when to his horror he saw that there was an additional ambulance parked beyond the row of seventy-one graves.

No one moved toward it; the driver was half standing.

"Damn it, you benighted bastards, get these bodies out. I'm done for the night and want to go home."

It had happened again. More had died during the night and word had not been sent over.

He could hear Meigs snarling an order to Russell, who came out from under the tarpaulin and up to Garland's side.

"Sergeant Major. See to those bodies please."

Garland hesitated.

"Two to a grave, sir?"

He could see the look of resignation.

"Yes, Sergeant, two to a grave; we'll sort it out later."

Sort it out later. It meant that sometime, a day, perhaps a week from now, maybe months from now, someone, most likely the men of this regiment, would have to dig the graves out, remove the decaying remains, and move them.

Garland motioned the details from the last four graves over and personally went to drop the tailgate. Even he recoiled at what greeted him. Whatever hospital had sent these men over had run out of coffins, yet again. The four dead within were wrapped in the bedsheets on which they had died. Bare feet were sticking out—the feet of three of the dead. The fourth man had suffered amputation of both feet, and from the stench it was evident that he had died of gangrene. One of the men of his detail turned away, sobbing and beginning to vomit. The others hesitated to touch the fourth body. Garland reached into the ambulance and pulled the burden out. Even without his legs the man was heavy, and Garland struggled to remain upright. Helping hands reached out to him, and he looked into the eyes of Lieutenant Grant.

Grant struggled to offer a reassuring smile.

"I've done this before," he whispered. "Antietam, Gettysburg. I can handle it. See to your men, Sergeant."

"Please let me help."

Beside Grant stood a tall lanky man, wearing a filth-encrusted officer's eleven-button jacket, hatless in the rain, dark red or perhaps brown hair plastered to his skull. His green eyes were deep set but hollow, looking as if he had not slept in days, and his face was pale, unshaved for at least a week or more. An oversized haversack dangled off his right hip, and his well-made, knee-high boots were scuffed and torn, as were his dark brown nonmilitary trousers.

He reached out to join the two as they carried the body over to one of the open graves and carefully set it down beside a coffin. All saw it, and Garland had to bite his lip to hold back the emotion of the moment. Young Grant was a veteran, and he wondered at that instant how many men he had carried in that same way. He did not know the civilian, who stepped back with bowed head, his shoulders beginning to shake.

"Sergeant Major." He turned; and it was Colonel Russell who stood with features taut. "After Fredericksburg, we stacked men three deep in open trenches. The ground was frozen solid and we had to pickax the holes. Bury them now. Tonight we'll try and give them their own graves. We can't leave them out here like this, and I want the men back in barracks as soon as possible and out of this weather. Enough of you are sick already."

"Battalion, attention!"

It was the chaplain for the cemetery, who had come out from under the tarpaulin and now stood in the middle of the row of open graves, open Bible in hand.

The rain had slackened somewhat, but as it did so the fog roiling up from the Potomac thickened, creeping up from its marshy banks, coiling around the assembly, and filling the graves with mist.

The chaplain raised his Bible, and an orderly came over with an open umbrella to ward off the rain. The man's high, nasal voice barely carried as he hurriedly raced through the all-too-brief service. Finishing with an "Amen," he turned and went back under the tarp. A guard detail dressed in clean uniforms from the 29th United States Colored—a regiment lucky enough to receive a detail to garrison a nearby fort, rather than the digging detail here—raised their rifles—the first rank firing, then the second, and then the third—the blank charges sounding dull and hollow.

The ceremony was over.

"Colonel Russell." It was General Meigs, motioning their commander to come over to his side. Russell did as ordered; there was a brief moment of conversation before Meigs handed a folded sheet of paper to Russell, and then, not even bothering to acknowledge the colonel's salute, Meigs rode off, heading back up to the mansion where a dry uniform and a warm breakfast awaited.

For the men of the 28th, however, there were still final labors to perform. Snaking the two lengths of rope under each coffin, the men began to lower the coffins into the ground. Garland stayed at the far end of the line to supervise the lowering of the coffins. After they were placed in the ground, the newest bodies, those wrapped in sheets, were lowered. At the third grave the civilian stood by the lip of the grave while Lieutenant Grant ensured that the body was lowered in with some semblance of respect.

As coffins reached the bottom of the graves, they sank into the muck, water rising up around them. The sight of it filled Garland with a sick, empty feeling. Before joining this army in this war, he had never pictured military funerals this way. There should be solemn processions, a band, men marching the slow step with inverted arms, each coffin draped with the flag he died for. Not this, merciful God, not this.

The ceremony was over, but not for Garland.

Men were looking toward him, but none had yet taken hold of a shovel.

Garland stiffened.

"Battalion, attention! Hats off!"

Garland let a long moment of silence pass.

"Men of the 28th. Look upon our comrades. Did they want to die for you?"

He paused.

"I do not think so. They were men just as we are, men who wished to live, to have families, to grow old, to be placed to final rest with dignity, with children and grandchildren by their graves. They wanted to live as much as we do.

"Look upon your comrades. I doubt, though, if many of them would have called us comrades, though some might have indeed gone to this war believing in our freedom. Perhaps only a few, but that does not matter now, for they are dead. Their war is finished forever; they rest with God.

"They died and you are alive, and I now ask you, my brothers: What do we owe them in return?"

There was silence for a moment.

"What do we owe to them?"

"Our freedom," came a reply, and the words were picked up; some whispering, others shouting it; some in tears, others standing silent, stoic.

"Our freedom."

"We owe our brothers and sisters our lives. We have made two pledges, my comrades. We have pledged to fight for the Union, and so we shall. In so doing, if need be to die as these men have died, we shall prove to the world, as Frederick Douglass said, that we will defy any power on earth that says we are not free and equal men. That, my comrades, I believe is worth dying for."

More than a few simply replied with one word: "Amen."

Looking down at an open grave, Sergeant Major Garland White stiffened and slowly raised his right hand to his brow in salute. He knelt down on one knee, scooped up a handful of mud, and let it drop into the grave before him.

"From dust we come and to dust we shall return. Thus is the will of God. Amen."

He stood back up and nodded a dismissal. At each grave one of the men knelt down and did the same, scooping up a handful of muddy earth and letting it trickle into the grave before they set to work with shovels. The ceremony—their ceremony—ended, and the men picked up shovels and started to fill in the graves.

Lost in prayerful thought, Garland White started to walk down the line of graves.

"Sergeant Major?"

He looked up. It was the man who had helped Lieutenant Grant carry the body out of the ambulance. The man stood before him, tears mingled with the rain. He tentatively raised his hand and extended it.

"Thank you."

"Sir?"

He was not sure if this man was military or not. Looking closer at his uniform jacket, he saw no insignia of rank on his shoulders, but from long experience as a man of color, both in and out of the army—and not all that long ago as a slave—he hesitated, not sure of the gesture offered to him. The man took a step forward, open hand still extended.

"Sergeant Major, take my hand and thank you."

He detected the hint of Ireland in the man's voice. The gesture of equality was at times offered by abolitionists, but in the bitter world before the war, with men of color competing for work with the millions of impoverished immigrants leaving their famine-afflicted isle to seek refuge in America, there was little love lost between the two.

A bit nervous, he took the man's hand, the grip solid. Looking into his eyes, Garland saw the emotion.

The handshake after several seconds became one of nervous embarrassment for both. Garland was not sure when to let go, but the man held his hand tight.

"That was my brother you helped to carry. Your prayer was for him."

"Sir, I am so sorry," was all Garland could say.

They released their grip. Garland was not sure what to say next, feeling that he should turn away and continue on with watching his men, but the man's gaze held him.

"My name is James Reilly, and yours, Sergeant?"

"Garland White, sergeant major with the 28th United States Colored Troops, and again, sir, my deepest sympathy."

James looked back at the grave, and Garland felt as if he should turn the man away. His men, now eager to get the job done and back to their barracks for breakfast, were hurriedly filling the grave in, half shoveling, half scooping the thick, wet mud back into the hole; the clods of earth and muddy water thumping against the body wrapped in cheap linen, covering it over.

James, as if in imitation of Garland, knelt down on one knee, scooped up a handful of mud, let it drop in, made the sign of the cross, and stood back up, nearly slipping as he did so. Garland instinctively reached out to steady him and prevented him from falling in.

"Thank you," James whispered as he stepped back.

"Patrick was my half brother," James said, voice flat, almost without emotion. "We were never close, but still, he was all the kin I had left in this world."

He paused. As a preacher, Garland had presided over many a funeral long before he donned the uniform, and he knew when it was best to just let a man talk.

"My mother died from the famine on the boat coming over from Ireland. Dad brought me here to America. Drunkard he was, though a good man at heart. He met Patrick's ma on the boat over here. She had no use for me, and I moved on a few years later. That was back in '46 or so. We were never close, but when I heard he joined the army, I tried to see him whenever I could."

"You are with the army, sir?" Garland asked after a long silence.

James shook his head.

"Artist. I'm with *Harper's Weekly*, covering the war."

James started to look back again to the grave, and Garland, seeing the way the mud and water were rising around the body, put a hand on James's arm and turned him away, walking slowly.

"Your brother, then, was a soldier?" he asked.

James nodded.

"Told the lad not to join, but he was all afire to do his part. He was wounded three days ago at Cold Harbor," his voice began to break again. "Lost his legs, both of them, by the time they got him back here to the hospital. Blood poisoning had him. I didn't even know he was on the same boat as me until just before we docked, and I heard him call my name. I should have found him earlier. I should have . . ."

Garland stopped walking, looking back into James's eyes.

"He is at peace now, sir."

"Some peace. They couldn't even give him a proper grave to himself."

"I'll make this pledge to you, sir. Later today I'll bring some of the boys down, we'll dig a grave, good and proper, lift him out of where he is now, rebury him, and make sure his cross is properly marked. Can you write his name down for me?"

"You would do that?"

"I would do that for any man," Garland replied forcefully.

James started to make the gesture of reaching to his pocket for his wallet, but a look, almost of anger from Garland, stopped him.

"I will do that for a comrade, sir," he said quietly but forcefully.

Embarrassed, James let his hand drop to his side.

"Thank you," James whispered.

"No, sir, it is I who thank you."

There was another awkward silence.

James looked past him to the long line of graves; the men filling them in.

"I'll give you his name," James said, and opening his haversack, he pulled out a battered sketchpad. Opening it, Garland could not help but see the man's work. Some of it was incomprehensible: a scattering of quickly drawn lines, vague outlines of men, a flag, numbers around them, but as he turned the pages, several made him draw in his breath. A man clutching his abdomen and, merciful God, entrails spilling out; the face of a boy, dirt smeared, but the eyes hollow, empty as if he was gazing off to some distant place thousands of yards away; a man holding another, whose face was contorted, crying; a fence row, bodies draped over the rails, a note in the corner, "memory of Antietam"; men crouched against a trench, and on the back of each was a white square of paper with a name on it; a priest, kneeling in a trench, surrounded by dead, hand held up as if in benediction or anguished lament.

James flipped through the pages, Garland stood gazing at the images.

"My God," he whispered. "Is that what it is really like?"

James looked up at him, eyes steady, and finally he just nodded, saying nothing.

He reached a blank page, took a pencil out of the haversack, and wrote down a name. He hesitated as he did so, his hands beginning to tremble.

"Are you all right, sir?"

James nodded, trying to force a smile.

"Just reminded me of something. I'm fine," but his voice betrayed the truth. With shaking hand he wrote down Patrick's name, age, and regiment. He tore off the corner of the sheet and handed it to Garland, who carefully took the piece of paper, folded it over, and put it into his breast pocket.

"I promise I shall see it done."

"Thank you, Sergeant Major."

There was another awkward silence as James looked down at the sketchpad, which was now splattered with raindrops.

"It seems like sacrilege, what I'm thinking."

"And what is that, sir?"

"James, just James, please."

Garland nodded.

"What do you think is sacrilege?"

"To sketch what I am seeing now."

Garland looked back at his men.

"I think you should, sir. You have the gift of the artist. Things like this should be remembered. A history of it, you might say."

"What?"

"Something I've thought about much," Garland replied. "I hope that someday an historian will remember this sacrifice in blood."

He hesitated, looking into James's eyes.

"I think your brother would want you to draw it."

James smiled.

"Thank you," he hesitated, "Garland."

"Men of the 28th!"

Garland turned and saw that Colonel Russell, surrounded by the other officers, was stepping out from under the tarp. Something was afoot, some of the officers were actually grinning, though more than a few were tight-lipped. The mixed reaction was hard to read.

Garland turned away from James and back to his men.

"Battalion, attention!"

The men laboring on, quickly filling the graves, looked up, falling silent.

Russell stepped closer, holding up a sheet of paper.

"Men of the 28th United States Colored Troops. We have received orders! We have been officially assigned to the First Brigade of the Fourth Division of the Ninth Corps. Men, we ship out tonight to join the Army of the Potomac! We are going to war!"

All stood as if struck dumb.

"Sergeant Major White. See that this detail is completed. March the men back to the barracks. All uniforms to be cleaned, all equipment packed, and ready to march to the docks at Alexandria by four this afternoon!"

"Three cheers for the Union lads!" one of the officers shouted. The cry was picked up—men holding up shovels, cheering, slapping each other on the back, laughing—some in their excitement all but dancing.

"Battalion!" Garland roared. "See to your work, men. See to your work!"

They fell back to their labor with enthusiasm, racing each other now to fill in their grave first.

"Merciful God."

It was James.

Garland looked back at him, sketchpad in hand, a few lines already drawn, numbers and symbols dotting the rain soaked paper.

Garland gazed down at the pad as if to comment on the horrors it contained of the world they were now marching toward, and then just shook his head, saying nothing.

Again James could only nod.

Garland looked back to the grave of James's brother, where all sense of ceremony had been forgotten. Men were eagerly pushing the earth in, mounding it over, tamping it down; one of them already hammering a single cross into the ground with the back of his shovel.

"I promise you before we leave, I'll bring some men down here and make sure he is given his own grave. I promise."

"I doubt if you will have time," James sighed. "I know you mean it. Perhaps someday, someday after this war is over, we'll do it together."

CHAPTER TWO

WHITE HOUSE

JUNE 6, 1864

8 P.M.

✳✳✳✳✳✳✳✳✳✳✳✳✳✳✳✳✳✳✳✳✳✳✳✳✳

CLUTCHING A LONG SCROLL OF FLIMSY TELEGRAPHY NOTEPAPER, President Abraham Lincoln stood by the open window of his office, head bowed, sheets of paper turned to catch the last light of the sun setting behind Arlington.

It was the latest dispatches from the fronts—all of them bad. In crises of the past, there had always been some glimmer of hope, except perhaps after Fredericksburg. A hope that a sharp riposte, an aggressive turn, could reverse fortune or news from one front counterbalance the bad news from another. He now had in place two of the most aggressive, tough, intensely willful generals of this war— Grant and Sherman—and they were stalled. A month into the campaign, started with such high hopes, the daily casualty lists were appalling—and there was no end in sight. Grant was just outside of Richmond, Sherman only halfway to Atlanta, and yet they were checkmated. Their armies were stalled in squalid trenches; the nation stunned by casualty rates averaging two thousand men a day.

He hoped the military telegraph line into the Treasury building

was truly secure, for today's dispatches portended far worse than usual—perhaps upward of ten thousand men lost in one futile charge, no more than twenty minutes in duration. At Fredericksburg it had taken eight hours to pile up such a casualty list; now it could be done in a matter of minutes.

He did not need to ask what the nation would say to this. Grant had ordered censorship from the front lines, arguing that revealing the casualty rate would provide useful intelligence to the enemy.

The argument was, of course, as hollow as a dried-out gourd. The enemy could count the bodies easily enough. And so could the reporters who were slipping back to their publishers with the truth. It was devastating news that could not be contained much longer.

At the cabinet meeting this morning, with rumors already swirling in the streets outside this very building, he could sense the mood. Stanton was melancholy. There was animosity between Stanton and Grant, the man who now commanded all Union armies in the field. The asthmatic lawyer was biding his time, waiting for the public outcry to reach a thunderous roar. Then he would make his move against Grant. If by some miracle Grant did take Richmond, Edwin would, of course, be the first to lay claim to that victory.

And then there was the little Napoleon, George McClellan. Even while leading the army to defeat—on nearly the identical battlefield two years ago—the press had hailed him, blaming the administration. McClellan's agents and supporters launched a whisper campaign that a sure victory had been thrown away by the President, an amateur at war, who had interfered with the carefully laid out battle plans and thus triggered a disaster—a disaster that was now bleeding the nation to death two years later.

In two months McClellan would, without a doubt, clinch his party's nomination. Though McClellan claimed he would support the war's continuation after winning the election, the party platform—which was being written at that moment by Copperhead Clement Vallandigham of Ohio—demanded an end to the conflict; a conflict led, the Peace Democrats claimed, by the abolitionists and "King Lincoln, the Butcher."

His personal secretaries, Nicolay and Hay, tried to conceal the worst of it from him; however, all he needed to do was walk down Pennsylvania Ave., to the corner by the Willard Hotel, and chat with "Ole Moses," a black man who ran the corner newsstand. There he could get the latest papers from New York and Chicago and learn the truth about public opinion. As he opened the papers, Moses would stand silent, head lowered, perhaps whispering, "Never you mind that, Mr. President, it ain't nothing to fret about, we are with you."

What would Moses' papers say tomorrow? Surely this news could not be kept hidden forever.

He looked back out to the river. Steam tugs were busy marshalling ships in and out of the docks at Alexandria.

Stanton had mentioned at the meeting this morning that a convoy of troop ships, actually empty hospital ships, would leave this evening. More troops were being stripped out of the garrison of Washington, over his personal objection, to be sent up as replacements, to feed the voracious appetite of war. In this case, however, Stanton was not very upset, because it was nine regiments of USCT who had filed into the city over the previous month.

"Mr. President?"

He turned. It was his secretary, John Nicolay, the door half open. "Your guest is here, sir."

Lincoln nodded, returning to his desk, dropping the dispatches. "Show our friend in, John."

Even Nicolay, trusted as he was, did not know the reason this visitor had appeared at a side entrance to the White House, presenting a note in the President's hand stating: ADMIT THIS BEARER WHENEVER HE SHOULD CALL AND BRING HIM TO ME AT ONCE REGARDLESS OF THE HOUR.

Nicolay opened the door wider and stood curious for a moment. The man entering wore a battered officer's jacket. It had been brushed clean, but it bore the well-worn look of a man who had been up on the front lines for some time.

"Thank you, John, and please close the door," Lincoln said with a smile.

Nicolay, obviously filled with curiosity at this strange visit, hesitated for a second, but a sharp look from his President caused him to lower his head with a nod and carefully close the door, which latched shut.

"James," Lincoln announced, coming around from behind his desk, right hand extended. "I am so glad you could finally come. Please accept my deepest sympathies for your loss."

Despite their being old friends, James Reilly stiffened slightly, almost coming to attention, and took Lincoln's hand. The President's grasp was warm and firm as Lincoln let his left hand go to James's shoulder, squeezing him tightly.

"I am sorry I did not report at once, sir. I hope you understand."

"James, sit down, I received your note. There is no need for apology."

He could detect the faint scent of whiskey on the man's breath. The curse of the Irish, some called it, but under these circumstances he could forgive it. He guided his friend over to a chair by the window, where they could sit and catch a hint of the cooling breeze wafting in after a hot day of humid rain and mists.

James settled into the chair with a sigh; Lincoln motioned to an ashtray by the side of the chair, and said, "It's fine with me if you smoke."

James nodded his thanks, pulled out a half-smoked cigar from his breast pocket, and struck a match on the side of his boot. Lincoln could see the man had made an attempt to clean up, albeit with little result, and waited patiently as James puffed the cigar to life.

He had known James for over fifteen years. A half-starved lad of eighteen or so, he had appeared at his office one day, looking for work, willing to trade a day of labor cleaning the dusty clutter of his office in exchange for a meal, a place to sleep on the floor, and after tough negotiations, twenty cents for his pocket. Illinois had been flooded with such men at that time. Bedraggled Irish by the thousands had come, streaming westward, looking for any kind of work. It had saddened him to turn so many of them away, but on that particular day the building's regular janitor had disappeared yet again, and he had just won a case with a handsome retainer. But despite that, there was something about the lad that caught his attention.

James had ensconced himself in the office, as if it had become his territory to defend with life and limb, rendering it spotless during the day. At night Lincoln would find him buried in a book from his library. He encouraged him to consider the law, but James showed another talent. One day he found the young man asleep on the floor and scattered around him were half-a-dozen sketches that made him sit down and burst out laughing, awaking James with a frightened start. They were the most remarkable, entertaining caricatures of himself, long limbed, sitting in his chair, leaning back, hugely over-sized feet plopped on his desk, pantlegs halfway up to his knees revealing socks that had snapped their garters and were sagging into his shoes. Another sketch showed him laughing, oversized head thrown back, and another—one he still had in his possession—was a serious study of him, looking out a window, as if gazing off to some distant land.

"Forget the law, my young friend," he had proclaimed. "Besides, there are too many of us lawyers already. You must be an artist!"

For the next six months James cleaned during the day, and at night studied art books that somehow, mysteriously, appeared in the prairie lawyer's office. He had no bent toward the classical art of the day and showed little interest in the works of Church, Cole, and Turner. His was more of a satirical wit, mixed at times with personal studies of folks sitting in a tavern or courtroom, or clients of Lincoln's who took delight in James's skill and sharp wit. One client gave James the unheard of sum of five dollars to do a serious pencil-and-charcoal portrait of himself, his wife, and daughter.

With the advent of the steam-powered printing presses, and with the public's insatiable demand for steel engraving illustrations, James at last found his calling, and an anonymous donor appeared. Lincoln smiled at the memory, for James would never be told the name of his benefactor. James spent a year of study in Chicago and never returned to Springfield, landing a job with a paper in the growing metropolis along Lake Michigan.

They had lost touch, as often happened, and Lincoln suspected that James, guessing who the "anonymous donor" had been, felt shame for so readily accepting the gift.

They did not cross paths again until 1858, when, during the first debate with Douglas, Lincoln had spotted the young man, now in his late twenties, sitting in the press section, sketchpad in hand.

It had been a warm reunion, rekindling a deep friendship, and it was, he had to admit, an investment well paid for; it was beneficial to have such a supporter with a national weekly. While some artists took to wicked, and at times enraging caricatures, Lincoln could always find the warmth in James's work. There was a certain homey touch that captured the spirit of a plainspoken prairie lawyer, carrying the burden of a nation sliding into the "inevitable crisis." Thomas Nast, though supportive of the cause, could be wickedly vile, especially in his portrayals of Irish, Catholics, and Negroes. Ward and Homer—although their work was superb—lacked something that James always seemed to capture: a very personal, and at times disturbing, vision of the war.

Shortly after the debates and their reestablished contact, James sent the defeated candidate a check for $120, the cost of his year's tuition at the art school. Lincoln had replied to him that he had no idea why such a check would be sent to him, but he would cash it and donate the money to a school for freed colored children.

They temporarily lost touch again until the week following the collapse of McClellan's Peninsula Campaign. James had shown up at the White House, unbidden, standing in line for hours to finally have a word with his President. He asked for five minutes of time to show him some sketches—not the sketches that would appear next week in *Harper's*, of perfectly aligned ranks of soldiers going forth to victory, but rather, drawings that would never be published.

For the first time, he had seen a glimmer of the true face of this war through James's eye and pencil, and it had left him shaken. Five minutes turned into four hours, and later that evening a plan was hatched.

"James, I'd like to ask a favor of you," he said slowly.

"Anything at all, sir."

"Whenever you are returning from the front would you visit with me?"

"A pleasure," and he then hesitated. "I wouldn't want to intrude on your time, sir."

There was a long pause.

"Actually, I take delight in seeing you as an old friend from Illinois, but this is about something else."

"And that is, sir?"

"I'd like you to bring your sketchpad along, share it with me, especially those drawings, which you say will never be published. It gives me a sense of things, things no official report, no newspaper account, can carry."

"Of course."

"But there is more, James."

"And that is?"

"I'd like you to talk to me as you just have. Tell me your impressions. What you see. What you hear the men saying. Unlike a lot of the newspaper writers the soldiers dislike, I can see from the drawings that the men trust you. They fancy when you sketch them, and you've told me what they talk about while you sketch them. I want to hear that."

"And?" he asked tentatively.

"And what you hear in headquarters as well. What the staff talks about. Find a way to sketch some of the generals now and then. Heaven knows they will sit all day doing nothing except posing like Napoleon himself while a battle is raging outside their tent if they think they'll wind up on the cover of *Harper's.*"

He had forced a smile.

"Share a drink, let them chat, hear what they say about themselves, about each other, about how they really feel the war is going. That is what I really want to hear from you, James."

His young friend had taken that in and remained silent for several minutes, looking down at his sketchpad, slowly thumbing through the drawings, stopping at a drawing of the field at Malvern Hill after the fighting ended.

"In other words, you want me to spy."

"That, my friend, is such an ugly word when so many talk about an honorable war, all glory and such."

He sighed.

"I want to hear the truth, James, not the whispers of a spy, as you put it. I want to hear from a man I trust, understand what he sees with the eyes of an artist, but also, what he hears. I do not think there is dishonor in that. It would be of tremendous help. Think of yourself as the President's eyes and ears in places I can't go."

His friend had finally nodded, pointing to the carnage drawn out on his pad.

"If it shortens that by one day, I'll do it."

It was James, returning to Washington the day after Antietam, who brought Lincoln the bitter news that two entire corps had remained idle throughout the fight, the men raging that if they had been sent in at the end of the day, they would have swept Lee and his army into the Potomac and ended the conflict then and there. The privates, sergeants, even some of the generals, had seen it—but not McClellan. He had reported the same about Chancellorsville and again after Gettysburg . . . lost victories and distant generals who had failed to see the possibilities.

But now, Lincoln could see that his friend was a man all but shattered by what he had seen over the previous month. His drawings were full of pathos and anguish. Gone was the light satirical wit.

Thumbing through the pages of drawings, Lincoln stopped at the one of the men, lined up in the trench, slips of paper pinned to their backs with their names on them.

"Tell me of this. What is it?" Lincoln asked.

He looked into James's eyes and saw that there were tears; the man all but breaking as he described the futility of the charge.

"That was the attack your brother was in?"

"Yes, sir." James did not offer any further explanation.

"I see," and he continued to thumb through the drawings, stopping at the last one, bodies carpeting a field, all of them with the sheets of paper pinned to their backs.

"Talk to me about this," Lincoln said softly. "Why the pieces of paper?"

James, head lowered, the cigar between his fingers going out, described all he had seen, his voice a monotone.

"They *baa*-ed like sheep, sir, like sheep as they climbed out of the trenches. These were veterans, sir: men who had seen three years of it. Many of their enlistments were up within a few more weeks and they had already done their duty a hundred times over. They knew what was to come, that it was the end of it all, and yet they went forward anyhow. That *baa*-ing was their last act of protest."

He sighed deeply.

"After Antietam, I no longer heard them sing, or cheer for the

Union when they charged, but they would go in like veterans, they would. However, three days ago, sir, it was different from anything I have seen in this war. I never want to see the likes of it again."

He looked into the President's eyes.

"I don't want to talk about that anymore, sir," he whispered.

Lincoln nodded, features drawn, filled with an infinite weariness. He slowly stood up, went to the door, opened it, and said something to John Nicolay, who was at his desk in the next room. Nicolay came in a minute later with a heavy crystal glass, filled halfway with whiskey. He offered it to James, who gladly took it.

"Not a word ever of this drink," Lincoln said, trying to make a feeble attempt at a smile. "If Mary knew I served liquor in this room she'd have my head, but I think we can forget that this time."

"Of course, sir," John replied, withdrawing and closing the door.

"Did Grant fail?" Lincoln asked, waiting for James to drain the glass and finally relight his cigar with a shaking hand.

James looked straight at Lincoln.

"Information from a spy?"

"James, just the truth as you see it."

"I honestly can't say. At the Wilderness, and even at Spotsylvania, the men were saying they trusted him even though the fighting was murderous. That he was knocking the stuffing out of Bobbie Lee, keeping him pinned in place and dancing to our tune. But North Anna, and then this accursed place, Cold Harbor . . ."

He fell silent again.

"I'm told he saw no other choice. Richmond was right before him, he thought Lee was battered enough that he could break through."

"Was that the official report?" James asked.

Lincoln did not reply.

"I guess it could be said that way but the men who had to do the charge knew different."

James looked into the glass and then back at Lincoln, but the President made no offer to have it refilled.

"The war's changed, sir."

"How so?"

"You could see it at Antietam. In a stand-up fight, the ghastly slaughter was equal, but give one side time to dig in, dig deep, real deep . . ."

His voice trailed off, and he looked out the window.

"Lee had entrenchments three lines deep. Deep falls, entanglements, and a moat in front if they had time. A fortress line, miles long. Gone are the days of trying to maneuver around it. The Rebs can dig as fast, even faster, than a corps can march to flank them, and when they attack, there are the trenches filled with Rebs waiting for us.

"General Grant gambled that he could batter his way through," James gestured to the open sketchpad of the casualties on the field. "And that is the price. Was it a mistake?"

He hesitated, Lincoln leaning forward, nodding in a reassuring gesture for him to proceed.

"Yes, sir," he replied emphatically, almost fiercely. "Rumor is there were the usual staff work mistakes, the result the attack went in twenty-four hours later than planned, and that gave the Rebs more than enough time to turn it into a killing ground with no hope of success. If the privates and sergeants could see it, why in hell . . ."

He hesitated.

"Excuse me, sir, but why in hell couldn't the generals see it?"

He muttered something under his breath, and Lincoln did not ask him to repeat it.

"Blame Grant? I'd say blame the whole mess on the chronic, bad luck Army of the Potomac. It always seems on the edge of victory and then someone goes off half-cocked, or does not do his job right, or gets drunk, or an order gets lost. Don't get me wrong, never blame the men, they are the bravest of the brave, and if just once leaders ensured that things were done right by them, I know they could win."

Lincoln nodded in agreement but said nothing.

"After Cold Harbor though, I must say this: No frontal attack will ever work again, sir, not against trenches manned by Lee's veterans, armed with rifles, and backed up by artillery packed with canister. Around Richmond itself there is nothing but layer after layer of trenches and forts. No, sir, not Grant, nor anyone else, will break through and take Richmond. I guess he believed he had to try and that was the result."

Lincoln whispered, "It's the same I hear from Sherman on the approach to Atlanta. With every flanking march, he finds another wall of fortifications waiting. It seems we are in a new age of warfare, as Ericsson's monitors have changed forever how navies will fight. Until some genius figures a new way of doing the same on land, or the will of the Rebels just falls apart . . ." His voice trailed off.

"Sir, I came to see you, but this will be for the last time."

"Why so?"

"I'm asking for a change of assignment after this. I want to get as far away from this damn war as I can possibly get."

He looked back at Lincoln and shook his head.

"Excuse my language, sir."

"I've heard a lot worse, James, no apology needed."

"Maybe go out west; I'd like to see that while it is still wild, open, and free."

Lincoln sighed and looked out the window. Darkness was settling, but the river was aglow with lights, distant echoes of steamboat whistles drifting in the still evening air.

"Another division is shipping out tonight," Lincoln said.

"The colored troops," James said.

"How did you know?"

"Some of them buried my brother this morning. Good honorable men they are, and God save them, they cheered when they heard the news that they were going up to the front lines."

"They feel they have something to prove and indeed they do."

"They'll be slaughtered. We've both heard what the Rebel government said about black troops."

"General Lee is an honorable man, even if he is the deepest thorn in my side," Lincoln replied sharply. "There have been communications, shall we say, in private and assurances conveyed, that regardless of what Jeff Davis and some others say, the rules of war will be observed."

"And what is it, you think, they'll prove?" James asked.

"The same thing the Irish Brigade proved at Fredericksburg, what hundreds of thousands from your isle proved."

"That we're equal? That we have brought our right to a claim to this land?" James questioned. "Sir, that might sound good in war time, but if and when this war ends, what then? And if we lose?"

"We will not lose," Lincoln replied sharply. "We cannot lose. And, yes, I do believe those men just might prove something once and for all," he continued, nodding toward the river and the boats heading downstream. "Believe me, I was one of the chief doubters when it came to arming Negro troops, but now? They are just about the only ones left willing to volunteer and their presence just might decide the issue. If that is the case it requires me as well to rethink many things about them."

"For their sake, sir, I pray it is worth something, given what they are about to face."

They sat silent for several minutes, James relighting his cigar and puffing it down to a short stub.

"I sent Grant a box of his favorites," Lincoln said, finally breaking the silence. "Are you at the Willard? If so I'll send a box over to you first thing in the morning."

"Yes, sir, but I'm catching the noon train for New York tomorrow to turn in my sketches, they want to run them next week."

"Which sketches?"

"The usual ones," and he shook his head. "My editor keeps saying the others are too grim, and the public does not want to see them."

"If both sides could see them in every detail," Lincoln replied, "maybe this madness would indeed stop. But that is never the case in war."

"Do you still think we can win?" James asked.

Lincoln simply nodded.

"James, there is no other choice. I pray the good Lord will forgive me for this price," and he pointed at the drawing still open on his lap. "I could end it tomorrow with a simple command for the armies to stop, turn around, and march home, and I daresay, at this moment, most folks in the North would cheer. But what of the future?"

He looked back out the window.

"In five years at most there will be more war," Lincoln whispered, voice distant as if remembering a dream or nightmare. "The fire-eaters in the South will plunge into Mexico, claiming they are going to kick the French and Austrians out, but in reality, they will attempt to seize more land for slavery. California and the west coast? We will wind up fighting over that someday, or they may also just decide to split away. Then we will be three nations, maybe four or more. Then we will squabble over everything in between. You know your history of what happened after Charlemagne died; it would be the same here.

"A hundred years hence? We will be like Europe, divided against itself, scheming with ever more cruel instruments of war against each other. A Shakespeare would indeed then proclaim that there was a plague on both our houses. It has to end here and now.

"That and slavery; it, too, has to end now, and I believe it is the burden of our generation to see it done. I will not pass on to my sons the curse of yet another war and to my grandchildren, Lord forbid it, yet another and another.

"And as for those men," and he gestured to the boats turning down the broad sweep of the Potomac, one after another in the line disappearing from view.

"There was a time, James, when I agreed with the recolonization movement, that the two races could not live side by side in peace. But those men, their blood drawn with the lash and the bullet, I realize now, have as much a place here as I do and as you do."

James sadly shook his head.

"There are neighborhoods in New York where I would be beaten to death as a Papist Mick. You see what Thomas Nast draws about us Irish and the Negroes," and his sarcasm was evident.

"Is there a man in any other regiment in the army who would say a word against the Irish Brigade?" Lincoln asked.

"Not unless he wants a thousand of us lined up and ready for a good bare-knuckled fight." Now James finally smiled for the first time.

"Guess you heard all the legends about me, Jack Armstrong, and his boys of Sangamon County," Lincoln said.

James chuckled.

"Who hasn't?"

"Some of it is actually true. It is the way of things."

"Except they weren't armed with fifty-eight-caliber Springfield rifles, deadly out to six hundred yards."

"No, but Jack wasn't above eye gouging or biting off a man's ear if he got him down. I had to tame him of that."

The President smiled as if recalling a pleasant memory.

He sighed and looked back at James.

"I want you to go back, James."

"Sir?"

"Just that. Your editor at *Harper's* might let you take an assignment somewhere else, but believe me, my young friend, in the end you'd hate yourself for it."

"You mean running away from a job that is not finished?" There was a cold edge now to James's voice. "You want me to go back and draw more pictures like *that*?"

Lincoln did not reply.

"No thank you, sir. I've had a belly full of this damn war. I did my part being there, and I've had enough."

"And who will replace you?"

"I don't care anymore."

"Thomas Nast, perhaps?"

James looked at him crossly.

"Hit a nerve there, didn't I?"

"That bastard? He keeps his distance from me when I'm in the office, and I keep my distance from him. Though for two cents I'd love to break both his hands good and proper so he wouldn't be able draw for a year or two."

Lincoln leaned back and chuckled softly.

"I'd like to see that fight, if it ever comes to that. But seriously, James, I need you back there. I can't order you, the way I would a soldier. But I need your eyes, and, yes, your ears. This war is not going to stop because of Cold Harbor. It will go on; God forgive me if I am wrong, but I believe with all my heart and soul it must go on to the end."

"And if McClellan wins the election?"

"We will have a victory, some kind of victory between now and then that will turn the political tide."

"Do you really believe that, sir?"

Lincoln gazed straight at him. In reality he was no longer sure, but if he voiced the opinion that he was truly going to lose and let that infection spread, he would indeed lose, and the nation would forever be torn asunder.

"I must believe we will win," he finally replied.

James did not reply.

"I want you to go back. Of course go to New York first, turn in your drawings, rest up for a week or two. Perhaps go back and fall in with that colored division for a while. It would be good for the nation to see how they can indeed fight. Your drawings of your Irish brethren at Fredericksburg, and again at Gettysburg, were nobly done and were as important as a victory itself. Keep an eye on these new men, perhaps you will find a moment that will immortalize them as well. I think that is a task you cannot turn down."

James's glance was actually one of anger.

"Mr. President, if it was anyone else in the world asking me this, I would tell them to go to hell."

Lincoln forced a homey smile.

"But you won't say that to your President and your friend."

"You know I can't refuse a request from my President," and he finally smiled again. "And my friend."

Lincoln slowly stood up and extended his hand.

"Thank you, James. Now back you go to Willard's. I can try to order you not to drink, but I don't want you to make a promise you will not keep. But do try for moderation."

"After tomorrow, but tonight . . ." He shook his head. "Sorry, sir."

Lincoln patted him on the shoulder again and guided him out the door. Nicolay looked up, holding a sheaf of papers, as James left the front office.

"New dispatches?"

"Yes, sir."

"Anything pressing I need to do right now?"

"I don't think so, sir."

"Tomorrow, then," and he closed the door to be alone.

He went back to the window. The last of the boats had turned the bend and were out of sight, five thousand more men for the front lines.

He thought of the song so popular only a year ago, but rarely heard anymore, "Battle Cry of Freedom," and the refrain: "And we'll fill our vacant ranks with a million freemen more . . ."

The nation was running out of men willing to fight. But then again, so was the South.

One victory, dear Lord, he thought, *just one good clear victory*. No mistakes by generals this time, no lost orders, and no bitter infighting. The men on those boats deserved their chance, and perhaps they would be the key to that victory, for they had a stake in this fight, if anyone did.

CHAPTER THREE

PETERSBURG, VIRGINIA
JUNE 25, 1864

✳✳✳✳✳✳✳✳✳✳✳✳✳✳✳✳✳✳✳✳✳✳✳✳✳✳

"That's it, Stan, just a mite higher; slowly now, slowly."

The boys watched expectantly as Stan Kochanski ever so slowly raised the stick with a battered kepi atop it.

"Come on, slow like. Bob it up, then down, and then back up again. Play it, damn it, play it."

Stan grinned, his newfound comrades almost treating him as an equal even though he was a "fresh fish," a new recruit to the 48th Pennsylvania Volunteers.

He edged the brim of the hat above the lip of the trench.

"Now down, quick, you dumb Pole, quick!"

He jerked it back down as ordered by his brother, Johann, a sergeant.

"All right, boys, now we move a few feet and catch ourselves a Reb."

The group crawled along the trench, Stan suppressing a gagging feeling as they passed an open latrine pit dug into one wall of their forward line.

"Here's a good spot," Johann announced. "Now again, but this time pop it up and keep it there."

Johann looked farther down the line.

"Michael, you ready?"

Private Michael O'Shay, purportedly the best shot with the regiment, was concealed in what the men called a "spider hole" dug into the forward side of the trench during the night, a narrow indentation, dirt piled atop the lip, then carefully leveled, a small aperture cut into the dirt, fixed in place with a few boards from a ration box and masked with canvas scrubbed with red clay so that it blended in. His rifle was laid in place, with the front of the barrel covered in grease so it would not glint under the noonday sun. Michael did not reply, merely tapping a foot in reply, stock of his gun set tight against his shoulder.

"Now, Stan!"

Stan did as ordered, raising the hat atop the pole up over the lip of the trench and waiting.

He didn't have long to wait.

A bullet caught the hat square, barely an inch to the right of center of the brow, the hat whipping backward, flying off the stick, the hit from the .58-caliber minié ball shattering the stick as well, knocking it out of Stan's grasp.

"See him," Michael hissed, shifting slightly; a little more than a second later his rifle recoiled with a sharp crack. He pulled the gun back out of the firing slit and flung himself down. A few seconds later, two minié balls slapped through the firing slit he had just vacated.

"Get him?" Johann asked.

"Think so," was all Michael replied, breathing hard, slumped against the wall of the trench.

"Good shooting, Yank!"

The taunting cry echoed in the hot midday air.

Johann stood up halfway, cupping his hand around his mouth.

"We get 'em?"

"He wet his britches, he did," came a reply. "But nope. Ya missed. What about your man?"

"You missed me, you sons of bitches!" Michael shouted.

"Now that ain't polite, you bastard sons of bitches, calling us that. We was born here, you wasn't."

"You started this sharpshooting," Johann retorted. "And I'm as good a man as you are, born here or not, by God."

"You started it, shooting poor Jimmy in the ass when all the lad wanted to do was shit outside the trench, him with the bloody flux."

"Sorry about that, Rebs!" Johann shouted. "It weren't us. We're the 48th Pennsylvania, it was them Connecticut boys that done that."

"We'll stop it if you stop it, Yank, even if you are some damn bohunk or Polack from the sounds of it."

Johann laughed.

"I'm Irish, damn ya," Michael shouted.

"Well, a son of the sod," came the retort. "Heard you gonna get darkies in the ranks next, once we kilt off all you white boys."

The men looked at each other in confusion.

"Ain't heard that," Johann finally replied. "No colored here with this corps."

"Well, we shoot to kill if they show up, Yank, and you, too, if you got the same corps badge as them."

"Ain't none of 'em here. So we got a deal, Reb?"

There was a momentary pause, echoes of voices debating and finally a reply.

"Deal, Yank. Nighttime no shootin', but during the daytime if one of you boys gotta drop his britches outside the trench, you gotta wave a white flag first."

"Hell, no," Johann replied. "No white flag. Our officers would hang us for sure for that. How about wave a cap back and forth three times."

Again a discussion on the far side.

"Deal, Yank, but there be a problem."

"And what's that?'

"We 'uns are the 25th North Carolina, but we can't speak for the boys to either flank."

"Ah, shit, Reb!" Michael shouted. "What good is a truce if we get shot in the ass sideways from farther down the line?"

There was a rancorous laugh from the Rebel fort above them.

"Well, we can be all democratic like and send delegations up and down the line, if that's what you want to negotiate out, fair and proper like. But that will be a heap of talkin' and a lot of delegations given how many different regiments stuck out here in this godforsaken place."

Johann shook his head and laughed sadly.

"We did that, I think we'd vote to end this damn war today and just go home, and the hell with this Petersburg."

"That we would, Yank, that we would," the Reb shouted back.

"All right, Reb. At least this: We don't shoot anymore straight at you; you don't shoot straight at us. If we go off the line, we'll tell you. You do the same for us, so there's no mistakes. Fair enough?"

"Deal, Yank."

"Does that mean we can stand up now?" Stan asked, and even as he spoke the new recruit actually did stand up to take his first look, in daylight, at the massive Rebel fort, poised on the brow of the ridge, 130 yards away.

"My God, Stan!" Johann shouted as he leaped forward, tackling his brother around the knees and knocking him down; as he did so a bullet zipped across the lip of the trench.

"You stupid ass! Don't you ever stand up like that. Never!" He then lapsed into Polish as he slapped his brother several more times before hugging him.

"But the Reb said," Stan gasped, mouth bloody from the drubbing dealt out by his brother.

"Sorry 'bout that, Yank. It was them damn South Carolina boys off to our left. They're meaner than snakes," a cry echoed from the other side.

"Tell 'em the next one of 'em I see they're dead. They damn near killed my brother!" Johann cried.

Silence from the other side.

"He must be a fresh fish standing up like that," and there was a chorus of chuckles.

Johann did not reply, holding his brother tight.

"I promised father I'd bring you back safe," Johann snarled, delivering an angry punch to his brother's side. "Don't stand up like that, ever."

Obviously shaken, Stan did not reply.

"Still safer here than some of the mines we worked in back in Pottsville," Michael announced, sitting against the wall of the trench, working a patch down his rifle to clean it out before reloading.

"Ya, that it is, that it is," Hans Lubbeck, a corporal with the company, replied, biting off a chew of tobacco and handing the thick, dark block of cured tobacco over to Johann, who, still a bit shaken, sat back against the red clay wall of the trench.

Johann bit off a chaw, offering it to his brother, who, ashen faced, shook his head, and then gave it back to Hans.

"Found it on a dead Reb last week when we took their first line," he sighed. "Doubt if we'll get any more for a long time to come. We stuck in this damn hole forever now."

A chorus of agreement greeted his words, the men falling into casual complaining about the war, the trenches, everything.

"That Reb was right," one of them offered. "If we all stood up, met in the middle, and talked it out decent like, we'd be going home by the end of the day."

"Home to what?" Hans replied. "The coal mines? Jesus, I don't know about you men, but I say, it is safer here."

"Cave in, it's quick and you already got your grave, just need a priest then to consecrate it," one of them replied. "Think about the poor bastards shot at Cold Harbor. No cease-fire, them screaming and begging for water under that hot sun. No thank ye, I'll take the mines."

The debate went back and forth, pausing as a watering party crawled out of the communications trench, lugging canteens refilled from the swampy creek a couple of hundred yards to the rear.

The temperature in the narrow confines of the trench, dug into the brick-red Virginia clay, was near 100 degrees or more; the noon-day sun beating down on the sweating, suffering men.

"To hell with going back to the mines," Michael announced, finished with cleaning his rifle, reloading it, and cautiously venturing a peek through the inch-wide aperture of his spider hole. "That damn Rebel fort up there will be the death of us anyhow. Some lunkhead general will get frustrated and finally order a charge, and then, me laddies, no more worries."

A minié ball buzzed over Michael's head. He stuck his hand up for a second to wave and then ducked back down. Several seconds later there was a dull thump.

"Mortar," Johann announced.

All eyes turned heavenward and a couple of seconds later they could see the shell arcing heavenward.

"Two bits say it's short and to the left," one of the men announced.

"I'll take that, long and to the left by twenty yards, is where my money is," Michael replied.

The round reached apogee, started its descent, and seconds later Michael was grumbling as he handed a quarter over.

He sagged back against the trench wall.

"Boys, I know how to get us the hell out of here."

"Don't start that desertion talk again, Michael O'Shay," Johann snapped. "I won't stand for it."

Michael grinned.

"No, seriously, Sergeant. I was a blaster in the mines; you all know that. Hell, after the war I'm going out west, make good money blowing tunnels when they build that railroad to California."

"If they build it," one of the men grumbled.

"So how does that get us out of here now?" Johann asked, feigning at least some interest. Poor Stan was still shaking and he wanted to divert the lad with talk of something else.

"That mortar shell just now. Packed with a couple of pounds of powder. What a waste. Even if it lands in a trench we usually got time to run from it. But down underground, you laddies know what a couple of pounds of powder will do to ya inside a tunnel."

There were nods of agreement. Nearly every man of the 48th had come up out of the coalfields of Schuylkill County.

Michael took the chaw from Lubbeck and bit off a piece.

"I was thinking on it last night while taking a look at that damn fort up there." As he spoke, half-a-dozen mortars back behind their lines opened from the fort called "fourteen gun battery," lobbing their rounds high, seeking out the Confederate mortar, which had just fired. Michael paused, a few casual bets were offered, but there were no takers; it was far too risky to venture a peek for the results, even if the Rebs up in the fort were claiming a truce.

Several of the shells detonated with hollow pops, the others were duds.

"So what was you leading up to?" Johann asked.

"Well, I was thinking. How long do you think it'd take us boys to dig a tunnel up under that fort?"

As he spoke, he pulled out a pocketknife, opened it, and stuck it into the wall of the trench.

"This ain't no hard Pennsylvania rock. It's clay and sand, boys. How long?"

A healthy debate ensued for several minutes. Stan at last spoke up, and the men listened since he was book learned, having spent a year at college studying engineering before running off, the month prior, to join his brother in the army.

"How far is it again up to that fort?" he asked.

"Figure about a hundred and thirty yards or so," Johann replied.

"Three weeks through clay and sand, I'd figure," Stan announced after sitting quiet for a moment, as if in deep concentration.

The others chuckled good-naturedly. Given that he was the younger brother of their sergeant, they did not ride him too hard, but peppered back with, "Suppose you hit a spring? This ain't no coal-digging tunnel," and the debate gradually petered out. The heat rendered all of them dull, listless, and forlorn; it was even an effort to swat the flies, which plagued them by the thousands.

"Colonel's comin'," a private announced, sticking his head out from the covered communications trench that led to the rear.

The men made no effort to spruce up; they were in the forward trench and thus excused from such foolishness. Crouching low, a couple of officers emerged, one a captain, uniform as worn and battered as that of his men. It was their own Captain Conrad, commander of Company A. He was one of them, a coal cracker before the war, joined as a private and promoted through the ranks.

Behind him was Colonel Henry Pleasants, mid-thirties. In spite of the years of war, his face had a certain gentleness to it, his frame diminutive; wearing spectacles, he looked more like a preacher than a regimental commander of a hard-fighting unit. A mining engineer before the war, he had joined with the regiment as a lieutenant. Whether he looked like a preacher or not, he had proven his mettle on every battle the Ninth Corps had faced, from New Bern to this godforsaken place, rising to command of the regiment after the Battle of the Wilderness.

Men half stood at his approach, and he made a gesture for them to stay low.

"How goes it, boys?" he asked, pausing to shake Johann's hand.

"Hotter than hell, sir."

"With the Rebs or that blasted sun?" and he made the gesture of taking off his hat to wipe his brow, nearly standing up.

"Be careful, sir!" several of the men cried simultaneously, gesturing to the lip of the trench.

"We got a deal with the boys over there," Johann announced. "But not with the regiments to either flank of 'em."

"Besides," Lubbeck tossed in with his barely understandable English, "they see an officer's hat, and they go bang."

He made the gesture of shooting, then stabbed at his forehead with a finger and crossed his eyes.

Pleasants chuckled, nodding his thanks. Unlike some of the officers, who were all full of fight, even when it was little better than murder—which was how he defined sharpshooting in a place like this—he had no problems with the informal truces the men might strike up.

"I hate to tell you boys this, but we're stuck on the line for at least another week," he announced, his statement met with groans and curses.

"Sorry, lads, orders from on high. All the regiments of the division are like us, half strength or less, and there's no reserves to replace us on the line for now."

"Then let's just blow the bastards up and be done with it," Michael interjected.

"Blow them up?" the colonel looked at him quizzically.

Michael grinned.

"Me and the boys have been thinking on it, sir. Take a peek through my hole for a second or two, sir."

He gestured for the colonel to come over to his sharpshooting position. The men around him fell silent.

"Suggest you take that hat off, sir," Johann interjected, and Pleasants forced a smile and handed his wide-brimmed officer's cap to Captain Conrad.

"Just eyeball the fort up there, sir, but not for too long."

Pleasants leaned up against the narrow hole, ventured a look for several seconds. A minié ball snapped overhead, sounding like an angry bee, followed by laughter from the Rebel line as Pleasants ducked down.

"No peeking there, Yank!" came a taunt.

"Thought we had a deal, Reb!" Johann cried.

"One of the boys changed his mind. Damn officer here said we gotta shoot ya."

"Tell that son of a bitch to go to hell."

"Sorry, Yank, but he said you is on our land, trespassing like, so it's back to shootin'. Just gave your boy over there a warning, but next time it'll be for real."

Johann sighed.

"So much for the truce."

He looked over at Pleasants, who was squatting by his side, handkerchief out, trying to clean his spectacles, sweat beading down his brow.

"Well, at least he gave me a warning," Pleasants offered with a smile, and the men around him laughed good-naturedly.

"It's that damn fort up there, sir," Michael said. "You saw how it sits up on that ridge."

"Yes, and?"

"Blow it up."

Pleasants sat silent, one of the men uncorking a canteen and handing it to him. He soaked his handkerchief, wiped his face, and then wrapped it around his neck.

A bayonet was sticking out of the wall of the trench, serving as a candleholder. He pulled the bayonet out and started to scratch the ground.

"The Rebs call it 'Pegram's Battery,'" he said, as if to himself. "A battery of six Napoleon cannons, garrison of a full regiment, anchored to either flank by at least two lines of trenches. We could throw the entire corps at it, and . . ." his voice trailed off.

"And we all die," Michael replied coldly.

Pleasants drew it out on the ground as he spoke.

A thump echoed.

"Mortar," someone announced. Johann looked up, but Pleasants continued to sketch in the dirt, not even bothering to raise his eyes.

"Long but it'll be close," Johann announced, eyes heavenward, tracing the line of flight of 4.5-inch mortar shell, fuse sputtering, passing just overhead and slapping into the ground ten yards to their rear, to detonate a second later.

"Hey, Reb, cut the fuse a mite shorter, and you'll kill us all next time!" Michael shouted.

Pleasants stared at his sketch for several minutes; Stan, kneeling by his side, added a few comments about distance.

"You the new recruit?" Pleasants asked.

"Yes, sir, joined two weeks ago."

Pleasants smiled.

"Heard you had a year of college."

"Yes, sir, my brother and father said they wanted me in the front office, not down in the mines."

Pleasants nodded.

"You study drafting?"

"Yes, sir."

"Come back with me then, Corporal; I just might have some work for you."

Michael leaned back and hooted derisively.

"Promoted to corporal after two weeks. Hell, you'll be a major general in eight weeks and me still a private."

Johann, obviously proud of the fact that his brother had been recognized, and inwardly relieved that he'd be off the front line for a while, glanced at Michael, but saw that his friend was just ribbing.

Pleasants stood up, again the men chorusing to mind his head in spite of his short stature.

"Boys, I think you just might be on to something," Pleasants said with a smile.

He looked over at Michael.

"And you, Private Michael O'Shay, how many times have you been up on charges of drunk and disorderly?"

Michael grinned.

"Colonel, darlin', I think you can keep count better than I. You see I was drunk at the time and you was not."

Pleasants grinned, reached into his haversack and pulled out a half-empty pint of whiskey and tossed it over to him.

"You do better thinking with this, Private O'Shay, so my compliments and enjoy the bottle, but be sure to share it with your comrades so you don't get charged again."

"How about a promotion instead, sir?"

"And tear the stripes off you a week later?"

The men around him laughed as Michael shook his head with mock sincerity, raised the bottle as a token of respect, and gulped down half of it before passing what was left over to Lubbeck.

"Now, keep your mouths shut about this, boys," Pleasants announced, and his friendly manner was gone, replaced by a cold sternness which every man in the regiment knew never to cross.

"I know how you banter with the Rebs. That's fine, but if one of you, just one of you, says a word across the line about blowing things up, I'll have you tied to a wheel, then bucked, and gagged, so help me God I will. If I believed in flogging I'd do that, too, and in this case I just might do it anyhow. Do you understand me?"

No one spoke.

"I want this to stay here, not a word to any other men of this regiment, and by God not a whisper of it to any man of another regiment. For this to work it has to be secret, and the surprise has to be complete. Do we understand each other?"

"Yes, sir," and all were nodding in agreement.

"Corporal Kochanski, come with me. Keep your heads down, boys. I'll let you know if anything comes of this."

Crouching low, Pleasants, followed by Stan and Captain Conrad, went into the covered communications trench that led to the rear.

"Boys, thanks to me, we just might be doing some real digging now," Michael announced, gesturing to Hans to pass the bottle back. Hans ignored him, passing it instead to Johann.

"Let's just pray we aren't digging our graves," Johann said quietly, taking a sip and then passing the bottle on and away from Michael.

HEADQUARTERS, GENERAL AMBROSE BURNSIDE
JUNE 25, 1864

✳✳✳✳✳✳✳✳✳✳✳✳✳✳✳✳✳✳✳✳✳✳✳✳✳✳

General Ambrose Burnside, commander of the Ninth Corps, assigned for now to the Army of the Potomac, stood silent outside his command bunker, just over a half mile from the front lines.

The sun was setting behind the Rebel lines, silhouetting Fort Pegram, revealing it in high relief, perched atop a low crest line. He studied it, as he did nearly every evening now, with raised field glasses, the red glow of the setting sun glinting off the polished barrels of the bronze Napoleon field pieces. Six hundred yards beyond the fort, cut along the side of a low hill, he could see a couple of Rebel ambulances daring a passage on the Jerusalem Plank Road.

That road was the main artery stitching the Confederate line together. Once darkness fell, if the night was still and there was a breeze coming from the west, it was easy to hear the rumbling of their supply wagons, jouncing along the plank-covered way, moving what meager supplies and equipment Lee still had in his possession. It was the one and only road just behind the siege lines that ran parallel to the Rebel lines. Cut it, and the Rebel army would be cut in half as well. The road was described to him by one of his staff as the "aorta of Bobbie Lee, cut it, and he and his army will be dead."

A week and a half ago they had come so damnably close to doing just that; their last futile charge going to ground in front of the Rebel fort atop the ridge; during the ensuing night his men digging in just below the lip of that ridge. Common sense dictated that he should have pulled the men back to here, the next ridge line over, but George Meade, in direct command of the Army of the Potomac, had insisted that the forward line be held, and it was now the closest and most dangerous position of the entire vast siege line that arced around Petersburg.

Even here, eight hundred yards back, his staff was not all together happy with his evening surveys. Just as he thought about that, a bullet hummed overhead.

A stray round, but Captain Charles Vincent, his adjutant, flinched and then made the gesture of stepping in front of him.

He smiled.

"How often do we have this argument, Vincent?" Burnside asked.

"Every damn night, sir. I tell you that Rebs over there can spot you easy enough, and well, sir, you do present a rather imposing figure."

He chuckled and shook his head.

Ambrose Burnside, unassuming as he was inwardly, knew that he was one of the more recognizable men in this army, in which so many vainglorious men strove to stand out. He did not so strive himself but achieved it, nevertheless, with his immense muttonchop whiskers, his towering frame, and impressive height—the same height as Lincoln, though stout, with a good sixty pounds more weight than the gaunt President—and, of course, his high conical hat, which he deliberately wore so that his men could easily spot him in the smoke and confusion of the battlefield.

The evening was hot, and it was good to be out of the bunker, which served as his command post. Unbuttoning his double-breasted

jacket, he pulled out a handkerchief and wiped the sweat from his brow and neck. A scar from an Apache arrow, picked up while serving on the frontier after the Mexican War, still troubled him at times, and tonight it was sensitive to the touch as he flexed the muscles of his shoulders and winced slightly.

"Vincent, I admire your loyalty, but you stand barely five two in your stocking feet, so unless you get a ladder to stand on, I doubt you will catch a bullet if it is meant for me."

"Sir, a Rebel armed with one of those Whitworth rifles could drill you certain."

"Why, at this range, he couldn't hit . . ." his voice trailed off, a touch of superstition evident. He was about to finish the sentence, which had been the last words of his old friend John Sedgwick of Sixth Corps, killed last month by a Rebel sharpshooter at Spotsylvania at nearly this same range.

A few more bullets whizzed past; it was obvious they were indeed aiming for him.

Fear for his personal safety had never bothered Burnside all that much. Far more frightening to him was the responsibility of his command. He loved the men of this army, especially those of his loyal Ninth Corps. His mistakes, and he was frank enough with himself to know when he was taxed beyond his ability, had cost many a life, such as at the infamous bridge at Antietam across which he had ordered suicidal frontal attacks, and especially when he briefly commanded this entire army a year and a half ago at Fredericksburg. Twelve thousand dead and wounded that day, and a day did not go by when he did not feel a deep and dreadful sense of inner torment over that tragedy.

He had not wanted the command when Lincoln offered it to him, in fact he had turned it down twice, only relenting when told that if he did not take it, it would go instead to Joe Hooker, a man whom he secretly detested as lacking in moral fiber.

Relegated back to command of his old Ninth Corps after Fredericksburg, he and his men had become the most "wandering" corps of the army. While the Ninth Corps served at Vicksburg without Burnside, he rejoined them for the Knoxville Campaign and served with the Army of the Potomac. Under his own independent command they had absolutely trounced Longstreet at Knoxville. Then Grant recalled him east for what was now known as the Wilderness Campaign. He and his men had gone through the toughest fighting of the war these last seven weeks, his command sustaining over 50 percent casualties in the ghastly bloodlettings.

Stalled in front of Petersburg, the army had tried one more flanking attempt and come within a hairsbreadth of success. Richmond's present survival was dependent on the Confederate supply line being kept open at Petersburg, where four railroads and several plank roads converged. Take Petersburg, and Richmond had to surrender. General Grant had seized on the idea at last, but then moved too slowly, allowing Lee to shift to meet this new threat. If only he had been ordered to attack a day earlier. The heights guarding the Jerusalem Plank Road had been all but naked, but a furious night of digging by the Rebs had thrown up a defensive line, and he had lost more than a thousand men trying to storm it. In the days since, every night one could hear them digging over there, strengthening the line which protected their one vital artery, an artery that connected the Rebel army together along a siege line more than a dozen miles in length.

Another bullet hummed by, close enough that he felt the concussive slap of the bullet.

"Oh, for heaven's sake, General," Vincent sighed.

He simply nodded, scanning the enemy position one more time. On the Confederate left flank of Fort Pegram, a third of a mile or so north, was high ground, crowned with a church, called Blandford. It predated the Revolution by nearly a hundred years. It was within range of his heavier guns, but he had issued the strictest orders that it was not to be molested. But . . . if only they could take that church- and cemetery-crowned hill, just beyond that rise, the city of Petersburg would be at their feet. Put a division up there, backed with a battalion of artillery, and Lee would either have to counterattack head-on and bleed himself out doing so, or abandon the city. Abandon Petersburg, and Richmond would have to be abandoned as well.

It would be the end of the war here in Virginia, perhaps triggering an entire collapse of the Rebel cause . . . and his men were the ones in the perfect position to do it. If not for that seething anthill, that fort atop the heights, which would turn any charge into a slaughter ground as bad, perhaps worse, than Cold Harbor . . . He paused in his thoughts . . . or, yes, as bad or worse than what he had tried and failed to do at Fredericksburg.

"All right, Vincent, let's go back in," and his adjutant sighed with relief, the poor lad flinching when, seconds after they stepped away from the low parapet he had been standing on, a couple of more bullets slapped the air.

He forced a smile to cheer Vincent.

"Not yet our time," he said good-naturedly, slapping the shaken adjutant on the shoulder.

They stepped down into the bunker, a log-sided structure cut into the earth along the main reserve line for the sector. The fourteen-gun battery, a quarter mile to his left, opened up, each piece firing in measured sequence, beginning the nighttime of harassing fire to be dropped onto the Jerusalem Road. The Rebel mortar battery inside the fort opened a reply, lobbing shells toward the heavy battery. The nightly fireworks had begun.

His telegrapher, sitting in the corner of the bunker, looked up and just shook his head, indicating no new messages from Meade or Grant. In the gloom, illuminated only by a smoky coal oil lamp, he took off his jacket, preparing to bed down for the night on a cot in the corner. But then he noticed someone had entered the bunker while he was out for his evening stroll and examination of the line.

"Colonel Pleasants?"

"Sir," and the man stiffened to attention.

He prided himself on knowing the name of every regimental commander and often many of the subordinates of the nearly forty regiments of his corps.

"To what do I owe the honor of this visit?"

"Sir, something has come up, an idea from some of my men, and I wanted to talk to you about it directly."

He hesitated. He wanted his men to feel he was approachable but some of the sticklers for regulations would, of course, object if

Pleasants had not gone through the proper chain of command by first going to brigade and then division before coming here.

"General, I'm taking the liberty of coming straight to you with this. Sir, you were an engineer before the war, and I think, sir, you'll grasp what I'm talking about. Going through channels . . . " he hesitated. "Well, sir, if I had gone to General Ledlie first, it might have taken days. I think this is too important to wait. Also, sir, you know how staff officers can talk when they're not supposed to. By the time my suggestion got up to you, dozens would be chattering and well, sir, this idea depends on complete surprise so thus I've taken this liberty, which I hope you will forgive."

Burnside nodded. Few had much love, or respect, for Pleasants's division commander. Good-natured and forgiving at heart, one prone to not like confrontations, Burnside was beginning to have to face the fact that the entire corps was filled with rumors that Ledlie's nerves were shot, that he had become a "bunker and bottle" general.

He hesitated.

"Let's just call this a friendly visit then," Burnside replied, and motioned him over to a small rough-hewn table, which served as his desk. Pleasants sat down across from him on a wobbly stool with a sheaf of oversized papers rolled up in his hand.

"Well, let's see what you came here about," Burnside offered, motioning to the papers. Obviously a bit nervous, Pleasants rolled them out, weighting down the corners with a couple of empty bottles, and Burnside leaned forward to look at the drawings.

"This came from talking with some of my men earlier today, sir. Remember, sir, nearly every man in my regiment worked in the Pennsylvania coal mines before the war. I thought about it, had some plans drawn up, and by God, sir, I think it just might work . . ."

It was past midnight when Pleasants finally stepped out of the bunker, Burnside following him, offering a cigar, which Pleasants refused. Burnside lit his up and puffed it to life.

"I want you to start on this at once. Only your regiment is to be involved. I'll have Captain Vincent draw up a provost detail to block off any approach to your front line position from even a single man outside of your regimental area. You are right, sir; this does depend on absolute secrecy. I'll compress your flanks in a bit to free up men for your project, but it must be kept secret."

"As I said, I have impressed that upon the men already, sir."

"I leave the details to you and your men. As you said, nearly all in your command were miners before the war. If anyone can figure out how to do it and carry the job through, it'll be them."

"Thank you, sir."

"Tomorrow, survey the site."

"I'll need a theodolite for starters, sir."

"The engineers at army headquarters must have one; I'll get it for you. But you don't need that to start; you can just do a compass bearing to begin with. Find a secure spot where you are absolutely certain the Rebs cannot see what is going on. As you said, a lot of things to be figured out, but I want it started now."

"Sir, a question."

"And that is?"

"If we do it and make it work, I don't want to see it just as an exercise in murder."

"What?"

"Just that, sir. I mean just blowing up the fort and that is the end of it. To me that is little better than murder. I think this could be far more, a way of breaking the siege and ending this damn war. That means, sir, a lot more than our just digging."

Burnside smiled.

"I already had something developing even as you set it out before me. A lot more, Colonel, a lot more."

"Taking the road and Blandford Church?" Pleasants asked hopefully.

"You worry about your project, which you are to start now. Let me worry about the rest.

"I'll go up to see Meade tomorrow." He hesitated. "I'm certain he'll approve. Colonel, you just might have come up with an idea to end this war."

Pleasants smiled encouragingly.

"I'll get back to you once I meet with Meade."

"Sir. Tools, picks, shovels—both long and short handled—shoring material, extra rations for the men doing the hard labor."

"I'll take care of it, Colonel," and his words, filled with confidence, also carried a tone of dismissal. Saluting, Colonel Pleasants withdrew.

In part he was buoyant; the former engineer turned general had grasped the plan within minutes and already expanded on how he saw a broader plan to exploit its potential. But this was the Army of the Potomac, and across three bitter years there had been dozens of plans put forth, all of them with the statement, "Boys, we can end the war with this one."

He sighed as he watched Pleasants disappear into the darkness. He then returned to his bunker to expand out on the plan, such a rich beautiful plan, which he would take to Meade come morning. Surely Meade, though there was no love lost between them, would see the elegance and simplicity of the idea—its rich potential—and then throw in his endorsement.

CHAPTER FOUR

CITY POINT, VIRGINIA
JUNE 28, 1864

✳✳✳✳✳✳✳✳✳✳✳✳✳✳✳✳✳✳✳✳✳✳✳✳✳✳

"ROUTE STEP, BOYS, KEEP IT AT ROUTE STEP," THE SERGEANT major commanded and then paused. "And look smart!"

Sergeant Major Garland White moved to the side of the column, looking back down the length of the 28th to see that orders were being followed. He then glanced over the side of the "roadway," filled with awe and, admittedly, nervousness as well.

They were crossing the James River over the great pontoon bridge, which spanned nearly a mile in length. After the disaster at Cold Harbor, the Army of the Potomac had been stalled in front of Richmond for another week. Their movement, which had started in early May, was halted. Nearly all thought it would now be a repeat of McClellan's disastrous Peninsula Campaign of 1862, with General Grant also conceding defeat and withdrawing back toward Fredericksburg.

But the western general, a veteran of maneuvering up and down the Tennessee, Cumberland, and Mississippi Rivers, had an ace up his sleeve after all. The massive bridge was constructed in secret, towed up the river in sections during the night, and, in less than a day, anchored in place. It had steam tugs placed at intervals to help keep it secure and a drawbridge in the middle to allow river traffic supplying the army to move through. Before the bridge was even completed, Grant had secretly abandoned his works in front of Richmond. Force-marching the entire army south, he had flung the Army of the Potomac across the river, and now in front of him was Petersburg.

It should have been obvious to everyone, all along, that Petersburg was the true key to Richmond, the back door into the Rebel capital. Four rail lines from the Deep South converged there, along with several major roads. From that bustling river town at the confluence of the James and Appomattox rivers came forth the supplies and replacement troops, funneled north into the beleaguered Rebel capital. It was now all so obvious: take the back door at Petersburg and Richmond will fall within days, like a decaying apple dropping from a tree whose roots have been torn out.

Now, it was obvious. Grant, for that brief moment, had shown, yet again, the strategic flair that had won him so many victories in the west, from Forts Henry and Donelson to Vicksburg and Chattanooga. But once across the river, although Petersburg was all but undefended, the Army of the Potomac froze, just as it froze after stealing a march on Bobbie Lee, not quite believing they had done so, giving the Rebels time to respond.

Grant had hesitated for three crucial days—compounded by the endemic disease of the Army of the Potomac: faulty staff work and communications. He launched only half-hearted probing attacks, which had easily stormed over the massive defensive works of the city, which were then manned by only a few thousand troops, but he stopped less than a mile from his goal: the center of the city. By that time Lee had rushed men south to meet the threat, and it had settled into yet another bloody siege.

Perverse as it seemed to have uttered a prayer for such continued violence, Garland White and the men of the 28th had openly prayed that the war would wait, just a few weeks longer, for them to arrive. Since ordered out of Washington, they had languished for nearly two weeks at a reserve depot behind the Richmond lines. With every dispatch from the front—the vast move to the south, crossing the James, the fighting in front of Petersburg—they had met the reports with frustration. They were so close, with victory obviously pending, but they were prevented from engaging in the siege.

Young Lieutenant Grant, and even Colonel Russell, both veterans of the hard fighting of the previous two years, had smiled wearily, shaken their heads, and offered reassurance, if it could be called such, that the fight was a long way from being finished, and they would still get their chance.

Other USCT regiments were coming into the depot. To their delight one of them was the 29th USCT, recruited out of neighboring Illinois. More than a few friends and kin had been reunited. Near on to four thousand strong, nine regiments, they had assembled, waited, and drilled until at last a vast cavalry column, under the legendary Phil Sheridan, came riding in with orders for the men to fall in with him and proceed south . . . to the war.

The day before Sheridan arrived they had even seen their first action: a brief tangle with some Rebel militia and cavalry. The regiment had taken its first casualties, two dead and half a dozen wounded. That evening their camp had been buzzing with excitement—at last they were in the thick of it—until some white cavalry troopers, walking through their encampment, dulled their enthusiasm with disdainful remarks that their experience was nothing more than a little mischief against a handful of rabble, and they would sing a different song when they finally went head to head with a real army led by Lee himself.

Garland had taken it upon himself to go personally to Colonel Russell to seek his opinion on the affair. The colonel had expressed his pride in how they had handled themselves under fire but then agreed that it was merely a foreshadowing of far more to come.

Russell was a good man, a good officer, proud of his regiment, and had devoted many an evening since the regiment first mobilized back in Indiana to converting Garland from a man of the cloth, but already a leader of men, into a man of war, a sergeant major who would lead men into battle. The bond was now close, one of mutual respect. In the breast pocket of his uniform, tucked in behind a Bible, Garland now carried "Scott's Manual of Drill," personally given to him by Russell and far more difficult to master than even the most confusing and obscure passages of Revelations.

Standing on the edge of the wooden road, resting high out of the water on barges anchored every thirty feet across the mile-wide river, Garland could not contain his amazement at this vast structure. His army had built it in a single night to span a mighty river and then fling across it a hundred thousand men, two hundred pieces of field artillery, and all the accoutrements of war that went with them. It made him think of the vast bridges built by the likes of Alexander and Caesar to move their armies, and perhaps blasphemously, that even Moses and Joshua might have found this useful in their marches, if they had not had the hand of God to part the waters for them.

The drawbridge ahead was down for the passing of the division. Steam tugs were on the down-river side, pressed up firm against the side of the bridge, their paddlewheels turning ever so slowly to help keep the bridge firmly in place. The roadway beneath their feet lurched and moved back and forth—slightly.

"Route step, boys; no marching, lads; just route step," Garland announced. He could see that more than a few of the men were nervous; the ones who could not swim were outright terrified, looking back and forth wide-eyed, exclaiming over the experience.

"Quiet in the ranks!" he snapped. "Just keep to route step and we'll soon be across."

He caught the eye of Sergeant Felton of Company A, motioning for him to keep the regimental flags up high and vertical. Felton nodded and whispered a command to the color bearers.

The regiment tramped across the hundred-foot span of the drawbridge, passing under the support trusses and the hissing steam engine used to raise and lower the bridge. The sound of the decking beneath their feet was different, the men bunching up nervously, trying to get across as quickly as possible.

"Keep in your files, boys. Just relax," he said soothingly, even though it did make his stomach knot up as he gave a sidelong glance back over the side of the bridge . . . He couldn't swim a stroke and knew that if the bridge should collapse, or if he fell over the side—burdened down as he was with pack, ammunition, NCO sword, and rifle—he would sink like a stone to the bottom of the dark muddy waters. It was one thing to be shot fighting for freedom. It was altogether more terrifying to imagine being drowned in that struggle in a dark muddy river.

The last of the regiment passed. Twenty yards behind them the men of the 29th approached, their colonel dismounted, leading his skittish mount by the bridle. Garland offered him a salute, turned, and double-timed along the side of his column, offering encouragement and a pat on a shoulder to a man here and there, finally regaining the front of the unit.

Russell, dismounted along with the other officers, looked over at him and smiled.

"All's well?" Russell asked.

"Yes, sir. Boys are a bit nervous though with this bridge."

Russell leaned over.

"So am I. Hate pontoon bridges; I can't swim."

"Nor can I, sir."

The two laughed softly, the column slowing for a moment, commands shouted to stand at ease, then moving forward again.

The opposite shore was drawing closer, now only a few hundred yards off. The sight before them filled Garland with yet more wonder.

City Point had been converted from a small whistle-stop port on the James into the sprawling supply center for the army besieging Petersburg. There were dozens of ships of every description: tugs and barges, packet boats, two- and three-masted ships, an old sternwheel boat flying a hospital flag, and two massive monitor ironclads, which were ponderously backing away from freshly built piers. A steam-driven crane was chugging away, lifting a huge stumpy-looking mortar that must have weighed half a dozen tons off the deck of a barge, swinging it over to a waiting wagon drawn by a dozen mules.

Scores of rough-made huts, hundreds of tents, and vast open-sided warehouses had gone up in just a few short weeks. Beyond the low bluff were hundreds of supply wagons, rows of guns, stacks of ration boxes, and pyramid-like piles of barrels. All along the waterfront, hundreds of men labored, moving crates and boxes of ammunition. With dismay, Garland saw that nearly all of them were colored and in uniform. They had labored this way in Washington when not on burial details, and again in the depot behind the lines at Richmond, and he had a momentary sinking feeling that this was to be their fate yet again: to have finally reached the front and then be sent to the rear, only to labor while other men, white men, got to fight for freedom.

As if reading his mind, Russell took in the vista before them and just shook his head.

"Generals ahead," he whispered. "I think it's Burnside and Meade. As soon as the men are off the bridge, marching step, eyes right, salute arms."

Still a hundred yards from shore, Colonel Russell stilled his misgivings about being mounted on a shaky pontoon bridge, swung himself into the saddle, and unsheathed his sword.

He looked down at Garland and smiled.

"Let's make a good first impression. Order the fifers to play 'Hell on the Wabash,' let them know we're Indiana men here to fight, Sergeant Major."

General Ambrose Burnside stiffened to attention as the head of the column cleared the approach ramp to the bridge, smiling inwardly as the fifers at the front of the column broke into a jaunty air, the theme song for men from the Hoosier state.

"That must be the regiment from Indiana," one of his staff, Captain Maury Hurt, exclaimed. He had always liked that tune, being a graduate of Oberlin College, and, though a Quaker, he had joined the fight for the ending of slavery.

"They look good, damn good," another of his staff exclaimed.

"Looking good and fighting good are two different things," one of Meade's staff retorted.

Burnside did not let the remark bother him, though he did look over his shoulder at the major who had made it, fixing him with his gaze for a second. The man just smiled defiantly. Turning back he caught a glimpse of a photographer with Brady trying to capture the scene, nearby him an illustrator with sketchpad out, working feverishly with quick strokes to try and capture the moment. Good, he hoped they would capture the truth of the moment.

"Battalion, prepare to pass in review!"

Although he did not recognize the mounted officer, he was obviously the commander of the lead regiment, and he spared a glance over his shoulder as he looked back at his column. Facing forward, sword resting on his shoulder, his mount nervously danced a bit as they came up the slippery, corduroyed road, paved with logs split in half and rough-hewn boards.

Flag-bearers of the regiment hoisted their colors high, the national flag and the distinctive sky-blue colored flag emblazoned with an eagle: flags unique to the regiments of the USCT. A light breeze was coming in off the James, flinging the colors out, so that they snapped and fluttered, the gold thread catching the sunlight so that the flag seemed to sparkle.

General George Meade, in direct command of the Army of the Potomac under Grant, stood with his staff a few yards away, showing no emotion one way or the other, but then again, he rarely did. He came to attention though.

"Battalion, eyes right! Pass in review!"

As one the men of the 28th stiffened, left hands crossing their breasts to steady their weapons, turning heads to the right, shifting from the route step, required on any pontoon bridge, to the march, keeping perfect time to the beat of the fifers and drummers.

"Very smart indeed," Burnside announced as he returned the salute.

Regiment after regiment passed by, the men of the 29th out of Illinois, followed by the 31st out of New York, their fifers playing, "We Are Coming, Father Abraham." Each regiment showing a smartness to drill, shoulders squared back, uniforms new and clean, muskets polished to a mirror-sheen.

They did not yet look like the true veterans of the Army of the Potomac did after nearly two months of solid campaigning in the

field. A scattering of those stood on the far side of the road, the dye of the dark blue of their jackets faded from the sun, sweat, and rain, cuffs of trouser and jackets frayed. Trousers once sky blue were now a dingy, faded, nearly indistinguishable color, heavily layered with the red clay of Virginia. Their knees were patched with whatever fabric could be found, and trouser leggings stuffed into heavy over-sized gray wool socks in a vain attempt to keep out the chiggers, fleas, and ticks that swarmed in the fields and trenches. Few of them wore the regulation kepi hat, a useless issue to soldiers if ever there was one. Most had tossed them aside for broad-brimmed floppy hats of black, gray, or brown to shade the eyes and the back of the neck from the blistering sun. The only thing about the veterans that was precise, clean, and obviously well tended were their rifles, which were casually slung, inverted, over their shoulders.

Most were unshaven, all of them lean and wiry, and their eyes had that strange hard gaze of veterans, as if looking off to some far distant land that only a veteran could truly see and understand.

The men of the nine new regiments of this, the newly formed Fourth Division of the fabled Ninth Corps, did not yet have that look, that "feel," no matter how proudly they now marched. More than a few derisive comments drifted from the other side of the road: "Fresh fish"; "You boys gonna see the elephant now for sure"; "Hey there darkie, you think you're a soldier?"; and far worse. The worn veterans of this worn army did not take lightly to new recruits until they had proven themselves in battle, and now they could complain further about the fact that they were black as well.

In spite of the insults only a few of the men marching by wavered, turning slightly to cast an angry glance at their taunters.

"They better get used to it," one of Burnside's staff whispered.

"No, we better get used to them," another staffer responded firmly.

Burnside ignored the comments, eyes fixed on these men, examining them with the practiced gaze of a general who had commanded men in battle for over two years and in nearly every theater of the war.

When in Mississippi, Tennessee, and the coast of Carolina, he had seen slaves by the thousands coming into their lines, but these men looked different. All nine regiments were recruited out of northern or border states, the muster rolls showing him that in fact, contrary to myth regarding the USCT, a very high proportion of them had been born as freemen in the North. The majority even had some education and could read and write. Those not born free had either been manumitted by their owners long before the war or had purchased their own freedom and then drifted north. Few had come straight from slavery into army blue. They looked healthier than the typical slave who had endured years of hard labor, usually with scant rations and few comforts.

Their officers, as he knew, were the pick of the army. When the USCT began to form after the Emancipation Proclamation, the decision had been made that all their officers were to be white. The criteria for their selection were rigid. They had to be combat veterans, preferably of noncommissioned rank, of good moral character, literate, with letters of recommendation from their company and regimental officers.

If they passed this first mark and were accepted by the examining board, it was off to a newly established officers' training school in Philadelphia, the first of its kind. The veterans were then drilled yet again, but now in how to teach drill to new recruits, along with classes ranging from history to military justice and proper etiquette of an officer. Only after testing and another review board were they recommended for promotion to either lieutenant or captain of a company. Potential regimental commanders, already commissioned, went through the same rigorous drill before at last being assigned to their regiments.

They knew the prejudices they would face; they had already faced them when they had first volunteered to serve with the colored troops. Those who had chosen service with the USCT to simply get out of the front lines for a while or for the shoulder bars were weeded out early enough. The men who remained believed in what they were doing and were as eager as their troops to prove their mettle.

The last of the regiments came off the bridge, men of the 32nd Ohio, fifers playing the traditional, "Rally 'Round the Flag." Burnside was deeply moved by it all. It had been a long time, a very long time, since he had seen and heard troops march to such music, showing such precision and fresh new pride.

The veterans who had been watching on the far side of the road stood silent, realizing that a bevy of generals were standing across from them. As veterans, they knew when it was time to make themselves scarce before being tasked with some additional duty. The contrast between the two, though, Burnside caught him yet again. To a casual civilian eye, regardless of race, the comparison would be that the men on the far side of the road were filthy rabble, the men who just marched by the true soldiers.

It was this "rabble," though, who had endured the forest fire in the Wilderness, the bloody charge at Cold Harbor, who had held their ground at Gettysburg and Antietam. It was they who had seen this army through three long years of bloody war. And once, long ago, a very long time ago, they had marched as the colored troops did now, uniforms clean and neat, flags held high, fifers playing, and singing together the patriotic songs.

A place like Cold Harbor or Antietam took that out of a man forever, emptying him and filling him instead with a weary cynicism, as well as a toughness for war with all its myriad horrors. Nearly all were volunteers or men who might have drawn an enlistment bounty but were then matched to hometown regiments. The "bounty men" and draftees were shipped down to the army in locked boxcars to form new regiments—many a man deserted with the first opportunity. Those who stayed were, in general, men ready to prove themselves; they were volunteers. The cowards had long ago run off. Many of the best of them were in shallow graves across Virginia, Maryland, and Pennsylvania. The ones that were left had no illusions: they knew that chances were high that a shallow grave was in their future.

And as Burnside gazed at them he knew what he had to do. Veterans, often far better than their generals, knew when a battle order, especially a charge, had some chance, no matter how small, of success. After the utter debacle at Cold Harbor, this army of veterans had all but mutinied. They had disobeyed orders out of a cold pragmatic sense of survival. Never again would there be a charge like the one at Cold Harbor. If ordered to take a heavily fortified position, more often than not the veterans would just stare in silence at their commanders, many times even joined by their company and regimental officers. They would stay in their trenches, or at best make a half-hearted demonstration of advancing a few dozen yards, then immediately fall back.

They were not cowards; they were the hardened elite of an elite army. They simply knew what was possible and what was next to impossible.

He looked toward the long, sinuous column of black men—four thousand of them—a column near to half a mile long, dust swirling up by their passage, as they marched to a reserve position a mile behind the main lines where they would camp tonight.

These men did not yet know what was possible and what was not. Such men, if ordered to charge, would do so without hesitation, filled with the new recruits' desires to prove themselves. Their veteran officers might know the reality, but they wished to prove their own worth as well. And finally, these were colored troops . . . if ever a division of men had joined this army with a burning passion to prove something, it would be this one.

"Burnside."

He stirred from his musings and looked to his left. It was Meade.

How much things had changed between them. Only eighteen months ago, Burnside had been in command of the Army of the Potomac in front of Fredericksburg, and Meade was just a division

commander. Meade's reputation then was that he was a brave leader from the front, but brusque, cantankerous, and in an army noted for giving nicknames, his men could only find terms such as "ole goggle eyes," or "the snapping turtle." He had to admit inwardly that both nicknames fit, especially "the snapping turtle." Meade walked with head drawn in slightly but when angered would lean forward as if ready to snap.

In a year and a half their positions had changed dramatically. In six months Meade had sprung from division command to lead a corps at Chancellorsville and then command the entire army at Gettysburg. Burnside had been demoted to command of Ninth Corps after the fiasco at Fredericksburg and the infamous "Mud March" a month later, and his corps detached from the Army of the Potomac and shifted west for over a year, keeping the two generals apart.

Meade made no bones about his lack of respect for Burnside. In his after-action report for Fredericksburg, he bitterly complained that his was the only division to pierce the Rebel lines, after which he had called for support to exploit the breakthrough, and Burnside had done nothing.

And with a humility rather unique for commanding generals, Burnside was the first to admit that at Fredericksburg the failure was his and his alone.

Meade, however, apparently would never forget or forgive.

"A word, Burnside," Meade announced, motioning for Burnside to come the last few steps to him. Of course he did as ordered; such deference was expected to the commander of an army, even one who was in the strangely unique position of being in command but essentially having little real power. For over them all was the presence of Ulysses S. Grant, commander of all the Armies of the Union, who had chosen to make his headquarters here, and in the field often took direct tactical command of this force. What little power Meade still retained he guarded jealously, especially when Grant was back in Washington to meet with the President or Secretary of War Stanton.

Meade gestured for his staff to leave and Burnside did the same for his, the two officers turning to slowly walk together down to the edge of the river. A long column of supply wagons was now on the bridge, their progress stopped as the drawbridge was raised to let a twin-turret monitor pass upstream.

"I've reviewed your suggestion, Burnside, for this scheme of yours about digging a tunnel," Meade announced without preamble.

"And?"

"I've passed it up to Grant, of course, but did so without my endorsement."

A bit surprised, Burnside slowed and looked straight at Meade.

"May I ask why?"

"My engineering staff says it is impossible to construct a mine of over five hundred feet in length beneath the surface, and keep it properly ventilated without poking breathing holes to the surface, which of course would reveal it to the Rebs."

Burnside sighed inwardly, saying nothing yet. It wasn't wise to interrupt Meade in mid-thought.

"Second, that your demand for ten tons of medium- and coarse-grain powder for the explosion is excessive."

He stopped, looking up at Burnside with a sidelong glance.

A casual observer not knowing the two might have been confused as to who the commander really was. Burnside towered over his commander, who was wiry, short, and round-shouldered. Meade, head cocked, protruding eyes gazing up at Burnside, had his neck now thrust forward like a turtle ready to snap.

"I assume there are more negatives," Burnside finally replied.

"Plenty more. You've taken a lot onto yourself, Burnside. Your plan states that three corps will be engaged in the assault and should be a single unified command, which you imply should be you. Good God, that is a third of our army here and would leave no reserves if things turn into a disaster."

He fell silent for a moment, shaking his head.

"And without my authorization, have you not already told your men to start digging?"

"They've gained thirty feet so far," Burnside finally offered.

"You ordered them to start digging this thing of yours without getting proper clearance from me?"

"Sir, respectfully, they are men of my corps and since the order to start in no way impacts the daily duties of the rest of my command, other than a minor adjustment to which regiment holds the front line, I see no harm in the exercise."

"It could build false expectations."

"Sir?"

"As I said, my engineers tell me that ultimately it is impossible."

"Sir, may I address the issues raised? That is of course if you are finished."

Meade grunted his assent, while fumbling in his pocket for a cigar, then muttering a curse that he had left his cigar case behind. Burnside reached into his breast pocket, pulled out a silver case containing half a dozen Cubans, and offered one to his commander, who muttered his thanks. Burnside took one out as well; the two bit off the ends, spitting them out. Burnside struck a lucifer on the sole of his shoe, offered the flame to Meade, and then puffed his own cigar to life.

The two stood silent for a moment, wreathed in smoke. Burnside hoped that the small gesture would calm Meade and be an indicator of deference and good will.

"May I respond to your objections, George?" he asked, venturing to address Meade by his first name.

"I assumed you would."

"First, regarding the assertion of your staff engineers that the task is impossible."

"That is what they say, and Burnside, these are mostly West Point trained men. If anyone knows military engineering, they are the ones."

"How many of them have ever worked in a coal mine?"

"What?"

"Just that, sir," deciding to drop the more familiar "George." "My men of the 48th Pennsylvania nearly all come out of the anthracite coal fields. Their commander, Colonel Pleasants, was a mining engineer before the war."

"So what does he know that my men don't?"

"Practical experience, sir. A lot of new techniques learned since you and I were at West Point. I raised the same question when Pleasants first approached me. He gave me a quick education on it all and had already devised a plan."

"Oh, really? Air, drainage if they hit a spring, keeping it all concealed . . . Those coal mines have steam engine pumps and ventilators, for God's sake. If we drag that equipment up, the Rebels will laugh themselves sick before turning a few dozen mortars loose on it."

"It's rather ingenious actually," Burnside replied. "A simple woodstove was all they needed. Also, the tunnel for its entire length will slope uphill, and if they hit a spring, it will just naturally drain out. Where they started is well concealed about sixty yards further back from the front line, near the bottomland that traverses the front, and all diggings will be hauled out at night to be dumped in a ravine so the Rebs can't see the difference in the soil. It is a well thought-out plan, and I urge your engineers to come up and look it over."

He did not add that perhaps it would be a damn good education for them as well as to what is and is not impossible, rather than making armchair decisions miles behind the lines.

Meade puffed meditatively on his cigar.

"They've already dug thirty feet?"

"Yes, sir, a good start in just three days."

"But that was without my authorization."

"Sir, your various corps commanders have a hundred thousand men digging all the time—new trenches, revetments, covered passageways, and even tunnels from front lines to the rear—clearing and corduroying roads . . ."

He fell silent for a moment.

"Surely they do not come and bother you with every detail of what they are doing?"

Meade stared at him sullenly without a reply.

"Regarding the amount of powder, that was the recommendation of Colonel Pleasants. And, sir, that came in turn from a number of men with experience blasting in mines and tunnels. Surely ten tons will not tax our supplies."

He pointed to a monitor pressing its way up the James.

"That ship boasts four fourteen-inch guns, each shell propelled by nearly a hundred pounds of powder. There must be several tons on board her alone."

"We're not the Navy," Meade grumbled.

It was a minor point at the moment, Burnside thought. They could argue it out later.

"As to the tactical plan, sir. It is straightforward. Once the mine is blown, there will be a gap in the Rebel lines a couple of hundred yards across. Everything gone, everything. It is fair to say that in the ensuing minutes, panic will reign to either flank for several hundred yards or more. We will be looking at a gap at least a quarter of a mile wide."

His voice was now raised with enthusiasm. Picking up a stick, he began to trace out his thoughts on the mud beneath their feet.

"The first division in will flank either side of the mine, but they do not stop! They continue on forward, six hundred yards, and seize the Jerusalem Plank Road. The regiments to the right will then pivot and race the third of a mile to the Blandford Church and the hill it rests upon.

"From the detonation of the mine to seizing that hill should take no more than half an hour at most—at most."

Burnside emphasized his point by punching the stick into where he had traced out the hill.

"We both know, sir, that if that hill is taken, Petersburg is finished.

"Behind the lead division, in column by regiments, will come my other three divisions. One of them to pivot to the left to hold the road against counterattack, one to hold the breach open, the other to pivot right to reinforce the position at the church and then surge on into the town, which will literally be below their feet.

"That is why I'll need two more corps, sir. Next corps in will widen the breach along the front line, secure the position, and ensure that a couple of battalions of field artillery are pushed forward to reinforce the hill. The third corps will serve as operational reserve to exploit the breakthrough and secure the town. Sir, before the morning is over, Petersburg will be ours, with Lee's army cut in half and its base of supplies gone. By nightfall the rest of the army

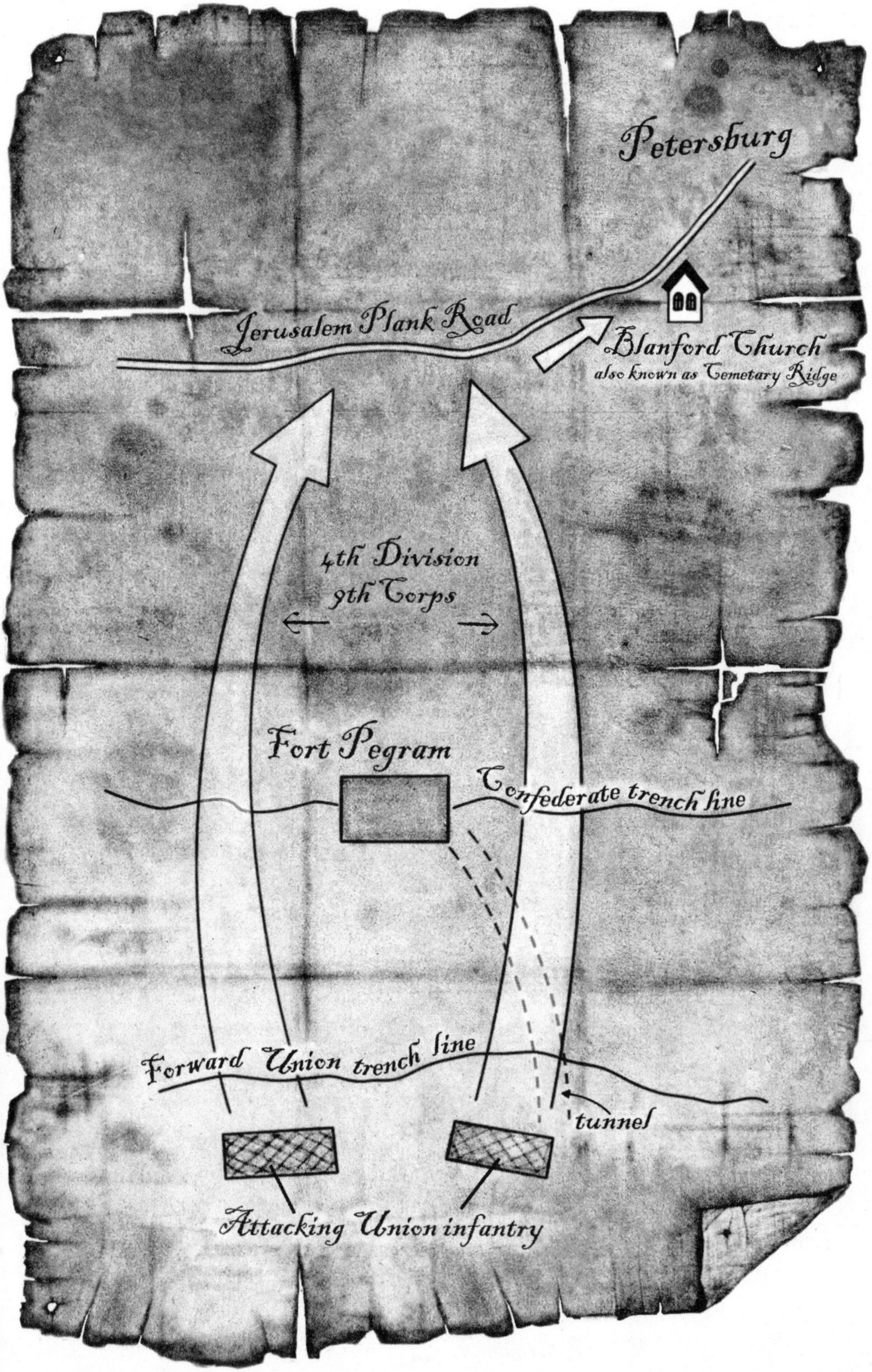

Petersburg

Jerusalem Plank Road

Blanford Church
also known as Cemetary Ridge

4th Division
9th Corps

Fort Pegram

Confederate trench line

Forward Union trench line

tunnel

Attacking Union infantry

Union Army plan of attack on Petersburg, Virginia, July 30, 1864.

could be pinning them against the Appomattox River and finishing them off. And as we both know, when Petersburg is ours, Richmond will fall, and by God, we could be looking at the victory that will win the war."

"That is based on a lot of assumptions, Burnside. You," Meade paused, "more than most, should know how plans collapse the moment battle is joined."

Burnside took the almost insulting comment without response. Every newspaper in the country had lambasted him for Fredericksburg, and in his heart he knew they were right. He had lost control of the battle before it had even started. What was so frustrating, though, was that of his victories, especially against Longstreet at Strawberry Plains outside of Knoxville, not one in a hundred knew of them.

"Sir, there are so many details we can settle later. I simply ask now for approval to move forward and at least prepare my corps for the potential of action. Pleasants states he can complete the tunnel in thirty days. I ask for those thirty days to let it go forward and to get ready."

Meade grunted, taking a deep draw on the Cuban and blowing it out.

"I told you I passed it up to Grant without endorsement."

He hesitated as if for dramatic effect.

"But Grant said to proceed with the digging." It was obvious that he was not pleased to have to give Burnside this approval.

Burnside could not contain a sigh of relief and a smile.

"But all the operational plans are still to be sorted out. First, let's see if your coal crackers can actually dig a real tunnel while at war. If there is even the remotest indication that the Rebels hear them, or get wind of what you are doing, the entire operation is off. Once completed, if completed, we can discuss details then."

"Thank you, sir."

Meade looked up at him, said nothing, and turned away.

Walking back up the slope, his staff gathered around him. They mounted and rode off.

Burnside's staff, a bit hesitant, slowly walked behind him down to the river's edge.

He looked back at them and smiled.

"It's on."

Smiles greeted his announcement, several adjutants their hands to congratulate him. He was warmed by their loyalty—many of them having served by his side since the start of the war—and by their evident enthusiasm for the plan.

They started back up the slope and one of them pointed to a man wearing a long canvas duster in spite of the heat, an oversized haversack by his side.

"Some reporter is pestering to see you, sir."

Burnside, with a remarkable memory for names and faces, remembered the man and nodded.

"Give me a few minutes with him, then back to headquarters."

He nodded for the reporter to approach and extended his hand.

"Reilly isn't it, with *Harper's Weekly?*"

"Yes, sir, surprised you remember me."

"I rather liked the sketch you did of me that your paper printed."

"Thank you, sir," James offered with a smile.

"The sketch was good, but the rest of the reporting of Fredericksburg . . ." His voice trailed off, and he gazed into Reilly's eyes. The man returned his gaze unblinkingly. A good sign he felt.

"Sir, I simply do the drawings. Others do the writing."

Burnside did not reply.

"Sir, we must admit, it was not the best of battles for our side."

Burnside sighed and shook his head. Would his name forever be associated with that debacle? Hooker had basically cribbed his plan for what became Chancellorsville but panicked and froze when, in those dark woods, his communications broke down. He had frozen in place, easy pickings for Lee and Stonewall Jackson. Burnside, himself, would have pushed on through into open land beyond. If . . . always if.

And now Hooker was out west, a corps commander again, but gaining a good name once more. Yet, Burnside always seemed to be saddled by Fredericksburg.

He shook his head.

"Not your fault, Reilly. Mine. I have and will always take the blame. I was in command and where the victory would have been mine so must the failure be. That is the nature of command."

Reilly seemed to relax, as if fearful that Burnside might have banished him because of the paper he represented.

"Reilly, I know your work. I don't hold much love for newspapermen, but I admire your drawings. You have an eye for the ordinary soldier as good as that of Ward. You don't glorify it the way Homer sometimes can. I've never heard a single complaint about you. You strike me as an honest man trying to do his job."

"Thank you, sir."

"I even remember some of your sketches of the Lincoln-Douglas debates and the 1860 campaign. It was obvious you were a Lincoln man even then."

He wondered if Burnside was probing; if there were any rumors afloat as to just how close he truly was. He said nothing in reply.

"And your reason for this interview now?" Burnside asked.

"Well, sir. I've been up here a few days. I should have checked in with you first, but let's just say there is a word going around."

"What kind of a word?" Burnside snapped.

"Just that something is up."

Burnside bristled. His cigar had gone out, even though he tried to puff on it. Reilly fished into a breast pocket, pulled out a cigar for himself, a lucifer, and relit Burnside's half-finished stogie.

"Sir, please. I am as loyal a Union man as you are and know enough when to keep my own damn mouth shut. Besides, I am only an artist, not a print correspondent."

"Assuming your hunch is even remotely correct," Burnside snapped, and then his voice trailed off.

"Sir, all I am saying is that you know how soldiers talk. A bit of a rumor going around your First Division is that something is up, but no one is saying anything specific."

He hesitated. He was trying to win this man over.

"Sir, I am simply telling you because if I can pick up on it, others will as well, and sooner or later some Reb picket will get wind, or some deserter or prisoner will spill about it. Or, yes, some reporter who will blow it back to the papers in Washington or New York."

"And you are asking me what it is all about? Perhaps give you, what do you people call it, an exclusive?"

"Absolutely not, sir," James replied forcefully. "And frankly, sir, I do not want to know until the lowest private in the ranks is given the details and not before."

Burnside filed that away. The men gossiped all the time between the lines when out on picket duty, and more than one plan had been revealed by a boastful private who met a savvy Reb in middle field during the night who was ready to share a canteen of good corn liquor, and by morning a report would be sitting on the desk of General Lee.

He would have to tighten the lid around the 48th, keep that section of the line totally isolated and their encampment isolated as well. Veterans at least did have one good instinct and that was to keep their mouths shut when their own necks might be on the line. and the men of the 48th, he hoped, could be counted on to keep their work secret and see the reason for it. In fact, he would go to their encampment tonight to impress that upon them.

"If you are asking for any further information, Reilly, I have none to offer, but I thank you for the warning I sense you are giving me."

"Well, sir, I actually wanted to ask a favor."

He felt better disposed to the man with the information given, but now he wondered if that was merely tossing out a bone to gain confidence for some bigger reward.

"Go on," he said coldly.

"The colored division."

"What of it?"

"Permission to visit their camp and sketch them for my paper."

"To what purpose?"

"They're a unique story, sir. The largest formation of black troops in the East, now serving with the Army of the Potomac. It is a special moment."

"You will give them a fair shake?"

Now it was Reilly who seemed to bristle slightly.

"Sir, I got to know some of them while in Washington earlier this month."

"How so?"

"They buried my brother," he said quietly. "Wounded at Cold Harbor, he died in Washington, and some of those men who just marched by buried him."

Burnside nodded.

"Sorry for your loss."

"We've all lost someone."

"That we have," Burnside sighed.

Burnside looked away from Reilly, back to the main road that led up to the front at Petersburg. The regiments of his new Fourth Division had disappeared from view, cloaked in swirling dust kicked up by their passage.

"Let's just say I am partial to them now, sir, and curious as well." He did not add that he was also under orders from Lincoln to see how they were received and treated by the high command.

"You ask for a favor. I will consider it if you provide one in return."

"Please ask, General."

"You have my permission to visit their camps, sketch them as you wish. But for God's sake, I will have you drummed out if I see your paper print but one illustration that is derisive of them. If you were that damn Tom Nast, I'd personally grab you by the neck and throw you in this river."

Reilly laughed softly.

"You can tell by my name and the occasional hint of the brogue where I come from. I have no more love for Nast than you do, and I promise you all my sketches will be respectful of your men."

"They are men. Soldiers, by God, and to be respected as such."

James again nodded in agreement.

Burnside sighed.

"Fine then. You draw them fairly and you stay."

"Agreed," and Reilly extended his hand.

"But there is something else," Burnside said before agreeing to shake.

He seemed to hesitate, as if mulling a decision over in his mind. He looked again toward the dust-covered road.

"I've reached a decision today regarding those men."

"And that is?"

"I want three things of you, Reilly. You draw them fair. Second, they will soon go into a special kind of training, unlike anything this army has ever done before. They will be kept off the line for a while and in isolation but that training will be damn serious. I will trust you to see it, but to keep your mouth shut. You do that and after everything is over, you can report it. But if you even attempt to leak a single word of it, by God I will have you flogged out of this camp."

Reilly nodded. "And the third favor?"

"Just drop in on me occasionally. Tell me how you see it all going. That's all."

He tried not to smile. If only this man knew that was already his task, a task for someone far higher than any general.

He wondered for an instant if there was something about him that elicited such trust, or whether it could be that this towering man, whom so many mocked, actually was outsmarting all of them, and by some means already knew the task Reilly had been assigned by his President. It did not seem possible, but it was worth pondering.

"All terms agreed to," Reilly replied and raised his hand. And this time Burnside took it and shook it warmly.

James could not help but wonder who had played a game on whom as he shook Burnside's hand. Regardless, and in spite of his reservations because of the debacle at Fredericksburg, he felt he could actually like and trust this man.

Farther up the road, halfway back to the front line, General Meade sat waiting impassively while one of his staff stricken with the two steps had run off into a woodlot to relieve himself, joined by several others suffering from the same "discomfort."

Burnside. It would have to be him coming up with such a scheme. He looked out across the open field to his left, heat shimmers rising. That day at Fredericksburg, it had been cold, so damn cold, the frozen ground flecked with snow, and carpeted with the bodies of men from his division, his division that he had led with such pride.

The plan of attack: all knew it was foolish. The Rebs held a long ridgeline that stretched for miles, paralleling the flood plain of the Rappahannock above the town of Fredericksburg. Of course the Rebs had let them throw pontoon bridges across the river . . . they actually wanted them to cross. Throughout that cold, bitter night the army had swarmed over, forming up rank after rank, with the arrival of dawn concealed beneath the mist that rose off the river on a cold winter morn.

And the order from Burnside, with all its lack of imagination, had simply been "Go forward."

No coordination, no maneuver, just go forward across the wide-open bottom land and then up the long slope, crossing 1,400 yards of open ground while before them waited near to 70,000 Rebs and 150 artillery pieces.

It was slaughter and yet he had obeyed. He had no choice: he was merely a division commander and that tall, fat fool in the conical hat was the commander of the Army of the Potomac.

And it was his division, his division alone, which had actually accomplished the foolish task. He recalled traversing the open ground, keeping formation and control as he rode back and forth along their length, urging them forward into the maelstrom.

They had pierced the Rebel line. Alone. As all the other divisions were charging not as one mass unit but like uncoordinated amateurs with no communication between the various divisions and corps. He alone had pierced the Rebel line, driving them back out of their position. It was then that he had sent back a triumphal note, informing headquarters of the breakthrough achieved, calling for reinforcements.

As the precious minutes ticked away he saw no columns coming up behind him out of the battle smoke and mist. Just emptiness. Another courier, and another, went galloping back, each appeal more desperate, that by God, we have a breakthrough, bring up the reserves.

But there were no reserves. None, not a single damn one. No artillery to anchor the flanks of the breakthrough, no fresh infantry to push on through and begin rolling up the Rebel line. While off to his right he could hear the continued roar of battle, of other divisions which, rather than pivoting to help him, instead continuing their own futile charges without any rhyme or reason other than because that damn fool had ordered a frontal attack.

He held the breakthrough for nearly an hour until the far more adroit Rebels, bringing up the reserves that any army should have in place for such a moment, swarmed over his men, and drove them back.

Drove him back, leaving more than half his command dead, wounded, or captured on that bloody slope.

And even as he fell back he half expected that at last someone, even just a fresh brigade, would be coming up in support, enough to rally his men around and open the hole back up.

Nothing, not a single man. It was the worst moment of this nightmare he had ever known. So many a good comrade was dead, lost for nothing, while the fat fool in that damn stupid-looking hat sat upon the far side of the river, like a statue frozen in place, never acknowledging even one of his appeals, nor ever once offering a word of apology or solace after that nightmarish day was over.

And now he wants me to give him a third of the army I now command and throw it into another frontal attack?

He shook his head wearily. Beside him his staff was coming out of the woods, one of them having to be held up by a comrade on either side, features sweaty and pale, grinning weakly and thanking his general for waiting and apologizing for the inconvenience.

More men die from that than from bullets, Meade thought, looking over impassively and judging that the lad had better be sent back to the hospital because there already was that pallor about him. *At least he'll die in a bed rather than facedown on a frozen field*, he thought grimly. *In fact they would all be home by now if only that bastard had supported me that day in front of Fredericksburg. If only . . .*

"James, Foch, would you please guide Captain Wayne to the hospital."

Wayne offered no protest, which showed indeed how sick he was.

"The rest of you, staff meeting in an hour to go over this scheme of our good friend General Burnside," he announced coldly.

CHAPTER FIVE

PETERSBURG, VIRGINIA
JULY 1, 1864
THE TUNNEL

****

"Officers coming."

"So what the hell are we supposed to do? Stand up?" Michael O'Shay said with a laugh.

He turned from the face of the tunnel and looked back at Sergeant Johann Kochanski, who had just passed the word up in a stage whisper.

"Keep your voice down," Kochanski hissed.

"Damn it, Sergeant, we're still eighty yards short of the Rebel line; they can't hear anything we say."

"Get used to keeping your mouth shut now," Corporal Lubbeck retorted. "We don't want the mistake of a drunken Irishman to kill us all."

"Then get someone else to dig if you don't like my chatter, and I can sit outside and have a pipe."

He knew he could always win on that point. He was the best digger in the Pottsville mines back home, bringing out nearly twice the tonnage of others, and he was the best here as well.

Lubbeck was the number-two man for this shift. The number one worked the face of the tunnel, digging with a short-handled spade. Prying the dirt loose while squatting or kneeling, the number-two man would scrape the dirt back and pile it into a box, usually an empty ammunition or hardtack box. It was already decided that once they got a bit closer to the Rebel lines they'd haul the dirt out in sandbags. There would be less chance of scraping, or worse, someone dropping a box and it clattering. The number two would then slide the bag or box back to a "crawler," who then, scuttling in a low squat, would carry or drag the dirt out, leave it by the tunnel entrance, get an empty box or bag, and crawl back up. Behind him came the shoring team, who carefully erected vertical supports, then put in ceiling and floor, rough cut timber for the shoring and overhead cross beams, and finally sidings from ammunition boxes between the beams and for the floor and ceiling.

The tunnel was about three feet to a side, high enough and wide enough so that when finished, the barrels of powder could be quietly maneuvered into place. As they got closer to the Rebel lines, it had already been decided, the men digging would shift to bayonets to probe with, and a shovel not much bigger than a hand trowel. The shoring team, which occasionally needed to hammer or shove a beam into place, would only work during the day, while guns from the Union side would keep up a slow but steady tattoo of fire to mask the noise. Fortunately the soil they encountered consisted of layers of either sandy loam, which required a lot more shoring, or the ubiquitous red Virginia clay, which cut away easily and remained stable. So far they had not hit any springs and only a shallow trickle of water ran beneath the flooring.

If they encountered rock or shale it would be harder. That was highly unlikely here in central Virginia, but anyone who worked beneath the surface had learned long ago not to be surprised by anything. Rock or shale would dramatically reduce their progress of nearly twenty feet a day and would also cause noise. In short, it would be impossible in the short time span requested by Burnside, and furthermore, they would have to go three or four times as deep to try to conceal the noise.

"So who are these officers?" Michael asked, as he helped shove dirt back to Lubbeck, who was rounding off a box to be hauled off.

"Come on out and see. It's time for a shift change and taking an angle and measurement anyhow," the sergeant announced.

Michael pulled a couple of candles out of his pocket and stuck them into the facing wall for the next crew. He put his hand against the opening of the ventilation pipe and warm air was definitely wafting out. They had to be careful that dirt falling away from the facing didn't jam it. The flames on the candles to either side of him looked bright; there had been many a day in the coal mines where the hooded candles were barely a blue flicker. Satisfied that all was in order, he stuck his spade into the facing, turned, and helped Lubbeck drag the ammunition box loaded with clay out of the tunnel.

They had made close to eighty feet so far, and by nightfall, with the change of shifts, it would be close on to ninety. As he crawled back, Michael cast a wary eye to the overhead shorings. Sandy loam was easy to dig through, but frankly he preferred hard anthracite; you could almost skip the shorings all together, the rock was so hard. Sand and loam constantly threatened to give way and cave in. More than a few overhead boards were bowed under the weight they now supported.

It took less than a minute to crawl back. He saw Colonel Pleasants in the shadowy light and then, to his surprise, a great bulk of a man came into sight. Damn, it was the general.

Dealing with Pleasants was one thing; their bond had been close across the war. Certainly he would get drunk on a regular basis, and Pleasants would admonish but then cut him loose. For in a battle he knew he could count on Michael O'Shay to do his duty and make sure others did theirs as well. And now Michael had arrogated unto himself the role of crew boss, for this was partially his idea and his tunnel.

But a general?

He had seen him often enough on parade and sometimes in a fight on the front line but not up this close. He hoped the scent of whiskey on his breath was not too evident.

"Don't repeat this outside of here," Pleasants announced, "but I'd say, sir, this is just about my best digging team."

General Burnside, sitting on the floor of the tunnel, smiled and nodded, then actually extended his hand, shaking Kochanski's, Lubbeck's, and O'Shay's.

"It was Sergeant Kochanski's brother, Stanislav, who thought this up," and Pleasants gingerly patted the woodstove that was cooking away, just inside the entry to the tunnel.

"Most ingenious, most ingenious indeed," Burnside chortled.

Michael saw that young Stan was squatting behind the two officers.

"Explain it," Pleasants announced.

It is typical of him, Michael thought, *ensuring that credit went where it was due and not taking it for himself, as too many officers did.*

"Well, sir, all that talk about it being impossible to ventilate a tunnel of this length without air holes, seems like nobody thought about convection and air flow with a fireplace or stove.

"I figured that at the face of the tunnel, we put an airtight door," and he motioned behind him to the wooden barrier. "We put this woodstove inside the tunnel right here at the entry and started a fire in it. That fire needs air and will suck it in, to fuel the fire, and, of course, the smoke and hot air will go up the chimney." He pointed to the tin chimney, soldered tight, that rose vertically and poked through the ceiling of the tunnel and out into the open.

"Then, it was simple enough," Stan continued. "We make an airtight pipe—we're making it out of cracker boxes—joined side to side with the facing to each side knocked out at the joints of each box; then we seal it tight with pitch. The start of the air pipe is on the far side of that airtight door."

He pointed back to the sealed door and where the cracker box pipe came through it, running along one side of the tunnel along the floor.

"That pipe goes all the way up to the face of the tunnel and the last box is left open. So, sir," and he cleared his voice a bit nervously, as if realizing he was talking to a high-ranking officer and not wanting to appear too boastful, "we all know the fire needs air, it sucks it in through the stove vents, that lowers air pressure here, and then draws air all the way down from the face of the mine, where fresh air from the outside comes rushing in, piped in from the outside."

He coughed nervously.

"That's about it."

"Works like a charm, it does," Michael announced. "You got regular miners here, General, not a bunch of sod-busting farmers."

Burnside chuckled, and taking out a handkerchief, he wiped his brow. Someone had suggested to him that coming this close to the front line, it was advisable for him to shuck his regular uniform and tall conical hat. He was now hatless and wearing a private's four-button jacket. If he inadvertently stood up outside the tunnel, he'd be an easy target with his great height and frame. Even if he survived that, if he was recognized it might start raising questions as to why a corps commander was up on the front line poking around. He found himself crouching and crawling the entire time he was close to the front. It was a new experience for a senior commander.

"While you're here, sir," Pleasants said, "let's take a measurement and check bearing and angle."

Moving to the far side of the narrow tunnel and several feet back to get away from the massive iron and tin bulk of the stove, Pleasants drew out a well-made compass with a sighting ring set into it. He put it atop a small flat board set into the side of the tunnel. Stan first checked that the board was perfectly level. Tying a string to a stake that was driven into the side of the tunnel just below the sighting board, Stan crawled up the length of the tunnel, looping the string around marking sticks that were set in place earlier, and then finally reached the facing.

"Bet two bits we made eight feet," Michael announced.

"I'll take six," Lubbeck replied.

"Eight and a half," Sergeant Kochanski whispered, and Michael looked over at him angrily, about to protest that there should be a foot between each bet.

"Hold the candle right in front of the string so I can sight on it," Pleasants announced.

All were silent watching him as he lay down and carefully adjusted the sighting ring, looking at the compass face to ensure it was properly aligned. Then back to the ring again.

"Drift from the wall?" he asked.

"About six inches sir," Stan replied.

"Rise?"

"Not sure, sir. I'm holding it level, and it is on the ground. Give me a few seconds."

By the flicker of the candlelight all could see him pushing a stake into the ground, wrapping the measuring string around it, laying down, and lightly putting a level on top of it.

"I'd say three- to five-degree climb, sir, but can't be certain."

Pleasants pulled out a small notebook and flipped it open.

"Length?"

"Eighty-eight feet, four inches."

Pleasants jotted it down.

The diggers waited expectantly while Pleasants ran a few calculations.

"I'd put the face at a real distance from here of eighty-seven feet, six inches."

He flipped the book shut and stuffed it back into his haversack. Michael sat counting on his fingers, from the measurement of yesterday.

"That's eight feet, nine inches of actual length," Lubbeck announced quietly, and the sergeant chuckled over his win.

Pleasants sat back and looked over at Burnside.

"Men, this is most impressive. I wish I could bring a few officers down here who just a week ago were telling me this was impossible."

"Well, sir, it will be impossible if we go much further without a proper theodolite."

Burnside sighed.

"Engineering at army headquarters claims they lost them during the march from North Anna to Cold Harbor. There's not one to be found."

Pleasants looked at him coldly, not saying a word.

"I wanted you to see how slapdash all these measurements are, sir.

I'm doing the best I can with what I have, but off by even a few degrees, and at four hundred feet, that could mean half a dozen feet or more out of alignment. And God forbid we start our gradual climb to compensate for the slope but get it wrong. And distance—I need to shoot at least a couple of good bearings, outside and to either side of this tunnel, to get an absolutely precise distance. Without that, we could very well wind up blowing a huge hole behind the fort, in front of it, or to either side, or suddenly pop out of the ground right under their noses."

"I know, Pleasants," Burnside replied, and there was a bit of a cross edge to his voice.

"I find it hard to believe there is not a single theodolite with the entire army."

"Both of us do, Colonel," Burnside responded with a growl of frustration.

He looked at the enlisted men, realizing they were taking in every word.

"Pleasants, you know what kind of instrument you want?"

"Yes, sir."

"If I sent you personally back to Washington, there are several instrument makers there. If you take the afternoon dispatch packet, you could be up and back in three days."

"Sir?"

"You know what you need. Go up and buy the dang thing and get back here with it."

"Sir, a proper instrument is damn expensive, a couple of hundred dollars at least. And I'd want a better compass and level, and some well-made measuring rods; using string the way we are, there's always stretching."

Burnside smiled.

"Remember, I was trained as an engineer at the Point before I got into gun making. I know how much it costs. I'll get you the money; you get the instruments . . ."

He paused and looked at the diggers.

"And you, lads, keep at it." He reached into his pocket, pulled out a pint bottle of whiskey, and handed it to the sergeant.

"After you are done for the day, men, and not before."

Squatting low he waited for Pleasants to pop the door open, and there was a rush of a breeze as the airtight seal was broken, the candles lining the tunnel flickering with the change in wind direction. As the officers got out, Burnside stood up to stretch, and Pleasants grabbed him by the shoulder and yanked him down with a warning.

With the hatch open, the morning digging crew crawled out into the boiling heat of midday, men now reaching in to grab the crates full of dirt that had stacked up inside the airlock, hauling them out into the trench and restacking them. After dark, work crews would haul them down into a ravine, dump them, and cover it all with top-soil just in case some Rebel managed to slip through the lines and spotted the difference in soil color.

More empty crates were loaded in through the airlock, firewood for the stove. The next crew of diggers, stackers, and crawlers were now ready to go in.

"Sergeant Rothenberg, we've angled over about four to six inches to the right," Pleasants said to the replacement crew. "Carefully work it back, keep an eye on your alignment."

Rothenberg nodded, bent low, leading his team in, the last of them pulling the door shut. Seconds later there was a burst of white smoke from the chimney sticking up out of the sod as someone opened the firebox and tossed more wood in.

"You men did good work today," Pleasants announced. "Just keep a sharper eye on your angle of deviation."

"Yes, sir," all chorused.

Burnside made the gesture of shaking their hands and patting them on the shoulders.

"My boys, you have no idea how much is riding on this," he announced and, ducking back down, he followed Pleasants into the communications trench that led to the rear.

"A gentleman he is," Michael said, reaching over to try and take the bottle from Kochanski, who stuck it in his pocket and grinned.

"Tonight, boys, tonight."

ACROSS FROM THE MINE ENTRANCE

✳✳✳✳✳✳✳✳✳✳✳✳✳✳✳✳✳✳✳✳✳✳✳✳✳✳

"Cap'n Sanders!"

Sergeant Joshua Allison, Company D, 25th North Carolina, looked back from his lair, a beautiful concealed sharpshooter's position carefully dug in under a fallen oak where the front line jutted out slightly from Fort Pegram. Men who occupied this post were under the strictest orders not to shoot, which would reveal its position, unless the target was truly special. Otherwise, they were to remain quiet and use it to keep an eye on the Yankee line.

Captain Bill Sanders, moving low, came up to the lip of the trench, where Allison was perched in a shallow depression dug under the fallen oak.

"I swear I just seen him," Allison announced.

"Who?"

"General Burnside."

"You certain?"

Allison did not remove his gaze from the narrow observation slit, eyes still glued to his field glasses.

"Sir, like I told ya a hundred times. I served with him out in New Mexico chasing Apaches back in '49. I'd know that man anywhere, and we all know it's Ninth Corps over there."

"You get a good bead on him?"

Allison hesitated, eyes still glued to the field glasses.

Could he have shot the man? Actually, he thought rather highly of him, not like most of his officers. And when he took that arrow he showed grit, staying in the fight, and helping to pull Allison out after he took an arrow in his leg, which still left him with a bit of a limp.

"I'd of tried," he lied. "His head was up for only a few seconds. But I'd know that man anywhere. Then caught a glimpse of him again, right there through that little culvert where you can see into their trench to the rear that they don't know we can see. I'm certain it was him."

Sanders took it in and nodded thoughtfully.

"Good spotting, Allison. Keep at it."

He started to turn away.

"Would you have shot him if you had the chance?"

Allison was purportedly the best shot of the regiment and at times would be loaned one of the precious Whitworth rifles for long-distance shots. He had claimed more than once to be able to spot Burnside a half mile back at their main lines, and had even lobbed a few shots at him more out of fun than with a real desire to hit him, though all laughed when he apparently had gotten real close, sending the knot of Union officers scrambling.

Allison took his eyes off the field glasses and looked back at his captain.

"No, sir. I owe him one."

And then he smiled.

"But I'd of scared him a bit for the fun of it."

Sanders smiled and turned away.

"Keep a damn close watch on that spot."

He hesitated and then decided something was up. Allison had picked up on it. Why a cooking fire, up in the front line, going day and night? Glimpses of men moving back and forth, more than was usual in their forward trench. And now a corps commander literally up on the front line.

Sanders ducked into the communications trench leading to his regimental reserve area and the headquarters of Colonel Ransom.

JULY 1, 1864
TWO MILES BEHIND THE UNION LINES BESIEGING PETERSBURG

✳✳✳✳✳✳✳✳✳✳✳✳✳✳✳✳✳✳✳✳✳✳✳✳✳✳✳✳

"My name is Captain Vincent, of General Burnside's staff. And this is Sergeant Major Kevin Malady."

The men of the Fourth Division Ninth Corps were drawn up in a huge semicircle, without arms, around the captain and sergeant major, standing at ease.

"What you see there before you," and he pointed over his shoulder, "was, until six weeks ago, the outer works of the Confederate lines defending Petersburg. These fortifications have been under construction since the beginning of the war, and I will say much of them were built by the labor of slaves."

There was a muttering of voices around Garland, and he looked around sharply to still the chatter.

"The works you see before you are similar in size and position to the inner line, which the Rebels now hold just short of Petersburg."

Vincent paused for a moment.

"The task of Sergeant Malady and me will be to train you men in how to storm those works and take them. Because, men, that is precisely what you shall do."

Excited voices now rose up, many of them jubilant.

"Quiet in the ranks, by God!"

It was barrel-chested Malady, stepping a few feet forward, his voice sounding nearly inhuman with its power and strength. He did not seem to care that he was addressing commissioned officers as well as enlisted men.

Vincent did not seem to mind the interruption by Malady. Garland gave a sidelong glance to Colonel Russell, wondering if he was offended, but the colonel, so long ago an enlisted man, actually had a slight grin.

Malady nodded to his captain and stepped back.

"We will do this training one step at a time. As you master each step, we shall move on to the next. You men shall be kept in isolation while doing this. Provost guards will ring your campsite behind the lines. I will be frank. I want the curious to think that it is because you are colored troops, and therefore you are being kept separate from the rest of the army."

A few muttered and fell silent.

"Secrecy and surprise are the keys to this attack. One leak could destroy it. You are to keep your mouths shut. You are not to say a word about this training to anyone other than your own immediate comrades. If anyone asks you what you are doing and you do not know the man, you are to collar him and find the nearest officer or provost. And by heavens, if any of you slip from your camp and speak but a single word of what you are doing . . ."

Vincent hesitated, as if what he was about to say was distasteful.

"By orders of General Burnside you will be shipped to the Dry Tortugas for the remainder of the war."

Some muttered against this, that they were not helpless slaves to be beaten, but others hushed them down, hissing that anyone who disobeyed the order deserved to be hanged and not just sent to the most distant, noisome point of exile in America.

"Have I made myself clear?"

There were nods of agreement.

"I want the Second Brigade to form to your right, by column of regiments in column by company. First Brigade over there, where the white marker flag is, two hundred yards away. Form as well in column of regiments in column by company."

No one moved for a moment. And Vincent nodded to the leather-lunged Malady.

"You heard the officer! Fall out and form up as ordered!"

Close to four thousand stood for a moment as if riveted. So much had just been imparted. Since their arrival to the encampment behind the lines, a few regiments had been allowed brief stints along quiet sectors of the front in the reserve line, but otherwise they were kept isolated. Rumors had been rampant that regardless of the promise of their officers, they would, in the end, be marched down to City Point, mountains of boxes pointed out to them, and instructed to get to work moving them.

But this?

Garland tagged behind Colonel Russell, who trotted up to Colonel Thomas, commander of their brigade; the other four regimental commanders gathered round as well.

Thomas looked at them, grinning; he had obviously been in on the secret.

"Colonel Russell, the 28th is to form the lead. I want the 29th behind them!"

Russell turned away before Thomas had even finished.

"28th column by companies, form on me!" he shouted, racing over to where a white flag atop a high pole had been set.

Garland broke away from his side, moving among his men, guiding them into place. They had, of course, drilled this way scores of times back at Camp Morton in Indiana, but this was different. For the first time it felt truly real.

"Uncase the colors!"

Color guards pulled the canvas sheaths off the National Flag and the sky-blue flag of the USCT, holding them aloft as a guide. Helping to chivvy the last of the companies into place, Garland went back to the very front of the column.

The front of the column, Garland thought, beaming with pride. *They would lead the charge!*

Malady, who had been standing with arms folded and equidistant between the two columns forming up, trotted over to where the Second Brigade was forming, stopped at one side, leaned over with an exaggerated gesture, closing one eye as if squinting to sight along a rifle, then straightened up.

"Now you bastards listen to me for I will only say it once. I might, someday, like you. Someday, you might like me. All I ask is that we get along. Do any of you have a problem with that?"

He gazed across the ranks and centered in on a corporal gazing at him angrily.

"Corporal, I don't think you like me."

The man stood silent.

"Speak up, or did your master geld you and cut out your tongue for good measure? What is it you want to say, you dark African son of a bitch?"

The corporal, a man with Company B, muttered under his breath.

"Think you can take me, boy?"

The corporal stood silent, but his anger was evident.

"Well, if you think you can take me, now is your chance."

The corporal looked around at his comrades, more than a few grinning at the thought of their burly leader beating the tar out of an arrogant mick sergeant.

"Come on, Corporal. What is it?"

The corporal looked over at Colonel Russell, who was making it a point to gaze in the other direction, as if not hearing a word of the exchange.

"Well, what is it?"

The corporal finally lowered his gaze at the sight of the burly Irish sergeant, built like a brick wall, fist half raised in anticipation.

"No, sir," the corporal finally whispered.

"I am not a sir, I am a sergeant, by Christ," Malady snapped. "Merciful Mary, you call this a column? I've seen drunken, dumb Polacks and micks line up better in front of a saloon, waiting for it to open, by God. Now get this column aligned straight!"

Without waiting for a reply from any enlisted man or officer, he stalked off to deliver the same chewing-out to the other column.

Russell looked over at Garland and winked; Garland was surprised that as a colonel he had not objected to Malady's tone and obvious lack of respect for rank.

"Irish sergeants, Garland. You might hate their guts, but usually they're right, so we all better get used to it. The man knows what he's doing."

Long minutes passed as Malady tramped back and forth, demanding proper alignment, cursing no one in particular, just the world in general. Then at last he seemed satisfied, walked up to Captain Vincent, who had been standing calmly throughout without uttering a word, and saluted.

"Columns ready, sir!"

Vincent stepped forward, his gaze sweeping from one column to the other.

"At my command, which will be a pistol shot," and he held up his revolver, "all of you will step forward at the same time. I want no breaking up of ranks, no spacing between regiments. All of you are to step forward and march up that slope. You will advance at standard march pace. I will fire my pistol twice more, which will be the signal for double time."

He pointed to the Rebel works.

"Your goal will be the white flags on the far side of the

entrenchments. You must go down through the moat, up over the parapet wall, then form on the far side. You must maintain ranks and intervals throughout. I will see all of you on the far side of the forti-fications."

Without waiting he held his pistol up and fired it once.

"Forward, boys, forward!" The cry was picked up from one of the columns to the other. Being at the fore, Garland could see it all, his heart racing. In his mind's eye he could see the flash of gunfire from the works ahead, wondering how he would react when this would be all too real. But at this moment, he was too excited to care, for if they were doing this drill, unlike anything they had ever tried be-fore, it was obvious that something was truly in store for them . . . a chance to prove what they were really capable of.

Two more pistol shots were fired, barely heard over the tramp-ing of four thousand men advancing in the two columns.

"At the double!"

The pace picked up. He heard loud cursing and looking back, Garland saw where a man of Company B had tripped up, falling; others stumbled to get around him.

They reached the front of the fortified line and now, for the first time, saw the mud-filled moat, at least ten feet across and several feet deep. The forward line hesitated for a second.

"In, boys, in and over!" Garland cried.

Men of the second, third, and fourth ranks began to bunch up behind the stalled soldiers.

They slipped down the slope. The mud was not deep but many were clutching at their shoes, more than one man losing a shoe com-pletely, but then being shoved on forward, unable to retrieve his pre-cious boot.

Hitting the slope of the entrenchments, they scrambled up, more men slipping, sliding back, those behind them cursing. Garland gained the crest and looked back for a brief second. The entire column was bunching up around the moat, regiments to the rear colliding into those which had slowed in front. Cursing and yelling erupted.

He looked forward and was surprised by the chasm that lay ahead. The parapet concealed a trench eight to ten feet wide, well built, with wooden floor, logs built up and staked in place, delineating the forward and back walls.

Even Russell hesitated for a second.

"In and over, boys!"

He jumped down into the trench, grabbed hold of the far wall, and climbed back up.

"Flag-bearers, come on!"

The first line of men did as ordered, but behind them the trench, within seconds, was piled up with men cursing, yelling, and trying to push forward. Back down the slope the regiments behind them were either tangled in the moat or spilling over to either flank of the column, trying to pick their own way across, free of the tangle.

He heard pistol shots and a loud bellowing voice.

To their left was a massive earthen fort, smack in the middle between the two columns. Standing atop the parapet was Sergeant Malady, holding a pistol straight up, shooting, emptying the revolver, and cursing some mighty curses in English and what he guessed was the Gaelic tongue of the old country.

The tangled mob fell silent.

"Stand in place, you benighted bastards! Stand in place!"

Some of the men down in the moat were still trying to push forward, and a fistfight had broken out between several men from different regiments.

Malady lowered his revolver and pointed it at the brawlers.

"You there. You want to have a fight? By God, come up here, and I'll kick your black ass clean back to whatever damn plantation you hauled it away from.

"Come on, do you want to try me?"

No one spoke.

Garland looked at Colonel Russell and could see that he was less than pleased—in fact furious—and that Malady's harangues were starting to get to him.

"Look at you, you damn fools. Look at you!" and he stood with hands on hips. "Now think about a bunch of Rebs sitting up where I am now, and just laughin' between taking shots at your woolly heads, smashing them like pumpkins with them minié balls. Look at you!"

He looked to heaven and made the sign of the cross.

"Sweet Mary, what sin did I do to have me cursed with this?" and Malady lowered his head and shook it. "You will now untangle yourselves. You will go back to where you started. You will advance at the walk with the first shot and double-time with two. You will get across the moat, over the parapet, cross the trench, and form on the far side, as ordered. And, by God Almighty, if it takes us day and night until Judgment Day—which believe me is coming damn soon for you—we will do this right! Now move it!"

"You heard the man," Russell said quietly. "Back we go, boys."

"Damn it, sir," and Garland saw Lieutenant Grant come up to the general. "This is insane. We both know what will happen if we have to charge works like this."

"Just follow your orders, Lieutenant Grant," Russell said calmly. "Let me worry about the rest."

As Garland climbed out of the trench and headed toward the rear, he caught sight of a civilian wearing a long white duster, sitting on the edge of the fort, sketchpad balanced on his knee.

He remembered the man. Reilly was the name; he had been back at Arlington that last rainy day before they moved out. Garland felt a pang of guilt. Their orders to move out had come so quickly he had not had time to fulfill his promise to dig a separate grave for the man's brother.

Reilly looked up from his pad and caught Garland's eye. There was hesitation, then recognition, and a nod of the head. Garland waved back, wondering what the man was doing here, behind the lines, when in the distance one could hear the steady rumble of the siege guns bombarding the Rebel lines.

The two groups of men, little more than a disorganized mob at this point, many of them filthy with mud, tramped back to the marker flag. A couple of medical orderlies were hauling off two men, one of them obviously with a badly broken leg, the other ashen faced—an older man who had just simply collapsed from exhaustion and the heat.

Long minutes passed until at last a pistol shot rang out, the column starting forward, thirty seconds later two pistol shots, and again they drove into the moat. From the corner of his eye Garland could see Malady standing atop the fort, taking his hat off, throwing it to the ground, cursing madly.

All could sense that under this particular tyrant it was going to be a very long day indeed.

CHAPTER SIX

WASHINGTON, D.C.
JULY 3, 1864

✳✳✳✳✳✳✳✳✳✳✳✳✳✳✳✳✳✳✳✳✳✳✳✳✳✳

"JAMES, IT IS GOOD TO SEE YOU," LINCOLN ANNOUNCED, COMING out from behind his desk and extending his hand, which James Reilly took warmly.

"I had just ordered some coffee," Lincoln announced, motioning for James to take the seat alongside his desk. After the long trip on the mail packet, which had no accommodations and meant sleeping out on the deck, James was glad to settle into a comfortable padded chair and was a bit fearful he might actually start to nod off.

A servant brought in the coffee. Lincoln, acting as host, poured James a steaming cup and pushed it over to him.

"Bit like the old days isn't it, James," Lincoln said with a chuckle. "But, back then, you were always the one greeting me with a cup of coffee as I came into the office."

James smiled with the memory of sleeping on a cot in Lincoln's law office back in Illinois, getting up early to build up a fire if the day was cold, and heating up some coffee to greet his boss.

"Let me see what you have," Lincoln said in a friendly tone, motioning to James's haversack. James drew out the sketchpad and handed it over.

"Now, talk to me while I look."

"Well sir, there's not much to say really. I got to the front to witness the assaults of June fifteenth to seventeenth."

He hesitated, and like any artist, a bit nervous when someone else is examining his work for the first time, half stood up, leaned over, and pointed to several sketches on the third and fourth pages.

And like any artist nervous about a first viewing of his work, James moved around to Lincoln's side, looking over his shoulder as Lincoln slowly turned the pages.

"I tore out the best ones that could be printed and sent them directly to my publisher. Those are the preliminary sketches you are looking at."

It was standard stuff: lines of men, drawn from behind, charging upslope; smoke-shrouded Rebel lines in the distance.

"What you are looking at there are the roughs."

"I see," Lincoln said noncommittally, turning the pages, and then he paused.

"That I couldn't send up, sir. I knew they wouldn't publish it."

"Merciful God, what is it?" Lincoln whispered.

"Those men there were the First Maine Heavy Artillery. They were garrison troops here, and then, because of the demand for reinforcements, traded in their hundred-pound Parrott guns for rifles and were sent to the front line. The poor damned souls, sir," he paused. "The poor souls didn't know the orders they had been given were suicidal. They were ordered to charge a Rebel fort frontally, in broad daylight. They did as ordered, climbed out of the trenches under fire, formed up the way it used to be done back at the start of the war, and marched up that slope."

He sighed.

"Eighty percent lost in ten minutes."

The mere sight of the drawing brought it all back. For three days the army had stalled to a near crawl. As so typical, the privates, sergeants, and company commanders had the true gauge of affairs. The

Rebel lines ahead, all but empty on June 15th, but on the 16th it started to fill out as Lee raced his men south to Petersburg, aware that for once he had been caught napping and had been flanked. By the 17th the Rebel trenches were damn near full.

It was as if a nightmare was unfolding within the quiet office of the President. Men who had been eager, begging to go forward on the 15th were grim but still ready to go on the 16th, but on the 17th, except for green regiments that did not know better, or men led by an exceptional commander who did so from the front, rather than directing from the rear, the fight was out of the veterans.

James recalled that the First Maine had lined up in traditional formation in a ravine. My God, here it was 1864 and they were going in as if they were fighting the First Battle of Bull Run, ranks aligned perfectly, shoulder to shoulder, just as they had practiced on the drill field. Veterans who had taunted them earlier in the day, as veterans loved to do with new troops, fell silent at the sight of this regiment preparing for their futile charge.

Taunts had turned to cries of protest and warning: "Don't do it, boys. It is suicide out there!"; "Once out there find yourselves a hole, lay down damn it! It's suicide!"; "Don't do it!"

Even as Lincoln gazed silently at the sketches, James felt as if he could actually hear the shouts, the yells, and then, merciful God, the long roll of the drum, the clarion call of a bugle, officers stepping forward, swords raised, the regiment coming up out of the swale in perfect rank, bayonet points gleaming.

They were scythed down in rows. As they advanced one of them had actually turned, looked back, and screamed a defiant reply to the veterans:

"You bastards, now you'll see how men from Maine can die!"

And they had died, less than one in five stumbling back into their own lines ten minutes later. The men from veteran regiments to either flank—which had refused to go forward—were openly weeping as they crawled over to offer succor, a drink from a flask. And as the fire slackened and died, the Rebs, grounding their weapons in a show of awe and pity, had shouted across that they would not shoot if the wounded were dragged in. The veterans had cautiously crawled out to help.

James had overheard one of them, coming through the carnage back to his own regiment, shaking his head, "You know what one of them said? 'Now we're veterans same as you.'"

The man had stared vacant-eyed at James. "Jesus, will this ever end?"

"It really was this bad?" Lincoln's question stirred him from his memory.

He could only nod in reply, unable to speak.

Lincoln stared morosely at the drawing. In the foreground was a body, draped upside down, lying backward into the trench, feet and torso up on the ground above, arms flung wide back into the trench, eyes still open as if staring straight at the viewer. The hurried sketch that filled most of the page was of bodies, blurring together, carpeting the ground, upslope as if the observer were peering over the lip of the trench, standing about five to ten feet back. In the foreground, sitting inside the trench and to one side of the body draped into the trench, was an officer, leaning over, hands covering his face. One could see he was sobbing, and next to him a boy was just staring off into nothingness, stunned by his immersion into volcanic violence.

"That bad?" Lincoln whispered.

"Yes, sir. Of course, *Harper's* will never publish it."

"Of course," Lincoln whispered, exhaling with a shuddering gasp. "I did see they published one of yours, a charge taking a Rebel fort the first day in front of Petersburg."

"That's what they want. That's what they publish."

"At least *Harper's* is still supporting the war," Lincoln replied. "Most of the press is howling now that word about the losses of the last two months is leaking out."

James looked at him with a penetrating gaze.

"Leaking out? I've been up on the front, so I haven't kept an eye on what is being published."

Lincoln hesitated.

"It seems some in high command have withheld the full casualty lists, and only now are they becoming apparent."

"Did you know about this, sir?" James asked.

The President sighed.

"I was told it would give the Rebels too much information if they knew the accurate numbers of how many men Grant has lost these last two months."

"How many?"

"At least seventy thousand," he whispered. "At least fifteen thousand more lost with Sherman."

"My God," James sighed. "I knew it was bad but . . ." and his voice trailed off.

"While you were back at the front, the country was getting into an uproar," Lincoln continued. "We have lost more than at Chancellorsville, Gettysburg, and Chickamauga combined. Support for the war effort is at an all-time low, worse even than after Fredericksburg."

He looked off for a moment, sighed, and then focused his attention back to the sketchpad, turning the pages.

"Good likeness of Burnside," Lincoln said, trying to smile. "How is he?"

"One of the reasons I'm here, sir."

"And that is?"

"Perhaps you should turn the pages first."

Lincoln did as requested, reaching the drawings devoted to the

Fourth Division of Burnside's corps. He smiled at the first ones, a rough draft of a long column of troops coming off the "mile-long bridge of boats," as some now called the wonder that had been flung across the James in a single day. Then he came to a more polished version, which Reilly would obviously forward back to his paper, with a note across the bottom: "Proud men of the Negro division pass in review before Generals Meade and Burnside as they join the Army of the Potomac."

He turned the pages to the sketches of the division practicing an assault on fortifications.

"This isn't a real battle, is it?" Lincoln asked. "I haven't heard word of their being in action."

"No, sir. They're being drilled for an assault. I spent most of yesterday and the day before watching it."

"How did they do?"

"As to be expected of green troops. Enthusiastic but confused."

He said nothing, again half straining to lean over and watch Lincoln's reactions.

"I think you are trying to tell me something," Lincoln finally said, closing the pad and handing it back to Reilly.

"Never could hide anything from you, sir," and Lincoln chuckled in spite of the seriousness of the conversation, looking up affectionately at James.

"Trying to hide the truth, are we?" Lincoln asked with a smile.

James tried to smile and both knew the event to which James was referring. Several weeks after he had started to work in this man's office, while cleaning and polishing his desk, he had come across a hidden drawer, within a handful of coins, obviously petty cash that the new lawyer tossed in there at the end of the day from his pockets. He had lifted forty cents from it, never figuring it would be noticed. A week later, after nights of wrestling with temptation, he had pried it open to take just a quarter, no more. There was more money than ever in the drawer, but also a note: I THINK YOU OWE ME FORTY CENTS. YOUR FRIEND, A. LINCOLN.

Abashed, he had slammed the drawer shut. Lincoln had paid him his fifty-cent wages without comment the next day and as soon as he had closed the office James had put all fifty cents back in with a note. PAID IN FULL WITH INTEREST. THANK YOU, SIR. IT WILL NEVER HAPPEN AGAIN.

Never a word was said between the two about it and yet both obliquely referenced it often.

James smiled at the memory, as did Lincoln.

"Something is up, sir."

"What do you mean?" Now they were serious again.

"I think a major assault is being considered, and these men will lead it."

Lincoln did not reply.

"Sir, are you being silent because you do not know, or because you cannot talk about it."

Lincoln just smiled.

"Sir, I hope this decision was a wise one."

"Why do you say that?"

"I have seen too many charges go straight in at a well-prepared Rebel position. In every case it has been a debacle. I've come to know some of those men. They're good men. In fact, in one sense, too good."

"How do you mean that?"

"More than any white troops, they feel they have something to prove. Where veterans or even new troops who are white would hesitate, they'll go forward."

"Perhaps it is exactly what is needed."

James nodded.

"But against a well-prepared line? I just wanted to give you that caution. I think, at heart, General Burnside is a good man, even if he does carry the burden of Fredericksburg. I think he has deliberately selected this division to prepare for something daring and complicated and done so with good reason. I just pray that whatever it is, it works."

Lincoln nodded, saying nothing.

"I've noticed a few other things. I tried to go up to the front line and provosts stopped me, even though I showed them my pass from General Burnside. Said, it was orders. Then on the packet boat,

I met a regimental commander with the Ninth Corps. A good man, name of Pleasants; I have run across him before. Solid regiment of coal miners."

"And?" Lincoln said, chin resting on folded hands, staring straight at James.

"Well, sir, this Pleasants was as tight as a drum. I couldn't get a word out of him as to what was going on. I tried my usual bribe of offering to sketch him and his men for *Harper's* and he flat out refused. I mentioned that General Burnside had given me permission to observe the training of the division of black troops and sketch them, as long as I kept the sketches secret until I was told they could be released. That made Pleasants downright nervous, it seemed. He cut me off and wouldn't say another word."

James smiled.

"I'm not complaining. He's a good officer and did the right thing, but it did get me curious."

"And?"

"Sir, we walked up from the dock together, and he checked into the Willard as I did. And well, sir, I was curious."

"So you played spy?" Lincoln said with a smile.

James nodded sheepishly.

"He came out a half hour later, dressed in civilian clothes, and I just sort of tagged along behind, just curious mind you. He went straight to a shop."

"What shop?"

"McGregor and Sons, Makers of the Finest Instruments for Surveying and Navigation."

Lincoln stared at him intently.

"I went into the shop after he left. One of the shopkeepers, maybe it was one of McGregor's sons, was very pleased. In minutes I was hearing how he had just sold three hundred and fifty dollars of surveying equipment, finest quality mind you. Something called a theodolite."

Lincoln leaned forward with a smile.

"It's an instrument for taking precise angles to measure distances. If you know the length of your base line and use a theodolite to shoot the precise angle from two other points along that base line to a distant object, you can calculate within a few inches just how far away that object is from any point along your base line. But you need a darn good theodolite to do it right and that thing costs a lot of money."

Lincoln sat back, a bit proud of himself.

"Before I decided to study law, I looked at being a surveyor, but found too many numbers to calculate for this thick head," he chuckled in his self-deprecating way. But then he was suddenly all seriousness again.

"Why are you telling me this?"

Reilly returned his gaze.

"Something big is being planned for the Fourth Division, and all I'll say is, sir, I hope it is well thought out this time. Surveying equipment bought in secret? Someone is trying to calculate something out, precise distances, maybe a new way to attack or . . ."

"Or what?"

"Maybe a tunnel?"

Lincoln did not bat an eye; he just continued to gaze at Reilly.

"I thought it curious as to how the troops were being drilled as two separate columns a couple of hundred yards apart. And smack in the middle between them is a fort. It is suicide to try and push a charge past either flank of such a fort; the enfilading fire would rip any attacker apart. So, it is either some massive bombardment being planned and someone wants to calculate the precise distance to a Rebel position so that the first volley of shells will hit with maximum effect or . . ."

His voice trailed off.

"Or what, James?"

"Well, sir, I thought about it and frankly that will not work against earthen works that are well prepared. Then it hit me that this Pleasants commands a regiment of Pennsylvania coal miners, and if anyone understands tunnels and digging it would be those men."

"James, all I will say is, not a word of what you think to anyone, not a word. Lives depend on it. Indeed the outcome of the war may depend on it."

"I know that, sir," and there was a slight note of reproach in his reply.

"Even if I did know something, you realize at times I cannot discuss it."

"I was not pumping you, sir. It is just that I wanted to put a caution in front of you."

"And that is?"

"Don't let this one be in vain. Too many times I've seen indecision, incompetence, or outright politics destroy a well-made plan. This might be a well-made plan or it might be insanity. I am suggesting you keep a careful eye on it, and that alone is the reason I felt I should make this trip to see you."

Lincoln nodded sagely, but said nothing.

"And also, sir, if I could so easily hit upon it, I daresay the Rebels will, too. We all know Willard's is a hotbed of drunken officers, and ladies a bit too compliant, who listen to every word and constant boasting."

"Was Pleasants drinking at the bar?" Lincoln asked sharply.

"No, sir. I went back, looked around, made an inquiry about him, claiming I was his brother, and was told that he had given strict orders not be disturbed; that he wanted to sleep until four and be awakened in time to catch the next packet back to City Point."

"Good for him."

"Though maybe someone should go and have a talk with Mr. Mc-Gregor that in the future his staff should keep their mouths shut as to what other customers are buying. Sir, I'm trying to say that if I could ferret this out, the Rebs will, too, at some point and then God save those men."

"I'll make sure it is taken care of."

Lincoln stood up, a signal that the interview was drawing to a close.

"I have another visitor shortly," he announced. "I'd like you to go back on that packet this evening and do as you've just done."

"Sir? I was hoping for a few days here."

"A certain Congressman's daughter?" Lincoln asked with a smile.

"Sir?"

"Maybe I have spies watching my spies," Lincoln chuckled.

James looked at him with surprise. Lincoln moved to reassure him.

"No, no. You know how gossip is. Mary told me of it months ago. Of course she doesn't approve, says you two come from different social classes."

James said nothing, for after all she was right.

"I agreed, telling her that the young lady in question is the daughter of a Democrat from Maryland, but I wouldn't hold it against her."

James smiled as the President showed him to the door.

Lincoln stood for a moment and then went to the window to look out, deep in thought, the drawing of the dead artillerist from Maine refusing to leave his mind.

There was a tap on the door.

He turned to look.

It was his secretary, Hay.

"Sir, we just got a message from General Grant. His courier boat had some boiler problems, and he won't arrive till this evening."

"No problem," Lincoln replied softly. "It'll give me time to think."

ON THE WAY TO THE FRONT

✳✳✳✳✳✳✳✳✳✳✳✳✳✳✳✳✳✳✳✳✳✳✳✳✳✳✳✳

Having cast off, the small packet boat began to pick up speed, water foaming up from under the stern. The small deck was packed, mostly with officers returning to the front line. What space was still available was stacked with crates and barrels. At least the weather promised to be fair, because except for a few of the higher ranks, most would be sleeping out on the deck tonight for the run down to City Point.

A few joked that they preferred the night boat; those running during the day would, on occasion, draw some long-range fire from Rebel militia. The militia, far behind the lines, enjoyed taking potshots at anything that steamed by. Recently, a major had been killed by just such a random shot.

"Damn bushwhackers, we should hang 'em when we catch them," someone announced, and there was a chorus of agreement.

"Aren't you Pleasants with the 48th?"

James saw a colonel approach and extend his hand.

"I'm MacArthur, 33rd Ohio. We were on your right in the Wilderness."

He extended his hand, Pleasants took it, and for several minutes MacArthur tried to engage him in conversation but was met with only monosyllabic replies. The Ohio man finally drifted away, and as he did, James realized that Pleasants was staring at him. There was no sense in pretending he had not seen him, so James smiled and came over to his side.

"We were on the same boat this morning," James said, extending his hand, which Pleasants shook for a brief instant. "James Reilly with *Harper's Weekly.* Remember?"

"Yes."

There was silence for a moment.

"Mr. Reilly, I am tempted to ask if there is a provost guard on this ship and have you put under arrest."

"Sir?"

"You followed me today."

"I don't quite understand what you are saying, Colonel."

"You most certainly do," Pleasants replied, his voice cold, tense. "We checked into the same hotel."

"No crime in that," James said easily. "I was in town to make sure my drawings went to a courier to take them to New York. Sometimes you have to do that yourself."

"Then why did you follow me when I left the hotel?"

"Sir, I am afraid you are confusing me with someone else," James replied, staring the colonel straight in the eye.

"You make a rather poor spy, Mr. Reilly. At least change out of that long duster you insist on wearing when following someone. I spotted you when I walked out of a particular shop."

James did not reply for a moment.

"I am a correspondent with *Harper's,*" James finally said. "But I can assure you I am not some damn Rebel spy."

"Then why did you follow me and go into that shop?"

"I will confess curiosity took hold. I've been with your corps for two weeks now."

"I haven't seen you."

"I am not allowed to see you. Your sector is sealed off from any reporters."

"With good reason, damn it," Pleasants snapped.

"I've mostly been with the Fourth Division since they joined the corps."

Pleasants looked at him with a good poker player's gaze.

"If you doubt me, sir, when we dock at City Point, call over a provost, have me put under arrest, take me to General Burnside's headquarters, and check directly with him."

Pleasants did not reply.

James sighed, drew out a flask, offered it, which Pleasants refused, and took a drink.

"All right, I was curious as to what you were up to. I think I have it figured out."

Pleasants looked past him and there was a nervousness about him.

"Sir, I am a Union man. I've been covering this war ever since McClellan's Peninsula fiasco. I hate loud mouths, boasters, and especially reporters who don't know when to keep their mouths shut as much as you do."

He hesitated and tried to smile.

"And officers who talk too much as well."

There was an ever so slight nod from Pleasants.

"And I lost a brother at Cold Harbor."

Already that battle was being buried and forgotten. No one spoke of it the way they did of Gettysburg, Antietam, or even the two Bull Run fights. Cold Harbor would be forgotten. It was too bitter and painful a defeat to be remembered or glorified. Its memory had been buried with its dead.

"The desk clerk told me that someone claiming to be my brother asked for me at Willard's as I checked out," Pleasants retorted. "He described you perfectly."

"That was me."

Pleasants gazed at him coldly, then finally nodded.

"So why are you interested in the Fourth Division of my corps?"

"The boys with one of the black regiments were doing burial detail at Lee's old mansion. I went there to see my brother buried, got to know a couple of their men, and asked if I could draw them as they got ready for whatever was coming up."

"Coming up?"

James extended his hand in a calming gesture.

"I want this war over just as much as you do. For what it is worth from a newspaperman, you have my oath I'll not breathe a word of what I'm thinking."

Pleasants did not reply.

"I'll say no more, sir. My offer stands. Report me if you wish when we get to City Point. I'll be camped with the men of the Fourth Division if you decide not to, but then change your mind later."

Pleasants seemed to hesitate and then finally spoke.

"What do you think of those colored soldiers?"

"Sir?"

"Is this some sort of stunt by the Abolitionists? I've heard mixed reports. Everyone knows about the charge of the 54th Massachusetts last year down in front of Charleston. They were courageous in the face of entrenched firepower. It was good press at least, but by God, they got slaughtered for nothing. Then, on the other side you hear reports that they panic easy, that if they don't have their white officers telling them what to do every step of the way they break down and run. What do you think of them?"

It was the most Pleasants had said to him on either leg of this journey.

"I think they're trying very, very hard to be good soldiers," James replied, after thinking it over for a moment. "Better than some, not so good as others. None of them have seen the elephant, of course, so they are all fresh fish. But on the whole I'd stack them up alongside any white regiment in this army who were going into their first fight."

"Will they charge into Hell, if ordered?" Pleasants asked and then he seemed to draw back slightly, as if knowing he had just said far too much.

Reilly looked at him closely. The moment was ironic, for the steamer was rounding the great bend of the Potomac past the run-down mansion of General Washington. He was a man who had owned slaves, and yet by the end of the Revolutionary War, had agreed to the enlistment of thousands of colored troops into the ranks.

"They have something driving them we don't have," James finally said.

"And that is?"

"They have to prove something."

Pleasants did not reply, as if wanting more.

"Look, it's obvious, isn't it? Well maybe for you it isn't as much, but for me it is."

"How is that?"

"I'm from Ireland," and he forced a smile. "Accident of birth not of choice, believe me. My parents brought me to these shores when I was fourteen back during the famine. Me ma . . ."

He paused, realizing he was drifting into dialect, "My mother died on the passage over. My father remarried and we moved to a godforsaken place called Chicago where he took work on the railroads. There was no place for me with them, so I lit out."

He smiled.

"I found a kindly lawyer who allowed me to sleep in his office in exchange for keeping it clean, plus four bits a week, which was all he could afford back then, and that was where my life started in a way."

"Kindly lawyer?" Pleasants laughed and then spat over the railing. "That's an oxymoron if ever I heard one."

James did not know the meaning of the word, but he caught the sense of it and continued to smile.

"There are a few, a precious few. The point is, we Irish have had to claw every inch of the way for what this country claims is the right of all men, but those rights get forgotten by a lot of people once they get those rights for themselves."

Pleasants said nothing, but James could see his words might sound like preaching.

"All I am saying is, you asked me if they would charge into Hell. And I say, hell yes. The same way the Irish Brigade charged and died at Fredericksburg."

"Ghastly fight," Pleasants sighed. "I was there."

"So was I, and I wept at the sight of it, the memory of it."

It would haunt him for the rest of his life, the way those men cried, *"Erin go bragh,"* as they swept up the blood-soaked slopes of Marye's Heights, died nearly to a man, and gained immortal glory and perhaps, just perhaps, the first step to the realization of many that the Irish were as much Americans as anyone else. He had personally carried the drawings of that charge back to New York, slammed them on his editor's desk, and was not ashamed of the fact that, in tears, he begged the man to print them, which he did. His everlasting shame in a way was that he had not gone in with his brothers from Erin and instead had fought that battle with just a pencil and a stick of charcoal in his hand.

"What I'm trying to say"—He realized his voice was slightly choked and was angry that emotion was getting the better of him. "I'm trying to say that the men of the Fourth Division have a fire in them. The first battle will most likely quench it, as it does with most regiments. Oh, they'll fight after that to be certain, but like all veterans, they will do so as their sworn duty, not with that fire of idealism in them. Those colored soldiers will charge into Hell because by going to Hell, if need be, they will prove they are men and as that Frederick Douglass of theirs said, with rifle in hand they will prove their right of citizenship to the entire world."

James fell silent and realized his voice had pitched upward and several others were looking over at him. A couple of them snickered; he heard a whispered laugh of "Damn, stupid darkies will run all right, straight in the opposite direction, to the rear." He turned but the man who said those words would not identify himself.

But one did nod and smiled.

"Bully for you, I'm with you, Irish," he announced, shook James's hand, and then after shooting a telling glance at another officer, walked off toward the bow of the ship.

James looked back at Pleasants.

The colonel stood silent in the shadows and then finally replied. "I pray to God you are right."

Without another word to James, he walked, off as did the other officers around him.

James was tempted to offer a taunt that he had a good quart of store-bought Irish whiskey in his haversack and would drink it with a man who would drink to the Fourth or the Ninth, but he knew better. No point in starting a personal fight on the deck of a boat going back to the war.

Summer darkness had descended. By dawn, they would be rounding Fortress Monroe and by midday be back at City Point. The quart should last him till then, he thought, and curling up in a corner between two barrels, filled with what he suspected was whiskey bound as priority shipment to some headquarters staff, he uncorked the bottle and rationed out his first long drink.

It helped to still the memories, and he was soon asleep.

THE WHITE HOUSE

****

Abraham Lincoln leaned back in his chair, scanning the papers and maps, turning them over one by one and then, at last, placing them back on his desk.

"Do you honestly think this will work?" he asked.

General Grant, who had sat while his President evaluated the proposal, was silent for a moment.

They had gone over why Sherman was stalled in front of Atlanta, the southern campaign wearily dragging into a third month, with no end in sight. The utter fiasco of an entire army venturing up the Red River out in Louisiana and Arkansas, rather than marching east to take Mobile as ordered, had been passed over. It was an embarrassment to Grant that a general in charge of an entire army had claimed to have misread orders and set off 180 degrees opposite from where he was supposed to go. In front of Charleston that pathetic siege continued without any end in sight. That the Rebels were dug in like ticks on a hound was now a well-worn and overused analogy.

The only hope of a shift of fortunes before the Republican and Democrat conventions, and with that any hope of winning the national election come November, rested on Petersburg, and what Grant had just shown him was the most radical of plans to end it.

"I will admit, Mr. President, I have not studied it as closely as I could have. I have delegated that to General Meade, who is in direct command of that army. But I think there is at least a chance of success."

Lincoln nodded.

"From some of your questions, sir," Grant ventured, "it seems you have had some foreknowledge of this idea."

Lincoln just smiled and said nothing.

Grant did not probe further, for it was not his place to do so. That was something Lincoln appreciated about him. He knew how to give honest straightforward answers without any "varnish," but also knew when not to ask or push. Grant was unlike so many of his generals, especially McClellan, whom he would undoubtedly face in the fall election.

"I feel it is time to make a few things absolutely clear," Lincoln finally replied. As he spoke, he raised his long legs and put them up on his desk, folded his lanky arms over his stomach and leaned back in his chair, with the forelegs rising off the floor so that he was perfectly balanced. Somehow, however, this casual gesture did not diminish his authority in the slightest.

"If this fails, it could turn into an absolute slaughter, could it not? The same as happened at Cold Harbor?"

Grant visibly winced at the mention of that fight.

"Yes, sir, it could."

"The lead division annihilated?"

Grant did not reply verbally but finally nodded his head.

"Choose them well then," Lincoln replied. "Please let General Meade know that the lead division of the assault must be the best possible to assure success. This scheme carries one of two things with it: either the promise of a success that just might end this war

before the elections, and thus assure the survival of the Union, or a disaster that will end any chance of this administration continuing into next year. I speak not for myself, General; you should know me well enough now to know how I view myself in relationship to this. It is about saving our Union and that is the task I have entrusted to you because I totally trust you."

Grant nodded, saying nothing.

"And you have delegated the details of this to General Meade?"

"Yes, sir."

"Why so? From the Wilderness on through you have often taken direct command of the Army of the Potomac."

"That was in the heat of action, sir, and frankly, at times I could not restrain myself. This, in contrast, is, what they used to call at West Point, a 'set piece battle,' one planned weeks in advance, something quite rare in this current war. Meade will have plenty of time to evaluate it, and besides, I cannot predict where I might be needed three weeks from now. I chose to place my headquarters in the field with the Army of the Potomac when the spring campaigns started, but circumstances might require me to decamp and move instead to Atlanta if need be."

He fell silent. The implication was clear. Sherman was his closest friend and ally in the field; otherwise Grant would never have entrusted his old command to him when called to Washington to take command of all armies in the field. But, if there should be a reversal there, or lack of a clear indication that progress was being made on that front, Grant might find it necessary to go and take back direct command, thus leaving Meade in complete charge of the events unfolding before Petersburg.

"Well enough, then."

Lincoln took his feet off the desk, picked the plans up, and thumbed through them once more.

He looked back at Grant.

"Please, General, no mistakes this time. No politics, jealousies, rivalries, or decisions based on blind prejudice. I know you understand me. Please ensure that General Meade knows it as well."

"Yes, sir."

"If we do not win the war with this one, General, I fear the backlash could be such that the country, the American people, might very well give up, and we will then lose the Union."

CHAPTER SEVEN

✳✳✳✳✳✳✳✳✳✳✳✳✳✳✳✳✳✳✳✳✳✳✳✳

"ARE WE READY?" COLONEL PLEASANTS WHISPERED.

His team was gathered around the observation position carefully prepared during the night. He had decided to shoot the angles precisely at dawn. The air was usually still then, and his veterans had pointed out that after midday the angle of the sun was such that light would glint off the lens of the theodolite and he might well be greeted a few seconds later by a .58 minié ball.

They had measured the first angle fifty yards to the right of the tunnel the morning before without incident. During the day he had made precise measurements down the length of the tunnel, finding that the crude instruments he had used when earlier measuring the angle and climb of the tunnel had deviated nearly three feet, which was being corrected now. This morning he would shoot the next angle fifty yards to the left of the mouth of the tunnel. Both distances had been laid out precisely with measuring rods rather than tape, so he would finally be able to report back to Burnside that they were proceeding with exactitude.

Captain Hurt would act as spotter a dozen yards to his left, watching for any hint of movement along the Rebel line, warning of any sharpshooter on the other side. With him were three enlisted men, one of them Corporal Stan Kochanski, whom Pleasants had already slated, in the back of his mind, for promotion to second lieutenant. Kochanski was diligent and had an excellent background in trigonometry, took care of the delicate instruments, and would note down his angles as he whispered them out.

Pleasants took a deep breath.

"Let's do it," he announced.

He ever so slowly pulled the canvas curtain, coated in red clay, away from the lens of the theodolite. He and Stan had checked and rechecked that it was absolutely level, the plumb line resting directly above the marker stake, laid out the evening before so that they were exactly 163 feet from the center of the entry to the mine, 3 extra feet having been added because of a slight rise in the trench line where a sharpshooter's position had already been dug in.

Colonel Pleasants leaned over, sighting through the scope ever so slowly, raising the elevation on the theodolite till he was sighted at the base of the fort. Next, he slowly traversed it to align directly with the center line of Fort Pegram, locked the hold-down screw in place, and then carefully raised the elevation angle a little more than a degree. It was hard to judge—constant artillery fire had rent the grand before the fort—but he felt he had a good shot on actual ground level and not the rising ground of the parapet itself.

"Mark," he hissed.

His assistant, kneeling by his side, noted down traverse and elevation and reconfirmed that the compass was set exactly.

He spared a look down to make sure the corporal got it right and took one more sighting just in case either of them had brushed against the delicate instrument, mounted on a heavy tripod, and had thrown the observation off.

He reached over and pulled the curtain shut. He would have preferred to take a second shot after waiting a few minutes, just to be sure, but knew that would indeed be pressing his luck.

"Captain Hurt, you can step down," and he turned to look over to the young officer, who was spotting for him against sharpshooters.

Hurt started to turn his head, smiling with relief, when at that exact instant the side of his head shattered, blood and gray matter spraying against the opposite wall of the trench.

"Merciful God!" Pleasants cried, ducking down as a bullet pierced the canvas screen, slipping past Pleasants's face by no more than a few inches. Tripping backward, he nearly knocked over the precious theodolite, but Kochanski reached over the tripod and, cradling it, pulled the instrument away from the canvas screen. Even as he fell, Pleasants noted the boy had made the right move, grabbing the precious instrument rather than trying to block his officer's fall. The bullet had creased the wood on one side of the tripod, but the brass mounting and the surveying tool itself had not been hit.

Pleasants scrambled over to Hurt, but knew the man was already dead.

"You goddamn sons of bitches!" one of the enlisted men, who had been standing back watching their commander at work, screamed. He stepped to the place Hurt had been just seconds before, poked his rifle through, and fired a shot blindly toward the fort.

He wisely ducked back as several more rounds zipped overhead, one of them striking the dirt where Hurt had stood.

"We warned ya, Yank," a reply came. "We un's got orders to shoot. No truce here." There was a pause for a moment. "Ever since we heard you got darkies with ya now."

Pleasants was kneeling by Hurt's side. He had seen hundreds of men die in battle, but this lad had been close to him. He had been a good adjutant, brave, had survived every action since New Bern without a scratch . . . and now to die like this?

Corporal Kochanski was still clutching the theodolite. *Thank heavens he grabbed it,* Pleasants thought, in spite of his grief. For even though he had finally worked out a proper measurement to the fort, he still needed it to check direction and angle of slope within the tunnel. The boy was pale faced, staring at Hurt and the pool of blood spreading onto the dirt floor of the trench from his shattered skull. He began to sway.

Pleasants jumped to his side and grabbed the instrument. Kochanski tried to mutter a thanks, then collapsed in a heap, fainting dead away.

The men around them were silent. The boy was "fresh fish," and this was the first time he had seen someone take a head shot. All of them, long ago, had been fresh fish as well.

Pleasants knelt down, unbolting the theodolite from the tripod, carefully putting it into its velvet-lined carrying box, and snapped the lid shut.

"A couple of you boys keep an eye on our young corporal there; help him back to headquarters when he comes around. Find a stretcher detail for Captain Hurt as well."

There were quiet nods of acceptance of his orders. He took the precious notebook, with all the calculations, out of Kochanski's clammy hands. Crouching low, he headed to the communications trench to the rear, leaving it to others on his staff to take care of the measuring rods, compass case, and tripod.

He wanted to get the final measurements calculated immediately and then double-check them. And he had yet another letter to write to someone's parents back home.

FORT PEGRAM

****

A couple of men were still chortling about Allison's incredible shot, but he said nothing. He had actually focused his Whitworth on the target a dozen feet to the left when the man, who looked to be peering through some sort of strange telescope, had closed the canvas curtain. It had only taken a moment to swing to the second man and finally squeeze off a round after a long twenty-four hours of being told by Captain Sanders to just observe and not shoot.

He felt no joy in what he had done. Some of the sharpshooters along the line sickened him with their damn boasting about how many Yankees they had put into graves since this siege started. It was not that he minded killing Yankees, he had been doing it ever since Gaines Mills, and they damn near had killed him more than once. It was just that there was something too cold-blooded about shooting in cover against a helpless target, especially when using the precious Whitworth hexagonal bore rifle with its four-power telescopic sight. That sight allowed him to see his target as if only thirty yards away, which meant he could see the man's eyes, whether he was young or old—a touch of his soul in a way.

Captain Sanders came up and squatted down by his side as Allison finished running a cleaning patch through the barrel, preparing for the laborious task of pushing a six-sided bullet down its tight hexagon twist.

"You got the spotter, didn't you?" Sanders asked.

"Think so, sir. I was just about to squeeze when the man I was aiming at pulled the canvas curtain over."

Sanders nodded.

"Could you see what he was looking through?"

"It sure weren't no field glasses. Just a single glass. But if it was a telescope it was mighty strange. Seemed to be mounted on something or other. Couldn't see much of it, sir, but I could see he didn't have his hands on it, so that meant it was mounted to something. A tripod or something like that."

"Same man we saw on our left yesterday, about a hundred yards over?"

"Can't tell you that for sure, sir, but whatever he was looking through was the same."

"No bother."

Sanders stood up as far as the safety of the trench would allow him and patted Allison on the shoulder.

"Good work, Sergeant. I'll bet, though, we don't see them again."

"'Cause I killed that man?" he asked quietly.

"No, because he measured at least two angles straight to here. That's all he needed. He won't risk it again."

Allison simply nodded, grunting slightly as he carefully rammed the bullet down the tight-fitting barrel.

Sanders fell silent, sitting in the bottom of the trench, oblivious to the stench, with the flies swarming about them and the heat of early morning building by the minute.

This was a hellhole if ever there was one. Back a year or two the campaigns had been out in the open, and though grueling at times, there had always been the excitement and anticipation of a march ahead, and, yes, if need be, a battle to be fought in open fields and woods. Here, they were confined to holes in the earth, little better than premade graves, enduring the constant fetid stink of latrines dug into the sides of the trenches. Everyone was filthy and dirt-encrusted because water was too precious to use for bathing.

And if we feel this way, surely the Yankees do as well, and hate it as much as we do. And surely they must be plotting something to break this infuriating deadlock. His instincts told him whatever they were plotting was aimed straight at this fort. It was the shortest route to Petersburg and, in the process, would cut the one east-to-west road that linked the Army of Northern Virginia together in its tenuous hold on this redoubt. Win here and the Army of Northern Virginia is cut in two, and the war is over for all practical purposes. This fort is the fulcrum of the whole war. Of course they will try to come here.

It was going to be here, and it was going to be soon. It was time to talk to his commanding officer.

"Be careful up there," Sanders said. "You got them riled up, and they'll be looking for vengeance."

"Soul of caution, sir," Allison said, but there was no smile, just the grim look of a man about to return to a distasteful job.

JULY 15, 1864

TRAINING CAMP

****

"All right, boys, do it right this time," Garland growled, stalking up and down along the flank of his column. They had been at it since dawn, the way they had been at it ever since dawn for the last two weeks.

Their once spotless uniforms, which they had been so proud of, were torn and mud-splattered, the red clay of Virginia ground in so deep that no amount of washing could get it all out.

Men were breathing hard, some bent over gasping in the heat, and he looked at them carefully. An order had come in to the brigade the day before reporting that nearly a third of the men of the 28th were to be detailed off for guard duty down at City Point. Russell had howled in protest, kicking it up to Thomas, their brigade commander, and had even gone to their seldom-seen division commander, Ferrero, with no results. At an officers meeting, which Garland attended, it was decided to cull out the men who were obviously not standing up well to the relentless drill and, at times, outright abuse showered upon them by Malady and the dozen other white sergeants Malady had brought in to assist with his brand of training.

Some of those sergeants were even worse than Malady when it came to the verbal abuse, and, now that the training had shifted, the physical abuse as well.

The hatred against the trainers was simmering to a boil. Even though Garland tried to reassure the men that these were veterans of such assaults, that they knew what it was like, and no matter how rough it got, the hard training was getting them ready.

Garland uncorked his canteen and handed it to a man who had just vomited from exhaustion and the heat.

"Here, rinse your mouth out, take a drink slowly, then go over yonder to those trees and lay down."

"Not me, Sergeant Major," the man gasped. "I sit down, they send me down to City Point to guard. I'm staying here."

Garland slapped him on the back and waited to get his precious canteen back.

"Sergeant Major White!"

He looked up. It was Lieutenant Grant, breathing hard, face pale.

He went up and saluted.

"Five minutes, we go in again."

"Yes, sir."

"I know what the boys are thinking; let's try not to have any trouble now."

"I'll try, sir, but their blood is up."

Grant forced a smile.

"Well, at least let's try."

A whistle sounded; the shrill sound picked up, blown by the other sergeants, who were spaced at intervals up in front of the "Rebel line."

Much had been added in the last few days. Eight rough-hewn wooden footbridges, several feet wide and twelve feet long, had been issued to the men of the 28th. Their task was to carry the footbridges up at the double, get across the moat, drag them up the face of the enemy parapet, and then fling them across the trench to serve as pathways. Men grumbled—why in hell had they not been given them on the first day? Suppose the bridges were lost or blown apart, for Malady seemed almost to relish telling them how their ranks would be torn by rifle and canister fire as they advanced.

New elements had been added three days ago, abatis and chevaux-de-frise. An abatis was nothing more than a maze of sharpened stakes driven into the ground, pointed toward an advancing foe. Chevaux-de-frise were logs, drilled out in a crisscross pattern, and stakes driven through, so the whole affair rested chest high like a spiked fence. These barriers now dotted the landscape in front of the moat and had been driven into the face of the parapet. Two men had actually been killed by them, pushed into the barriers by comrades shoving from behind, and dozens more had endured various cuts and bruises. They had been placed there during the night between exercises. The first time the advancing columns came to them, so proud of their progress up to that point, they had ground to a confused halt.

Malady continued to shower abuse on them to find a way through.

After several failed attempts he at last relented. A wagon pulled up, offloading a hundred axes, which were handed out to the men at the front of the column. The moment the signal was given for the advance, their job was to sprint ahead and smash the barriers clear before their comrades reached the line.

It had worked reasonably well the first time, though all grumbled when they had to rebuild and replace the barriers themselves before falling back for another go.

This morning, two new elements had been added. The first was the object of lively speculation among the men. What about the earthen fort smack in the middle between the two advancing columns? This morning that fort was now marked off with a circle of marker flags and cloth strips nearly two hundred yards across. Malady announced that any man who stepped into that circle was a dead man and would spend the rest of the day repairing the barriers after each practice charge and would get no rations. He also announced that his new assistants would block men at random, and if blocked, the man was to fall to the ground and remain there.

All knew what that meant.

And then the trouble started. The white sergeants were less than gentle standing in the way of the charging column, tripping men as they ran by, knocking others over. Men getting too close to the "dead man's circle" were shoved into it by the sergeants screaming they were dead and had to fall out for work detail.

Brawls were starting, and several men had already been dragged off by provosts for striking a noncommissioned officer.

Garland was at the front of the line, looking back at his men and then eyeing the sergeants, who seemed eager for the fracas to begin.

"Keep calm, boys," he cried. "Follow your orders!"

But he could tell that tempers were wearing thin in the boiling heat.

Beyond everything else the men were now heavily burdened down. Full uniforms, rifles slung over shoulders, backpacks, and cartridge boxes stuffed with forty rounds were part of the load, as well as an extra forty rounds stuffed into haversacks and pockets. Canteens were filled and many an officer and sergeant was carrying an extra, some even a third.

Garland looked over at Russell, who just smiled calmly.

"They want you angry, Garland, remember that. No matter what they do to you, it is only a taste of what the Rebels will do when this is for real."

Captain Vincent stood atop the fortress wall, his pistol replaced by a small mountain howitzer, which could be more clearly heard and seen.

The gun recoiled.

"Axmen forward!" Russell cried.

The men of the lead ranks, axes held high, leaped forward like demented medieval warriors, advancing at a full run. Men of the second and third ranks hoisted up the wooden footbridges and started forward at the double behind them, while behind them the rest of the column started to advance at the walk.

Garland put himself forward, running alongside six men hauling a footbridge. Russell was in front of him. Garland looked up the slope, but vision was difficult with sweat streaming into his eyes.

The axmen were already into the barriers, swinging blades wildly, smashing a way through. The white sergeants had let them pass, and he smiled, wondering if they were more than a little afraid to confront and stop the biggest men of his regiment—wielding axes and with their blood up.

A sergeant sprinted in front of Colonel Russell, shouting, "You are down, sir!"

Russell did as ordered, first moving to one side of the column so he wouldn't be trampled and then sitting down and taking off his hat to wipe his brow. A look from him told Garland that he, more than any other man in the regiment, was expected to see it through.

That moment had filled Garland with a stomach-knotting horror. He had served under Colonel Russell ever since the day he had enlisted, December 24, 1863. Russell had singled him out on the very first day, knowing Garland's record as a political activist, as a literate man who could read and write, and as a man who had worked as a recruiter for both the 54th and 55th Massachusetts. He knew Garland had been offered the rank of sergeant major in both those famed units.

Russell had tutored Garland for months, grooming him for command; even many of the white officers who had joined the regiment over the ensuing months deferred to Garland or sought his advice when a particular recruit was proving difficult. Usually Garland had been able to talk the recruit around; on several occasions, though, he did what sergeant majors had done since the armies of Pharaoh: he passed a quiet word to a couple of corporals, walked the other way, and ignored the sound of a man getting a good thrashing.

The quick look from Russell spoke volumes: "This might happen for real, and if it does, you've got to lead them." It was a fearful thought but one that filled him with pride, as well: to have such trust placed in him by a white officer, whom he respected in turn.

He offered a quick salute as he ran by.

The sergeant who had stopped Colonel Russell zeroed in on the men with the footbridge: "All of you, down!"

Some of them stopped, but Sergeant Felton, leading the team, looked less than pleased and continued to drag the bridge forward.

"You are down!" the sergeant screamed, shoving Felton with both hands.

Garland started to approach, ready to order Felton to drop the bridge and lie down as ordered; behind him, the rest of the regiment was closing in quick, already advancing at the double.

"Sergeant!" He was trying to address Felton, but the white sergeant turned and pushed him hard.

"You, too, boy, you're dead!" He shoved Garland with both hands, nearly knocking him over.

Garland stood there incredulous.

"You heard me, you damn darkie!"

"You are talking to a superior rank!" Garland shouted, and now the main body of the charge was up and around them, pushing forward.

The sergeant, fists balled up, took a step toward Garland and then went sprawling. Sergeant Felton, standing behind the man, coldcocked him with a single blow against the side of the head.

Felton was grinning.

"Come on!" Felton shouted, and Garland ran with him, picking up the footbridge and dragging it forward.

"Knocking me down is one thing," Felton gasped as they hauled the bridge. "But you is the best damn sergeant in this army, and I'll be damned . . ."

"You'll be damned if you keep talking like that," Garland said, the preacher in him coming out even as he grinned.

Others fell in, hoisting the bridge high, nearly running with it, crossing over the moat, which fortunately had dried out over the last week of unrelenting heat. Others were already atop the parapet, reaching out, grabbing the bridge, throwing it across the trench, men of the main column storming across within seconds after the footbridge was dropped in place. Garland and Felton scrambled up the far side of the parapet and pushed their way to the front, where the regimental flags marked their position.

They were no longer being ordered to stop just beyond the trench. They now had to sprint nearly six hundred yards, then deploy out into the line of battle at a right angle to their line of advance, the second regiment behind them already doing so to cover the flank of the column, the remaining regiments coming up behind the 28th and then deploying out as well.

Two hundred yards to their left, the second column was doing the same, deploying to face in the opposite direction and shake out into battle line.

There was not a man in these two columns who did not know his task by this point, and around the campfires in the evening they could all, easily enough, surmise what would soon await them. They were practicing to be a lead division, a breakthrough force, seizing some objective six hundred yards or so behind a Rebel line. What left them worried and questioning, though, was the fort in the middle that they were bypassing. They also wondered if they were to be the only division to charge or if more men would come pouring in behind them for support once they had established the perimeter behind the Rebel lines.

If their officers knew something, they were keeping mum about it. Garland could sense, however, that many of the officers—even

Colonel Russell himself—were questioning and worrying, but they did not share this with their men.

Six hundred yards, at the double, with full gear; rifles now unslung and carried at the charge, though without bayonets to prevent men impaling each other in a practice drill. But when the time came for the real thing, it would be with fixed bayonets, though their rifles would be unloaded.

Men were breathing hard, some staggering to keep up, but they held together, and he caught a glimpse of Captain Vincent running alongside them, pocket watch in hand.

They reached a set of marker flags and without orders—with Colonel Russell sitting this one out—the men knew what to do. Company A pivoted to their right and the flag bearers held their colors high, shouting, "28th form up on us!"

In the mad dash companies had become intermingled. Russell had told them repeatedly that if that happened, to hell with falling in with your own company; just fall into line of battle and later, if time permitted, things could be sorted out.

What looked like a disorganized block of 250 men was transforming itself. Orders were being shouted, officers holding up swords, and within seconds, the men melted from the block column into a battle line two ranks deep and nearly a hundred yards wide. Behind them came the men of the 32nd doing the same thing, thirty yards to their rear. Behind them, the other regiment of the brigade. Back at the entrenchment, the 29th stood solid and ready, facing the same direction.

Malady came walking up, ramrod straight as always, surrounded by a dozen or so of his sergeants. It was obvious more than one of them had taken a drubbing in this last charge. The one who had confronted Garland was rubbing the side of his head and gazing at him with a cold eye. Garland tried not to smile as he looked straight ahead.

Malady went over to Vincent, who showed him his watch; Vincent was obviously pleased, but Malady's expression did not change.

He stepped in front of the formed regiments.

"I bet you think you are getting good at this!" he shouted, and the men looked sidelong at each other. It was the kindest thing he had said to them during the last two weeks.

"For a bunch of benighted darkies, I guess you are getting good at it."

He slowly shook his head, looking down at the ground.

"Being a Sunday you have the rest of the day off."

Now there were murmurs of approval from the men.

"One thing more, though."

And now he was smiling.

"Starting tonight, form up where we usually do. I want ranks formed at nine this evening, no torches or lanterns."

"They can smile at each other," announced one of the sergeants— the man Felton had knocked out. "Darkies can always see each other in the night when they grin them pearly whites."

No one spoke. Malady looked over at the sergeant but did not say a word. Garland wondered if, in fact, he really approved and wanted to believe he did not. None dared to speak, but Garland could see their white officers bristling and knew words would be exchanged once the men were dismissed.

"You are going back to step one and will relearn everything, but now you will do it at night."

He smiled.

"By the way, I think I smell rain in the air. Hope so, that ought to fill the moat back up with mud."

He actually smiled at them and then turned and stomped off to inform the regiments who were deployed on the other side of the field.

Colonel Russell had come up to join his men.

"Battalion, stand at ease."

The men grounded their rifles, grumbling—cursing this sadist who controlled their lives—but Russell was smiling.

"Night?" he announced. "Men, this is beginning to make a little more sense. Back to camp with you; take the afternoon off and try and get some sleep."

They broke ranks, gossiping among themselves. Garland felt a hand on his shoulder; it was Russell.

"Let the men know how proud I am of them," Russell said quietly.

"Tell them if we're going to do this charge, something like this has never been done at night, and it just might give us the chance of surviving after all."

"But that fort in the middle?" Garland asked.

"I know, Sergeant Major, it is a puzzle to me, too, but I believe someone is really thinking this thing out. This time, I hope the generals have something up their sleeve."

"Yes, sir; I'll pass the word. It'll be good for the men to hear it."

"And, Garland."

"Sir?"

"Felton sure knows how to throw a punch."

Startled, he looked at his colonel, who only smiled and then turned to go over to speak to some of the other men.

THE TUNNEL

****

Michael O'Shay was glad to finally be working the night shift. The air wafting out of the ventilation shaft was cooler, not laden with the suffocating heat of midday. Besides, it meant they had the daytime off and could skip morning parade. They had found a cool spot behind the lines, down by a spring. It was well shaded, and they could wash off, and then loll about in comfort while others stood guard in the front trenches or worked on the tunnel.

By today's measurement they were nearly three hundred feet in, less than thirty yards out now from the main Rebel line. This evening they had been ordered to change how they dug. No more broad spades; the ground was to be probed first with a bayonet, loosened up, and then carefully worked out with a trowel. The number-two man, up by the side of the digger, would hold up a sandbag to catch the dirt as it fell so that it didn't rattle against the tunnel floor. It had cut their pace of advance by a third or more. To make it worse, the soil had shifted to a sandier composition, meaning that the shoring crews had to work close behind them, carefully slipping in upright supports and cross planks of boards torn from ammunition and cracker boxes. There was not to be any hammering; it would have to be brute strength, shoving the posts and slats into place.

And now the inevitable happened.

Michael could sense it, a few seconds before the ceiling let go, a trickle of sand from where the shoring team had yet to set their supports in place.

He barely had time to hiss a warning to Lubbeck and to cover his own head when the ceiling let go—a ton or more of sand and loam crushing down on them. He had just enough time to brace his hands around the back of his neck, trying to get up on his elbows to form an air pocket. He wasn't sure about Lubbeck, though, and could feel him kicking and thrashing by his side.

Michael wanted to scream at him to be still, but it would only cause him to lose whatever air pocket he had, and might cause him to lose his own as well. If this was anthracite the whole thing would be moot; he'd be dead, or with luck, just have some broken ribs. In this soil it was about suffocation, and praying that the cave-in had not caught the shoring team behind him, or that it wasn't an entire shaft of earth letting go, clear up to the surface.

He fell back upon the instincts of childhood, saying a quick Act of Contrition and then, lips barely moving, reciting Hail Marys one after the other. Then Michael sensed that, try as he might, he was breathing too fast, the small pocket of air under his face turning fetid.

Don't panic, don't panic, he kept thinking between prayers, "Now and at the hour of our death, amen."

And then at last he felt it, a hand grasping his left ankle. Another hand on his right. Seconds later, they had pulled him out.

In the fluttering candlelight he saw a man frantically clawing at the dirt to the left of where Michael had just been pulled out.

"Got him," the digger hissed, sliding back, holding on to an exposed ankle. Someone else crawled up, grabbed hold as well, and they pulled Lubbeck out. The man was still, one of their rescuers rolling him over, putting his head to the man's chest.

"He's still alive," and then he slapped Lubbeck's face several times and thumped his chest hard.

"Come on, laddie, spit it out, spit it out."

Lubbeck stirred to life, rolling onto his side, coughing, spitting out dirt, gasping, and then coughing again.

"Get them out of here," Sergeant Kochanski hissed.

It was easier said than done. Half a dozen men had scrambled forward to the rescue when the cave-in hit; they were all tangled together, but finally managed to push Michael and Lubbeck back. The two crawled on hands and knees to the entryway of the tunnel, Lubbeck coughing loudly like an asthmatic.

"Stay here," the sergeant hissed. "Don't need you coughing like a dying man out in the open. The Rebs might hear you. Just stay here and get your breath."

"Sergeant, darlin'?" Michael asked, and Kochanski relented. It was a tradition as old as mining. You survive a cave-in, you get the rest of the shift off and a bottle to calm your nerves. Kochanski popped the air-tight door, went out for a moment, and came back with a pint bottle, handing it to Lubbeck first, who took a drink, coughed, and spat it out. Michael managed to keep his gulp down.

"You boys all right?" Kochanski asked with genuine concern.

Both just nodded.

"Not too bad," one of the shoring team announced, coming back to join them. "A pocket about six feet across and several feet upward gave in. Think it will hold."

"Double shore the spot and get some heavy planks in beneath it rather than those cracker box boards. More of it might let go at some point."

"Right, Sergeant."

"At least it didn't go up to the surface," Kochanski sighed.

"Imagine some Reb out on picket crashing down on top of me, that would have been a sight," Michael whispered, trying to act steady and not doing a very good job of it as he took another drink.

FORT PEGRAM

****

Colonel Robert Ransom of the 25th North Carolina and Captain Sanders looked at each other without a word. For a long half hour they had sat on the ground up against the southeastern wall of Fort Pegram. The men within and along the line to either flank had been ordered to stand in place and not speak. Both had felt increasingly foolish while staring at a foot-wide tin pan, filled to the brim with water. There was a cork from a wine bottle in the middle of the plate, kept in place by a thread attached to a one-ounce lead weight resting on the bottom of the pan.

Of course the Yankees had not been cooperative in the slightest. For the last three weeks, with the coming of sundown, their artillery from a battery up on their secondary line would fire at regular intervals. Sanders found it fascinating that the water in the pan would actually register the concussion of the gun firing, as it raced through the earth long before the shell finally screamed overhead, displaying an ever so slight ripple emanating from the cork anchored in the middle.

Ransom was just about to give up and offer some compliment to Sanders about his diligence keeping watch and all that, when it happened.

The cork had bobbed ever so slightly, a ripple puckering the water filled to the brim of the pan, so that a few droplets of moisture had splashed over the side. Sanders flung himself to the ground, pressing his ear to it, and laid there, holding up a hand for everyone to remain silent.

"There," he hissed. "I think I hear voices."

Ransom was down by his side, imitating his posture. They waited for several minutes. Sanders held a finger up in front of Ransom, then held it to his lips to indicate silence.

Another few minutes passed and finally Sanders sat back up.

"Did you hear that, sir?" he asked.

"I'm not sure," Ransom whispered.

"It sounded like someone coughing and other voices."

"I'm not really sure," Ransom said slowly, but then nodded his head.

"How far do you think they are, if indeed they are there?"

"Sir, first there was my report about observing someone taking observations on this fort from at least two different angles and now this. Sir, I'm convinced they're digging a tunnel under us and it's getting damn close, fifty yards, maybe thirty, maybe under us already. I wish we could find some old miners with this army to give us some advice on it."

Ransom sat back on his haunches, face illuminated by the lantern resting by the tin pan, which shook as a mortar shell detonated on the far side of the fort.

"I'll not discount you, sir," Ransom finally replied. "But I've been assured by a couple of the officers at corps headquarters that digging a tunnel of such a length without ventilation holes is impossible."

Sanders shook his head.

"Sir, I'm no engineer, but could you at least ask a couple of them to come down here tomorrow night and take a listen and report what we've seen?"

Ransom nodded.

"We don't want to appear jumpy."

"Let's just say cautious, sir. We are the closest position to the Yankees on this entire line. We are also almost a straight line right into Petersburg. At the very least, maybe a reserve position should be dug in back along the Jerusalem road and up on the Blandford Church Hill."

"That's for corps to decide," Ransom replied. "We barely have the tools, as is, to keep our forward lines intact."

"Just a thought, sir."

Ransom did not reply.

"I'll send some engineers up tomorrow night—if they'll come," Ransom finally replied.

The colonel stood up, climbed up on to the parapet of the fort to check on gun positions, and said a few words to the men, who were obviously dying of curiosity. Why were two officers on their bellies at midnight, staring at a tin plate of water, and then putting their ears to the ground? It didn't take them long to figure it out and for rumors to begin to fly. They rotated position in the fort with a South Carolina regiment and soon bets were flying as to which regiment would be the losers.

HEADQUARTERS, ARMY OF THE POTOMAC
10 P.M.

****

"Those are my concerns and objections, General Burnside," Meade announced, finishing a fifteen-minute lecture through which Burnside had remained silent. Anyone who served under Meade knew it was best to let him vent first, then try and counter later.

He had not been offered a drink, and Burnside felt he could sure use one at this moment. The evening was hot and stuffy. The thunderstorm of the previous hour had at first cooled the air slightly but now the mugginess had returned, made worse by the swarms of mosquitoes and biting gnats that had become a plague to this army.

Burnside sighed, looked down at the sketches he had brought along for Meade to review, and began to stack them up.

"Nothing to say?" Meade finally asked.

"Plenty, George," and he looked Meade in the eye, deciding to go for the familiar tone shared between generals at least technically of equal rank.

Meade's features did not shift or show insult, so he pressed on.

"You seem to object from nearly every point, George. The amount of powder, the consolidation of the men to participate in one unified command . . . you even raise questions about using my Fourth Division first."

"They're green troops. The administration in Washington has expressed some concern to General Grant about the number of casualties this army has endured."

"They've been training hard for two weeks now."

"I heard."

"You should ride out and inspect them. They're shifting to night drill starting tonight. I tell you, those boys are responding well, perhaps even better than white troops to the drill. Veterans? They'd just stare at us at this point and tell us to go to hell."

"And suppose something goes wrong and they get slaughtered."

"Nothing can go wrong if we follow the plan as outlined."

"Damn it, Ambrose, everything goes wrong in every damn battle we've ever fought. Nothing follows plan after the first shot."

"It seems to for Bobbie Lee, most of the time."

He knew he had misspoken, for Meade bristled at that.

"And they're not even really men of the Army of the Potomac yet," Meade said coldly. "And by God, if this scheme of yours does work . . ."

His voice trailed off.

Burnside leaned back from the table. He had always thought of himself as a bit slow on the uptake; the kind of man that would not grasp the full implications of what others said until long afterward, especially if intentionally veiled. But this?

"Is this about who gets the glory of taking Petersburg?" Burnside asked, voice pitched low. "The rest of this Army of the Potomac has never really looked at the Ninth Corps as one of 'theirs.' Most of the time we are shipped off somewhere else. Is that what this is about?"

"I don't know what you mean," Meade said coldly, eyes narrowing.

". . . and now made worse in that I have agreed to take the col-ored division into my corps."

"That was not popular with some. I didn't see any of my other corps commanders leaping for them to join."

"Their loss, my gain," Burnside retorted. "I don't give a good damn what color they are as long as they can fight."

"And will they fight when this scheme of yours blows up?"

"Hell, yes, they will fight. They have every reason to fight."

"We'll see," Meade replied, his voice pitched low. "We'll see. Just remember, this country can't stand another Fredericksburg."

CHAPTER EIGHT

＊＊＊＊＊＊＊＊＊＊＊＊＊＊＊＊＊＊＊＊＊＊＊＊＊＊

IT WAS AN HOUR BEFORE DAWN, ORION RISING OVER THE EASTERN horizon but already beginning to be washed out by the first faint streaks of sunlight, which promised another scorching day.

In spite of the cool morning chill, the men standing to either side of Garland were panting hard. They had run through the drill four times during the night.

He could see the faint outline of Sergeant Major Malady, standing with the commanding officers of the five regiments of their assault column. The other four regiments were just two hundred yards away to the west, yet nearly invisible in the early light.

All could sense that something was different, that something was in the air. The drills had gone almost too perfectly, the cussing of the sergeants had diminished. In this last charge, they had just stood back and let the men go through their paces. Signal to attack . . . axmen race forward, followed by men carrying footbridges, followed by column. Clear obstacles, cross the moat, up the parapet, lay down the footbridges, charge across, sprint six hundred yards, pivot and turn to the right deploying into line of battle.

It had gone like clockwork.

The officers broke away from the conference, calling their men to attention. The men of the 29th, who had the task of pivoting at a right angle as soon as the trench was crossed, were coming across the field, falling in with their comrades of the First Brigade of the Fourth Division.

Malady stepped before them, the order being shouted for the men to ground arms and stand at ease.

"You black bastards . . ." he started, and some of the men stiffened. When the hell would this man ever relent?

"Your drills with me have ended," he continued.

"Well, thank Jesus for that," some wag grumbled from the ranks, and there was a low ripple of laughter.

Malady ignored him.

"The next time you do this, you will be doing it for real—for real. It is not many days off, so those of you thanking Jesus now better start praying good and hard, because more than a few of you will be standing before him soon enough."

There was no laughter now.

"Within the next day or so you will all be briefed on the exact details of this charge and any questions you still have will be answered."

Malady acted as if he was beginning to turn away, then he paused and looked back at the men standing in the shadowy twilight.

"I am going in with you. I have volunteered to stay with your brigade commander. I am doing that because, God and all the saints help me, I must of lost my mind but I think you are some of the finest soldiers I have ever trained."

They stood there stunned.

"Dismissed!"

HEADQUARTERS, GENERAL AMBROSE BURNSIDE
10 A.M.

****

"That, gentlemen, is your objective," Burnside announced, pointing westward.

The nine regimental commanders of the Fourth Division, most of them with some of their staff and sergeant majors, stood around him, joined by brigade commanders and their division commander Ferrero.

Russell stood with field glasses raised, trained on the Rebel fort eight hundred yards away. Garland, shading his eyes, leaned against the parapet of this, the main Union defensive line.

The ground before him sloped down rather sharply. Before war had come, this had most likely been pasture land. There had been a few stands of trees, all of which had been cut away within a matter of days for fuel, for the building of parapets, and to clear fields of fire. At the bottom of the open valley a stream meandered, with foot-bridges crossing it every hundred yards or so. There was also a rail-road line, or what was left of it. It had once been one of the four main lines that came into Petersburg, but it had been seized and cut in the opening days of the battle and rails and ties had been torn out by the men to use for building positions.

The ground then sloped up sharply until, about two thirds of the way up the slope, there was a raw jagged line of red earth and sand, the forward Union trench. At regular intervals, zigzagging "cov-ered ways"—communications trenches covered over with boards, logs, and planks, which in turn were mounded over with dirt—linked the main line to the forward trench. The covered way di-rectly in front of where they stood had been widened out over the last month so that men marching four abreast could quickly move its entire length up to the front line.

What now held the focus of Garland's attention, though, 130 yards beyond their forward trench, directly on the crest of the opposition ridge, was the Rebel line. In a straight line directly across from them was Fort Pegram, a high, earthen-walled compound 40 yards or so wide and half as deep, a full battery of guns within and garrisoned by an entire regiment. That one fort alone could hold off an entire division. A line of well-built entrenchments and parapets jutted from either flank of the fort, running along the crest of the hill. In front was a jumbled maze of the ubiquitous abatis, chevaux-de-frise, and trip holes. Even to Garland's unpracticed eye, it looked as if not just a division but an entire corps could be slaughtered trying to take those heights.

"I call your attention to the road beyond the fort," Burnside announced, gesturing back toward the Rebel lines. "It is six hundred yards beyond the fort. That is the Jerusalem Plank Road. To our left, that road is the only link to Lee's forces holding the line further to the west. Cut it and they are cut off. To our right, going northeast and then north, the road leads straight into Petersburg, little more than a mile away. Its strategic worth is obvious and that shall be your goal. That is what you have drilled for."

No one spoke for a long moment.

"And, sir, you think charging at night with our men will achieve that?"

It was the commander of the 32nd, and his voice was filled with doubt.

"I think it is time to tell you the rest of the plan, gentlemen, the ace up my sleeve," and he smiled at what he felt was a little joke, but no one chuckled.

"A tunnel has been dug under Fort Pegram. It is being finished today. Starting tomorrow ten tons of powder will be packed into its galleries, which fan out underneath that fort. Three days from now, at three-thirty in the morning, just at first twilight, that charge will be detonated, the largest explosion ever witnessed on this continent. Fort Pegram is doomed; all that will be left is a gaping crater nearly two hundred yards across."

The doubts and dread of but a few minutes before were now replaced with excited chatter. Burnside grinned at them as if having just presented a coveted gift.

"That is what you have been drilling for in secret," Burnside announced. "That is why there was a fort between your two columns, but you were not allowed to step near it. Rather than a fort there will be a smoking crater thirty to forty feet deep. I think, men, that thirty seconds after that explosion, the Rebels for a quarter mile to either flank will be fleeing in terror, and many of them will be in need of changing their britches."

Now there was some laughter.

"It is during those moments of panic that you will charge. I think the chances are high that you will hit trenches and parapets devoid of a single living Reb."

He gestured down to the open valley below them and between the two lines.

"Four hours before the assault is to begin, your regiments will be positioned down there, in the open, on the far side of the creek closest to the Rebel lines.

"Your positions will be staked out, guides assigned to get your men into place. Backpacks, blanket rolls, tin cups to be left behind. Full cartridge boxes with forty additional rounds in pockets. Canteens are to be topped off full and strapped under your belt before departing. Bayonets will be sheathed, and every weapon inspected to ensure it is not loaded.

"You must impress upon your men that if but one man coughs, talks, trips, or makes a noise it could very well alert the Rebs and place the whole plan in jeopardy. Do we understand that, gentlemen?"

There was a chorus of assertions.

"The moon?" one of them asked.

"That is one of the reasons it is so urgent to do the attack this week. If we go in on the thirtieth, it will be three days from a new moon. The attack is to begin at three-thirty just as it is starting to rise and it should not pose a threat. We will be into their trenches and past them, and at that moment, the bit of light we get from the moon plays to our advantage."

"Still, sir, to deploy that close, out in the open little more than three hundred yards from their lines?"

"I've weighed the risks and benefits," Burnside said solemnly.

"Your men are well trained. They will know to keep absolutely silent, and besides, the field all the way from here down to the creek will be packed with men as well."

They were silent, looking over the crest of the parapet. Several dull thumps echoed and three mortar shells rose up from the Rebel line, arcing up, obviously aimed at them. No one spoke, judging the flight of the shells.

"No loss of dignity, men, if we duck down," Burnside announced and they needed no encouragement. One of the three shells impacted within a dozen feet of the front of the parapet and detonated, spraying them with dirt.

There were some nervous chuckles as they stood back up, brushing the dirt off their uniforms.

"Someone's taking an interest in us," one of them announced.

"As I was saying," Burnside continued, studiously ignoring the occasional musket round that zipped nearby. "The other three divisions of the Ninth Corps will deploy directly behind you. Even before you reach the Jerusalem Plank Road, those three divisions will follow. The next in column will push through to reinforce those of you holding the road and together push on to seize the high ground of Blandford Church Cemetery, while the next division will widen the breach at the point of breakthrough. The last of the four divisions will move forward as our active reserve."

He hesitated, but then smiled.

"There has been some debate, but it is all but certain that following us will be two additional corps. But gentlemen, you will be in the lead. Do you know what that means?"

Some nodded, all were silent.

"Your signal to go will be the instant the mine detonates. And believe me, it is something you can't miss and you will tell your great-grandchildren about. The instant the Rebel fort begins to lift into the air, your men are to be up and going forward."

"That does seem mighty close," one of the colonels offered. "Shouldn't we wait till the explosion settles down?"

"My engineers tell me that it could be a minute or more and debris might be thrown several hundred yards or more. Frankly, there is some concern it just might panic some of our own men, as well, so make sure you carefully brief your men that this is going to be one hell of an explosion. But it will also clear the way for them. They must leap forward instantly and with élan. This is going to be one hell of an explosion, the biggest any of us have seen or will ever see. I've decided we don't wait, we will be up and going in."

He paused.

"And, yes, I do expect some casualties in our own ranks from debris raining down, but I believe they will be fewer than what we will take from enemy fire if we wait. Besides, the sight of the explosion going off and your two columns emerging out of the smoke and confusion will only add to the Rebel panic.

"Those of you in the column to the right will be in the vanguard of the breakthrough. You will lead the way. Gentlemen, it will be your troops who will seize Blandford Hill and from there be the first to storm into Petersburg."

He smiled expansively.

"And it will be you of the Fourth Division of the Ninth Corps who will go down in history as the ones who led the charge that took Petersburg, and then on to Richmond. With Richmond gone, this war will be over. That is an honor you and the men of your command, the men who were once slaves or the descendents of slaves, will carry with pride to their dying day."

Another shell winged in, and they ducked. One of Burnside's staff suggested it was time to get back into the bunkers and no one objected.

Garland saw that his colonel was not yet ready to leave, though. He was leaning against the parapet, gazing out across the valley and to the fort beyond. Garland went up and stood respectfully to one side.

Russell seemed lost in thought and Garland remained silent until finally his colonel stirred, looked sideways at him, and tried to smile.

"Sergeant Major, what do you think?"

"Sir, the 28th is ready. We will be in the lead, sir, and think of it—" He could not contain his enthusiasm. "Sir, we will be in the lead clear into Petersburg. It will be the 28th that does it. I say, by the great Jehovah, we can do it if any men can."

Russell turned to face him.

"Sergeant Major White, I have been in this war since the beginning, and I've heard such things said too many times . . ."

He looked at Garland, drew closer, and put his hand on the sergeant major's shoulder.

"Never mind, Garland. This evening you tell the men the plan and let's pray it goes as planned."

"Sergeant Major White?"

Garland turned and saw the artist, James Reilly, approaching, extending a hand.

Garland took it warmly and then introduced him to Colonel Russell.

"I noticed you hanging around, watching the training and such," Russell said, and there was a touch of wariness in his voice.

James smiled, and, as he explained he was an artist for *Harper's Weekly*, drew out his sketchpad and handed it over. Russell thumbed through and, after looking at a dozen or so pages, relaxed slightly.

"Well done, and most respectful of my men," Russell finally offered.

"So you heard the briefing?" Russell asked.

"He had a separate one for several of us correspondents just before you came, but not as detailed. So, yes, I know the plan."

"Trustful of him," Russell said.

"I'm on the same side for this, sir," Reilly said forcefully, "and will not release anything until after the battle."

He forced a smile.

"Besides, I guess you haven't heard. General Grant, starting this morning, forbade transport for any correspondent on the packets and any man who tries to send a dispatch by some other source will be drummed from the camp."

"Sir, I'd like to ask a favor of you, if you will indulge me."

"And that is?"

"Do you mind if I camp with your regiment until after the battle? I'd like to do some more sketches of them, before and after this fight."

Russell looked back down at the sketchpad, thumbing back through it and then turning at last to an earlier one. James looked over his shoulder. It was the one of the men of the 1st Maine. Russell was silent, just staring at it, and then closed the pad.

"Merciful God," he whispered, then looked back at James, closing the pad before Garland could see it.

"Yes, you can stay until after it is over."

THE TUNNEL

****

The digging crew sat expectantly at the T junction of the tunnel. Two days ago they had reached the point that Colonel Pleasants declared was directly under the Rebel fort. There had been no need for them to be told that. Every time one of the artillery pieces inside the fort fired, a shower of dust sprinkled down on them. They could clearly hear men moving above them, some even whispering that they could catch snatches of voices, singing, and laughing.

It was nerve-racking because they had started to hear something else as well . . . digging.

At first they had tried to dismiss it as work being done on the fort above them, but the sound was coming closer off to the north side of the tunnel.

Even now as they waited for Pleasants, who was measuring the length of the gallery dug at a right angle to the main tunnel, Michael and the others would look at each other wide-eyed, nodding when it sounded like a shovel or pick had struck something nearby.

Long minutes passed and at last Pleasants could be seen, crawling on hands and knees, returning from the west end gallery. He stopped before the waiting diggers and extended his hand.

"Congratulations," he whispered. "It's finished."

Of course there was no cheering, or even backslapping, just a quiet shaking of hands.

"The powder, fuses, and detonators are supposed to arrive back at our encampment this evening. We start packing the tunnel to-night. Moving ten tons of powder, which we're supposed to receive in twenty-five and forty-pound barrels, is going to be delicate, tricky work. I've managed to get a couple of mining lanterns made that are spark-free but that will be our only illumination. I only want you men who worked digging this tunnel to load it up. Others crawling around in here and not familiar with it might trigger an accident. You figure out the best way to move the powder into place. And re-member, for God's sake, absolutely no metal on you. If you have hobnails in your shoes either trade them off or go barefoot. Brass isn't as dangerous but still could pose a problem, so all uniform jackets and belt plates must be removed as well. You're all experi-enced miners; you know how easy it is to trigger an explosion in a confined space."

"We were thinking about some sort of relay," Sergeant Kochan-ski said. "A barrel is passed in, first man rolls it up to the next man about twenty feet ahead, passes it off, goes back and gets the next one, and so on up the line."

Pleasants nodded.

"Good enough. Just remember you'll be working in near total darkness, especially once you start packing them into the galleries.

"I've done some calculating. Once the powder is set and the deto-nating wires and backup fuses laid, the rest of the galleries are to be sandbagged shut. Then back down at least twenty feet of the length of the tunnel as well, otherwise the blast will just blow back out. The tamping has to be at least one and a half times or more the distance to the surface."

"That's a lot of dirt, sir," Kochanski offered.

"I'm figuring about forty-five cubic yards or so; something like two thousand or so sandbags will have to be filled, brought up to the mine, then pushed in to block it all off."

The men were silent; moving that much powder and dirt without someone banging into a shoring or some other fool mistake was going to be rough. And as they sat in silence they suddenly heard it again. Someone was definitely digging; it wasn't them, and it was nearby, perhaps only feet away.

"We should start tonight," Pleasants whispered. "The sooner we get it done, the better. Now let's get going."

TRAINING CAMP

✳✳✳✳✳✳✳✳✳✳✳✳✳✳✳✳✳✳✳✳✳✳✳✳✳✳

"Care for a drink, Sergeant Major?"

"No thank you, sir, I'm not the drinking kind, but I sure would like to stand up and stretch for a moment."

James nodded an assent, putting down his stick of charcoal.

Garland smiled, stood, and stretched.

"I've done a lot of things in my life," Garland announced, "but never figured sitting to have my picture made would be one of them."

"Some find it relaxing," James replied, while uncorking his flask to take a sip, "most are a little bit tense, and some find it downright tedious having to remain still for so long without moving."

Garland put his hands against the small of his back and stretched backward until James could hear the bones pop. Garland groaned softly with delight.

"Ahh, that's better. If you'll just excuse me a few minutes, I'd like to walk around and kinda check on things a bit."

"Take your time," James replied. Garland walked off into the shadows to do his unofficial rounds. The camp was nothing less than jubilant tonight. Just before sundown Colonel Russell had paraded the regiment, had them break ranks to gather around, and then explained exactly what he and Garland had seen.

That announcement had set off a true celebration. Morale had been high throughout the day. Before, the men had detected a sense of uneasiness in the way many of their officers acted, despite the officers' best efforts to convey confidence. But now the men had begun to celebrate. They had heard the description of the size of the explosion, shared the belief that the trenches without doubt would be empty and the Rebs would be fleeing in panic, and were excited about the prospect of leading the charge into Petersburg,

Impromptu celebrations reigned in this camp and in all the camps of the division. Where, only the night before, if one listened closely they could hear muttered threats against Malady and his crew, now there was nothing but words of praise, many promising if they saw him after the fight they'd give him a drink from the whiskey they were sure to seize in the Rebel town. And regarding whiskey, more than a few, as soldiers had throughout history, found a way to obtain a bottle, most likely purchased from provost guards at a premium price.

Reilly smiled, watching in the flickering firelight, as Garland was admonishing one such soldier, holding his hand out firmly, the soldier, head down, handing the bottle over. Garland tossed it into the fire, there was a flaring flash of light as the brew nearly exploded, laughter rippling around the camp as others quickly scrambled to hide their own bottles.

Garland, smiling, at last returned. James picked up a few more split logs and placed them on the fire, bringing up the light so he could finish his drawing.

Garland settled down on a low camp stool, leaning forward slightly, hands clasped between his knees, staring into the fire as James had asked.

James picked up his stick of charcoal, sharpened it with his razor pocketknife, and resumed his work.

"Garland, I know so little about you," James said. "Just that before the 28th formed up you worked as a recruiter for the 54th and 55th Massachusetts and turned down noncommissioned rank with both. Mind telling me a bit more about yourself?"

"Sir?"

"I'm not an officer, James will do."

Garland looked up at him for a moment and there was a flicker of a smile.

"Not many white men make that offer."

"You might be surprised once all this is over. Besides, I'm Irish, been through some hard knocks myself."

"I've found that some of the Irish hate us even more than white folks born here."

James did not reply to that.

"Just James. Remember, I asked that before, all right?"

Garland nodded.

"Where are you from originally?"

"Georgia."

"Strange, you don't have much Georgia in your voice."

Garland laughed.

"Most white folks say it's hard to tell us colored apart and we all sound alike."

"Well, the same is true for us. Cork and Galway are as different as night and day to someone born there."

Garland nodded.

"So you were born in Georgia. When?"

"Not sure really. I guess around 1830 or so."

"Family?"

He shook his head.

"Never seemed to have time or be what the Lord wanted of me. Last I heard my mother was still alive though."

"And how long ago was that?"

Garland looked off.

"More than ten years since I last saw her."

James felt a kinship with that. His own mother was dead, buried at sea. His father, last he had heard, had died a drunk, killed while working on the Illinois Central, and he had felt precious little emotion over that loss. His brother . . . well, Garland knew that story.

"In 1853 my master was selected for the Senate by the state legislators and he took me with him to Washington to be one of his house servants."

"Your master was a United States senator?" James asked with surprise.

"Yes, sir," he paused, forcing a bit of a nervous smile. "Yes, James, Senator Robert Toombs."

James could detect just a trace of pride in his voice, the way a man might speak of a regimental commander whom he respected as a leader.

"The same Toombs who was secretary of state for the Confederate government and then a general?"

"One and the same."

"Well, I'll be damned."

"Well, there were times I damned him," Garland said, and now he did smile. "He presented a strange argument. Said he was for keeping the Union together at all cost and against secession, but at the same time said slavery should be allowed to spread clear to California."

Garland chuckled.

"Funny how masters at times never quite figure out that servants and slaves have mighty big ears while standing there silent in a corner of the room, all dressed up in finery, and ready to step forward and quietly refill a glass of brandy for a gentleman or punch for the ladies gathered in the next room.

"For over five years I can't say I sat in, but I most certainly stood in, on nearly every debate held in that house of his, only three blocks from the Capitol. On many a day, I accompanied him to the Capitol itself carrying his umbrella, taking his coat, and then waiting, but while waiting always listening to the debates from the other side of the door. I can't say I met, but I most certainly served a drink, opened the door for, and at times spoke to nearly every famous man of that time in the Senate, Congress, and even from the White House. Jefferson Davis himself was there more than once, and even northern men like Sumner, before he got caned so wickedly, and the man who is now secretary of state."

"You mean Seward?" James asked, now truly taken aback.

Garland smiled.

"Even carried on a correspondence with him after the war started, urging him to mobilize black troops."

"You knew Seward, so you could write to him?"

Garland grinned.

"You act like you never met someone famous or high up before. And you the famous artist for *Harper's?*"

James just smiled in return and figured it was best to let that line of the discussion drop.

"When the Senate wasn't in session, and the Senator went back home to Georgia, I stayed on to oversee the house and maintain it. That's when I learned to read and write though I already had the basics of it from Bible lessons while still in Georgia. Some fine Quaker ladies in Washington had set up a school for colored folks to learn, and I spent many an evening there studying, God bless them."

"So how did you get free?"

"Easy enough," and Garland pointed to his feet. "One morning I just packed a bag. I am a tad ashamed to admit it, but I felt after all those years of service I was owed at least a few dollars, so I withdrew from the petty cash box, that was kept to pay delivery boys and such, just over thirteen dollars. Actually all that was in there. That purchased me a train ticket as far as Buffalo.

"So it was easy enough. I went to a colored printer's assistant down on K Street, he made up a fancy-looking document saying I was a free man with papers of manumission, and signed it for me with a real fancy signature. I packed my bag, walked out the door and down to the Baltimore and Ohio station.

"I had a lot to think about on that walk. I posted a letter for my mother to a white preacher near the plantation, who I knew would read it to her. I doubt if I will ever see her again in this world."

He paused and for a moment it seemed as if emotions would take hold.

"Do you have any idea how many men of this regiment cannot tell you tonight where a parent, a wife, or a child is?"

James did not reply.

Garland sighed and stared back into the fire.

"I have no idea if she is alive or dead. And she has no idea of my fate other than that I was most likely cursed as a runaway."

He was silent for a moment.

"If you don't want to talk about it anymore," James offered.

"No, I like to finish what I start."

He shook his head.

"I knew I'd be branded a thief for taking the thirteen dollars. Toombs was a good man in many ways to his slaves, or servants as he called us, in the house in Washington. He even talked about granting me freedom after he died.

"That did bother me, though. You see when I learned to read I started to read things Frederick Douglass was already writing. I read the Declaration of Independence and how it said all men were created equal. This was just after the Dred Scott decision, which Toombs applauded, but which said I was not even, in the capital named after Washington, considered to be the equal of a mule or a horse.

"There was a lot to think about as I took that walk to the station. That train took me to Buffalo and from there I walked to Toronto on the other side of the river where I knew I would be safe from slave catchers. I lived there and I waited."

"What were you waiting for?"

"This is my country, too," Garland said fiercely. "How could I enjoy my freedom, with the knowledge of so many of my race, or to those of but half race, quarter race, or one-eighth race, still in bondage in a nation that says it was founded on certain self-evident principles derived from God."

James said nothing.

Garland took a deep breath and exhaled noisily.

"I hear a lot of the men calling you preacher or reverend rather than sergeant," James urged, and as he did so, he worked quickly to try and catch the serious, almost tragic look in Garland's eyes. He noticed the way Garland's comrades, sitting in the shadows of the campfire, sat in respectful silence, listening to his story, more than one nodding as if they were hearing their own story as well.

"The preacher in me? Well there are precious few schools in this land where a black man can actually be ordained and given a certificate of some kind. I was a runaway from a rather famous man, who had posted a notice that I had stolen money and silverware from him as I left his employment."

He actually chuckled and shook his head.

"Now that did bother me a bit. I figured he owned me near on to thirty years, so taking fifty cents a year or so wasn't a sin, but the silverware as well? That was just plain wrong to claim that against me."

He laughed softly and more than a few commented that he should have taken every silver knife, fork, and spoon in the house.

Garland looked back at them smiling and then just shook his head.

"The thirteen dollars was enough to get me to freedom.

"So there I was, in a strange city, in another country no less.

"I felt it best not to draw attention to myself, but I had always felt the calling to preach the word of God since I was a boy. That white preacher I mentioned would read Bible stories to us slaves, and I was able to remember them by heart. Once I did learn to read the Bible became my guide. I read it and reread it. It taught me much. Not just about God and salvation, but about how this language can be shaped to form men's hearts and men's ideals."

"You do a good job of it," James responded and there was evident respect in his voice. "I heard the way you talked to the men tonight. You know when to be a sergeant major, and you know when to be a darn good preacher."

"Thank you," and again he hesitated, "James."

"And the rest of it?" James continued to work on his sketch, now using a fine pencil to hatch out the remaining lines of the drawing.

"Then the war came. I returned to New York first. I wrote to everyone I knew in Washington . . . Seward, Welles, Sumner, even the President himself."

"What did you write?"

"That, but give the word, and two hundred thousand black men would spring to the call. This war was not just about the Union, but about freedom long denied as well. I do wonder if the President ever read my letter."

James made no comment, but felt he most likely had. Unless the letters were from outright cranks, potential threats, or scallywags looking for some government job, Lincoln tried to read or at least scan all his mail every day. John Hays most certainly would have singled out a letter from a former slave for notice.

"I think he would have," James finally ventured.

Garland smiled at that, deep lines streaking his face as he did so, and James wondered if he should somehow change the face in his drawing from somber and reflective to more cheerful, but he had already decided that he would title this one, *A Colored Sergeant on the Eve of Battle*, and would send it in to *Harper's*. Smiling could too easily be turned into a caricature by an engraver back at the publisher. Publishers, even *Harper's*, were notorious for changing around what an artist or writer did.

"When I heard that Governor Andrews of Massachusetts decided to jump the gun, and actually mobilize two colored regiments even before the Emancipation Proclamation was made official, I sat outside his office door for two days before getting an audience and offering my services as a recruiter.

"Not many people knew this, most never will, that in reality there are precious few colored folks in old Massachusetts. I wandered as

far afield as Ohio and Indiana, recruiting men, getting them vouch-
ers for train tickets, and sending them back to that old Bay State. I
bet there are more men in those two regiments who claim Ohio as
their home than Boston."

He chuckled at the thought of it.

"And that gave me the idea."

"Which was?"

"Well it was evident, wasn't it? I think I can honestly claim I
personally recruited over two hundred men to the Cause. And yes,
Colonel Shaw, God rest him, hearing of my work and after meeting
with me, offered me the post of sergeant major in the regiment. It
was then that I met Frederick Douglass and he urged me to take it
as well. But I refused."

"Why is that?"

"Because I saw a higher goal. Just say the good Lord pointed me
a certain way that led to here."

Garland paused for a moment and raised his head.

"Did you hear that?"

James had not really noticed it until Garland stopped and called
his attention to it.

The camp was beginning to settle down for the night. Rather
than be up till dawn drilling, they were at last to go back to a regular
soldier's schedule, already filled with the dire certainty that after this
day off, on the following morning it was back to regular inspections,
clean uniforms, polished brass, and drills.

A rhythmic clapping had started. During the time they had been
talking there had been the usual background chatter of a regimental
camp, more enthusiastic and animated than usual this evening because of the news given this day. And though James had to admit it
did seem somewhat alien to him, there was something even more
different, that the way men talked, joked, bantered, and now sang
was born out of a different culture.

He had no words to define it. It was not like some stout and taci-
turn regiment from New England deciding to sing "Rock of Ages,"
or some other hymn. It was not a group of Ohio boys laughing to
some raucous and perhaps bawdy riverboat man's song accompanied

by a fiddler, or an Irish regiment singing a lament of a lost homeland across the sea, or a German regiment lustily cheering a good drinking song or a favorite hymn.

This was unique.

It was a rhythmic clapping; others were joining in. Snatches of words could be heard to the beat, sometimes picked up by others; sometimes, after a few repeats, the refrain would stop. A few lines of a more familiar song would be voiced, a few more voices joining in, then that would drift away as well.

Someone was speaking a line when Garland, as if listening all along, had hushed him to silence.

"We look like men a-marchin' on . . ."

The line was repeated and repeated. Other voices joined in. What had been spoken words began to pick up a cadence, a marching cadence, but also inflections, notes rising and settling, the first one to call it out a baritone, then a tenor joining in, then a bass, counterpointing, the words echoing.

Garland, as if lost in the rhythm, was nodding his head, beginning to clap his hands.

And then it happened.

A second voice made a counter reply.

"We look like men of war."

It was repeated instantly, as if fearful that the words might be lost. Some broke into approving applause at this new refrain, others increased the tempo. A drummer boy picked it up, beating to each step; a fifer struggled to add notes, following the rise and fall of the two-line chant.

We look like men a-marchin' on . . .
We look like men o' war.

Garland turned to look back at James, and he could see that the man's eyes were bright, struggling to hold back tears.

"This is what I was called to do," Garland said quickly, as if afraid he too might lose the words he had to speak.

"I could have gone off with the 54th, maybe died in that charge down in front of Charleston, and I would have been content, but I had learned something while recruiting in Ohio and Indiana."

"And that is?"

"Politics."

"God save you," James said, trying to smile but with one ear still cocked to the chant.

"Don't you see?" Garland said excitedly. "Politics. In the early days of the war, there were volunteers aplenty for the government ranks. A call would go out for more men, a quota would be assigned to each congressional district, and it was up to the governor of each state, by any means possible, to meet that quota.

"Well, by the spring of 1863, with newspapers filled page after page with the casualty lists of Chancellorsville, Vicksburg, Gettysburg, and by that autumn Chickamauga and Chattanooga, unless you bribed a man a thousand dollars or more in bounty, which each state had to raise again and again, no one was volunteering. All the good men, well the white men with a stomach for the fight and a belief in the Cause, be it for Union, against slavery, or both, were at the front lines. We all know what a disaster the draft has proven to be. And yet there were hundreds of thousands of men eager to answer the call, if only the governors would listen.

"In a way I was 'poaching' on recruits in the Midwest. Every man, every black man out of Ohio, Indiana, Illinois I recruited for Massachusetts was one less man for the governor of the state I took him from. So I started writing letters to the governors. I'd tell them how many men I had loaded aboard trains leaving from Columbus, Indianapolis, Springfield, to fill the quotas of Massachusetts and ask if it wasn't time they counted those men as their own instead."

James could not help but chuckle. The chanting was dying down; in a few more minutes tattoo would sound, and then, fifteen minutes after that, the new call the army had adopted for lights out, which had been written by Dan Butterfield the year before.

He pulled out two cigars, and held one up to Garland, who hesitated and then nodded a thanks, reaching over to take it. Both bit the ends off; Garland put a stick into the fire to light the end, held it over to James as he puffed his cigar to life, and then lit his own.

"Good Cuban, thank you, sir."

"James, please."

"Well, it isn't every day a man gets a good Cuban. How much do those folks at *Harper's* pay you?"

"Not enough," James chuckled. "Publishers never do, and believe me, they smoke far better cigars than I do while I'm up here with you men getting shot at."

"Well, thank them for me."

"The rest of your story, Sergeant Major. We have only a few minutes."

"Oh, yes," and he puffed on the cigar for a moment, holding it out to look at it, the way any aficionado would when enjoying a good smoke.

"I finally got a rise out of Governor Morton of Indiana. I must say he wasn't too pleased to hear that at least a hundred or more men had been snatched off by me and by a less than scrupulous rival working for the state of Rhode Island where, believe me, you can count the colored on one hand."

He chuckled at that and shook his head.

"And so I, along with a Doctor Revel, a colored doctor from Indianapolis, helped to talk him into forming this regiment here. The men of the 28th."

He fell silent and looked away from James, and it was evident he was feeling a deep sense of pride.

"I got an audience with him. Gave him my ideas, and he asked me if I would work for the state of Indiana, help mobilize the regiment, and be the sergeant major, the highest rank a colored man is allowed to hold."

He looked back at James.

"After the years of exodus, I had a sense that, it was there in Indiana, that, with these men, I had found a home at last, and so that is why I am sitting here now with you."

"That is quite a story, Garland."

Garland just shook his head and looked at his cigar.

"This is quite a cigar."

He leaned over, rubbing the glowing tip on a stone at the edge of the fire, putting out the glow, and without comment, put the rest of the cigar into his breast pocket, saving it for later, and stood up.

The chanting was increasing again, the men knowing that in another few minutes they would have to fall silent and go to their tents.

"Garland."

James set his sketchpad down, stood, and extended his hand.

"God be with you. You are a good man and when this is over I'll buy you a box of those cigars, and we'll smoke them together in Richmond."

Garland forced a smile.

"If the plan works. And if we are still alive," he said softly.

He held James's hand firmly and there seemed to be a tremor of emotion.

"Good night . . ." again the pause, "James."

He walked off and only seconds later was clapping his hands in rhythm with the rest of his men, the chant rising again.

We look like men a-marchin' on . . .
We look like men o' war.

James stood silent, as somehow this song was theirs, not his. He turned and saw where Colonel Russell stood looking out at his regiment, but his features were fixed, solemn, and he knew in his heart what this man was thinking at that exact instant.

How many of his men would still be alive to sing this song three days from now?

And then from a distant camp it sounded. Dan Butterfield's bugle call for lights out and the end of day . . . "Taps."

It echoed and reechoed, one of the buglers of the 28th raising his instrument to join in the call.

The chanting died away into silence . . . until only the echo of "Taps" remained.

JULY 28, 1864
ENCAMPMENT OF THE 48TH PA VOLUNTEERS
DAWN

✳✳✳✳✳✳✳✳✳✳✳✳✳✳✳✳✳✳✳✳✳✳✳✳✳

"Son of a bitch!"

Colonel Henry Pleasants was out of his tent, hoisting suspenders over his shoulders, leaving his jacket behind, the furious cursing having awakened him.

A group of his men were gathered around a wagon; nearly twenty more wagons were weaving up the road into the encampment and coming to a stop as well. Half asleep he had heard the excited calls of sentries that the supplies were coming in, and had decided to let one of his adjutants handle the beginning of unloading while he tried to secure a few more minutes of precious sleep, but the ever-increasing cursing finally drove him from his cot.

"All of you!" he cried. "Attenshun!"

The men of his command looked over as he approached. In their eyes he could see that they were like a crowd of expectant schoolboys, waiting for a favorite teacher to set things straight against an unfair teacher. But, miners that they were, they waited for their foreman to stand up for them against an infringement of their rights.

An officer, a major, was dismounting, and shoulder tabs indicated he was staff. Pleasants recognized the officer, now glaring at the men who had surrounded the first wagon, as someone with Meade.

The major made a show of stalking over to the crowd that was gathering.

"All of you bastards stand back and out of the way, this is dangerous cargo."

"We know that better than you do, you pompous ass," someone in the group cried, "but it ain't the right equipment!"

"You there!" the major cried, pointing at Sergeant Kochanski. "I want the name of that man and want to have him bucked and gagged!"

Pleasants stormed up, moving between the major and his sergeant.

"You will come to attention as ordered, Major!" Pleasants roared.

The major glared at him.

"And who the hell are you?" he sneered, and made a pointed display of scanning Pleasants's sweat-encrusted shirt, devoid of any uniform jacket.

"That's the colonel of this regiment, it is," Michael O'Shay, who had moved up behind Kochanski, announced.

The major hesitated.

"You will stand at attention, Major," Pleasants said, voice pitched even, "when addressed by a superior officer."

The major ever so slowly stiffened, even as he shot an angry glance at the crowd gathering behind the colonel.

Pleasants made a deliberate show of slowly turning around and facing the crowd that was gathering.

"I heard no call for assembly. Now, all of you disperse; get in proper clothing for the day. No metal whatsoever, jackets and belts removed, any with hobnailed boots to go barefoot, all rifles, ball, and caps to be left in your tents. Now move it!"

The men broke up and dispersed, except for Sergeant Kochanski and his brother, who were peering into the back of the first wagon after carefully dropping the tailgate. The miners knew caution when moving explosives, and were horrified to see that the tailgates of all wagons were iron chained.

Stan had already dragged a box out on to the tailgate and was using a lever made of bronze to pry open the lid.

"Your shipping manifest?" Henry snapped, looking back at the major at last.

He snatched the proffered papers and scanned them quickly, lips pursed, anger slowly beginning to build.

"It's like it said, sir," Stan interjected, "priming fuse, slow burn, ten-foot lengths."

Pleasants extended his hand for Stan to fall silent, continuing to examine the shipping list, then looking back to the other wagons slowly climbing up the slope to fall in behind the first one in line.

"Please sign, sir, so I can be on my way," the major announced, offering a pencil to Henry.

Pleasants tore his gaze from the manifest and fixed the major with a cold glance.

"I was told to expect, last night—not this morning—but last night, a shipment of ten tons of blasting powder, semi-coarse grade to be packed in barrels of twenty-five to forty pounds. Instead I see only four tons here of coarse grade. That I was to receive eight hundred feet of insulated copper wire, galvanic batteries, and detonating plunger. I do not see that listed here at all. That, as backup if the galvanic detonators fail, I was to receive six hundred feet of fast fuse, in hundred-foot lengths, and six hundred feet of waterproof leather hosing to house that fuse; I do not see that."

His fury began to grow.

"And instead, I see this!"

He walked over to where Stan was holding up a ten-foot length of slow fuse, snatched from his hand, returned to the major, and waved it in front of his face.

"Instead, I find this! Ten-foot sections of slow fuse. What in hell am I supposed to do with it? The tunnel is exactly five-hundred-and-eleven-feet long! It will take a half hour for this to burn."

"Splice them together, I suppose," the major said haughtily. "You're the miners, not me."

"Fifty-one damn splices! You ever try that, Major?"

"It's your plan, not mine."

Henry flung the shipping manifest back at the major.

"I'm not signing," he snarled.

"I have my orders, sir," the major retorted. "Accompany these supplies until delivered and then report back directly to General Meade that it is accomplished."

"And damn you, sir, you will stand here and count off every barrel down to the last ounce, and every box of fuse down to the last inch before I sign. So you can damn well wait! And then I'll sign."

Pleasants stalked back to his tent and reemerged five minutes later. He left his jacket behind because of the brass buttons, boots barely on so that he walked awkwardly, and shouted for his orderly to bring up his horse but to keep him wide of the wagons because of his iron shoes.

Work crews were falling in, some of them barefoot. He snapped orders to his adjutants to see that the powder was properly organized and ready for transport up to the covered way, and from there to the tunnel. His rage had spread throughout the entire camp, and he inwardly cursed himself for letting his temper explode.

"All of you, shut the hell up!" he shouted, and his regiment of miners fell silent.

"You dug a damn good tunnel lads, and I am proud of you. And by God I will ensure the army does this right for once. Get to work, be careful, I don't need to tell you the danger. Loading detail for the tunnel itself, you know how to do it. The rest of you on sandbag details. Keep at it and move them up along the side of the covered way so they can be packed in quickly. I'm going to straighten this out with the horse's ass that shipped this trash to us."

There was a muffled cheer from the men.

He turned his mount and rode over to the major, who looked at him with barely suppressed rage.

"You have just insulted General Meade himself, sir, and I shall report it as such."

"Oh, I wasn't aware of that," Pleasants replied, trying to act apologetic and innocent even though he knew precisely who he was insulting.

"Tell me, Major, what headquarters did you say you were with?"

"You heard me," the major snapped, trying to regain some authority. "I am a staff officer with the headquarters of the Army of the Potomac."

Henry looked at him coldly.

"Funny, I thought you were with the Army of Northern Virginia."

He spurred his mount and rode off to see what he might be able to salvage through General Burnside. At least he felt he could still trust Burnside.

CHAPTER NINE

✳✳✳✳✳✳✳✳✳✳✳✳✳✳✳✳✳✳✳✳✳✳✳✳✳✳

"I WILL SEE GENERAL MEADE NOW."

Colonel Andrew Humphreys, Meade's chief of staff, looked up at him with exasperation.

"General, I have told you he is busy at this moment."

The bombproof bunker which served as Meade's forward headquarters was well situated, dug deep, several rooms connecting, illuminated day and night with coal oil lights, the fumes of which only added to the hot stuffiness of the damp room. Several telegraphers occupied the other corner of the room, each one of them linked by wire to the various corps headquarters along the front and to Grant's main headquarters back at City Point.

The door—looted from some farmhouse—to Meade's private room opened, and the general stepped out, jacket off in the heat.

"Can't this wait, Burnside?"

"I don't think so, sir." He was now taking a far more formal tone.

"All right then," and Meade gestured to the steps that led up to the surface, lighting a cigar as he stepped out into the open, both of them squinting under the blazing sun.

"It's about the powder and the fuses and everything else, isn't it?" Meade pressed, and his voice was low pitched. The headquarters encampment was alive with enlisted men and officers. There were couriers and the ever present reporters, who were looking over expectantly, but were being held back by provosts. Meade gestured to the high parapet, which faced the Rebel line 1,200 yards away. At their approach the sentries, keeping a bored watch, knew to withdraw out of earshot.

"I just met with Pleasants," Burnside began without preamble.

"Who?"

"Colonel Pleasants. Commander of the 48th, the regiment that thought up this tunnel project and have been digging it," he paused, "even though your own engineers said it was impossible."

"Oh . . . him."

"He told me that rather than the ten tons of blasting powder needed, he has received only four, of a too-coarse grade. Worse, the fuses are not the kinds that were ordered. We were to have a galvanic detonator to ensure an instantaneous explosion, precisely as planned, and with a backup of quick fuse. Instead we receive slow fuse in ten-foot lengths. General, you were trained at the Point as well as I was on blasting obstacles. Lengths of ten-foot, slow fuse almost guarantee something will go wrong."

Meade looked at his cigar, inhaling deeply, blowing it out.

"Ambrose, you have to work with what you have. This is the army, not some treasure chest you can pop open with an open sesame, and find everything you want."

"Sir, I put this request in a month ago. Surely, somewhere, some depot had what was needed?"

"We are talking about today, Ambrose," Meade retorted. "Today."

"I must press this," and Burnside's voice began to pitch up. "I had to send Pleasants to Washington to buy a theodolite and did so out of my own pocket."

"Most patriotic of you."

Burnside bristled.

"I knew that if I put in a requisition, even if I were lucky, it would arrive as a Christmas present. If I had known there would be a problem with the detonating systems, Pleasants could have gone to Pennsylvania, to his old mine, and there purchased wire, electric detonator, and quick fuses by the mile."

"My engineers put in the requisitions to ordnance as ordered and this is what was shipped to them. So this is what you will work with."

"And what exactly was the order back to ordnance supply?" Burnside asked.

"Are you questioning my integrity, General?" Meade snapped, a threatening tone in his voice. He had spoken loudly enough that onlookers had turned, attention fixed on what was obviously a confrontation.

"If I had known this would be the result, I would have purchased the items myself, damn it."

"With what budget?"

"My own money, if need be."

Meade stiffened and Burnside received the message that, though talking to a fellow major general, Meade was nevertheless in command.

"Are you proposing, therefore, to set this operation back until you get these extras you are demanding?" Meade asked brusquely.

Burnside shook his head.

"Colonel Pleasants reports that the Rebels are digging countermines even now. One of them might be only feet away from our main gallery. If they break through, it is over. We have to go now, as planned. If we delay even one more day, I am fearful of their finding us."

"If they do break through into your tunnel, your orders are to blow the mine immediately."

Burnside sighed and looked over the parapet to where Fort Pegram stood, 1,200 yards to his left.

"It will blow the fort, if we get the powder packed in by today, even if it is only four tons," Burnside replied, his bitterness obvious, "but the plan, that will be lost, and with it a chance to win this war."

Meade looked at him coldly.

"Do you honestly believe that?" he asked.

"What?"

"That this scheme of yours will end this war?"

"Yes, I do," Burnside replied sharply. "If we take the Jerusalem Plank Road and Blandford Church Hill, Petersburg is untenable and Lee's army is split. With dash and luck, by the end of the day we could be finishing off Lee's army out in the open, along the banks of the Appomattox, not trying to dig him out of those damn trenches over there. Even if some of his forces escape, the Rebels will have to abandon Richmond. Lose that, they lose Virginia. With Sherman knocking on the door of Atlanta, especially after the heavy fighting down there we've been hearing about over the last week, I think, sir, this fight right now is in our hands. The war-winning move."

He looked at Meade and at that instant wondered if he had said too much.

Meade just stared at him coldly.

"I have heard that too many times, Burnside. Hooker at Chancellorsville, McClellan before the Peninsula, and," he paused as if for dramatic effect, "your own words before Fredericksburg, and then that damn mud march you dreamed up: a campaign in January, when rain was all but certain, a month later."

Burnside returned his cold gaze.

"You still blame me for that, don't you?"

"Yes, I do," Meade said coldly.

"If that is what you feel, then why in hell did you ask for this corps to join your army?"

"I didn't," Meade snapped. "General Grant did. Grant insisted, but I will tell you this, Burnside, it was agreed for political reasons that you stay in command of this corps and that, sir, is the only reason you are standing before me now with this mad scheme, rather than someone else in command of the Ninth."

"Damn you," Burnside, whispered, turning away.

"What was that?"

Burnside turned back to him, ready to scream the words. All of it, all of the sly comments, the behind-the-hand whispers, the disdain after Fredericksburg, all of it had trailed him every step of the way. Nobody seemed to remember his triumphs at New Bern, how he bested Longstreet at Knoxville. Yet here was this man in command, only a division commander when Burnside had commanded this entire army. The man who let Lee escape from Gettysburg and whom it was obvious Grant did not fully trust and thus traveled with this army, always looking over his shoulder.

He struggled to control his temper; it would serve no purpose.

"And tactical command on the field of action once the assault begins?" he finally asked, deciding he had to shift away from a topic that surely would give Meade the excuse to relieve him of his beloved corps right now. Meade stared at him as if daring him to speak out and thus provide an excuse in front of witnesses.

"You will control your corps in the initial assault. But command of Fifth Corps, Tenth, and Nineteenth will remain under my direct control, not yours."

"May I ask why? At Fredericksburg I delegated operational command on the wings to subcommanders."

"And look what it got you," Meade said, his voice dripping with sarcasm. "I am commander of this army and I will decide when to commit our reserves, if at all, not you."

"So that's it," Burnside finally replied after a very long minute of silence.

Meade simply nodded, inhaled, and blew out a wreath of smoke.

"I have sent up to General Grant all your various requests, which you demanded be expressed to him. I will tell you, Burnside, I did not give them my endorsement, but acting upon his orders I shall see this operation through. Tonight and tomorrow Grant will have his troops near Richmond as if preparing for an attack, in order to draw Lee's reserves northward from here. I thought that news would at least please you."

Burnside realized that all the hangers-on of the headquarters were watching the two of them.

"So nothing changes," Burnside said.

Meade simply nodded and did not reply.

Burnside, rage barely suppressed, saluted, turned, and walked off. Meade stood, hands in pockets, and watched him leave.

Meade went back down into his bunker, ignoring the shouted questions of the correspondents. One of his telegraphers was standing there, holding out a sheet of paper.

"Sir, from General Grant."

He nodded, took the sheet, and retired back into his small room, carved deep into the earth. It was stuffy, but the earthen walls still held a touch of coolness when compared to the heat outside.

He scanned the single sheet, smiled at first, but then wondered what the real meaning was.

Grant was informing him that the diversionary operation to draw off Lee's reserves was even now being launched, in spite of the defeat of Hancock's Second Corps in the tangled ground of Deep Bottom on the far side of the river over the last two days. The crucial line of the message, though, was that rather than checking all orders, Grant was delegating to him all decisions of a tactical nature for the forthcoming battle to be initiated by the detonation of "Burnside's Mine."

THE TUNNEL

5:00 P.M.

※※※※※※※※※※※※※※※※※※※※※※※※※

"That's the last of the powder," Colonel Pleasants whispered.

The entire work crew let out an audible sigh of relief. To a man, all of them were miners and every last one of them had lost many a friend or relative in a mine they had been assured was safe, confident that the blasters knew their jobs and nothing could go wrong.

The 320 barrels, equally divided between the two side galleries, had been carefully stacked in near pitch blackness, the men working by feel. As each barrel was positioned, a hole was cut into each barrel with a bronze awl to allow the blast from the initial detonation instant access to the powder within.

Now came the frightful part, with Pleasants announcing he would do the task himself. He did it with a single miner's lamp

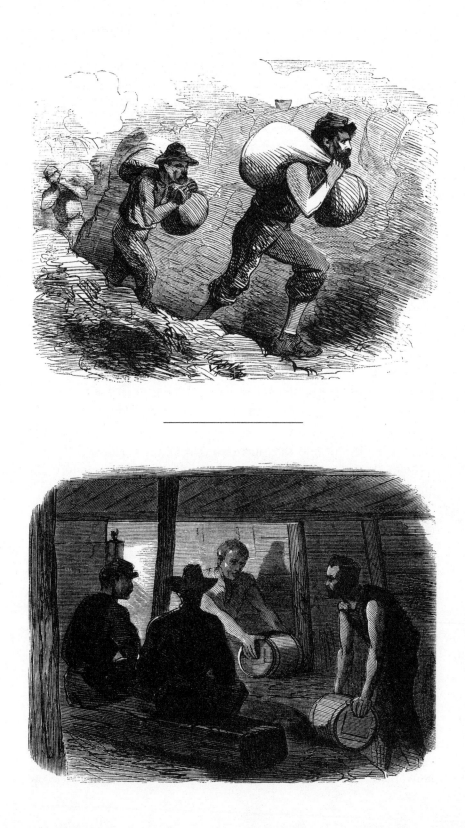

placed at the T intersection of the tunnel, and therefore was working in deep shadows. The wooden barrels, with a thin coating of nonconductive lead to keep out moisture, were stacked from floor to ceiling, lined nearly twenty feet deep. Unscrewing the cap of one of the barrels, he felt the wooden plug grabbing against the lead and, even though he knew it was safe, it still set him on edge. He laid the barrel on its side, making sure that it was wedged in tight against the other barrels behind it and to either side. On a heavy wooden plank he had laid out a piece of canvas covered in wax and, tipping the barrel slightly, he let a pound or so of powder spill out on to the cloth, banking the powder with his hand up to the open cap. Reaching back, he took the coil of fuse, careful not to pull too hard. The men had been working all day on the damn splices, making sure they were well woven and then carefully covered with a dripping of hot wax.

He laid the fuse into the banked powder and then carefully slipped a foot-long section of it into the open barrel. Then he draped another sheet of wax-impregnated canvas over the top of that, in case any moisture might drip down from the ceiling of the tunnel. A wooden stake had been driven deep into the ground and he made sure the fuse was coiled around that stake, so that, if any back pressure was accidentally applied while stacking up sandbags or splicing the main fuse in place, it would not be pulled free from its final destination.

Ever so carefully, he crawled backward out of the tunnel. This would be the part covered over with sandbags and the section he was most worried about. The fragile fuse, rather than a sturdy insulated copper wire, could easily be dislodged. Along this section, the fuse was raised off the floor of the tunnel. One of his scroungers had come back triumphant after prowling around the waterfront at City Point for several hours, having stolen a couple of hundred feet of canvas hose from one of the firefighting units positioned along the dock to protect the vast warehouses. The hose had been cut into two lengths to protect the fuse as it snaked through a carefully made opening, set into the mounds of the sandbags, leading to either wing of the tunnel.

He now replicated the same task in the other gallery. Yet even as he worked, every minute or so he would hear something, close on, just to his left. He paused in his work, put his hand on the wall, and after about thirty seconds felt the vibration. He put his ear to the wall, waited, but heard nothing distinguishable. Nevertheless, it sent a chill through him. They were close, maybe twenty or fifteen feet away. It was only a matter of time before this tunnel was found.

He carefully played out the fuse, making sure it was staked in place every three feet, as he crawled backward to the main tunnel leading back to the Union lines. He didn't speak, merely gesturing toward the sandbags that were already lining up opposite the wall along which the fuse would be laid. His men quietly got to work forming a relay, his most experienced men—Kochanski, O'Shay, Lubbeck, and half a dozen others working closest to the powder—building up a layer of sandbags from floor to ceiling. The only opening was just a few inches across, for the canvas hose containing the fuse. First layer firmly set, they slipped back a foot and started on the next layer, working in darkness. His greatest anxiety was that the fuses would somehow be dislodged, or far worse, in the final feet to detonation, the splicing would be pulled apart. For want of six hundred feet of copper wire, or just six-hundred-foot lengths of fast fuse, he was now laboring with this anxiety. He silently cursed whoever it was who had either misplaced, delayed, deliberately derailed, or just through sheer incompetence had failed to meet his specific request.

His only consolation was that, if at least one charge blew, while it would not all go up at once; hopefully at least some of the flame would blow through the opening left for the fuse and a second or so later strike the other gallery and set it off as well, even though the combined effect would be lost.

Like Burnside, he would have far preferred ten tons; he dug the length of the gallery out with that in mind. But it was too late now to change; he would have to replace that missing powder with yet more sandbags to tamp the charge in place. With that would come all the additional risks of dislodging the fuses or alerting the Rebs.

Pleasants ever so carefully turned around, knowing the job was in the good hands of his experienced miners, and crawled the 511 feet back out of the tunnel. Once the sandbags were in place, and only then, would he connect the rest of the fuse.

He reached the woodstove. Once all was in place, and before the fuse was laid, it would be damped out. Left in place, it would be buried with the rest of the tunnel. Perhaps someday an historian might dig it out, and he tried to smile at the thought.

He opened the airlock door and crawled out. Work details were hunched down, lined up back through the covered way leading to the rear. Men were bringing up more sandbags. Now that the charges had been set, it was their nerve-racking task to form a relay and carefully pass nearly two thousand sandbags, each weighing over forty pounds, up the length of the tunnel to the crews sealing off the four tons of explosives. A single mistake—a man dropping a bag so that it fell against an upright shoring, knocking it out of place—could trigger a disaster. Men could be buried alive, or it could make so much noise that the Rebels would locate the tunnel and finally be able to bore through the last few feet and discover their secret.

Henry was surprised to see General Burnside at the entrance into the covered way. As was custom on the front line, he did not salute, but did stiffen and offer a nod.

"The powder is set?" Burnside asked.

"Yes, sir. And I personally laid the fuse."

"That fuse, that damn fuse. Are you certain it will carry the flame?"

Pleasants was a bit surprised by Burnside's question and obviously nervous attitude. Enlisted men by the dozen were gathered around, bent over or squatting on the ground, some beginning to file into the tunnel to establish the relay, each of them hauling a sandbag of dirt and sand as they ducked low and went into the tunnel.

All of them could hear every word Burnside was saying and within minutes the rumors would start again that the general himself was now worried.

"I am confident, sir, the fuses will work. I supervised all splices connecting the two galleries to the main fuse into the tunnel."

Though he didn't fully believe his own words, he felt he had to say them in front of the men. Confidence had been sky high last night, and then collapsed this morning with the arrival of the powder and fuses. He could not help but hear the muttering that, yet again, the Army of the Potomac was preparing for defeat.

"It will work, sir," Pleasants repeated.

"Good, good," Burnside muttered even as he shook his head.

Pleasants finally had to motion him to step away from where the men were working and go back up the length of the covered way. Both remained silent as they passed the men of his regiment, laboring with the sandbags.

"I had to beg, borrow, and steal just to get those," Burnside announced, pointing at the bags. "Supply said there was a shortage. There's always a shortage."

"At least you got the sandbags for us, sir. As for the rest, there's nothing to be done about it now," Pleasants replied, feeling strange that, as a regimental commander, he was reassuring his corps commander. "Even if by some miracle additional powder and electric detonating equipment appeared, it is too late to set it in. We're already packing off the tunnels."

He did not restate his anxiety that the Rebel counterminers might be drawing closer. With all the work that had to be done in the tunnel over the next day, it would be a miracle if they didn't hear and bore straight in on them. If additional powder did materialize now, he would advise against setting it. It would only be a matter of days, perhaps hours, before they were discovered.

"I wish we had one of Professor Lowe's balloons right now," Burnside sighed.

"Sir?"

"I actually suggested it when all this started, but Meade dismissed it out of hand," Burnside said hurriedly. "Professor Lowe's balloons; one anchored behind our lines could easily tell us if the Rebels are digging reserve lines behind the fort or on Blandford Church Hill.

"He actually laughed and then just dismissed it."

Burnside turned away from Henry to look back at the men who were now relaying the sandbags into the tunnel.

"It will work," Pleasants said. "Sir, it will work."

Burnside looked back at him, his features drawn.

"It has to work," Burnside said softly.

TRAINING CAMP

11 P.M.

✳✳✳✳✳✳✳✳✳✳✳✳✳✳✳✳✳✳✳✳✳✳✳✳✳

Camp had at last settled down. The quiet whispering after the play-ing of "Taps" had died down and all was silent. Garland White, with James Reilly by his side, walked through the encampment area, neither saying much.

There had been excitement, to be certain, in the camp tonight, men singing the song about being men of war, which had sprung to the other regiments so that it echoed and reechoed across the en-campment area of Fourth Division. But there had been an increas-ing sense of somberness as well.

Officers had gone from group to group, urging the men to turn in promptly and get a good night's sleep. In the morning they would be allowed to sleep in until eight, an unheard of luxury in this army. The noonday meal would be fresh beef and the first of summer corn rather than the usual rations. But tomorrow evening they were to settle down at dusk, to be awakened at midnight and then move up to their positions for the attack.

Tomorrow was to be spent cleaning weapons, stacking packs and all unnecessary equipment into a common depot, and drawing eighty fresh rounds of ammunition and three days of marching ra-tions. The men were to drink as much water as they could hold, then top off their canteens, which were not to be touched once darkness settled. A full canteen was silent, a half empty or, worse yet, an empty tin canteen would bang and rattle.

James had stood silent, deeply moved by the number of men who had come to Garland during the evening to ask if he would pray with them for a moment, or if he could find the time to pencil a few lines to a wife or parents saying that they would meet in Heaven and not to mourn, for death had came honorably.

James had tried to sketch one such moment, a drummer boy and a young soldier who might have been his older brother, asking for help with a note back to a Quaker school mistress in Indianapolis, thanking her for her kindness to them.

Then he felt he was invading something sacred and poignant, and he gave up and turned away.

The scenes had, as well, reminded him far too much of Cold Harbor, but at least these men, not yet veterans, had yet to learn to pin the notes to their backs.

All was quiet now. A few who could not find sleep and did not wish to disturb their tent mates sat silent in front of smoldering fires. A small group was gathered around a lantern, a gray-bearded soldier whispering a verse from the Bible: "Though a thousand fall by thy side, and ten thousand at thy right hand, it shall not come nigh unto thee . . ." Another sat sideways by a fire, using the flickering light to write a letter, which was already several pages long.

Garland did not admonish any of them to turn in. He would simply nod, put a finger to his lips to indicate silence, and would walk on, hands again clasped behind his back.

"Do you think it will work?" Garland finally asked, breaking the long minutes of silence.

James did not reply. How could he? How many nights had he spent like this? He could not even count them anymore, so many nights before battle. Once they had been filled with anticipation and hope, but then merely resolve, and finally, in this last campaign, only a tragic resignation. These men believed; they wanted to believe. How could he answer honestly?

"If anyone has a chance at it, you do," he finally said.

"You didn't answer my question."

James forced a smile.

"Why don't you get some sleep, Garland?"

The preacher-turned-sergeant shook his head and smiled.

"When the last of my flock are asleep, maybe then—maybe then."

James felt that to stay longer was to intrude. The man wished to be alone with his thoughts, his prayers. He took his hand, grasped it firmly.

"I'll see you tomorrow night before you go in."

"Thank you, sir."

"It's James, remember?" and he smiled.

JULY 28

FORT PEGRAM

11:50 P.M.

****

"The sound is different," Captain Sanders whispered, looking over at Sergeant Allison.

"They've stopped digging, but they are still down there," Allison replied nervously.

"Exactly."

Sanders sat back on his haunches, looking at Allison.

"It's when we don't hear anything that we should start to worry."

"They won't withdraw us out of the fort?"

"At least our regiment isn't inside the fort," Allison whispered. "Thank God we switched places with these poor South Carolina boys . . . God help them."

Sanders shook his head.

"Ransom thinks there might be a tunnel, but we can't abandon the line," and he nodded back toward the Jerusalem Plank Road. This night, like every night, the Yankee heavy mortars were lobbing shells at random back onto it, hoping to hit the supply wagons that could only move at night.

"We lose that, we lose Petersburg, so we stay here."

"And get our asses blown off?" Allison retorted.

Sanders could only smile, pat Allison on the shoulder, and stand up.

"I'm gonna try and sleep. Give me a holler if the noise stops."

"Oh, I'll holler all right," Allison sighed. "And you can holler right along with me, as we either get blown to heaven or hell."

JULY 29, 1864
HEADQUARTERS, ARMY OF THE POTOMAC
1:00 A.M.

✳✳✳✳✳✳✳✳✳✳✳✳✳✳✳✳✳✳✳✳✳✳✳✳✳

George Meade, hands in his pocket while chewing on an unlit cigar, stood looking out across the valley to the Rebel lines beyond. There was a flash of light, followed long seconds later by a hollow thump. The nightly bombardment of the Jerusalem Plank Road. Rarely did it hit anything, but at least it kept the bastards on their toes and let them know we were watching.

Far beyond, to the west and north, the skyline flared, settled, and then flared again, a distant storm marching down, perhaps to arrive here in a few hours. If so, it would be a cool comforting relief after the days of such intense heat. Once this war was over he never wanted to see the South again. Before the war he had worked along the New Jersey shore, supervising lighthouse construction. Perhaps he would return there to settle down after all this was over.

Even a fool could realize how things would fall out once this was done. Grant would aggrandize himself with the glory of victory and pull his trusted companions from the West—Sherman and Sheridan— along with him. When the war ended and the army demobilized there would be no room for him. The mistakes that had been made, the butchery of the Army of the Potomac from the Wilderness to this godforsaken place, would be laid to him. He was pragmatic enough to know that if victory was ever won, the Westerners would get the credit, and he would get carping about how he had not pursued Lee after Gettysburg.

He thought of the note, carefully folded away in his breast pocket for future reference if need be. That tactical control of the forthcoming operation rested solely with him.

It had been masterful on Grant's part. A victory won, and of course the correspondents would all rush to Grant for his views and comments. Grant, with that outwardly humble nature of his, would say the glory was due to the Army of the Potomac. *"His" Army of the Potomac,* he thought bitterly. And if it were defeat? The note said it all: "tactical control of the forthcoming action" would rest in his hands.

I will take the blame; he will take the glory.

Another shell detonated somewhere near the road, the hollow thump washing over him six seconds later.

Damn that Burnside, he thought, almost whispering the curse out loud.

This army was fought out; Grant had bled it out. And yes, he had bled out Lee as well and pinned him in place. It was not masterfully done the way a Napoleon would have done it. It was like a battering ram relentlessly slamming away until the wall around Richmond collapsed. And it had bled his army out.

If that meddlesome fool, Burnside, had left well enough alone with his madcap schemes the siege would have played out. We just keep extending the lines farther and farther west until Lee is finally overstretched and snaps. This was again placing it all on one shake of the dice, another damn Spotsylvania, or Cold Harbor, perhaps even a Pickett's Charge in reverse.

. . . And then Burnside pulls out what he thinks is a trump card with his colored division, claiming they were fresh, eager, full of piss and vinegar and would carry the day. The fool—didn't he realize that either way he and this army would lose with such a gesture?

Who would win this victory, if there was even a remote chance of victory? Every damn abolitionist newspaper would trumpet that it was not his comrades, his army, his Army of the Potomac that had won the crowning glory. It had finally taken colored soldiers to do it. If there was to be a glory at last well earned, by God, it would be by his men, not them.

And if it went down to defeat, as he feared the chances were it would, he would be the one blamed for having approved such madness. And again the abolitionist newspapers would scream that he, George Meade, was more than happy to sacrifice colored men in yet another Cold Harbor. While every anti-abolitionist paper would mock him for having trusted such a task to "darkies" in the first place.

He could see the handwriting on the wall, and inwardly he cursed

Grant. A slaughter and Meade carries the blame, Lincoln blames him, and he finds himself quietly removed and stationed out in Nebraska or some godforsaken command the way Pope and others had been exiled.

Victory and it would not be the Army of the Potomac that could claim it.

The storm coming down from the northwest drew closer and for a moment he actually wished that it would pass directly over them, that a bolt would strike the ground directly above the mine and set it off here and now. It would blow the Rebel fort to hell; dispatches the next day would claim it had accomplished its purpose and the entire scheme would be forgotten.

But he knew fate would not deal him such a kind hand.

He thought again of the dispatch and the authority it gave him and at that moment he decided to well and truly use it.

CHAPTER TEN

✳✳✳✳✳✳✳✳✳✳✳✳✳✳✳✳✳✳✳✳✳✳✳✳

"MOUNTED AND MOVING AT A SLOW TROT, GENERAL AMBROSE Burnside rode the length of the battle line, a line of nine regiments, nearly four thousand men. They looked fit, proud, and ready. They seemed far tougher than the men who had marched across the bridge and first passed in review little more than a month ago. He could sense their spirit, their eagerness to get on with the task.

He had no words to say to them. He knew he was not, like some generals, an orator who could inspire. He rode the line, hand raised in salute, somehow wishing that this final gesture before battle would convey the respect he held for them. Reaching the end of the line he slowed, turning to look back at Ferrero, their division commander, and Thomas and Siegfried. The brigade commanders.

"We all know the plan," he announced. "Tell the men I am proud of them and tomorrow evening it will be my honor to shake the hand of each and every one of them in Petersburg."

The three did not reply.

"Don't let the rumors affect you. The good news is that I just received a message from Colonel Pleasants. The last of the sandbags have been placed, the mine is still secure, and he is confident it will go exactly as planned.

"I will meet you gentleman at my headquarters at eleven tonight for a final review."

The three saluted and he turned to ride back to his headquarters a half mile away. He was surprised and then increasingly unnerved to see General Meade with his staff, dismounted and obviously waiting for him. He slowed, and finally came to a stop; an orderly came up to hold the reins as he dismounted. Stomach knotting, he approached Meade, who simply gestured for him to follow, the two walking off toward the burned-out farmhouse near his headquarters.

Without any preamble Meade stopped and turned to face him.

"Did you receive my memo?" he asked.

"No, sir, I was out inspecting the troops."

"It should have been sent up to you at once."

"Sir, I was inspecting the troops and had said I would return by noon."

There was a long moment of silence.

It was obvious that Meade was displeased with this response.

"Then I will tell it to you, here and now. I am pulling the Fourth Division out of the attack."

Burnside stood as if struck, started to say something, then actually turned and walked away from him.

"Do not turn your back on me, Burnside," Meade snapped. "Do you understand the order I have just given you?"

General Burnside turned, glad that a dozen feet or more now separated them.

"Yes, damn it! Yes, I heard you. But understand it? No, damn it, I do not understand it!"

"One more outburst like that and I am relieving you of command as well," Meade retorted. "And by God, if you had said that in front of our staffs I would have relieved you!"

"Relieve me of what? An attack you have just doomed to failure? Maybe that would be a blessing. Now you can take the full responsibility."

"Then go ahead and resign, if that is how you feel," Meade replied, "but I will forward that resignation without recommendation other than that you did so in the face of the enemy on the eve of an attack."

"You would dare to call me a coward?"

"You are daring to be insubordinate," Meade retorted heatedly.

Burnside took a deep breath. He was cornered and there was only one hope left of getting out of it. He stepped back toward Meade, head slightly lowered.

"Sir," he began, "I beg you to reconsider this order."

Meade shook his head.

"I am at least entitled to know why, then."

There was almost the flicker of a smile, Meade having obviously regained control of this confrontation.

"You might place great store in this plan of yours, General Burnside, but there are few beyond you that do. From the beginning every engineer on my staff has warned against it."

"And they were proven wrong by the fact that the tunnel exists, built by men, who, it is obvious, know far more about mining than all the West Point–educated engineers with this army."

"Perhaps on that point, for the moment, but there are still sixteen hours to go. We know the Rebels are countermining. Even as we stand here they might very well break in and then we must blow the mine immediately. At that point any plan of attack is off anyhow."

"I do not see that as a reason to change the order of battle."

"I am ordering these changes for other reasons."

"Because they are black, is that it?" Burnside snapped. "They're not part of us, not of the Army of the Potomac as you see it. Is that the real reason?"

Meade bristled and Burnside fully expected that the next words spoken were that he was relieved of command.

"I will explain this once, and once only," Meade said coldly, "and then you will accept the order as given and follow through on it without any damn abolitionist accusations.

"The Fourth Division is green. I don't care how much you've trained them. They are green and we both know what that means the moment they are hit, and hit hard. You seem to presuppose that once your mine is blown up every Rebel will be gone and those colored regiments will just walk across the field and take Petersburg.

"No, it will be a slaughter. The sight of Negro troops will only redouble the fury of the Rebels to fight back. Therefore I want veteran troops to lead the way. Veteran white troops."

"Are you saying my men will turn and run the moment things get hot?"

Meade stood silent.

"You are calling them cowards."

"I have yet to see where men such as they have fought in a pitched battle against veteran Rebels and won."

"A brigade of them with the Army of the James took some of these trenches during the first day of the fighting here."

"Against mostly militia."

"The 54th Massachusetts, surely that proved something."

"Yes, that they were slaughtered and did not take the fort. The Southern press said it made their men fight twice as hard. The abolitionist press might make much of it, but it was a senseless slaughter. At Fort Pillow everyone knows they panicked and ran."

"So you are saying my men will fail, and therefore you are pulling them out without giving them their chance."

"I am pulling them out so that, if there is any hope whatsoever that your scheme actually does work, it has the best possible chance of doing so. And that is final."

"Those men trained for a month solid. They know it like clockwork."

"Clockwork for trained soldiers? And the moment the plan starts to go awry, and surely it will, they will fall apart."

"It is going awry, sir, because you are making it go awry by changing the order of attack only hours before we go in."

"You are pressing my patience, Burnside," Meade said coldly.

Burnside stood silent and then took a deep breath.

"Sir, I wish to speak with General Grant about this."

Meade, without saying a word, reached into his breast pocket and drew out the message of the night before.

"You can see from this that General Grant has already authorized and given me full control on this action. He has other things to do this day than listen to the protest of a subordinate, when this letter makes clear he will reinforce the chain of command, and that means my decisions are lawful and enforceable."

Burnside scanned the note, including the time and date. It was all so much clearer now. He knew, as well, that if he went around Meade this afternoon and rode to City Point to find Grant, that Grant, by custom and tradition alone, would endorse Meade's decision. And beyond that, there had never been any love lost between Grant and himself. If he were a Sherman or Sheridan it would be different. But the last thing Grant would ever want to see was a newspaper report that he had sided with "Burnside of Fredericksburg" against "Meade of Gettysburg."

He was trumped and just lowered his head, handing the memo back.

"None of my other divisions are trained for this. Their orders were to simply follow the lead of the Fourth Division, secure the breakthrough, and back up the Fourth as its first brigade advanced on Petersburg."

"When was the last time we fought any kind of battle where we had days or weeks to plan and train?" Meade replied. "I would suggest you have an officers meeting now, rearrange your order of battle, and see that they are ready to go by . . ." He hesitated and then asked, "What time was it set for?"

"It was three-thirty A.M. Less than fifteen hours from now," Burnside said bitterly. "That is if the slow fuses your staff supplied work."

"Call your officers together."

"It will mean having to entirely rearrange where they will deploy during the night."

"For God's sake, man," Meade shouted, "you have your orders, now see to them."

He turned and stalked off. Burnside just stood there, thunderstruck. Silent, he watched as Meade mounted, along with his staff, and rode off.

Finally, one of his adjutants slowly came up to him. It was obvious to all that something had transpired. The man was clearly nervous.

"Officers call," Burnside whispered. "I want all four of my division commanders to report to me immediately."

2:00 P.M.

✳✳✳✳✳✳✳✳✳✳✳✳✳✳✳✳✳✳✳✳✳✳✳✳✳✳

"So that is it," Ambrose Burnside said morosely, leaning forward, hands clasped, head half lowered. His four division commanders, James Ledlie, First Division; Robert Potter, Second Division; Orlando Wilcox, Third Division; and Edward Ferrero of the Fourth sat in silence.

The bombproof they were in was hot and stuffy with the afternoon heat. The only light was provided by the open door up to the surface. A shell crumped nearby. The Rebel batteries seemed to be a bit more active today.

Burnside waited for some kind of response, any response, but there was only silence. He finally raised his head, scanning them to gauge response.

What caught him were two things. Ferrero actually seemed to be relieved. As he had spilled out Meade's orders to them, Ferrero had blown out noisily, as if ready to voice something, but then just leaned back on his stool, looked to the ceiling, and was absolutely silent.

That had startled him. For God's sake, Meade had directly insulted this man's troops. He would have expected a bitter retort, a challenge back, an angry cry that by heavens his men were the best in the army and were being denied their chance, their honor besmirched.

There was only silence, and it was becoming clearer by the second that Ferrero was inwardly delighted with the news. His reaction was stunning. Ferrero, at the start of the war, had raised a regiment at his own expense. For three years he had risen steadily through the ranks, repeatedly cited for bravery. Some thought it a bit ironic that before the war his family had owned a rather famous chain of dance instruction studios, but Ferrero would grin and reply that learning drill under fire and trying to teach an overweight woman the latest craze, such as the polka, required just about the same skills and the same courage.

He had not hesitated when offered command of the Fourth, though there were rumors that Ferrero had claimed it as a path for further promotion; as more black regiments came into the army, they would be formed into their own corps, and by seniority he would gain that command position. He had seen to the task of drilling the men of the Fourth with some skill, bringing in a crew of tough and competent sergeants from his old regiment. To Burnside, however, he had appeared to be increasingly withdrawn from it all.

Like so many veterans of three years of war, had this man seen one battle too many? Perhaps he feared he had gone to the well once too often when it came to the luck of being a general on the front line. Was he now glad to be pulled from that line?

At the moment the concern struck Burnside as moot. Ferrero's division was out of the front line, though within the last hour he had at least wrangled from Meade the concession that the Fourth could serve as the corps reserve—if a breakthrough did indeed occur.

Ferrero knew he was out of the discussion as well. He just sat back silently, gazing at his three compatriots the way a man might after folding his poker hand and who, out of curiosity, wished to see what would transpire next for those still in the game . . . in this case a game where lives were at stake.

No one expressed outrage other than a few muttered comments about "high command," and how this most certainly threw plans awry, but nothing beyond that. Not one of the other three stood up to denounce the decision, then "beg" for the honor of his division leading the charge.

As he looked from Potter, to Wilcox, to Ledlie, all three avoided his gaze.

Burnside finally broke the silence.

"Gentlemen, we cannot reverse General Meade's order. Ferrero's division will be pulled to the rear of the column. I need one of you to volunteer for his division to lead the assault and to start to prepare that division for the task."

He paused, pulled out his pocket watch, and flipped it open.

"In nine hours. That is when your men will begin to break camp and move into position for the attack."

Again silence; none even dared to make a reply.

"Surely, one of you will volunteer?" Burnside asked, and there was a note of pleading in his voice.

Wilcox cleared his throat. Burnside felt that surely he could count on this man.

"Sir, you are asking which of us wishes to commit suicide. We have all been in enough frontal assaults to know the odds. I will not willingly volunteer my men to such a task without first consulting my brigade commanders and through them my regimental commanders. These men have been through pure hell the last three months. Perhaps you are now asking the impossible."

The other two quickly nodded their assent to Wilcox's bold words, which were essentially telling their commander to go to hell.

"I wondered, all along," Ferrero whispered in assertion, "when has any operation with this army gone according to plan? At least when we were an independent command, things always went well for us. But with this army?"

Burnside shot him an angry glance, ready to ask why in hell then had he accepted command of the division and the task that was laid before him.

"They always do this at the last minute," Potter interjected. "Just once, I'd like to see them stick to something. Damn them, we see how Lee does it, but not in this army. I wish we were back in Tennessee with you in independent command, General. You ran the show around Knoxville and the hell with Grant, or even worse this damn Meade."

Again nods of approval.

Burnside sighed, unclasping his hands, extending them, and if not for the dark shadows of the stuffy bombproof, all would have seen that they were shaking.

"We can sit here until doomsday, gentlemen, and argue the rights and wrongs of it. But I need a volunteer."

"Why not delay it a week?" Potter interjected. "That would give us time to train a division the way Ferrero trained his."

"There is no more time. The Confederates have started counter-mining activities and could discover and destroy the tunnel at any time. It will be a matter of luck if we get through the next thirteen hours. If we wait for a week, surely they will find it," Burnside snapped angrily, holding up his pocket watch as if to hurl it at them. "The attack goes in, in little more than thirteen hours. Meade committed to that at least, and to place Fifth and Tenth Corps into reserve support."

That was not quite true and he knew it. Meade had insisted that the other two corps would remain under his command and that he would commit them if a breakthrough was achieved.

"Then blow the damn fort, kill several hundred Rebs, strike fear into the rest of them, and be done with it. At least it will serve that purpose," Ferrero said dryly.

"I want this to end this damn war," Burnside snapped. "It is the best chance we shall ever have to do it. Either we do it by surprise in this way, or we will be doomed to a long and bitter siege ahead, perhaps well into next year, and ten times as many will die over time as we will lose in this assault."

He paused.

"I need a volunteer."

Again he was rebuffed.

He looked down at the floor of the bunker. Planked over, it was covered with rushes and straw to absorb some of the moisture. He stared morosely at it, looking again at his pocket watch, snapping it shut as if he had made a decision.

He looked back up at the three division commanders. Ferrero of the Fourth was no longer of any concern and he wondered now as to the wisdom of appointing him to the colored troops. The man had seemed eager enough when approached and offered a second star. Had that been the only reason, and, in reality, had he held no faith in them?

The other three stared at him in silence.

He was tempted to point at Wilcox and tell him the task was his. The man was able. His regiments, though battle weary, consisted of good troops. Wilcox led from the front, having been wounded and captured at First Bull Run. Exchanged, he had gone on to command his division at Antietam. At Fredericksburg he had directly commanded all of Ninth Corps while Burnside commanded the entire army.

His name was even now being recommended for this new decoration, the Medal of Honor.

It was surprising that Wilcox returned his gaze without saying a word.

Burnside looked back at the floor and finally saw only one choice left. Reaching down he picked up several straws, the three generals at first looking at him in confusion. He turned his back to them, broke one of the straws shorter than the other two, then turned back, holding the three straws in his fist.

"Draw."

He could think of nothing else. His mind and will were exhausted after so many long months of campaigning, of daily casualty lists, of so many letters sent to wives and parents of young comrades who had loyally stood by his side in so many fights. Unable to sleep for the last two days out of worry, and now this vicious and malicious blow dealt by Meade, he could think of nothing else to do.

"Draw a straw!" he almost shouted, holding his fist toward Wilcox.

He hoped that somehow this gesture would shame one of the three into at last relenting, and volunteering his division to lead the attack. Ferrero continued to just sit and stare with a slightly sarcastic grin, so enraging Burnside that he was ready to scream at him that he would be transferred to whichever division would lead the attack and that he expected to see him in the front line.

Wilcox, features cold, reached out and drew a straw. He turned next to Potter, who started to touch one, then hesitated and took the other. Ledlie did not move, just sat there, and Ambrose finally opened his hand and gave him the short straw.

Ledlie looked down at the straw and then, as if feeling he needed confirmation, looked to the straws held by Wilcox and Potter.

"Order of battle," Burnside said, nodding to Ledlie. "Your division goes first. They shall move into the starting point that would have been occupied by General Ferrero's division."

He looked over at Ferrero.

"I expect you to establish liaison with General Ledlie and ensure his men know the jump-off position, that they are properly instructed and equipped."

Ferrero nodded.

Ledlie was visibly shaken by the new development, letting his straw drop to the floor.

"The other two divisions are to move forward, occupying the positions originally planned for the division ahead of them. That means, Wilcox, your division goes in second; Potter, yours is third."

No one spoke.

"See to it immediately. Report back to me at two A.M."

They just sat there staring at him.

"Is that it, sir?" Wilcox finally offered.

It looked as if Burnside was in as deep a shock as anyone. His thoughts had drifted off to some other place. There were a dozen additional details to see to here and now, but he just sat there silently, head lowered, and simply nodded.

"That is all; I expect you men to see to the details now."

The four generals stood and filed out.

A crowd was gathered outside the bunker. No secret lasted for long in this army. It was amazing that word of the tunnel had been kept concealed as long as it had, but now the entire corps knew of it, knew that the assault was slated for 3:30 the following morning, and that there had been some major upset in the plan. Otherwise, why the very public confrontation between their general and Meade? And now this meeting of the four division commanders?

"The old man is ready for Bedlam," Wilcox whispered, coming out of the bunker. Potter looked back nervously, fearful that the injudicious words might have been overheard.

"Well, at least we didn't draw the short straw."

Wilcox looked over at Ledlie, who stood wooden, like a statue, features pale, as if he had just been given a death sentence, which in all probability was exactly the case.

"Better him than you or me," Potter replied. "Damn fool hasn't been through what we have. Why Old Whiskers even gave him a division is beyond me."

Ledlie had hardly seen any action since the war began. Most of his time had been spent commanding remote garrisons; his one prior nomination to high command was never confirmed by the Senate, which meant either someone knew him to be incompetent, or he did not have the right connections, or he had not bribed enough to see it through.

It was indeed a mystery why Burnside had taken him in and then given him a division during this campaign.

"We were simply told to follow the colored boys in once it began," Bob Potter said. "Now what the hell do we do?"

"We follow James Ledlie in."

Orlando Wilcox walked away, called for his horse, mounted, and rode off.

Ferrero just stood gazing off, looking toward the distant Rebel fort, which had been the center of so many nightmares throughout the last month.

So fate had intervened and had answered his prayers. The recurring dream that, when it was finished, his body would be found surrounded by his darkies and shoveled into an unmarked grave would not come to pass. He had seen far too many mass graves in this war. When he volunteered to take command of the Fourth, he had assumed, as did nearly everyone else, that they might draw some light picket duty along the line but would never be trusted in a combat role, let alone be given the nightmare assignment of leading an attack that was little better than a forlorn hope.

He would live out tomorrow.

He saw his two brigade commanders, Joshua Sigfried and Henry Thomas, waiting expectantly. Nearly the entire brigade command and even some of the regimental commanders had come in, waiting to hear their fates.

The two approached him, and he offered almost a cheerful salute.

"It's off for us," he said quietly.

"What?" Thomas gasped. "What do you mean, 'off'?"

"We don't lead the assault and have been placed in reserve." He almost added, "Thank God."

"Damn all of them to hell," Thomas cried, and took off his hat and threw it to the ground.

Ferrero startled, gazed at him, as did others.

"What are you saying, Thomas?" Ferrero retorted. "We knew it was suicide, and I say thank God someone else is going in first rather than us."

"Damn it, sir! My men are ready. As ready as any men would ever be, and ready to die to the last man to see it through. Just who in the hell ordered this?"

"You are talking about General Meade, sir," Ferrero said coldly.

"Then I say that General Meade is a damn fool and should burn in hell for this. We could have ended this damn war tomorrow without his meddling."

"Sir," Ferrero snarled, "you will watch what you say or by God I will relieve you of your command, here and now."

He looked around, as if to make sure others had heard the threat, in case word of this confrontation was carried back.

"We can do it. Sir, we can do it," Siegfried added in, but at least his voice was pitched lower. "Go to Meade. Go to Grant. They can change it back."

"It's been changed and that is final," Ferrero announced. "Our men are to assume the reserve position. We will be committed if and when the breakthrough occurs. And those orders are final."

The two stood before him, both obviously filled with rage.

"Go tell your men."

Thomas shook his head.

"I'll wait until they are awakened tonight at eleven," he said coldly. "They are ready, more than ready. At least I'll let them have a few more hours of believing in what they are to do. Even now, they are supposed to be bedding down to get some sleep. If I tell them this news now they will be in an uproar and then exhausted tomorrow. Telling them now or later won't change a damn thing other than when we break their morale."

"Your decision, then."

"Thank you for at least allowing me that," Thomas retorted sarcastically, turned, and stormed off, Siegfried falling in by his side.

"General Ferrero?"

He turned. It was Ledlie, face pale, coming up to his side.

"What is it?"

"You trained for this. Now, exactly what in hell am I supposed to do?"

"Go back and ask Burnside, not me."

"You saw the Old Man. He's broken. I doubt if I could get a coherent command out of him at this point."

General Edward Ferrero raised his hand and pointed at Fort Pegram, 1,200 yards away.

"You see that fort," he snapped.

Ledlie stared and simply nodded.

He reached into his vest pocket, pulled out his watch, and snapped it open.

"In just about twelve hours from now, that will be blown to hell. If indeed the mine blows at all."

And then he spoke words he would regret the rest of his life.

"Your job is to take it."

He turned from that trembling man and just walked away.

11 P.M.

※※※※※※※※※※※※※※※※※※※※※※※※※※

"You are joking," James whispered, incredulous at what he had just been told.

Colonel Russell stood before him, illuminated by a single lantern hanging from his tent pole, the only tent set up for the entire encampment, the rest having been struck during the day and sent back to be placed in depot.

"I wish to God I was," Russell replied somberly.

James could not find a reply. He felt a tightness in his chest. In one sense, what Russell had just told him was a blessed relief. These men, including this colonel with whom he had become so close over the last few days, would be spared now. The plan was a good one, but he had long ago learned not to put his trust in plans.

Never had he seen men so eager to trust in a plan, even if that eagerness was born out of naïveté. Still, at times belief was the key component to victory, even if the price demanded was a supreme sacrifice. History was replete with such examples, from Caesar, to Joan of Arc, to Henry at Agincourt, and to Washington at Trenton. Men such as Garland, Sergeant Felton, and the young drummer boy writing a thank-you and farewell letter to a beloved teacher, believed they would succeed. They actually seemed eager to make that sacrifice if, by so doing, what they believed in would come to pass. It was about far more than just preserving the Union; it was about Freedom itself, and they were ready to die for it. They might not themselves taste the full sweetness of that precious commodity, a celestial gift as Thomas Paine had described it, but they were ready to die so that others would.

It was such belief that won battles, even wars—that won victory for causes that could change the world.

He had resolved to go in with them. That was completely at adds with the rules he was operating under. An artist for *Harper's* could sit back with the generals to sketch a battle. Most did, though a few like Ward and he had more than once ventured into the front lines to capture in their minds an image that would later be converted into print. It was these vivid, realistic images that distinguished them from the others covering this war.

James had decided to go in with them for more than that. It was a responsibility he bore beyond his apparent task. He wanted to be able to report directly to Lincoln exactly what he had seen with his own eyes as to how these men could fight, whether they were willing to die, and whether perhaps the actual fate, the weight of responsibility for the survival of the Union, rested in the hands of black soldiers. Whether, in fact, these men were willing to carry that burden, wanted to carry it to prove to the world, and to themselves as well, that they were worthy of it.

"I have to tell my men," Russell sighed, and stepped away from Reilly.

Minutes before the sergeants had moved among the regiment, almost gently, telling them to wake up, repeating the litany a dozen or more times during the day, while they bedded down under the open sky, their camp gear having been taken down and sent into depot.

"Sergeants, check the weapons of every man, rifles empty, no percussion cap in place. Eighty rounds of ammunition and one hundred percussion caps per man. Do not touch canteens, which are to be filled, straps tucked under your belt. No talking, men, no talking. Silence in the ranks from now on. Form up on your company."

In the darkness, illuminated only by starlight and the single lantern hanging from Russell's tent, James could see 250 ghostlike apparitions fall into formation with practiced ease, not a word said, not a whispered command required.

Russell waited until all were in place.

"Men of the 28th, know that I am proud of you. No, more than that, I am honored to be able to lead such men as you into battle."

No one replied. They had been cautioned before dark that there were to be no spontaneous demonstrations, no cheering, and commands to be given at a whisper.

He took a deep breath.

"The order of battle has been changed. We are not to lead the charge and have been placed in reserve."

There was utter silence for several seconds, and then a low murmuring began, men turning to each other as if not believing what they heard. Surely they had misheard and would hear the needed assurance of a comrade by their side that the plan was still the same.

"Silence in the ranks," Russell said, voice pitched low.

James stood behind him, and in the pale illumination of starlight he could see other blocks of men receiving the exact same information, murmuring arising from them as well, even a shout of protest, which was instantly hushed down.

Though 1,200 or more yards from the Rebel line, voices could carry far on a still night.

"We will take up the position to have been occupied by the Second Division under Potter. Assume the formation you would have taken if in the front ranks of the attack."

He paused.

"Company commanders, prepare to guide your men. That is all," and he half lowered his head. "I will see all of you in Petersburg tomorrow."

He turned away and James thought he could actually hear a choke in Russell's voice.

No one moved for five minutes, then ten; officers whispered for the men to stand at ease while they waited for a guide who was supposed to come from corps headquarters to lead them to their newly assigned position. But no one came.

Ten minutes turned to a half hour and, regardless of hissed commands, the angry murmuring in the ranks began to rise.

"James?"

He saw Garland coming out of the shadows. James extended his hand, which Garland took.

"Why?"

"Why ask me?" James whispered.

"Because the colonel would not say a word to me. He just said those were the orders and that was it. So I am asking you. Why?"

"I know as much as you do, Sergeant," James finally replied, realizing he was lying. Of course he knew. It was politics, and rivalries, and jealousies—the continuing bane of the Army of the Potomac. Something had happened further up the chain of command. But he could not say that now. Not to this man, who, though in reserve, would be committed to the battle at some point.

"I will try and find out, though," James whispered.

Garland merely nodded.

"I promised to go in with you men," James finally said, and he felt shamed by what he would say next.

"But?"

"I think I should stay behind for this one, and I pray you understand."

"Why?" and he caught a note of cynicism in Garland's query that was so sharp that James reached out and put his hand on Garland's shoulder.

"Please listen to me. I want to go forward with you and if all had stuck to the plan I would have. Something has gone dreadfully wrong here. I think my duty now is to stay near headquarters, and perhaps by the end of the day I can tell you why."

And he did not add that he could tell his President what happened as well.

"28th?" a shadowy figure queried.

"Here."

"Follow me," and the shadow that addressed Russell, without waiting for a reply, set off.

"What about the footbridges, the axes?" Russell asked. "They were supposed to be transferred to Ledlie's division."

The shadow before him hesitated.

"I know nothing about that. Leave them here; I'll see that someone comes back to pick them up."

"Maybe we should take them with us," Russell offered.

"I have no orders for that. Once in position you are not to move. Ledlie's men will most likely look for them where you were last camped. It'd be absolute chaos trying to hand them over once in line for the attack. There will be over twelve thousand men packed side by side. Moving that equipment around will be chaos. Just leave the damn things here."

Russell sighed, turned, and looked back at his command.

"Drop the footbridges and axes by my tent. Now move out."

Garland stayed behind for a moment, whispering instructions as to where the men were to leave the equipment. The last company in column finally passed and started up the short distance to the top of the slope, which led down into the valley where they would form up for the charge.

As men dropped the equipment, James could hear their muttered protests, their anger, and indeed, their rage.

"I better get along now," Garland finally whispered.

"Garland."

The sergeant looked back at him.

"I promise, for the sake of your men, I'll try my best," James whispered. "God be with you."

Garland stepped back and took his hand.

"And may the good Lord guide you to the truth this day," Garland said solemnly, and then, releasing his grip, he disappeared into the night.

He had not cried when he watched his brother's body lowered into the watery grave at Arlington—but now? James Reilly lowered his head and wept.

JULY 30, 1864

FORT PEGRAM

1:00 A.M.

✳✳✳✳✳✳✳✳✳✳✳✳✳✳✳✳✳✳✳✳✳✳✳✳✳✳

"I think it will be tonight, at the latest, around dawn," Captain Sanders whispered, looking over at Colonel Ransom. Ransom sighed.

"I've passed the warning up repeatedly. Orders are we must stay in place."

"For God's sake sir, let's get the men out of the fort, move them back just a bit. God save them, they can draw lots for who stands picket for an hour at a time. If there is just a surprise attack we can be back in the fort in a minute at most."

"Do you know how that would play?" Ransom retorted. "This brigade, your regiment, the men of the battery in there would be the laughingstock of the army. I cannot order that."

"I'd rather have them alive as laughingstocks than dead."

"I cannot order that."

Sanders sighed, shaking his head.

"You are to come back to brigade headquarters with me. At least some reserves are to move back here at dawn. General Lee has surmised that Grant's attack north of the James River is nothing more than a demonstration. A feint."

"A feint to draw Lee's attention from what will happen here," Sanders snapped.

"General Hill said he would come up tomorrow to inspect and if your suspicions are confirmed by him, he'll order construction of a reserve line at once."

"That is a great comfort," Sanders replied.

"That is the best I can offer. Now let's go back to my headquarters."

"I'm staying here."

"Captain, you heard my orders."

"And leave my men? No, sir. I am staying here."

"I am giving you an order."

"You can give it to me in hell, sir."

Ransom said nothing, until finally he reached over and patted the young captain on the shoulder.

"I will see you in the morning," he whispered. "I have to report back. I'm ordered directly by General Mahone to do so."

Sanders did not reply. He knew his commander was not a coward and besides, what good would it do them if he were blown to hell? He would be needed to rally what was left.

After but a few yards he disappeared from view.

"Cap'n sir, you are one fool of an ass."

Sanders could barely distinguish the head sticking up out of the hole in the ground. It was Sergeant Allison.

"I thought I would stick around, Sergeant. Just once, just once, I'd like to see you actually frightened by something and see you wet your britches."

"Then come down in this hole with me and listen to how quiet it is," Allison replied. "I've wet myself three times tonight already."

Sanders laughed softly, reached into his haversack and handed over the quart bottle of whiskey that Ransom had so thoughtfully brought up to what he must know was a captain with a doomed command.

"Perhaps it is time to just get drunk," Sanders whispered, as Allison sighed with delight, took the bottle, uncorked it, and gulped down half a dozen ounces before handing it back.

"I don't think Saint Pete will hold it against us," Sanders whispered, taking a long drink as well, in fact the first one he had ever taken in his entire life.

WAITING ACROSS FROM THE FORT
3:00 A.M.

****

"It's three o'clock sir," one of his men whispered.

Colonel Pleasants did not need to be told. By the dim starlight he was just barely able to make out the face of his pocket watch.

How the troops, which had been forming up in the valley behind him ever since midnight, had not been heard by the Rebels was beyond him. Batteries were firing at their usual intervals to mask the noise, but several rifles, loaded against orders, accidentally discharged. Someone—either drunk or hysterical—had started to scream that he didn't want to die, and been beaten into silence, but from the Rebel side there had been no response, other than the occasional call of sentries, and the regular taunts between pickets.

That had been a tricky detail tonight. Men specially briefed by him had gone out after dark, as they did every night, to shallow dugouts between the lines, often not more than a rock's throw away from their Rebel counterparts. Usually the forward pickets agreed to truces and at times would even meet and trade Southern tobacco for Northern newspapers, cherished both for the news but also for other more fundamental uses, or a tin of canned milk sought for a sick comrade. The disappearance of these pickets might elicit alarm, so they were to play their normal roles, if need be to chat with the Rebs and trade as usual.

Three hoots of an owl, now expertly given by one of Pleasants's men, was the signal for them to disengage, and as quietly as possible creep back into the main line. If questioned by the other side, they were to simply say they were being relieved or were feeling too sick to stay on the line.

Pleasants waited nervously as, one by one, the men came slipping over the lip of the trench and dropping down. No alarm was being sounded.

It was just after three. The slow fuse, he had calculated, would take twenty-eight minutes to reach the magazines. Puffing his cigar to a hot glow, he looked at those gathered around him.

"Good luck to us all," someone whispered.

Without any ceremony or flourish, Colonel Pleasants touched the glowing tip to the end of the fuse. It sputtered to life and began to race forward. He watched as it reached the first splice just inside the now open door to the tunnel, passing easily through the well-made junction, and continued on into the tunnel.

He stood up and stepped back.

"Perhaps we should move away from the entrance," he whispered.

Some chuckled softly, others were silent, a few of the men patting the entryway as if saying good-bye to a friend.

"This better be worth all that digging," was all that Private O'Shay could say.

CHAPTER ELEVEN

✳✳✳✳✳✳✳✳✳✳✳✳✳✳✳✳✳✳✳✳✳✳✳✳✳

"IT SHOULD HAVE BLOWN BY NOW," BURNSIDE WHISPERED ANXiously, unable to contain his concern, standing atop the parapet in front of his bunker. In the silence of anticipation, all could hear the clattering of a telegraph from within his command bunker.

A moment later a telegrapher came running out, holding a sheet of paper. Burnside stepped down from the parapet, as a staff officer held a hooded lantern so he could read it.

He turned away, features taut.

"Meade wants to know why it has not blown yet," he snapped.

He crumpled the paper up and threw it on the ground, then turned to the telegrapher.

"Tell him that if he would come to this command post rather than remain eight hundred yards away . . ." As he spoke he gestured with an angry wave of his hand to his right, "he could see for himself. Communicating this way by telegraph, when a battle is about to start, is absurd. Damn it! It is absurd!"

The telegrapher just stood there, knowing better than to send such a message.

Burnside sighed.

"Tell him I am inquiring," he finally replied.

James Reilly stood but a few feet away, overhearing the exchange. He turned his gaze back to the valley below, where over twelve thousand men were waiting. Looking back to the east, he saw that the shoulder of Orion was beginning to fade with the first faint indication of approaching dawn. Just below the crest of the ridge, at the rear of the column, the men of Fourth Division were becoming visible in the pale light of the rising moon.

IN FRONT OF FORT PEGRAM
3:55 A.M.

✳✳✳✳✳✳✳✳✳✳✳✳✳✳✳✳✳✳✳✳✳✳✳✳✳

Unable to contain himself, Garland stood up and went to his colonel's side. Company officers were gathered around Russell, whispering softly, falling silent as Garland approached. He suddenly felt nervous. Orders were for all men to remain lying on the ground; only officers were to stand.

He formally saluted.

"Sir, I think I should tell the men something," he ventured.

Russell sighed and nodded.

"I know no more than you do." He had his pocket watch out, gazing at it intently, its face now nearly visible in the early twilight.

"Just tell them to remain calm. It's still dark enough that the Rebs can't see us.

"Tell them to stay calm. It should go up any second now."

4:10 A.M.

****

"Sir, a message from General Burnside."

The runner was out of breath, having just emerged from the covered way leading back to the rear.

The officers surrounding Pleasants noisily hissed for the messenger to be quiet.

"I know," Pleasants replied, "he wants to know what the hell has gone wrong."

"Something like that," the messenger whispered, looking nervously past Pleasants, in the direction of the entryway to the mine.

Sandbag barriers had been erected across the trench, fifty yards back from either side of the entry, to protect them from the potential of any blowout emerging from the tunnel. A single lantern rested on the floor of the trench, directly in front of the entryway.

"It's the damn fuses," one of his diggers whispered. "It must be one of the damn fuses."

Pleasants, stomach knotted, said nothing. He had personally inspected each splice, running his fingers along every foot of fuse as it was uncoiled from the T intersection back to the entryway.

When confronted with the problem of the fuse yesterday morning, he had entertained the idea of a volunteer. He intended that it would be himself, just lighting the last thirty feet before the intersection, giving him a couple of minutes to scramble out. But after inspecting the splices and the condition of the fuse, he had decided to play it safe for all concerned and light it from the entryway, timing it to go off at 3:45 as planned.

"I have to take something back," the runner gasped. "They're hopping mad back there."

Pleasants looked at his men, who had labored so long and hard on this. No one spoke. He dared a glance up over the lip of the trench, looking back to the east.

Merciful God, the eastern horizon was brightening, the first faint traces of the approaching sunrise. The stars of Orion were fading, the thin crescent moon beginning to fade as well.

The ground behind the trench, clear back to the main line eight hundred yards away, was carpeted with an entire army corps. The men lay down, as ordered, but too many damn fool officers were up, pacing back and forth. The sounds of nervous whispering were rising by the minute.

The swale was deep enough that the western slope, the side closest to the Rebel line, was almost entirely concealed by the low ridge upon which the Union's forward position was dug in. But farther back, on the eastern slope, looking closely he could now discern something different about the land, a darker darkness of thousands of men lying prone.

He looked back up toward Fort Pegram. In a few more minutes surely they would see or hear something.

"Sir?" It was the runner.

"Give us a few more minutes," he said, voice tight. "Just a few more minutes; the fuse must be burning slow."

He wanted to shout out that if they had been given a damn galvanic battery and proper detonator the fort would already be gone. The road would be taken, the way to Petersburg and beyond that to Richmond already open.

Did I do all of this in vain, he wondered?

The runner saluted, forgetting the protocol of the front-line trench, and turned to dash back down the covered way, obviously glad to be the hell out of a position directly in front of four tons of powder that could blow at any second.

HEADQUARTERS, NINTH CORPS
4:25 A.M.

❋❋❋❋❋❋❋❋❋❋❋❋❋❋❋❋❋❋❋❋❋❋❋❋❋❋

The telegrapher handed up another message. He no longer needed a lantern to read it.

𝔘𝔫𝔦𝔱𝔢𝔡 𝔖𝔱𝔞𝔱𝔢𝔰 𝔐𝔦𝔩𝔦𝔱𝔞𝔯𝔶 𝔗𝔢𝔩𝔢𝔤𝔯𝔞𝔭𝔥.

It is evident that the mine has failed. Your forces are already positioned. I am ordering you to attack now.

"This is insanity," Burnside cried, looking down at the preemptive order from Meade and back toward Fort Pegram, which was now clearly visible as a dark line on the western horizon.

"My God, if the men go in now and then it detonates, the entire corps will be annihilated."

He took a deep breath.

"Hold this telegram," he replied sharply. "I did not see it."

He looked back to his staff.

"One of you, go. Damn it, run! Tell Pleasants to send someone in and find out what has gone wrong!"

An officer climbed up over the parapet and started off at a run.

4:28 A.M.

❋❋❋❋❋❋❋❋❋❋❋❋❋❋❋❋❋❋❋❋❋❋❋❋❋❋

"I'm going in," Pleasants announced, peeling off his uniform jacket.

"Sir?"

It was one of his diggers, Kochanski.

"What is it?"

"Regiment will be in one hell of a fix if we lose you before the fight even starts. I'll go."

Pleasants started to shake his head. But Kochanski, jacket off, was already up over the safety barrier.

"O'Shay, come with me."

"Oh, God bless you, Sergeant, and the saints watch over you, of course," O'Shay snarled, tearing off his jacket and following Kochanski, the two running to the entrance.

"If I wind up getting blown to hell," O'Shay hissed, "I'll curse you forever while we're sitting down there, you damn Polack."

Kochanski almost chuckled as he picked up the lantern, bent low, and stepped into the dark chamber.

4:30 A.M.

✳✳✳✳✳✳✳✳✳✳✳✳✳✳✳✳✳✳✳✳✳✳✳✳✳

"My God, they must see us by now," Russell gasped, looking back to the east, then back toward the Rebel line.

"Are they blind?"

FORT PEGRAM

4:35 A.M.

✳✳✳✳✳✳✳✳✳✳✳✳✳✳✳✳✳✳✳✳✳✳✳✳✳

Captain Sanders stood on the parapet. In a few more minutes that would be suicide, but it was still dark enough behind him that he felt relatively safe.

Shading his eyes against the increasing glow of light, he carefully scanned the ground. Something seemed different on the broad open slope leading back to the main Union line. The landscape looked darker somehow.

He opened his watch and looked at it. Sunrise was little more than thirty minutes away. With dawn, he knew he could most likely breathe easy for another day, and perhaps his team of diggers would at last find whatever it was the Yankees were doing beneath them.

INSIDE THE MINE
4:37 A.M.

✳✳✳✳✳✳✳✳✳✳✳✳✳✳✳✳✳✳✳✳✳✳✳✳✳

"Hail Mary, full of Grace . . . Hail Mary, full of Grace . . ."

"The next damn line is, 'The Lord is with Thee,'" Kochanski snapped, without bothering to look back at Michael. Holding the lantern up, he pressed forward, O'Shay behind him, running his hand along where the fuse had been laid. All that was left was a blackened trail. Now, by the glare of the lantern, they could see the sandbag barrier ahead at the intersection into the two galleries.

"It's burned; it's burned through to the other side of the sandbags. Sweet Jesus, now what do we do?" O'Shay hissed.

Kochanski struggled against absolute terror, against just turning around and running. If it had burned this far, they were little more than thirty feet from the tons of powder. There was a fleeting thought: *Would the explosion kill me instantly, before next breath? Am I going to be standing before Saint Peter? Dear God, don't let me be burned, buried.* He had pulled out too many bodies from faulty blasts, their faces blue, contorted in agony. *Make it quick; please make it so quick I don't even know it.*

"God, please forgive me my sins . . ."

"Fuse!" O'Shay gasped.

There it was. Just before the beginning of the canvas hose that snaked the fuse in between the sandbags.

They stopped, both staring at the end of the fuse, dangling out of the canvas hose; this last splicing, just before the fuse disappeared into the built-up wall of bags, had failed.

The other possibility had terrified Kochanski, because, if they had not found the break by this point, it would have meant tearing into the sandbag barrier and trying to worm into the explosive-packed gallery.

Both were panting for breath, since the ventilation had been cut off. They stared at the charred end of fuse sticking out in front of them.

"It could still be a partial burn," O'Shay gasped, "part of it could still be burning in there."

Both had seen it, or the results of it, before. A fuse appears to have failed, a blaster goes in to find out what went wrong, and the last thing he ever sees is that the fuse is still dangling there, but a "partial" burn is still sputtering along inside of it.

Kochanski pulled the cover off of the lantern, held it up, and puffed the half-chewed cigar in his mouth to life. Hand trembling, he touched the tip of the cigar to the fuse. God, if it did not sputter then O'Shay was right, there was a partial burn still going on . . . and they were dead men who were still breathing, at least for a few more seconds.

The fuse flashed to life.

"Out!" Kochanski cried. "Run!"

In his excitement, O'Shay dropped the lantern, with coal oil spilling out as it overturned. Flaring up, the open flame added to their terror.

Squatting low, the two set off at a run. Kochanski, at one point, banged into a shoring with such force that it dislodged, triggering a partial cave-in, just as O'Shay pushed through behind him.

Ahead they could see the dim square of the tunnel entrance, illuminated by the rising light of dawn.

The two burst out, standing up.

"It's gonna blow!" O'Shay cried, racing for the safety barrier as Pleasants and others reached out to pull them over.

FORT PEGRAM

4:45 A.M.

✳✳✳✳✳✳✳✳✳✳✳✳✳✳✳✳✳✳✳✳✳✳✳✳✳

"Get Captain Sanders!"

Sergeant Joshua Allison, twenty feet down into the counter tunnel, was looking up anxiously. After long hours of silence he had heard something: voices and then something falling.

He turned to press his head back against the wall of the tunnel.

"Merciful Lord, please watch over me," he whispered.

Less than ten feet away, the burning fuse had already reached the split and had raced the final twenty feet up the two chambers. The flame in the southwest chamber reached the open pound of powder carefully laid out by Colonel Pleasants a few seconds before its counterpart in the northeast chamber hit its open charge.

The pound of powder flashed. No explosion yet, just a lurid blue burst of light igniting with a dull thump rather than a blast, for it was not contained. The flash burst into the open barrel of twenty-four pounds of powder, which ignited a quarter of a second later.

Sergeant Joshua Allison was the first to hear the beginning of the greatest explosion yet recorded on the American continent. He did not even have time to recognize it for what it was . . . as he was dead. A merciful Lord had answered his prayer, bringing him a death so quick that it did not allow even a moment for fear.

HEADQUARTERS NINTH CORPS
4:45 A.M.

※※※※※※※※※※※※※※※※※※※※※※※※

"Tell General Meade . . ."

General Ambrose Burnside was interrupted in mid-sentence.

"My God, there it goes!" someone cried.

He pivoted, looked west. The ridge appeared to be rising up, like a distant wave coming into shore, distorting the horizon, rising higher and higher.

No noise yet. Just the ground rising upward, and then suddenly breaking apart into ten thousand fragments that continued to soar heavenward.

Still no noise, but all could feel the shock wave racing through the earth, shaking them.

"Merciful God!" some screamed. "This is it!"

James Reilly stood up, sketchpad in hand, blank page ready to record the moment. Only seconds ago, he had feared that the pages he was about to sketch would be only of confusion and terror. He had been afraid that the Rebels had finally seen the mass of over twelve thousand men deployed and that then all hell would break loose. He had heard Burnside arguing about Meade's order to charge even without an explosion and had seen the agony Burnside was feeling. To charge without the mine going off would be to create yet another debacle. To charge and have the mine explode while thousands of Union soldiers struggled to surround the fort only yards away would be nothing less than murder.

But now the earth was lifting up. He knew he would have only seconds to register his impressions, impossible to make any clear sketch as it happened.

What had been Fort Pegram was now rising heavenward, an explosion at least a hundred yards wide igniting, tearing the Confederate position asunder. It was all darkness for another second or so, and then twin columns of flame rose up out of the earth, combining together a split second later, spreading up and out.

He tried to keep focused, to soak in every detail. He had been under fire scores of times and had learned to fix attention on a particular detail, imprint it in memory, then draw it later.

But this?

It was almost beyond his powers of observation. The first detail to catch his mind and hold for a brief instant was an entire field piece, weighing more than a ton, tumbling end over end as it continued to climb toward the sky.

The illumination from the flash grew in intensity, for a second or so like that of a rising sun as some of the powder, blown clear out of its place deep beneath the earth, was tossed upward, some of the barrels now bursting apart with brilliant flashes.

The explosion reached a climax. Around the edges fragments of earth, some half as big as houses, were now tumbling back down. In the center of the explosion, the column of thousands of cubic yards of earth, contained six artillery pieces, the caissons of which were exploding as well. Tentage, rifles, and more than three hundred men were being blown apart.

Captain Sanders barely had enough time to register what was happening to him. There was a brief instant of conscious thought, that he had been right and this now proved it, the beginning of a prayer for the good Lord to watch over his young wife and newborn child and then darkness for him as well, as he slammed into the ground fifty yards away from the fort where he had been standing but five seconds earlier.

Hunkered down behind the sandbag barrier, Pleasants heard the men around him cheering, shouting, even as some of the blast, which had raced down the collapsing tunnel, burst into the trench and was finally stopped only by the safety barriers they were positioned behind.

The shock wave raced through the earth and was followed less than half a second later by the sound of the explosion. It was not the sharp crack that many expected, some saying it would be like a volcano blowing up, though none had ever experienced such an event. It came more as an over-pressure punching into their lungs, a heavy thump like a giant door being slammed shut with a rush of air ahead of it.

Pleasants looked straight up, his horizon blocked off by the top of the trench in which they were lying. And then he saw it, a rain of debris climbing upward, reaching apogee, and then starting to come down. He had expected some of the wreckage to wash over their trench. And now it was, as he had expected, coming down upon them.

Garland White just stood silent, the explosion mushrooming outward, and then collapsing back down, the sound of it having washed over the regiment seconds before.

In spite of orders, every man was on his feet, shouting, cheering. The officers were as amazed as the men. Many of them stood dumbstruck, not shouting orders, for clearly no one could hear them through the noise of the explosion and its aftermath.

Though eight hundred yards distant, he thought he could actually see men, or what was left of men, tumbling through the air, carried aloft by the blast and now slamming back down into the earth.

He stood silent and offered a short prayer for God to grant them swift and painless deaths, for surely no man deserved to die in such a manner.

The rumble of the explosion washed over them. Then the noise just gradually died away. The vast mushroom cloud of dirt was disappearing, small fragments of it still raining down, while a dark cloud of dirty, yellowish-gray smoke, made lurid by the rising light of dawn, climbed a thousand feet or more into the morning air.

He stood silent, while around him men continued to cheer. He knew he had just watched several hundred lives being snuffed out . . . it was nothing to cheer about, even if they were the enemy.

The pillar of smoke appeared to detach from the ground and

slowly drifted, a cloudy mist hanging over the Rebel line. But after a minute or so it began to break apart.

And still no one was moving.

They had been trained again and again in what they were to do. When finally told what was to happen, that ten tons of powder would detonate under the fort, that it would disappear in a single heartbeat, to be replaced by a crater upward of two hundred yards wide, they had expected to already be moving forward.

"It will look like you are charging into Hell itself," Colonel Russell had told them, "but better that than Rebel bullets and canister at point-blank range.

"The moment the explosion starts, I want every man of you up and racing forward as you have drilled over and over. Every man of you! Do not hold back. Yes, some of you might be injured, even killed by the falling debris, but I want you into the Rebel lines to either side of the crater before the dust even begins to settle and the smoke to clear. They will be running the other way, I promise you, and we must latch onto their coattails and run with them, clear into Petersburg!

"You must charge, and keep on charging!"

Instead of charging, the men of Ledlie's division were on their feet, jumping up and down, gesturing, and to Garland's utter disbelief, falling back! In the face of the debris raining down, their forward lines were actually pulling back, some of the men turning and running.

"For God's sake," he heard someone scream. He turned and saw that Sergeant Malady, true to his promise, had fallen in with their brigade and was standing at the side of General Thomas.

"Charge, damn you! Charge!"

With his cry more and more of the men of the Fourth took notice for the first time that the men of the division which had replaced them, rather than going forward, were recoiling back. A universal shout of rage began to rise up from the ranks. Officers turned, some raising their hands for the men to fall silent, but the sight was so overwhelming to them as well that some of their voices joined in protest.

Two minutes had passed, then three, and not one man had crossed the forward trench line. By this point the entire 28th would already have been across the Rebel trenches and racing toward the Jerusalem Plank Road.

And so they stood, and raged, and not a single man advanced.

4:51 A.M.

✳✳✳✳✳✳✳✳✳✳✳✳✳✳✳✳✳✳✳✳✳✳✳✳✳✳

"In the name of God! Get your men moving!"

In his rage Colonel Pleasants had climbed out of the trench. The air around him was thick with the dust that had slowly boiled down the slope, but which was now beginning to clear.

He scanned their lines to either flank of the crater, half expecting to be shot as he stood up. There did not seem to be a single man in the trenches for at least a hundred or more yards to either flank of the smoking wreckage of what had been Fort Pegram. As he and Burnside had predicted from the first, the massive explosion had triggered a panic, understandably so.

Would more such explosions follow all along the Rebel line? Had the Yankees planted infernal devices along the entire front?

He could see scores of Rebels, out of the trenches, running pell-mell back toward the Jerusalem Plank Road. To either flank, for a mile in either direction, every Union artillery piece available—160 guns—had opened up as well, from the sharp bark of three-inch rifles, up to the deep thunderous cough of the huge fourteen-inch mortars, blanketing the Rebel lines with explosive and solid shot.

He turned back to face Ledlie's men. They had fallen back a hundred yards or more in some places, all packed together. Debris from the explosion had fallen nearly as far back—clumps of dirt, equipment, unidentifiable wreckage, and bodies as well. Amazingly, one of the Rebels was still alive, staggering around just in front of his trench; several men climbed out, grabbed him, and then with a show of gentleness actually helped him down to cover. The survivor was an oddity that filled them with curiosity as to why he lived when nearly every other man in the fort was now dead.

The sight of several of Ledlie's men who had been hit by the debris falling back when they should already have been over the enemy line filled Pleasants with rage.

He leaped over his own trench, and with arms flung wide, pointed to the enemy position.

"Charge, damn you! Charge!"

Some of his men, those who had labored so long for this moment, came out of the trench as well, pointing up the slope, screaming for their comrades to "Move, damn, it move!"

And finally, by ones and twos, and then in disorganized clusters the men of the First Division began to come forward. Only then did Henry realize that none of them were carrying footbridges to traverse the Rebel trench, and that none had been brought up during the night, to be thrown across their own trenches in the first seconds after the explosion. And not a single man with Ledlie was carrying an ax to clear away the abatis and chevaux-de-frise that were still intact on either flank of the crater.

Pleasants ran down the length of his own trench, drawing out his sword, holding it up high, waving it, pointing it toward the Rebel line.

"Do it! Do it now! Take it!"

The first of Ledlie's men reached his trench. Some managed to leap across, while many just lowered themselves down, then scrambled up the other side. Whichever units still had any cohesion now broke apart.

Raging, Colonel Pleasants found himself literally grabbing men, shoving them forward, leaping back over his trench and then turning to grab hold of men trying to climb up and out, yelling at them to keep moving.

Several hundred were now out into what would have been a killing ground only fifteen minutes before, walking slowly, cautiously, as if expecting at any second a blazing volley to erupt and give them reason to turn and dive back into the protection of their own trenches.

Not a single shot greeted them, and now more men, emboldened, began to push forward. But many stopped to gawk, to gather around a three-inch rifle, nearly intact, lying inverted halfway up the slope, others slowing to look at the bodies and parts of bodies of dead Rebels blown out of the fort.

"Keep moving!"

"Who the hell are you?"

He turned and saw a star on an officer's shoulder, but did not bother to salute.

"I asked, who the hell are you?"

Pleasants realized that the explosion must have affected his hearing; it was hard to catch what the man was saying.

"I'm Colonel Pleasants, 48th Pennsylvania. My men dug the mine. Why in hell are your men not advancing?"

He looked into the man's eyes, and saw that, for a general, he was quite young, not more than in his mid-twenties.

"Because we have no orders, that's why!"

"And who the hell are you?" Pleasants cried.

"General Bartlett, First Brigade of the First Division."

Startled, Pleasants could not help himself, and looked down. General William Bartlett was leaning on a cane, the straps of his artificial leg visible beneath his uniform trousers.

The man was something of a legend with Ninth Corps, and Pleasants realized that he himself must be in shock, otherwise he would have recognized Bartlett immediately.

Enlisting in the first days of the war as a private with the famed 20th Massachusetts, the same regiment which had produced Robert Gould Shaw, Bartlett had risen to company command by the spring of 1862. A Rebel sharpshooter had nailed him during the opening days of the Peninsula Campaign.

Losing his leg above the knee, Bartlett had finished his college education at Harvard while recuperating, gone back into the army, this time raising a regiment to go with him, and had then been wounded twice more, nearly losing his other leg, and having a hand permanently crippled after his wrist was shattered. He refused to allow the surgeon to cut it off, saying he had given enough of his body to the damn Rebels already. While Bartlett was recovering from those wounds, Burnside had recruited him to take over a brigade under Ledlie, and nearly every man of the division had looked forward to the day that Ledlie was finally booted out and a real fighting general like Bartlett took over.

It was therefore shocking to Pleasants that Bartlett, leaning heavily on his cane, apparently did not know what to do.

"What do you mean, you have no orders?" Pleasants asked, voice going tight, not believing he was asking such a question of this man.

It wasn't just the explosion that was making it difficult for Henry to hear. All along the Union line every gun was firing as rapidly as possible, the cannonade a continual wave of thunder.

"Just that!" Bartlett shouted. "My orders were to form and then advance after the explosion of some sort of mine; that once formed my men and I would be briefed. I waited all night for further instructions, but there wasn't a word and then suddenly this!"

He pointed at the still smoking crater.

Pleasants reeled with this blow. He could sense this was no coward or fool standing before him. The man was out in the open, confused, but obviously enraged as well.

"Where is General Ledlie? He was supposed to be leading this!" Pleasants asked.

"Damn him! You tell me!" Bartlett cried.

And even as the two stood out in the middle of what had been a no-man's-land but minutes before, they saw the first of the men reach the crest, look about, and then just disappear, jumping down into the crater.

"You had no orders to take the road and the hill beyond it?"

"What road? The Jerusalem Plank? That's what we're supposed to do now?"

"Merciful God," Pleasants gasped, not even realizing he was clasping Bartlett by the shoulder and nearly knocking him off balance.

"Once blown, the plan was for the lead brigades to charge around the crater, not into it!" and he pointed to where more and yet more men of Bartlett's command were doing just that, jumping down into the crater, or still poking around at the wreckage, like boys exploring a shipwreck after a storm.

"Well, this is now one hell of a time to learn that," Bartlett shouted.

Pleasants did not know how to reply.

"If I had had some such orders to give the men before . . ." Bartlett looked back up the slope over which hundreds of men of his brigade and that of the other brigade of his division now swarmed.

For the first time Henry heard the buzz of a minié ball snapping by. A few seconds later one of the men near them doubled over as another round clipped in. That began to set off a rush forward. As if by instinct, the veterans of so many forlorn charges raced for cover, with the crater ahead of them the best shelter of all.

"The road?" Bartlett asked.

"That was the plan."

He nodded.

"I'll see what I can do in this madness," he paused, "and if you see that son of a bitch Ledlie, do me a favor."

"What."

"Shoot him."

Leaning on his cane, Bartlett began to limp forward, remaining upright while around him men were beginning to duck, even though only a few miniés were whistling in.

"Keep them moving up!" Bartlett shouted, looking back. "I'll see what I can do up forward!"

Pleasants, ignoring custom on the front line, this time did salute as the man limped off.

Even as he turned to face back toward the rear the first Rebel mortar round came hissing down, detonating a scant dozen feet away. Pleasants ignored it, stepping through the smoke, calling on the men of his regiment to keep pushing the attack column forward, to pass the word that they were to push for the road, the precious road, just six hundred yards off. The road that even now was all but undefended and ready to be taken.

Behind Ledlie's division he saw the standards of Wilcox's division, as disorganized as the lead division, remaining in place, some of the men already lying prone as the volume of fire from the Rebel lines began to increase.

"For God's sake, charge!" Henry cried.

HEADQUARTERS, ARMY OF NORTHERN VIRGINIA
5:20 A.M.

****

General Robert E. Lee stood silent, field glasses raised in the direction of the plume of smoke rising beyond the Blandford Church Cemetery.

The first courier had come galloping in just minutes before, bearing news of what had happened. There was no need to awaken him. The distant rumble, the tremor passing through the earth, reminding him of the frequent earthquakes experienced while serving in Mexico, had caused him to spring from his cot, even before his adjutant, Colonel Taylor, had come to waken him.

Officers of his staff were gathered around, waiting as he leaned over a map table, the courier breathlessly describing the destruction of Fort Pegram.

It could be the signal for a general attack all along the line. He had thought the Union Army was pretty well fought out, but they had had a month to recuperate since the last of their major attacks. Grant might be venturing another bloody blow.

"General Mahone is our only reserve in that sector," Lee announced, looking back at his staff. "Send word to him that he must hold the Jerusalem Plank Road at all costs. Only if he feels overwhelmed should he call for more reserves. I will stay here for now because this might be the beginning of a general attack along the entire front."

He looked at his staff, all nodding in agreement. Walter Taylor jotted down the order to Mahone. Lee signed it and passed it to the courier who, seconds later, was off at a gallop back up the Jerusalem Plank Road.

"Gentlemen, remain calm. Remain calm and we shall handle this situation, no matter what arises."

CHAPTER TWELVE

JULY 30, 1864

THE BATTLE OF THE CRATER

5:30 A.M.

✳✳✳✳✳✳✳✳✳✳✳✳✳✳✳✳✳✳✳✳✳✳✳✳✳

THE THREE WHITE DIVISIONS WERE AT LAST GOING IN, BUT THE orders still stood that the Fourth was to stand in reserve, to be committed only by direct order and otherwise to remain in place.

Random fire was now plucking the air about them, rifle balls from eight hundred yards away arching in, joined by occasional mortar rounds that were aimed more deliberately, so that Colonel Thomas was at last able to convince his frustrated men to lie back down . . . and wait.

"Is that who I think it is?" Colonel Russell asked, tugging on Thomas's sleeve and nodding to his right as a lone horseman trotted toward them, unidentifiable in the plain four-button jacket of a private, but recognizable nevertheless by every man in the army.

"Maybe, at last," Thomas sighed with obvious relief, stepping forward to meet the rider, coming to attention and saluting, Colonel Russell by his side.

"Why have you not yet gone forward?" the rider asked.

"Sir, our orders were to remain here until told to go in."

The general looking down at them was silent for a moment, shifting his unlit cigar, looking past them to the crater, where thousands of soldiers swarmed about. Yet few had advanced more than fifty to a hundred yards toward the road.

Thomas pointed back to the battle.

"Sir, my men were trained for this fight. You have the authority. Release us. Send us in now!"

The rider continued to look at the growing chaos around the crater even as Thomas made his appeal.

He was silent, as if taking in what Thomas was saying, then shook his head.

"I will not interfere with orders given. It only will add to the confusion."

Stunned, Thomas knew better than to argue with the general in command of the armies, Ulysses S. Grant.

"Wait until your immediate superior orders you in; otherwise, it just might make things even more confused and chaotic than they already are."

He turned his horse and rode away at a trot. Thomas was silent, shaking his head, Russell cursing softly under his breath.

Even as Grant rode off, a courier came galloping past him and Thomas's spirits rose.

"I think this is it."

The courier reined in, looking about.

"General Ferrero? I have orders for him."

Thomas and Sigfried, commander of the other brigade of the Fourth, looked at each other.

"Just give it to me," Thomas said coldly, not mentioning that Ferrero was nowhere to be found, and in fact had not been seen since the officer's meeting the day before.

He opened the note. Men of his brigade were beginning to stand back up, in spite of orders, knowing with certainty that this was it, their order to go in and straighten out the chaos.

Thomas scanned the message, handed it to Siegfried, and looked back at the courier.

"This is it? This is all that you were told?"

"Yes, sir."

"Convey that I will comply," Thomas said bitterly, then turned to an adjutant, motioned for a note pad, and scribbled out a line.

Sir. We are waiting to go in. The situation can still be retrieved. We beg you to send us forward at once. General Ferrero is not with his command, so I am assuming control of the division in the field.

He showed it to Siegfried, who nodded and handed it up to courier.

"Ride like hell," he snapped, and the courier was off, galloping back to Burnside's headquarters, little more than a quarter mile away.

Thomas looked back to the commanders of his regiments.

"No orders to advance. Instead we are ordered to take shelter in the covered way and there await developments."

As the order was passed, more men were standing, moving the hundred or so yards to the covered tunnel that led to the front, the murmuring of anger and frustration continuing to build.

The covered way was nearly ten feet in width, six to eight feet deep, and covered over with planks, with earth heaped on top to protect the line of communication. Even as Thomas ordered the men down into its confines he raged at this new stupidity. The men would feel cut off, trapped inside. If ordered to go forward they would either have to run the length of the tunnel, or pour back out into the open field to reform. With this single order the entire formation for the planned assault, which still could work even now, had completely unraveled. To make matters worse, the first casualties were coming back from the front line, along with scores of demoralized men, pushing their way through, cradling bloody limbs, cursing, crying that the battle was already lost.

From an opening to one side of the tunnel, Thomas and the other commanders climbed out, Garland taking it upon himself to follow. As long as he was not ordered to go back with the enlisted men he could at least see what was transpiring.

All stood silent, sick with anger and grief. The roar of battle was building by the minute. It was now obvious that the Confederates were regaining their nerve, starting to try to push in from either flank. Another distant skirmish line was now barely visible through the smoke and haze forming along the Jerusalem Plank Road.

And the veterans, thinking they knew where safety could be found, were filling the crater, thousands of them, seeking its temporary shelter and hunkering down.

One of the regimental commanders, cursing violently, finally just lowered his head and wept.

Garland, standing silent, awestruck, and numbed, continued to pray.

HEADQUARTERS, NINTH CORPS
7:00 A.M.

✳✳✳✳✳✳✳✳✳✳✳✳✳✳✳✳✳✳✳✳✳✳✳✳✳✳

Sitting in his bunker, Ambrose Burnside, unable to conceal his rage, thumbed back through the telegrams sent by Meade, less than eight hundred yards away, during the last half hour.

Shortly after six, a preemptory order came from Meade to throw in every man, regardless of loss, "black and white." Freezing inwardly at that, Burnside had climbed out of the bunker to look across the valley. So much smoke was now boiling up from the gunfire that it was impossible to discern anything that was going on.

He had finally replied that it would take hard work, but that he still believed the crest would be taken. As for the black division, he was not sure what to do with them anymore, if anything at all. They had been trained to a specific task, but the opportunity of that moment had been squandered. Would sending them in now alter anything?

And then Meade's latest volley came:

What do you mean by hard work to take the crest? Do you mean to say your officers and men will not obey your orders to advance? If not, what is the obstacle? I wish to know the truth and desire an immediate answer.

As the telegrapher tore off the sheet of paper and handed the note to Burnside, sitting only a few feet away, it was obvious the telegraph operator was startled and nervous.

Burnside scanned the sheet of paper and threw it down.

"Damn him! Take down the following!

"The main body of General Potter's division is beyond the crater. I do not mean to say that my officers and men will not obey my orders to advance."

He paused, taking a deep breath, outraged by the insult to him and the men under his command, and then he continued.

"I mean to say that it is very hard to advance to the crest. I have never, in any report, said anything different from what I conceived to be the truth."

He waited for the telegrapher to catch up while taking down the note. The bunker was now packed with his staff, standing rigid and silent.

"Were it not insubordinate, I would say that the latter remark of your note was un-officerlike and ungentlemanly."

"Sir." It was one of his aides, Vincent.

"Sir, perhaps, sir, you should drop that last line," but Burnside cut him off with a vicious wave of his hand.

"Send it!"

Even the telegrapher hesitated, looking up at Burnside appealingly.

"Send it exactly as I said it, by God, or you will be relieved and I will find someone who will send it. I have had it with that man, his insults, and insinuations. If he had not altered the plan we would already be into Petersburg by now!"

The telegrapher dutifully put fingers to the key and started to tap out the message. Outside the bunker the guns from the nearest battery, firing in support of the attack, continued to thunder, trickles of dust falling from the ceiling by the constant vibration.

The sun, now two hours up, was beating down on the battlefield, the temperature already well into the eighties and rising fast. Some of the men within the bunker had already taken off their uniform jackets.

No one had noticed James Reilly, squatting in the far corner of the room, sketchpad out, acting as if he were drawing the scene. But after every few pencil strokes across his pad, along the margin he jotted down, word for word, everything that was being said.

The message sent, all stood silent, Burnside turning his back on the men.

His mind raced with confusion. *Should I just mount up and go forward,* he wondered. *I have led from the front before. That's it, go forward and rally the men. But this damn telegraph binds me, binds all of us, too far behind the lines.* Some had thought this new technology would give corps commanders greater freedom and instant communication with their field commanders. Instead, it was tying them to their bunkers and headquarters rather than following the old tradition of leading from the front.

But this was no longer like the open battlefields of New Bern and Antietam. It was a rabbit warren of trenches, revetments, covered approach tunnels. He would get lost in it, and how then to command?

He now recalled having ordered the Fourth Division to take shelter in the covered tunnel. He had all but forgotten about them in the confusion and controversy with Meade.

Order them in? Or should I just swallow my pride, ride up to Meade's headquarters, and see if this can still be straightened out? Where was Tenth Corps? If I had control of them, I would already be sending them in to try and flank the chaos at the crater. Surely they could still carry it?

The conflicting thoughts, the myriad of details racing out of control so overwhelmed him, that he just stood silent, making no decision at all. At last the telegraph key began to chatter in reply, with the telegrapher, pad on table, jotting down the letters as they came in.

United States Military Telegraph.

I demand a copy of the previous dispatch you reference, since I did not keep a copy, intending it to be confidential. Your reply requires I should have a copy.

Burnside glared at the telegrapher as if he had somehow created this message out of thin air. The implication was all too obvious. Meade was documenting every word for future reference in a court-martial for insubordination in the field.

He no longer gave a damn.

"Send it back to him again," he snapped and, putting on his over-sized high-crowned hat, stormed out of the stuffy bunker and into the blazing Virginia heat.

James remained quiet. Drawing attention to himself would only wind up with his being ejected, so he remained squatting in the corner, sketchpad out, furiously jotting down notes of the exchange that came flying back just minutes later from Meade, demanding an immediate apology.

Inwardly he raged. He had held Burnside in some regard until these last few hours. A general like Winfield Hancock would have just seized control of the moment, put himself on the front line out of the reach of Meade and the telegraph, and from there directed the battle. The story of Admiral Horatio Nelson raising his telescope to his blind eye to a signal to withdraw his fleet during battle, then proclaiming that he had seen no such signal, was known by all with an interest in history.

Burnside could have personally pushed the men of the Fourth forward in the first minutes, regardless of what Meade had ordered. If he failed, he might of course be hanged, but no one hanged a victor.

"This is worse than Antietam," someone whispered nervously, and James looked up to see that Captain Vincent was the speaker. "He's locked up inside with this. The battle is out of control. The same thing happened at Fredericksburg, he locks up."

No one dared to speak, the telegrapher standing silent, like an accusing ghost, holding out the telegram from Meade demanding an apology, obviously fearful of delivering it himself.

"I'll take it, damn it," Vincent finally snapped, snatching the flimsy sheet.

He hesitated.

"Write back the following," Vincent said. "Sir, no insult was ever intended on my part. The situation at this moment is difficult in the extreme. Please accept my apology."

He hesitated.

"Sign it, Burnside."

"I'll be the one in a court-martial if I send that without his authorization," the telegrapher replied, voice elevated to a nervous squeak.

"I'll take the responsibility, now send it!"

Vincent raced out of the bunker, the room breaking into nervous chatter, and James was suddenly filled with a vast loathing toward all of it. Eight hundred yards away, the supreme chance of victory and an ending to this war was being thrown away, and men were dying by the scores every minute, while this staff gaggle stood and argued among themselves.

He stood up and went out of the bunker.

As he did so, Vincent came back, features drawn, nearly bumping into James.

"What are you doing here?" Vincent snapped.

"For heaven's sake, I am on your side," James replied sharply.

"Leave this bunker, now!"

"That is what I am doing."

But he still blocked the entryway.

"Where is Burnside?" he asked.

"Just leave him alone!" Vincent cried.

James nodded.

"Listen, I'm on your side in this. Just one thing. You still have the Fourth Division. They know the plan. I heard the order come in an hour ago to send them in and for whatever reason it was not passed forward. Send them in."

Vincent seemed ready with a retort.

James put his hand up in a placating gesture.

"I stayed with those men for weeks. I know them. They're ready. They are tough, gallant men eager for battle. If anyone can retrieve this now, it is they. Send them in!"

Vincent hesitated, gaze fixed on James. He turned without comment and ran back up the steps of the bunker.

James followed slowly, seeing Vincent standing with Burnside, pointing to where the battle continued to rage, all now obscured by rolling clouds of smoke from musketry and artillery fire.

Vincent appeared to press his case, and finally Burnside just nodded. Vincent saluted, and seconds later was scrambling up over the wall of the parapet. James set off, running after him, not even bothering to look toward the pathetic, forlorn figure of Burnside, who just stood there, silent, as if gazing off to some distant place beyond the battlefield.

He ran after Vincent, passing wounded who were streaming to the rear, noticing as well that for every man bearing a wound, two, three, four were just heading to the rear, some having discarded their weapons.

Vincent slipped down into a side entry into the covered way, James right behind him.

"Ferrero. I'm looking for General Ferrero!" Vincent shouted over and over.

"Here!"

In the semi-darkness of the covered tunnel, James saw an officer, Colonel Thomas, pushing his way back through the press of men crowded together, mingled with wounded begging to be allowed to pass to the rear.

"Ferrero?"

"I don't know where that son of a bitch is," Thomas cried. "I've taken command of the division in his absence."

Vincent took that in, hesitating for a moment. James wanted to scream with rage, push his way forward, fearful Vincent would fail to act now based on some obscure military protocol. Rumors had already hit corps headquarters that both Ferrero and Ledlie could be found in a nearby bunker—a forward medical aid station—drunk, having taken some whiskey from a surgeon.

"Send them in," Vincent shouted. "General Burnside orders you to send the division in, retrieve the situation, and take the Jerusalem Plank Road."

"Thank God!" Thomas cried.

It would, however, have been one thing for Thomas to then have simply stepped in front of the two brigades out in an open field, nearly four thousand men, and cry for them to stand up, fall in, and prepare to charge. Instead, they were jammed six to eight deep inside a covered trench, the column several hundred yards in length.

Thomas, shouting for the men to fix bayonets, pushed and elbowed his way through the press, trying to gain the front of the column, James falling in behind him.

"Fix bayonets! Fix bayonets!"

Garland White, standing near the head of the column packed into the covered trench, looked back through the gloom. It was nearly impossible to discern anything between the thunder of battle outside, the press of men inside, the lamentations of the wounded, and the cries of the panic-stricken.

He saw Thomas struggling through the press of men.

"We're going in!" Thomas roared. "Follow me!"

He set off at a run, a cry sweeping through the confines of the covered way, men shoving, banging into each other, Garland looking over his shoulder. He suddenly became frightened that a man behind him, carrying a bayoneted rifle at the charge, could very well stab him from behind if he should slow.

The swarm surged down the tunnel, Thomas, Russell, and several other officers shouting for the wounded crowded in their way to clear back.

Garland suddenly wanted to laugh at the panic-stricken look of the white soldiers, wondering what they must be thinking as this swarm of armed black men came thundering forward, screaming and yelling.

Ahead he could see the light marking the end of the covered way and then the battlefield beyond.

"Here they come at last, thank God!"

Colonel Pleasants, crouched down low on the lip of the trench, looked to where his men were pointing, then scrambled back from the entry to the covered way.

Several officers emerged, and then a dark volcanolike explosion of men emerged behind them . . . and for a moment stalled.

The covered way terminated in the trench of the forward line, not on open ground. Inwardly he groaned at the sight of it. The month of digging, of planning, of going over the details with Burnside, should have meant that within seconds after the explosion, two solid phalanxes of colored troops would come storming forward at the double. Those two columns, as unstoppable as battering rams, would sweep up the slope and even before the debris settled would be up and over the Rebel entrenchments to either side of the two-hundred-yard-long gash torn into the enemy line.

But the explosion had been but half of what he had planned for. No charge had gone forth. They were now three hours into the battle, with the Rebels closing in from every direction. Now, at last, the men trained to lead the way were coming up, but coming up as a confused mass, pouring out of a covered trench with no semblance of formation or control. The men should have been racing across an open field in solid phalanxes, led by officers and NCOs who knew what was to be done, every man behind them knowing his position and duty as well. Instead, they were pouring out into yet another trench, disoriented, not even sure which way they were to go.

"Up here!" Pleasants screamed, catching the eye of an officer in the lead.

"48th! Help these men up!"

Men of Pleasants's command, who had stood impotent, watching the attack collapse, now pointed the way, trying in any way possible

to help push the attack forward. Many of them climbed out of the protection of their trench, turning back, reaching down to extend helping hands to their black comrades, pulling them up out of the trench.

Pleasants pulled Thomas up, then Russell. The two officers of the Fourth Division paused for a second, looking at the chaos 130 yards ahead of them.

"Oh, God," Russell gasped, instinctively ducking low as a minié ball zipped between him and Thomas.

Russell turned to pull up Lieutenant Grant and then Garland White. The two were standing upright, with Garland most likely not even aware that he was drawing fire.

"We will form up here, then go in!" Thomas shouted. "If we feed them in piecemeal, they'll get lost and slaughtered up there. Hold your men here, Russell!"

Russell seemed to hesitate, but then nodded agreement. Thomas jumped back down into the trench and pushed his way back toward the covered way, out of which men were spilling in a continuous rush.

"Sergeant Major White! Get the column formed up and keep the men down!"

Russell stepped away, looking back at the swarm of men.

"Colors of the 28th to me!"

The two flag-bearers, flags cased, poles held at slope arms, pushed out of the covered way, climbed up out of the trench, and tore off the canvas covers, tossing them aside, twirling the flag staffs to reveal the National Flag and the gold flag of their USCT regiment.

"28th to me!" Russell kept screaming, over and over.

As quickly as men climbed up out of the trench, Garland shoved them forward, showing no deference even to the white officers, shouting to them to gather their companies in by column and then keep down.

As they worked to get organized, the first casualties of the 28th were already falling. As Garland was pulling a man up out of the trench, the top of his head disintegrated into a pulpy mist of blood and brains, life going out of his eyes in an instant, his grasp on Garland's hand relaxing.

White had seen death before. The skirmish they had been in, which at that time he had thought to be a full-pitched battle, had claimed only two killed and ten wounded of the regiment. But this was beyond anything his training had prepared him for. He had seen death many a time as a preacher, called to sit by the bed of a friend about to breathe his last. But this? The soldier was an older man, flecks of gray in his beard. He had been a corporal of Company C and his life had just been snuffed out; he had accomplished nothing in this fight other than to be added to the roster of the dead after it was over.

Garland let go of his grip, the dead man falling back into the trench.

He saw another hand reaching up and was almost fearful to grasp it. Was he becoming the angel of death? The hand was white; he looked past it into the man's eyes . . . it was the artist, looking up at him, features contorted in a tight grimace as if trying to smile.

"Help me up, Sergeant Major," he gasped.

Garland all but pulled him up out of the trench, James gaining his footing and with the instincts of a veteran squatting low as he looked about.

Men crowded the trench now, spreading out, looking for a foothold, a hand above to help them up. Garland caught a glimpse of Sergeant Malady, standing upright, walking up and down the length of the trench line, at times lapsing into Gaelic, swearing the most obscene oaths, now directed at the Rebels. He then turned to shouting encouragement to the troops swarming up out of the trench: "Come on, my brave laddies, you damn black sons of bitches, now is your chance to get even! Come on, damn you, get ready!"

Russell, standing tall, flag-bearers by his side, looked up and down the line. Men of the 29th and 31st were coming out of the covered way, piling in behind his own command. Confusion was starting to take hold as the various commands mingled together.

"I'm taking them up!" Russell shouted to Thomas.

He turned back again to face his men.

"Up 28th, up! Now is your time! Charge!"

The men had waited for nearly four hours for this moment, indeed all their lives. They came to their feet, a cheer rising up from their throats.

James stood up with them. He thought he was a veteran newsman, impervious to emotions other than cynicism and grief and self-preservation, but for this moment, this brief instant, he believed. And his soul was one with them.

"At the double quick, forward!" Russell screamed, holding his sword aloft.

The colonel started up the slope, the 250 men of the 28th swarming in behind him.

"Guide on the colors!" Garland cried, repeating the litany over and over. "Guide on the colors, boys!"

Sergeant Major Garland White, once a reverend, felt a thrill of exultation unlike anything he had experienced in his entire life. Directly ahead of him was the glorious flag of his regiment; even as he gazed at it, the colors were being torn by bullets and shrapnel. But his eyes lingered and his heart swelled with passion on the flag next to it. The national colors. His flag. This was now clearly his flag. Never again, never could any man ever say that this was not his flag as well.

A storm surge of men swept up the slope, bayonets flashing in the sunlight, men cheering, screaming, some in tears of emotion, their voices commingling, overcoming for this brief instant the roar of battle.

The Rebel line was eighty yards away, fifty, then thirty. Garland could see men rising up, rifles poised, lowering the barrels, flashes of light, a man next to him screaming, collapsing, clutching his stomach, and dropping. A drummer boy next to him was shouting hysterically, beating on his drum. Russell had ordered the drummer boy to stay to the rear but the lad was with them anyhow, beating out the tattoo of the charge.

Ahead were the dreaded abatis, rows of sharpened stakes. They charged into them, men slowing, pushing their way around and

THE BATTLE OF THE CRATER

through. Ordered to leave the axes and footbridges behind, they were using the butts of their muskets to knock the barriers aside to clear a path for themselves and those who followed.

Men dropped to either side of Garland, one of them tumbling forward after being shot, impaling himself on a sharpened stake, screaming. The sight of it only enraged Garland, pushing him forward into the dry moat, for a brief moment beneath the rifle fire of the Rebels occupying the opposite trench. They were but a few feet away, on the other side of the earthen embankment.

Men piled into the moat around him. They could not stay here!

"Charge, men, charge!" Garland screamed and with rifle raised high he scrambled up the last few feet of embankment. Scores followed him, Russell in the middle of them, flag-bearers still flanking him.

As they came up to the crest of the parapet, a volley slammed into the 28th, a dozen or more men dropping, some dead before they hit the ground; others crying out, screaming. Some were silent, trying to suppress the agony of a minié ball having cut through an arm, a leg, or lodged fatally in their chest or stomach.

"Don't stop!" Garland screamed.

Climbing over the parapet he jumped down into the Rebel trench, the trench which throughout a month of training they had been told would be empty, the panic-stricken occupants having fled in the minutes after the mine exploded.

Scores of Rebels now occupied the position. What ensued in the next few moments truly fulfilled Garland's worst visions of hell.

There was no quarter. The pent-up rage, the insanity of a world that had driven them to this moment, was unleashed, both sides screaming "No quarter, no prisoners!" as they shot, cut, and slashed at each other.

More and more men of the 28th, now joined by men of the 29th and 31st coming up in support, piled into the Rebel trench, until at last the Rebels broke, falling back, dodging down narrow trenches and their own covered ways that led to the rear.

Murderous acts were perpetrated by both sides, as men fought, gouged, kicked, and bayoneted each other. Garland for a moment stood still, horrified, an inner voice screaming at him to somehow stop the insanity that was being unleashed.

And then the Rebels were simply gone. They had abandoned the trench to the men of the 28th, and the men swarming up from their brother regiments, and to the dead and dying of both sides piled in twisted tragedy, from the ghastly struggle to take the trench, flanking the smoke-shrouded crater.

Some semblance of survival instinct had at last held James Reilly back—for after all, what could he do if an enraged Reb came at him with bayonet lowered? Hold up his pencil and offer to draw him? During those few desperate moments, Reilly reached the Rebel trench— ducking low, crawling up over the embankment, and sliding down into the trench's relative safety.

What greeted him was a nightmare of bodies clad in blue, butternut, and gray—black men and white—piled together; some crying out piteously for help, for mercy.

Those still standing seemed like the living dead; dark features drawn, sweat soaked, gasping for air in the ever-increasing heat. One of them was sobbing, cradling a comrade who was writhing in agony; another was bent double, vomiting, and then just collapsed.

"We can't stay here!"

He looked up. It was Russell, half standing out in the open on the far side of the Rebel trench.

"Come on, boys. We must take the road and the hill with the church beyond it! Keep moving, keep moving!"

Russell grabbed the shoulder of the flag-bearer carrying the standard of the regiment, pulling him up to his side.

"28th, on the colors! Charge to the road! Charge!"

James, stunned, felt as if he would collapse, his legs unable to respond to the command of his mind and heart to stay with these men.

The regimental flag-bearer came up out of the trench, holding the golden standard aloft.

"Come on!" he screamed, holding the colors high over his head, waving them back and forth.

A wild shout of primal rage, of fear, of exaltation roared up from the men. James caught a glimpse of Garland standing atop the trench, rifle in hand, holding it aloft, gesturing with it for the men to keep moving, to just keep moving.

The renewed charge began to surge forward. A second later, dozens of men were down: doubling over, collapsing face down, screaming, clutching a torn arm, leg, face, stomach. The charge was being mowed down by Rebel fire. A white officer, Lieutenant Grant, grabbed Russell as if to restrain him. Just then, the officer was nearly cut in half, a blast of canister from their flank tearing his body. The lieutenant shielded Russell as he died.

The attackers fell back into the captured trench.

James pulled back from the lip of the trench, shamed by the fact that he was terrified. In the lost hours, the Rebels had managed to throw up a cordon around the torn, devastated hole of the crater, were boxing it in, and would die if need be to contain this ugly wound, this break in their lines.

Russell fell back into the trench, the flag-bearers still by his side.

More men were coming up the slope from the Union line and the covered way. But tragically, there would not be a gallant rush of all four thousand men of the Fourth. Because of the order to wait in the covered way, they were pouring forth in ragged clusters. Instead of a tidal storm sweeping all before them in the immediate aftermath of the mine being blown, they were coming on in small, weak groups. Their officers had tried to gather a cluster of their gallant command about them, but then, unable to wait any longer, led what men they had into the inferno.

Russell, eyes wide, near hysteria, looked at those filling the trench behind him.

"My God, men!" he cried. "We can still do it! We can still do it!"

The words came out as a strangled cry of hope, but also of frustration and rage.

"Get ready! Load and get ready!"

James could see that nearly all were ready for this final try. But he could also see the desperation in their eyes, the trembling of their hands as they fumbled to load their rifles. The drummer boy, caught up in the fury, continued to beat his drum, the sound of it echoing in the confines of the trench.

To their right James could hear increasing fire, and with it the dreaded Rebel yell. Whatever Rebel regiments had fled the line in the first minutes of battle, or had tried to hold and been pushed out by the first rush of the 28th and their comrades, were now rallying as well, preparing to charge in from the flank and close the breach.

"Ready with the bayonet!" Russell screamed.

A shout went up from the men clustered around him.

"Charge!"

Again Russell scrambled up the embankment of the trench, flag-bearers flanking him. The sergeant carrying the regimental colors reached the crest, holding his precious banner aloft, waving it high overhead. James looked up at him, awestruck. And then the man seemed to spin around like a child's top, staggering to keep his footing.

His right arm had been blown off just below the shoulder, the impact throwing him back into the trench. As the man fell, to James's horrified disbelief he landed on a broken rifle barrel, bayonet still fixed, impaling him through the chest.

Russell looked back at him, eyes wide.

"Take him to the rear. My God, someone take him back to the rear!"

And then Russell turned to face forward.

"Charge boys, charge!"

All around James, hundreds of men, for a moment transfixed by the sight of their flag-bearer going down, now let loose with a wild roar of rage and swarmed up out of the trench.

James stood, unable to move, though with all his heart and soul he willed himself forward. The agonized cries of the flag-bearer, still impaled on the upright bayonet, tore into his soul. He went up to the impaled soldier, grabbing him around the waist.

"Grab hold of my shoulder with your good arm!" James cried.

As he stood up, he could almost feel the grating of the bayonet as it slid back out from between the man's ribs. He held the flag-bearer tight, feeling his warm blood pulsing from what was left of his arm.

He saw a canteen on the floor of the trench, beside it a soldier of the 28th, who just started at the two of them as he clutched his side, blood leaking out between his fingers.

"The canteen!" James cried. "Cut the strap!"

The wounded—in fact, dying—man roused himself, picked up the canteen, using the upended bayonet as a blade, and sawed the straps off. James wrapped it around the stump of the flag-bearer's arm, tying it off the way he had seen it done on so many other stricken fields. Picking up a broken ramrod, he stuck it through the twisted strap, using it to twist the strap tighter and tighter until the pulsing flood of blood was stilled.

"Back to the rear," James gasped, and somehow he managed to help push the two back over the side of the trench toward the Union lines.

"For God's sake, don't stay here. Don't stop! Get to the rear."

The two set off, leaning against each other for support.

They disappeared into the smoke, out of which yet more men of the Fourth were advancing.

Reilly looked back to the west, where the men of the 28th had gone. In the smoke and confusion they had disappeared from view, and for that moment he seemed all alone on the battlefield, in a trench filled with horrors.

Sergeant Major Garland White had heard men describe battle as like being in a nightmare, the type of dream where all seems to move painfully, frightfully slowly, as if struggling to move while waist deep in mud and filth.

The field ahead was not as it had been described to them during their training. There were many bunkers, some shallow trenches, the shattered earth confusing. Every step he took, weaving his way around bunkers and leaping over trenches, seemed to take an eternity.

Garland, at the front of the charge, kept looking back; men were still following, many from the 28th, mixed with troops of other regiments, even a scattering of white soldiers, who, seeing the USCT go forward, had at last ventured out of the shelter of the crater to join in the assault. He caught a glimpse of an officer, standing awkwardly, leaning heavily on a cane, sword in the other hand, pointing forward, and men rising around him to join in the attack.

"We can still do it!" Garland cried, urging all of them on. They were nearly halfway between the crater and the Jerusalem Plank Road.

And then he saw it.

A dark-clad column of men was coming down the Jerusalem Plank Road at the run. Then, like a well-oiled machine, even while running the Rebels swung outward to either side from column to line of battle.

As, charging, they swept toward him like apparitions, men not fifty yards ahead seemed to rise up out of a raw slash of earth cut across the field. They had lain in a shallow trench, not more than knee deep; perhaps it had been cut even as the three divisions that were supposed to charge had remained stalled in the crater.

"Damn! Damn all this!" Garland cried, the first time such a word had escaped his lips in years. He looked back. The men of his regiment and brigade were indeed advancing, joined by a fair number of white troops coming out of the crater, urged on by the crippled General Bartlett. But they were scattered, broken up, across a couple of hundred yards of field.

Russell had taken it in as well, and he turned and reached for the flag-bearer still holding the national colors; the regimental flag had disappeared.

"Form volley line! Form line on me!"

But the men were too spread out, too disjointed. Some of the 28th was most likely still all the way back in the covered way. Men of other regiments who were mixed in were separated from their officers and NCOs in the confusion.

Russell's voice carried authority and, with back turned to the charging Rebels, Garland looked at him and could only feel awe for such leadership and courage.

He started to turn, to grab men, to create some semblance of a cohesive front to meet this countercharge, when the advancing Rebels suddenly seemed to disappear behind a cloud of dirty, yellow-gray smoke. A split-second later their volley of .58-caliber minié balls slashed across the field at nine hundred feet per second. The minié balls slammed into the men of the USCT and their comrades from the other divisions who had joined them.

Dozens collapsed. The flag-bearer, struck several times, sank to the ground, and Sergeant Felton leaped forward to grab the colors and raise them back up. Garland saw that the drummer boy had kept pace with them, but that one or more rifle balls had pierced his drum, shattering it. The once taut head of the drum was now limp, yet he still continued to beat on it.

"Give it back!" Russell cried. "Independent fire at will. Give it back!"

Those still standing raised rifles, leveled them, and fired, triggering a momentary resurgence of morale. For many of them it was the first time they had actually fired their rifles in action.

They were not much stronger than a skirmish line but more men were coming up every second, falling in on either flank, broadening the line out. Garland took position behind the line, pacing it as he had been trained, giving advice, repeating the litany:

"Load 'em right, boys, and then aim low. That's it. Aim low, aim low!"

He heard another voice repeating the words and looked down the line to see the barrel-chested Sergeant Malady also pacing the line, grabbing men who were coming up and pushing them into position. Their gazes locked for a second and Malady actually gave him a nod. For Garland it was perhaps the most meaningful salute he had ever received.

Then another volley tore into them, men staggering backward, some collapsing to their knees and pitching forward. The blow was shattering.

"Keep at it, boys!" Russell screamed.

And then they heard it. They had been told often enough of it, their officers trying to describe it, but now they heard it for real— the Rebel yell. It was true; it sounded like wolves baying at the scent of blood and now charging them at the run.

Back on the road Garland saw a battery of Rebel field guns was swinging into position. These were the dreaded Napoleons, which could deal such deadly work at short range. Two of the pieces had already unlimbered and were firing, recoiling as they hurled blasts of canister into the far-left flank of the Union line.

"Charge them!"

It was Russell, stepping forward, pointing toward the wall of smoke, and Garland knew it was the only command left to give. This attack had to be met head on.

"Come on!" Garland pushed the man ahead of him and grabbed another who seemed about to turn and run.

"Stay with me!" Garland cried.

The thin line hesitated for a second and then, as if shocked by an electric current, appeared to leap forward in one last act of desperation.

The range closed within seconds. If they had been the solid block formation as they had once trained, they would have battered through the thin Rebel line with barely a pause. Sheer weight and momentum alone would have carried them through. But now?

A half thousand men, scattered in knots and clusters, a few following a trusted sergeant, others around a flag or trusted officer, surged forward in the confusion. Some were tripping into the dugouts, moats, and bunkers that mazed the field behind the main line. They had almost reached the freshly cut trench, when out of it, troops holding up the flags of Virginia arose, joined now by the reinforcements pouring off the road. The Rebels came straight in at them, bayonets leveled.

Both sides were screaming foul oaths of hatred and rage. Centuries of slavery and the cruelty and fear it engendered, combined with three years of bitter war with no end in sight, unleashed a pent-up fury on this day as both sides screamed: "No quarter, no prisoners!"

The thin ragged line of blue collided with the thicker, better organized, and more cohesive tide of butternut and gray.

A Confederate officer, pistol raised, pointed it straight at Garland's face from ten feet away and squeezed the trigger. The hammer fell on an empty chamber and, with musket butt raised, Garland knocked the man over backward with a blow to his face. It landed with such violence he could hear bones crunching.

Garland had struggled long with the question of whether he could ever strike another man to kill him. The question had just been answered. He found himself filled with a wild rage, but also a pain so frightening that he only wanted to scream for all of them to stop.

Even as he struggled with that thought, he dodged to one side as a Rebel lunged at him with a bayonet. One of his men grabbed the weapon by the barrel, pulling the man forward, while another clubbed him down.

More and more Union soldiers swarmed into the melee, but for every Union soldier it seemed that two, three, or more Confederates pushed into the fight. Garland could feel the men around him giving ground, backing up.

He saw Malady, just a dozen feet away, swinging his musket like a club, while several Rebels closed in around him. He tried to push toward the man to help him, screaming his name, ducking a clubbed musket aimed at him as well. Then a Rebel leaned in toward Malady and shot him in the chest at point-blank range. Malady staggered backward, falling into a shallow trench.

The dam now broke, his men falling back, Rebs pushing in, screaming obscenities, a primal rage unleashed that to Garland did not seem to be war at all, but instead a devilish exercise in mass murder.

He jumped down into the ditch where Malady lay gasping, trying to pull him up.

"Get out of here!" Malady cried. "Leave me for Christ's sake and get out of here!"

"No!"

"Look out!"

With his remaining strength Malady pushed Garland to one side. A Rebel was aiming down at him. If he had squeezed a second earlier, the bullet would have struck Garland in the back. Instead it hit Malady. Garland lashed out with his rifle butt but the Rebel had jumped aside and was gone.

Malady's eyes unfocused and he looked up at Garland.

"Damn proud of you," he whispered. "You're as good as any man of Ireland this day."

Fighting back tears, Garland squeezed his hand, released it, and climbed out of the trench.

There was no semblance of order left. Some men of the USCT were still trying to come up but the veteran line of Confederates continued to push forward, pausing to reload, fire, then push forward again. He was nearly behind them. He caught sight of the drummer boy, who was helping a wounded soldier limp to the rear, and ran to him. Garland nearly scooped him off the ground, pushing the wounded soldier ahead of him. He started to run, bursting back into the confusion of his comrades, who were falling back but still trying to fight gamely.

Together they tumbled into the rabbit warren of trenches and dugouts just to the west of the crater. There was a moment of near-blind panic when he turned a corner and saw a swarm of Rebels, closing in on their flank, pushing forward.

Turning, he shoved the drummer boy in the opposite direction. The ground ahead was a jumbled mass of earth, in some places piled high, like boulders tossed by a giant. Scattered before it was wreckage, debris, dead men, and parts of dead men. There were many wounded, some trying to crawl toward the Confederate side, others up the sloping lip of torn earth.

He looked back.

The few men still standing against the Rebel charge were going down, shot from front and flank. Up toward the road the full battery of Napoleon field pieces now in play, firing case shot set to burst as the twelve-pound rounds skimmed over the ground.

The field was carpeted with Union and Confederate dead and dying. The only ones now standing and moving forward were Confederates.

"Garland! Get in here, you damn fool!" someone screamed.

He looked up the slope. There was the artist, beckoning to him.

Garland shoved the drummer boy and the wounded soldier he had been clinging to toward James. He scrambled up the hot red clay, following while minié balls smacked the earth to either side of him.

As he reached the crest, James extended a hand to pull up the drummer boy and then Garland.

Sergeant Major Garland White cleared the lip of the crater, and slid down into its relative protection. Gasping for air, he looked down into its depths and then swept his glance over the steep-banked slope. It was nearly a hundred yards wide, fifty across, and thirty or more feet deep.

Within its confines were packed nearly ten thousand men, crowded so tightly they could barely move. Those still with fight in them were manning the lip of the scorched hole, firing at the advancing Rebs, at last breaking their charge. They were tossing empty muskets down to the men behind them, who would pass up loaded replacements. When a shooter was finally hit—usually in the head, throat, or shoulders—and slid back down into the pit, he was replaced by another.

Garland took in a deep breath, gasping for air. It was scorching hot, as if the ground itself was still burning from the explosion; overhead a red-hued sun beat down upon them with a pitiless intensity. Garland reached for his canteen. It was gone, where he did not know, and he was grateful when James offered him a full one.

"We're trapped in a sunlit picture of hell," James whispered.

CHAPTER THIRTEEN

✳✳✳✳✳✳✳✳✳✳✳✳✳✳✳✳✳✳✳✳✳✳✳✳✳

"Sir, this is from Meade again."

Ambrose Burnside barely stirred, took the offered telegraph, and scanned it.

In the last half hour Meade had peppered him with repeated queries and then at 9:30 had announced that it was increasingly evident that the attack had failed.

Burnside replied that if only the reserve corps were released and thrown in against either flank, the situation could still be reversed.

And then, fifteen minutes later, came the death blow: an order to withdraw all men currently engaged.

He looked again at the telegram just handed to him and could only shake his head. Now it was another contradictory order, from Meade's chief of staff, to pass a command to the troops still in the crater to hold and dig in.

"Now what?" Captain Vincent asked, taking the telegram from Burnside's trembling hands.

He looked up at Vincent, eyes red-rimmed. It was obvious the man was in shock, bitten by what his staff privately called "Burnside's black dog."

"Tell Humphries I no longer have any discretion in this matter as per General Meade's previous orders to withdraw."

"Sir?"

"You heard me," Burnside whispered. "First, he tells me to attack whether the mine is detonated or not, this after changing the order of battle. Then he makes it clear that, somehow, I have insulted him, and it is evident he will have to bring me up on charges. He refuses to send in the other two corps and push them to either flank, when we have at least made a lodgment in their center. Then he orders me to withdraw. Now his chief of staff tells me to pass the order for the men to hold on and dig in?

"Tell me, Vincent. Which one of us is insane?"

Vincent stood wooden, unable to reply.

"Do you honestly think you can get a message up to those men now in the crater?"

Burnside knew Vincent to be a brave man.

Vincent hesitated.

"If you order me to do so."

"Would you order others to try and get up to them, other than in a mass charge?"

Vincent stood silent and then finally shook his head.

"No one can get ten paces up that slope now, sir."

Burnside sighed, burying his face in his hands.

"Send back to Humphries what I just stated. I no longer have such discretion, after being ordered but fifteen minutes ago to withdraw. Unless these instructions are countersigned by General Meade himself, his prior order stands."

He sat in silence, staring off. Through the open door, down from the surface, the sounds of the continued bombardment from the Union lines began to slacken. This was not out of any desire on the part of the gunners, who could see the desperateness of the situation, but from the simple reality that after more than five hours of heavy fire they had depleted their huge reserves. They had been told that they would fire in support for one hour at most—not five.

THE CRATER

11 A.M.

****

"And I tell you, if they catch us in here with them damn darkies, we're all dead men!"

Garland and those around him looked back nervously at the troops from Ledlie's division, who were packed in a vast seething mob at the bottom of the crater, more than thirty feet below them.

The crater was a bedlam, a madhouse. The sun was beating down mercilessly, the sky overhead the color of copper.

Around ten thousand men were packed into the crater, a hundred yards in length, fifty or more yards wide, and thirty feet deep.

It was hard to hear anything because of the din of musketry blazing along the entire rim. Those men still with fight in them, mostly from the Fourth Division, were interspersed with white troops. Artillery shells from the Union side were winging in, close overhead, in a vain attempt at support. Rebel fire was increasing by the minute. After the repulse of the last charge, the Rebs had settled into a semicircle, in some places not more than a few dozen feet away, hidden in adjoining trenches. At least half a dozen of their mortars had found the range—several of them light "Cohorns" that could be manhandled along a trench by several men, and which lobbed twelve- or twenty-four-pound shells. The range was so close that all they needed to do was drop in several ounces of propellant, and the ball would arc upward just fifty feet or so, then tumble down into the crater to detonate with devastating effect.

The heat was debilitating, even to those veterans inured to months of hard campaigning in the Virginia summer. Their water was all but gone and many of the men had already torn off their wool jackets and cast them aside.

The dead littered the sides of the crater and carpeted the ground around it. The wounded slid down to the bottom, trying to find some semblance of shelter. They crawled into the crevices cut into the raw earth by the explosions, some still venting wisps of smoke after five hours. The men were enveloped by the rotten-egg stench left by four tons of detonated black powder, as well as that from the musketry of the defenders and those encircling them. In many of those crevices, more than one wounded man died, or was trampled and buried by the panicked pushing and shoving of comrades.

Groups of men would cluster along the eastern lip of the crater, closest to the Union lines. Together they would spring to their feet make a break for their own lines, but few made it unscathed.

Garland glared at the knot of men below, gazing up at him with such hatred.

Colonel Russell, hearing their comments, turned toward them.

"Get up here, you damn cowards, and fight!" he cried, but none of them moved.

"I'll kill the first man who attacks any of my men!"

As they fought to keep back the Rebels along the rim, many soldiers of the Fourth gazed back anxiously; over the years, more than one had heard such talk and knew that at times it had ended with a rope and a tree.

11:45 A.M.

✳✳✳✳✳✳✳✳✳✳✳✳✳✳✳✳✳✳✳✳✳✳✳✳✳✳✳✳

"I said to start digging!" Henry Pleasants screamed, but his words came out as barely a strangled whisper.

His men, soaked with perspiration, some of them down from the heat, dragged back to the covered way, just looked at him, numbed.

He pointed up to the cauldron, the damn crater—the crater he had created.

Another burst of men burst from the crest, some running full out—rifles, cartridge boxes, and jackets cast aside. A few were moving more slowly, dragging along wounded comrades . . . nearly all were white troops.

In that inferno of noise he could hear whoops from the Rebel line. Shouts rang out that more were breaking, and then men suddenly began to collapse—many caught in full stride, shot from behind or from the side, falling, rolling over; some staggered back up. In some cases the Rebs took pity after winging a man and would let him limp the last few yards to tumble into Pleasants's section of trench.

But if it was a colored soldier, he would be absolutely riddled. Of the several hundred men of the Fourth who had tried to make a break to the rear, fewer than one in three were making it unscathed.

"We've got to dig to them!" Pleasants cried. "Those are your comrades up there!"

"Dig a hundred yards upslope?" one of his men replied wearily, obviously spent.

"Damn it, yes," Pleasants gasped. "It doesn't have to be deep, just a few feet across, a foot or two deep, enough to give them some cover. We can cut our way up there in three, four hours."

He knew he was lying. His regiment was one of the very few out of the entire corps which had been exempt from the charge. After their labors on the tunnel, their job had been to hold the forward line just in case something went wrong with the attack.

Men of the regiment that had been out of the trench in the first minutes watched the effect of what they had labored so hard for. They urged their comrades forward, helped pull them up and out of the forward trench, pushed them up to the attack, and now acted to aid the wounded. No one back at corps had arranged for a cadre of medical orderlies to be waiting in the covered way to help the wounded to the rear. In the grand plan of it all, once Petersburg fell, sections of pontoon bridges would be laid over the trenches to facilitate the moving of artillery, followed by wagons of ammunition and ambulances for evacuating the wounded.

All those ambulances were now parked a thousand yards back behind the lines.

Nearly half of Pleasants's regiment had by now been detailed off to help drag or carry wounded through the covered way and back to the aid stations behind the main line. More than a few of those men, in spite of the good discipline of his regiment, were not coming back, or were doing so as slowly as possible. All could see the deba-cle, and as veterans, none would be surprised if the Rebs decided to launch a surprise counterstrike into their trench to ensure complete encirclement of the four divisions, or what was left of them.

Several men, armed with shovels, finally stepped forward, one group led by Sergeant Kochanski. Without a word to their com-mander, they began to chop away at the forward edge of their trench. They were keeping low, for harassing fire was now begin-ning to skim the top of their position as well.

"Come on, I need more of you," Henry pleaded. "I want a half dozen crawlways up that hellhole!"

By twos and threes, his weary men, who had not slept in more than a day, began using short-handled shovels and bayonets—with which they had dug nearly six hundred feet of tunnel—to construct pathways to save their trapped comrades.

And then, to his absolute amazement, Henry saw a knot of sev-eral dozen colored soldiers leap out of the crater and set off at a full run. None were armed, most still wore their heavy blue jackets, but what amazed him was that each of the men had eight, ten, a dozen canteens slung over his shoulders or around his neck.

The fire that closed in on them was merciless. Henry wanted to stand up, to scream at the Rebels: "For God's sake, is it not obvious what these men are doing?"

Many were struck by well-aimed head shots, others wounded and knocked over. As they tried to rise they were hit again and again.

Little more than half of them made it to the lip of Pleasants's trench, his own men standing up, cheering them on, and pulling them in as they leaped or slid to safety.

Faces sweat soaked, they looked at each other, some with tight-lipped grins, all of them silent until one of them, a sergeant, looked up at Pleasants.

"Boss . . . I mean, Colonel, sir. Where can we find water?"

Unable to speak, Henry could only point to a fifty-gallon barrel that had been laboriously rolled up through the covered way for the benefit of his men in this blazing heat.

His own men stood silent, then eager hands reached out to these men who had just sprinted from hell and obviously intended to go back into it. And then words of encouragement:

"Here, you rest, I'll do it"; "Give me them canteens"; "You just sit a spell and get your breath."

And in the eyes of more than one of his men, Pleasants saw tears of admiration, a sight rare indeed with veterans.

His men, carrying the dozens of canteens, gathered around the barrel, plunging the canteens in to fill them. Others in his command ringed the dozen colored soldiers; squatting down by their sides they took off their hats to fan them. They offered them their own canteens, which they drank from greedily. A few made the ultimate gesture, one comrade to another unknown comrade, offering a pint of whiskey; some of the black men took it gladly, others refused. One of his officers lugged up a bucket and upended a quart or so of water over the head of each man to help him cool off.

The men of the Fourth looked up at them in amazement, for here were white men waiting upon them, eyes filled with admiration and wonder.

Soldiers of the 48th reached into haversacks, pulling out chaws of tobacco, whispering words of esteem and encouragement . . .

The men who had filled the canteens came back, one by one, and solemnly handed them back to the bearers.

Pleasants tried to control his voice.

"You don't have to go back," he finally said, voice choked with emotion.

They looked up at him, breathing hard.

"Sir, we got friends back there. Friends hurt real bad," one of them replied. "Wounded men crying for water, and they need it now."

Another sighed, shaking his head.

"I told Bobby I'd bring him back water," and the sergeant's voice was choked. "I ain't gonna let him die a-thirsting for a drink. Owe him that, don't we?"

Pleasants, too choked with emotion to speak, could only nod.

"I want covering fire for these men," he cried out. "For these brave comrades!"

The men around him, who minutes before had been so reluctant to start digging, leaped to pick up their rifles, and climbed up onto the firing line, weapons leveled.

Pleasants looked at the sergeant who was leading the water bearers, his comrades of the Fourth. It was a picture he knew he would carry to his dying day.

It was Pleasants who saluted first. The sergeant looked up at him, shocked by the gesture, and rose to return the salute. Pleasants put a hand on his shoulder, trying to force him to rest for just a few more seconds before confronting his fate.

"Ready, boys?" the sergeant shouted.

No one spoke.

"Go!"

The dozen scrambled up over the side, each of them burdened with a dozen or more loaded canteens; rather than going downhill, they were now going upslope.

As if waiting for them, a scathing volley swept the lip of the trench. One of the men barely cleared the parapet before he fell back in, hit in the chest, gasping out a final breathful of air, blood frothing his lips before he was still.

One of them started up the side of the parapet, then hesitated, and slid half down.

He looked up at Pleasants, not much more than a boy of sixteen or seventeen, shaking like a leaf.

"Stay," the colonel cried, trying to restrain him. "It is all right. Stay with us. You've done enough today."

The boy gazed at him for a second, then shook his head, squeezing his eyes tight shut.

"No, sir; no, sir. I ain't no coward," and pulling away from Henry's grasp, he scrambled back up the parapet.

The dozen who had started up the slope were within seconds just eight, then six, then five . . . The sergeant leading them almost reached the lip of the crater, then fell backward, shot in the head.

Pleasants could not contain his rage, half climbing out of the trench.

"For Christ's sake! They're a watering party for the wounded!" he screamed. "Show mercy!"

He would have been dead, if not for Kochanski and others of his command who climbed out after him, grabbed him, and physically threw him back into the trench.

Before being pulled back he saw only four make it back into the relative safety of the crater. The frightened boy was not one of them. He lay sprawled in the middle of the field; the shot that killed him had pierced a canteen filled with a precious quart of murky water, which now gurgled out of the shattered tin, mingling with his blood.

"Oh, God," Pleasants sobbed, sitting in the safety of his trench. "Forgive them, make this stop."

Around him he barely noticed that his men were now digging with a will, trying to cut a trench to their comrades, 130 yards away.

The pitiless sun glared down upon them.

12:30 P.M.

****

"General Meade, you know there will have to be a court of inquiry about this disaster."

Meade displayed not a flicker of emotion. He had learned long ago that Grant was the ultimate poker player when it came to not revealing what he was really thinking.

"I am due for a conference first thing tomorrow, back in Washington with the President. The packet is already late. I leave the field to you."

The thunder of battle continued to roar little more than a mile away. Meade had ridden over to meet Grant when summoned by one of his aides.

"Make sure good, fair men sit on it. I'd recommend Winfield Hancock for one."

Meade took that in. There was a degree of enmity between him and Hancock, whom some reporter had tagged with the moniker "Hancock the Superb." Some had even whispered that at Gettysburg, it should have been Hancock in command rather than Meade; for then surely the battle would have been fought to an end in which Lee, pinned against a flooded Potomac, would have been forced to surrender.

But Hancock was a fair man, who would render a good decision when presented with proper well-organized facts.

"Convene the court as soon as decently possible. I want a full inquiry as to what went wrong and why."

Grant leaned forward slightly, fixing Meade with his gaze.

"I think that for whatever reason, a fair chance to have ended this war today has been lost. I want to know why."

"Yes, sir."

"Fine, then we understand each other. Good day to you, sir."

General Ulysses S. Grant turned his mount toward City Point—toward the packet to Washington, toward meetings in Washington that would consume his time for many days to come—leaving General George Meade with the responsibility of sorting out the truth, of what had happened and of what was happening even now.

THE CRATER
1:00 P.M.

****

The shot had struck Private Jemson in the back; James Reilly could see that clearly enough. Turning, he saw in the mob of men clustered in the bottom of the crater a man glaring at him defiantly, having just murdered the soldier next to James—a black soldier who had been valiantly trying to hold back the Rebels for hours.

"For God's sake!" James cried, half standing, pointing at the murderer.

The man disappeared into the riotous press of panic-stricken soldiers trapped in the bottom of the crater.

What had only hours before seemed like shelter had instead turned into a spider hole, a death trap, the type he remembered seeing on an assignment out West before the war. The spider would dig a pit rather than a web, conceal itself. An unwary victim would fall into that pit, try to crawl out, and the spider would strike.

To either side of him, colored soldiers of the Fourth held the rim of the crater, freely intermingled with those white soldiers of the other divisions who still had fight in them.

Men shared cartridges when a comrade ran short, offered a sip from a precious canteen, and together cursed the Rebels and the damn generals who had got them into this nightmare. They were comrades, while behind them men filled with terror were now shooting black soldiers in the back out of fear that they might be executed in a final killing frenzy if taken prisoner with them.

When one was wounded or dying his comrade would stop for a moment, cradle a man whose name he might not even know to comfort him, pray with him, and hold his hand until death relaxed the grip, before he picked up a rifle and resumed the fight.

Reilly felt absolutely useless in this inferno. His precious sketchbook, still in his hand, had taken two neat bullet holes. Well, his friend Lincoln might be impressed by that, he thought with a wry smile.

But at least he could watch the backs of his comrades who still held the rim of the crater, beyond which the pressure was building, minute by minute. He was veteran enough to know that the Rebs were nerving themselves up for a final rush, and that, if they gained the rim, it would be an absolute slaughter pen. Passions were out of control on both sides; there would be no prisoners in this fight.

Colonel Russell was a few feet away, and James crawled over to his side.

"Your revolver, sir!" he cried.

"What?"

"Your revolver!"

"For God's sake, why?"

"Because one of your men just got shot in the back by those bastards down there. I'll cover them!"

Russell looked back at the seething mass, then peeked over the lip of the crater, and ducked back down; only a few seconds later a couple of minié balls impacted where he had just been.

He reached into his belt and pulled out a Remington.

"It was Lieutenant Grant's," Russell cried, "I took it from his body after he fell. Didn't want some Reb to get it. Check the load!"

James held the pistol up, half cocked it, and spun the cylinder. There were four rounds left.

"You know that as a civilian if you are caught with arms you will be executed?" Russell shouted.

"Hell, I'm going to be executed anyhow once they see my sketchbook and me alongside your men!" he replied.

Russell patted him on the shoulder and turned back to the fight.

James turned to face down into the crater, held the revolver up so those nearest him could see it, and cocked it, his intent clear. He assumed he might be shot within the next few seconds. Some shouted obscenities at him, but they drew back.

At least his comrades on this small section of the front were safe from being shot from behind.

BLANDFORD CHURCH HILL
HEADQUARTERS, ARMY OF NORTHERN VIRGINIA
1:45 P.M.

****

"Finish it," Lee said, looking at Mahone. "For heaven's sake, they are cornered. Bag the lot, and finish it. If we wait until dark they will escape. For that matter, I am stunned they have not yet brought up reserves to strengthen their line and perhaps threaten another section to draw us off. I want it finished now, before they can launch another attack and stretch us too thin to hold."

"Yes, sir."

"And General . . ."

"Sir?"

"Is it true a colored division was in the assault?"

"Yes, sir."

Lee stepped closer to Mahone and in an uncharacteristic gesture put a fatherly hand on his shoulder.

"I want the full honor of war observed. Those who surrender are to be treated as proper prisoners, with respect, their wounded tended to, their officers shown the respect due their rank."

Mahone looked at him, as if to reply.

"I know what our President has said, but in this army, sir, my orders on this day carry full weight. We are Christian soldiers, sir. Do you understand me? Passions must not rule, even in the heat of battle. If I hear of any atrocities, I will ensure that those involved shall face court-martial and the full penalty of military law."

He drew Mahone a bit closer.

"Do we understand each other, sir?"

There was only one answer Mahone could possibly give to such a man.

"Yes, sir."

THE CRATER

2:00 P.M.

****

"Oh, my God, here it comes!"

Garland braced himself. He had pulled three rifles to his side, all of them loaded, prepared for this moment.

A swarm of Rebs came charging up out of the trench they had seized in the first assault... How long ago was it? If it had been charged in the beginning minutes of the battle, the trench would have been empty altogether.

He aimed square at the chest of the officer leading the assault, squeezed, and to his rage and delight—but also to an inward horror that would haunt him later—he saw the man tumble backward, breath knocked out of him.

He threw the rifle aside, picked up another, aimed at a sergeant who, screaming with rage, had pushed the officer to one side, looked back to urge his men on, and then pressed forward. In the smoke and confusion he was not sure if he had hit him.

He dropped that rifle and picked up the third. There was another man, towering above him; he pointed the rifle skyward and squeezed, but the percussion cap had fallen off, and the hammer just clicked. The Rebel above him was aiming straight down, squeezed, and somehow missed.

Garland threw the misfired gun aside and picked up the last one. From the corner of his eye he saw the drummer boy, screaming with rifle in hand, and a Rebel dropping in front of him.

"Good lad!" Garland cried to him.

You've just killed a boy, and you are a good man.

The thought barely had time to register. The Rebel who had missed him was lunging down with a bayonet. Garland half rose to his knees, parried the blow, knocked the Reb's rifle upward, and pressed his gun into his chest, squeezing the trigger.

The Rebel jerked backward.

And then the swarming attack was upon them. Men were screaming, cursing, sobbing, mingled together, Rebel and Union, black and white. Men from both sides were shooting, lunging, and swinging clubbed muskets.

He had thought that surely there must be something noble in war, but at this moment, it was a fight in a gutter, in a sewer, among men driven mad by heat, rage, and the lust for blood.

The men of the Fourth, holding the crest of the crater, unsupported by the thousands clustered below, were beaten back; their temporary advantage, of holding ground under cover, had been lost at last to a surging tidal wave of Rebels. Gaining the crest of the crater, the Confederates were now pointing their rifles downslope, shooting into the seething mob of confused, leaderless, terrified men.

One of the few officers who could have led them, General William Bartlett, was down, his cork leg blown off by a bursting mortar round. He screamed for his men to rally, to carry him if need be, to charge back up the steep slope of the crater and retake the rim. But there were too few to listen, too few with the strength, let alone the will, left to fight after nine long hours of that madness. They were finished, cartridge boxes empty, canteens empty, wilting in 100-degree heat.

Garland stood defiantly, empty rifle raised, driven half a dozen feet down from the rim.

"Garland!"

Two voices called to him at once. He spared a quick glance back. It was Russell and Reilly, falling back into the mob that carpeted the bottom of the crater.

Garland looked back up. With each second, more and more Rebels were gaining the rim, falling flat, aiming into the crater, and tossing empty rifles back to men behind them, who handed loaded weapons forward. He was stunned to see a crew of four men dragging a Cohorn mortar to the very edge of the crater, and others lugging boxes of twelve-pound shells. As if realizing the absurdity of their efforts to drag the mortar forward, given their hold on the rim, they simply took the shells out of their wooden sabots within the ammunition boxes. One Rebel pressed a lit cigar to the fuses, which sputtered to life, and then heaved them into the seething mass of Yankees below them.

"Garland!"

He saw at least two Rebels aiming at him, firing; he flinched but by some miracle they missed him. He caught a glimpse of the drummer boy, hanging on to a wounded comrade and refusing to retreat. Garland grabbed him by the ankle, pulling him back.

"Come on, boy!" he screamed.

They slid down the face of the crater, Colonel Russell screaming over and over, "28th to me! 28th to me!"

A quarter of the men who had surged forward with him were now falling in by his side.

General Bartlett was at Russell's side, braced up by two men of his command, minus his cork leg.

"For God's sake get out! Get out!" Bartlett screamed, his voice edged with hysteria. "Take your men and get out while you still can!"

Russell looked back up at the lip of the crater and made his decision.

"28th, back to our lines. Follow me, my men; follow me!"

It was as if his cry set off a vast wave that had been building for hours. By the thousands the men trapped in the crater, seeing that at last the Rebels had gained the rim to their right and center, started to claw their way up the eastern slope, in a desperate bid to get back to the safety of their lines.

2:05 P.M.

※※※※※※※※※※※※※※※※※※※※※※※※※※※

"Another telegram from Meade, sir," Vincent whispered, holding the sheet of flimsy paper.

"Just read it," Burnside replied in exhaustion and defeat.

Vincent sighed.

United States Military Telegraph.

Inform the men within the crater to dig a trench out and thus escape before sunset. I expect you to pass this order on immediately.

Burnside looked up at him and said nothing in reply. Could not the man simply walk out of his own bunker and see that the men of the Ninth, by the thousands, were fleeing the crater and, without fire support, were being slaughtered as they tried to regain their own lines?

2:15 P.M.

✳✳✳✳✳✳✳✳✳✳✳✳✳✳✳✳✳✳✳✳✳✳✳✳✳✳✳

The surge of men, black and white, most of them panic-stricken, swarmed up the east slope of the crater, while only fifty yards away on the opposite slope Confederate infantry poured devastating fire into them.

"Let my men help you!" Russell yelled, looking at Bartlett.

He was greeted, strangely, by a smile.

"I stay here with my men. Godspeed and good luck to you and your men, sir. Now get the hell out of here!"

The offer made, Russell nodded and held his sword aloft, shouting for the men of his regiment to rally to him. Miraculously, the national colors were still in their possession, and he pushed the flag-bearer up the nearly impossible slope, men above them sliding and falling, some of them unable to climb another step, others collapsing with a rifle ball in their back.

Russell gained the lip of the crater, screaming at the flag-bearer to save the colors and run. He hesitated, looked back, stifling his own terror, and reached down to haul up Garland and then the artist. Garland in turn reached back to pull up the drummer boy, and after him a wounded comrade that the drummer boy would not abandon.

Within seconds, hundreds and then thousands of men were swarming across the field at a run, while from either flank the Rebels were pouring out of their entrenchments, slamming in a devastating fire to either flank as the tormented souls ran the gauntlet of hell.

Garland saw the young man the drummer boy was pulling along go down, shot in the head; the drummer boy screamed. Garland turned back for the boy, who collapsed a few seconds later, clutching his arm. He went for the boy, but James was on him, shoving him away.

"Run! For Christ sake, run!"

Shamed by his terror, Garland ran. With each step he was propelled by rage, a desire to turn, to somehow reverse all that had been done this day, all that had been done across a lifetime, all that had been promised . . . all that had been lost.

Together with James and Colonel Russell he reached the edge of the trench that meant the safety of their own lines. Men of the 48th reached up to pull them in, the trench piled thick with men, in places two and three deep. Soldiers of the 48th were shouting for them to head for the safety of the covered way while they themselves stood, rifles poised, pouring fire into the Rebel flank, which had swarmed out of their trenches, and finally driving them back.

The exodus of thousands from the crater decreased to hundreds, then scores, and finally only a ragged few who would rise, sprint a few feet, and then drop.

Cries for mercy and surrender could still be heard from within the crater, begging for quarter.

And then, finally, a merciful silence. Silent except for the pitiful thousands of groaning wounded who still lay on the field.

2:45 P.M.

✳✳✳✳✳✳✳✳✳✳✳✳✳✳✳✳✳✳✳✳✳✳✳✳✳

Colonel Henry Pleasants, forlorn and alone, sat by the collapsed entryway to the tunnel which, just thirty-four days ago, he had started with such hope, with even the dream that perhaps he might be an instrument to bringing this war to an end.

His gaze took in hundreds of men piled into his trench, dead men and wounded men too exhausted now to even move.

"Merciful God," he whispered through his tears. "What have I done?"

4:00 P.M.

✳✳✳✳✳✳✳✳✳✳✳✳✳✳✳✳✳✳✳✳✳✳✳✳✳✳✳

Vincent held the telegram but did not even bother to take it over to his commander, who sat in the far corner of the bunker, whispering to himself.

United States Military Telegraph.

All records of communications of this day are to be preserved and delivered to this headquarters, no later than 6:00 p.m. this evening. The telegrapher of your headquarters is to report to me immediately. All regimental, brigade, division, and corps commanders are to submit to this headquarters, no later than 6:00 p.m. tomorrow, their after action reports.

This is to inform all of you, that upon the direct orders of the Commander of all Union forces in the field, a court of inquiry into this debacle shall convene within three days.

General George Meade

CHAPTER FOURTEEN

AUGUST 1, 1864

11 P.M.

****

"HEY, YANK, GOT ANOTHER ONE OF YOUR DARKIES OVER HERE. He's still breathing."

James Reilly, with Sergeant Major Garland White by his side, followed the stretcher bearers over to where Rebs stood, gazing down at a man lying still, barely visible by the light of torches and lanterns.

Garland raced to the prone man, and knelt down by his side.

"It's Corporal Barnes," he cried, taking the man's hand. "He's one of ours."

"He won't be for long," one of the Rebs replied coldly. "Gut shot from the looks of him."

"Back off, and just leave us be," Garland hissed.

James was now at Garland's side, followed by the stretcher bearers.

"Dead one, anyhow, waste of effort to carry him back." Two of them walked off. The third Rebel, an officer, stood silent.

The weary orderlies, men from the 28th, put down their stretcher. They knelt around Corporal Barnes, one of them beginning to weep.

James stood silent, thinking he should have his sketchpad out to capture this moment, but it was far too personal, too painful. It was obvious that Barnes was near death. In the cold calculus of war, the Rebs were right; it was a waste of effort to carry him back. They should husband their strength for men who could still be saved, or better yet, saved and returned to combat duty.

They gently lifted the corporal onto the stretcher, and he groaned weakly, able to say only one word.

"Water."

One of the men opened his canteen, and the Rebel officer finally spoke.

"Gut shot like that, it might not be good for him."

James, surprised by his compassionate advice, looked at the man, and found something familiar about him. If Barnes was indeed shot in the stomach, the water would only pour out into his abdominal cavity and make things worse, but he was dying anyhow. After lying out here for a day and a half, nearly every man found alive was begging for a drink.

They gave him the water, picked up their burden, and set off, with Garland holding a lantern to guide the way.

"Why in God's name didn't your general ask for a truce yesterday?" the Rebel officer sighed.

James stepped closer.

"Don't I know you?" he whispered.

"Captain Sanders, 25th North Carolina."

"James Reilly, with *Harper's Weekly.*" James hesitated. "You were a correspondent for some paper out of Raleigh. Remember? We had more than one drink while covering the Democratic Convention down in Charleston back in 1860."

There was a moment's hesitation on Sanders's part, and finally he extended his hand.

"Of course I remember you, Reilly. What a tragic farce that was. We both knew where it was going to take us."

James took Sanders's hand and the man winced. Looking down in the darkness, he saw it was bandaged.

"Got burned a bit by the blast."

"So you were in it?"

Sanders nodded and sighed.

"Strange. I was actually inside the fort when it blew. One of my men . . ." he hesitated and for a second James thought the man was about to lose his composure. "A lot of my men."

He sighed.

"Why did I live?" he asked, and it was obvious to James that the man was in shock. "But nearly all my men . . ." and his voice trailed off.

"I'm sorry."

"Oh, really? You're sorry and that's it?"

There was a bitter edge now to his voice, and he started to turn away.

"Sanders, for God's sake, I am sorry. Sorry for this whole damn madness, and if I remember you correctly, you are, too. You no more wanted this damn war than I did."

Sanders stopped, turned, and looked back at him.

"Got a drink? I remember you as a drinking Irishman and damn all, I could use one."

James reached into his haversack and pulled out a pint of whiskey. He had been saving it for later, after buying it from a sutler for two dollars, so that once this night was over he could indulge in a damn good drink. Seeing this man he had known and had befriended some years ago caught him in the moment. He also figured that a drink or two might allow him to hear the other side of what had happened. If Sanders was any kind of gentleman, he would not just take the bottle and leave.

Sanders took the bottle without comment, pulled the cork, and took a very long drink.

"Good stuff," he whispered. "Strange, you sometimes dwell on one thing to drown out your misery, and all I could think of was that I needed to get drunk, damn good and drunk."

"Well, I doubt if there is enough there for both of us for a good drunk, but it could be a start."

He handed the bottle back to James, who forced himself to take only a sip before handing it back, watching as Sanders gulped down several more ounces.

"Smoke?" Sanders finally asked.

Though he still had several halfway decent cigars of his own, James muttered agreement, and Sanders pulled out two cigars, handing one to James. After fumbling in their pockets for a lucifer to light them, they approached a stretcher bearer team carrying a wounded Rebel back toward their lines, and each got a light from a torch.

"Did you see any of it?" Sanders asked.

"Yes. I was back at headquarters when it started, then went forward with one of the colored regiments."

"Who, in God's name, thought this one up?" Sanders snapped, almost a snarl, before taking another drink.

"Bill, you know I can't talk about that," James replied while puffing his cigar to life. It was fairly good Virginia or Carolina tobacco.

"Of course I know that, but this is madness! For Christ's sake why didn't you ask for a truce a day ago? A lot of these men were still alive then."

On this question, James no longer cared if he were giving a Rebel information or not. Besides, their high command most likely knew already.

"Burnside asked for one as soon as the fighting was over. Even hoisted a white signal flag."

He spat out the tip of the cigar and looked down at the ground.

"But then Meade fired off a telegraph message to Burnside demanding to know who authorized the truce, and stating that it was the prerogative of a commanding general only, that he had not authorized it, and to resume firing on your lines."

"Goddamn him," Sanders hissed. "We lost a couple of men out in the open who were giving water to the wounded between the lines. Damn him."

James took a sip of the whiskey and handed it back.

"All right, then, I told you something. Now, you tell me something.

We've been hearing rumors that colored troops were executed after the fight."

It was Sanders's turn to sigh and look at the ground.

"It was madness, all of it madness, James. Look, I've been in damn near every fight since the Peninsula. When men are out in the open, a hundred, two hundred yards apart, there's room for mercy when a man is down. But here?"

He pointed back up the dark slope to the lip of the crater, to the trenches on either side.

"You come across an enemy when you turn a corner and he is only five feet away, it becomes madness. Men become like animals, kill first or be killed."

"That was during the fight," James replied sharply. "I was in the final charge and saw that. Yes, I saw it, from both sides. No prisoners."

Sanders was silent for a moment.

"I was knocked cold from the blast. Think I got a cracked head, a concussion from it. It's still hard to hear. So I was out of it for most of the fight."

"I'm not asking about you, personally, Bill, though I am sorry to hear you were hurt."

There was a long moment of silence.

"Yes, after our boys retook the lip of the crater, the cry went up to kill all the colored. But if you write about this, for God's sake, report that General Lee passed specific orders that all troops, colored or white, and all officers of colored troops, were to be treated according to the rules of war."

He took another long drink.

"As you know, I was against slavery. My family refused to own them. We hired free blacks to work the fields of our farm. So, yes, I tried to stop it, so did most of the officers. It is bastard reporters from papers like the *Richmond Examiner* who call for more blood, and I bet your paper will, too."

"I can't deny that," James sighed.

"And I heard that some of your white troops turned on the blacks toward the end."

James could only nod, too ashamed by what he had seen to speak.

"Why didn't they send those colored boys in?" Sanders asked.

"What?"

"Why? I'm just guessing here, but the way they charged, it was like they knew what they were doing, but your white troops didn't."

James felt he couldn't reply.

Sanders finally nodded.

"All right. Yes, some of the prisoners opened up, and for God's sake, make sure someone reports that we took over two hundred colored men as prisoners, and in spite of what the Richmond papers say, or what that fool we have in Richmond as a president said, General Lee's orders have been and will be obeyed. But yes, some of them talked and said they were supposed to go in first and if they had they would have won the battle."

Hearing that again filled James with a cold sense of rage, but he felt he could not comment.

"I'll tell you this," Sanders whispered. "If they had gone in first right after the explosion, those boys might have crushed us clean through to Petersburg. Then, rather than us standing here picking up dead, I think this war would be all but over."

He took another long drink, and James inwardly sighed, sensing that the bottle was nearly empty.

Sanders handed it back, and James could see the man actually smiled.

"Being an old newspaper man myself, Reilly, I'll have to ask that you don't quote me on that. I think it'd cost me my rank."

"Agreed." The two stood silent for a moment.

"Have you seen inside the crater yet?" Sanders asked.

"I was in it during the fight."

Sanders looked at him appraisingly.

"I'm glad you got out alive."

"A lot of my friends didn't."

Sanders turned and motioned for James to follow.

Again memories resurfaced: of Cold Harbor; of so many battlefields at night; of lanterns bobbing up and down as the bearers stopped before each prone form, looking it in the face in hopes of finding a live comrade, then moving on.

Last night had been an utter horror. Hundreds were spread over the slope separating the Union line from the crater. In the darkness they had cried out for water, for a friend, and most heartbreakingly of all, for their mothers. So very many, in their last minutes, turned back to childhood, calling their mother to come and comfort them. James had prayed and wanted to believe that indeed the spirit of more than one mother did hover over that field to embrace their dying sons and then bear them away from their nightmares.

A brave few had ventured out laden with canteens to try and bring succor, but under orders from the high command, sharpshooters were to drive them back. Most, with no stomach for such action, would just put a warning shot close to a man. However, more than a few, still filled with the mad frenzy that lingers after a bitter fight, aimed and shot to kill.

And thus, come dawn of the next day, the wounded still lay out there in the boiling heat. Some had the strength to try and crawl to safety, and rage filled both sides because too often these men were shot, rather than shown the tradition of compassion, which had so far ruled on most battlefields of this war once the fighting was over.

If this damn war does not end soon, he had thought throughout the day, *this hatred will finally burn so deep we will never recover from it.*

They walked past more prone, motionless forms—veterans of so many fields—as they approached the lip of the crater.

James was used to the stench of death, but here it was so overpowering that he stopped and gagged, fearing he would vomit.

He pulled out a bandanna, as Sanders already had, Sanders splashing a bit of the precious whiskey on his and then James's. Tying the bandannas around their mouths and noses, they pressed forward, the whiskey blocking at least a bit of the stench.

They reached the crest.

"Oh, merciful God and all the saints have pity," James whispered.

With the truce, the Rebels who had reoccupied the crater had finally had the chance to "clean it out."

The lip of the vast crater, which covered nearly an acre of ground, was rimmed with torches. Several hundred men were at work, and the image was frightful, as if the men lining the crest were literally mining for the dead.

Ropes were tossed down to the bottom, where men laboring like the damned in some Dante's hell were looping the ropes around bodies, then shouting for the men above to haul away. Most of those who worked on the bottom were prisoners, black prisoners, armed guards standing and just watching. The bodies being hauled up the sides of the crater had been there for more than a day and a half in 100-degree heat.

Like all the dead he had seen on so many battlefields, after a day under the summer sun of Virginia, Maryland, or Pennsylvania, their bodies had so bloated up that their uniforms looked small, tight, constricting; in some cases jacket buttons and flies on pants had burst.

But this was worse, far worse. For these dead, hundreds of them, had been trapped inside a cauldron that held in the heat. Some of the bodies literally burst asunder as they were being hauled out, overwhelming the living men laboring to drag them out. The universal sound around James was one of gagging, vomiting. Men gasped for air. Some, in spite of orders or the threat of a bayonet prod, were breaking down, staggering away, or just collapsing into sobs.

Along the far rim of the crater, wagons were drawn up in a row, and as the bodies were finally dragged out, they were hoisted up and dumped unceremoniously into the back of the wagons until, fully loaded, the driver could set off with his load.

"We're burying them all in a mass grave up by Blandford Church."

Sanders hesitated.

"It's consecrated ground at least."

"Got another live one down here!" a cry came up from below. "Yanks, it's another one of your black boys."

On the near rim of the crater, James saw that Garland was again at work. He and one of the stretcher bearers were sliding down into the hellhole. James watched anxiously, for what was to distinguish them from the prisoners?

Sanders seemed to read his mind.

"They'll be all right. Your prisoners are wearing white armbands. As long as they keep them on, they'll be treated fairly. Again, orders of General Lee. But if any try to sneak off, they'll be shot."

James said nothing, taking in the Stygian nightmare, knowing he had to sketch it later, and knowing as well that no newspaper would ever print it.

Garland grabbed hold of the wounded man, called for a rope to be tossed down, and set to work.

"I've been in a dozen pitched battles," Sanders whispered. "My regiment was all but annihilated at Sharpsburg, but I've never seen anything like this."

James could only nod in reply, moving the bandanna aside to take a deep puff on his cigar and then regretting it. The smell had overwhelmed him; he dropped the cigar, turned away, and vomited.

He was stunned when Sanders actually patted him on the back and offered him the bottle so he could rinse the sour taste out of his mouth with another drink. It was the last of the bottle, which he let fall to the ground.

"Damn, I'm still not drunk enough," Sanders sighed.

"Nor I."

"So what next?"

"It continues," was all James said.

He looked over at Sanders.

"You know you can't win. We will just keep wearing you down."

"You call this wearing us down?" Sanders snapped, pointing to the crater. "If every one of you damn Yankees could be brought here, to see this, that bastard in the White House would be driven out tomorrow, and we could all go home."

"What about the bastard in your White House?" James retorted angrily. "He was the one screaming about no prisoners and selling these men back into slavery. Bill, I have to fight against that."

"Then I will see you on the next battlefield, if we survive."

The two glared at each other for a moment, as if about to fight the war on a very personal level, then James just lowered his head sadly.

"Sorry, James," Sanders whispered.

"We're all infected with it," James replied.

Sanders fetched two more cigars out of his pocket and handed them to James.

"Keep your head down, James."

"You, too, Bill."

There was a moment's hesitation, then James reached out and, rather than grasp his old friend's burned hands, he just patted him on the shoulder.

"Maybe, after this war is over, we'll see each other again."

"Doubt it," Sanders replied. "We'll keep fighting. You know I have nothing against the colored, but using them in battle like this . . . First of all, it was murder the way they were thrown into this fight. Second, there's many a boy in the ranks here who was not fighting for slavery, but will be damned if any colored troops are going to beat him down."

James sighed, watching as Garland continued to labor to hoist yet another comrade out of the crater.

"They're only men, just like us," James replied. "And that, I think, is worth fighting for."

He patted Sanders again, regretting as he did so because the man winced. By the torchlight he could see that his head was heavily bandaged and burns had swollen his face. In another world this man would be in a hospital, but not this world.

"After the war, I'll buy you a drink."

"A gallon at least," Bill whispered. "Maybe with enough of it, we can forget."

He turned and walked away into the darkness.

James moved along the rim of the crater to where the rescue party was laboring, lending a hand as they finally hoisted the wounded soldier out of the hell pit. His leg was gone below the right knee, the tourniquet which someone had put on over a day and a half ago still bound tight. By torchlight he could see that the shattered stump was already swollen to twice the normal size. The poor man would have to endure another amputation, most likely at mid-thigh, to stop the spread of gangrene.

James extended a hand to Garland, who, gasping for breath, reached up to him for help getting out, triggering a flash memory of the assault, the two helping each other up out of the trench, which was supposed to have been spanned with footbridges.

"Thank you," was all Garland could say. It was obvious he was on the point of getting sick to his stomach as well, but his attention was focused solely on the wounded man, now being gently laid on a stretcher.

Garland uncorked his canteen. The injured man was barely conscious. Garland offered him a drink, which he finally took, replying with whispered thanks.

"What regiment are you?" asked Garland.

"31st," was all he could whisper. "I'm a soldier of the 31st by God."

"Yes you are," Garland replied, and reaching into his haversack he pulled out a pocket Bible. The haversack was bulging with them.

"This is the good book, son," he said, pressing it into the wounded man's hands.

"Remember the Twenty-eighth Psalm?" Garland whispered. "'The Lord my strength and my shield; my heart trusted in him, and I am helped.'"

The wounded soldier could only nod.

"Hold the good book tight, it will make you feel good, son."

Garland could barely contain his tears. The man he was comforting was obviously old enough to be his father, and yet he called him "son."

Garland looked up at the stretcher team.

"Run. Run!" he cried. "Get him to help now!"

The stretcher team set off as ordered.

Garland stood back up, taking James's proffered hand.

"James Reilly, do I smell whiskey on you?" he asked.

"Just to cover over the smell," James replied.

Garland looked straight into his eyes and James, to his own surprise, felt a power and with it nearly a sense of guilt.

Garland finally relented and put a hand on his shoulder.

"For the first time in years, I wish I had a drink," he finally said.

He looked back down into the crater.

"God, how can we keep doing this to each other?"

He turned his gaze back to James.

"Remember this. Draw it. Tell the world of it and never let them forget. Never!"

His voice was filled with anger.

"Hey, we got another live one down here," a voice rose from below. "At least this one's white; I think he's one of ours."

Without comment Garland slid back down into hell to offer a hand.

HEADQUARTERS, NINTH CORPS
AUGUST 2, 1864
12:15 A.M.

****

"Colonel Pleasants, thank you for coming. Sorry if I disturbed your rest."

Henry Pleasants stepped down into the command bunker. It was empty except for General Burnside, who sat alone, in a corner. A tin cup, from the smell of it filled with coffee and whiskey, was sitting in front of him.

"No problem, sir; I couldn't sleep anyhow," Pleasants offered a bit woodenly. In fact, for the first time since the battle, he had finally drifted off into exhausted sleep a few hours ago.

"Take a cup of coffee, it's over in the corner there. Open the desk drawer and you'll find something stronger to put in it."

Pleasants took the cup and filled it to the brim with what was now, at best, a tepid brew, but ignored the suggestion to pour some sour mash in. When summoned by a corps commander, even one might have had a few drinks himself, it was best to keep a clear head.

Burnside motioned for him to sit down.

"First off, Henry, I want to commend you and your men for the job they did. It was exceptional, courageous, and I only wish it had achieved the effect originally intended."

Pleasants could only nod his thanks, taking a long sip of coffee in hopes it would clear some of the cobwebs in his mind from being awakened after not sleeping for nearly three days.

Burnside sighed and looked off.

"Originally intended . . . intended . . ." and his voice trailed off.

Pleasants took another long sip and as he gazed at the general he felt a surge of conflict. Burnside was a corps commander whom he had followed into battle for years, and whom he respected in spite of the scoffing of men from other units. Nearly all the men of the Ninth felt this loyalty and saw a side to him that others did not.

But after this fiasco? This nightmare?

Burnside was silent for a moment, and then stirred, as if snapping out of a dream as he drifted asleep. In front of him was a pile of papers, and he shuffled them nervously.

"After-action reports. I am supposed to forward them to General Meade; actually they were expected more than six hours ago, though I tried to explain that the demand was nearly impossible so soon after such an action."

He sighed.

"I was told they are expected anyhow."

"Sir, I sent mine in by one of my adjutants before six this evening," Pleasants replied, wondering if that was why he had been summoned.

Burnside smiled and shook his head. To one side of the stack were several sheets of paper. Even glimpsing it upside down, Pleasants recognized the handwriting as his own, shaky as it was, since he had barely been able to keep awake while filling it out.

"That was part of the reason I called you in, Henry," Burnside replied, and he picked up the report.

"Is there a problem with it, sir?"

"Yes."

Pleasants did not know what to say, and then was shocked to full awareness when Burnside tore the report in half and then in half again, tossing the papers to one side of the table.

"Sir? What was wrong with my report?"

Burnside smiled.

"Henry, don't you understand what is about to happen?"

"Sir?"

"Ever seen a man hanged?"

"Yes, sir."

Serve in the army long enough and of course you would see at least one. The punishment was meted out to men for crimes so heinous that they did not even deserve the honor of a firing squad. Before the war he had seen more than one hanging back in Pottsville. Miners were a tough lot, and on a fairly regular basis there would be a murder, a quick trial, and a public hanging.

"Well, Henry, there is about to be a hanging."

"Who, sir?"

"Me."

Pleasants did not know how to react, hiding his confusion by taking another long sip of coffee.

Burnside chuckled and shook his head.

"Oh, metaphorically of course. We only hang privates in this army, never officers, and especially not generals. If anything, when you make enough of a mess of things, you can get a promotion at times. Either that or you are sent off to a nice safe posting, say commanding a depot or prison camp in New York, where you can safely sit out the war and be forgotten."

"Sir, by God, we know where the truth lies," Pleasants replied, and now his voice was tinged with anger. "If the colored troops had been sent in first, as you planned, we wouldn't be having this conversation now. Tonight we'd be in Petersburg, maybe even Richmond, celebrating the approaching end of the war."

"But we are not," Burnside said sharply. "And someone will shoulder the blame and that will be me."

He seemed so calm as he said the words, as if talking about some impending reward or promotion rather than disgrace.

"I will shoulder the blame."

Pleasants was silent at that. At this moment he did not have the willpower to argue that, indeed, there were points of blame. Rumors were sweeping through the encampments about the now infamous "drawing of straws." Surviving veterans of all four divisions were declaring that if they could but set eyes on their division commanders, they would shoot them dead on the spot, especially the unfortunates who served under Ledlie, and the black soldiers of Ferrero's command. Word was already out that, while men were falling by the thousands, those two had been safely behind the lines, a thousand yards off, already drunk.

For that, Burnside was responsible. But at this moment, Pleasants did not have the heart or stomach to tell him to his face that, on that score at least, he had utterly failed.

Those who had escaped the crater spoke with admiration, some with tears in their eyes, of the courage of Brigadier General Bartlett, his cork leg blown off, trying to take command of the fiasco, to organize the fight while several of his men carried him around. In the end, Bartlett had refused to be carried out, saying that come what might, he would stay until the last soldier, white or black, escaped. If necessary he would go into captivity with them, and if captured he would try to ensure fair treatment for the prisoners.

A brigade commander had been doing the job of a division commander. With some corps, such as that of Winfield Scott Hancock, the corps commander would have been in there with them as well.

"As to your report, Henry," and Burnside motioned to the torn-up paper, "I am not submitting it."

"I think I have a right to ask why, sir."

"Because I have too much respect for you, Colonel, to see you throw yourself on your sword."

"What?"

Burnside chuckled and leaned back in his chair. He was a man known for mood swings that could be confusing at times. Often he was cheerful, encouraging, ready with a joke, always quick to praise, but then suddenly he would sink into a black funk. He would become withdrawn, morose, all but paralyzed when it came to a decision. That had been abundantly clear when the plan had unraveled and straws had to been drawn. Rumor was, as well, that throughout the battle he just stood at the parapet of the reserve line, bombarded by telegrams from Meade.

You should have gone forward, Pleasants thought inwardly. *Gone forward; to hell with Meade and the damn telegraph. You could have seized control, sent the colored troops in immediately, and led them yourself. You could have won the war by doing so. History never casts blame on a winner of wars.*

"Your report, Henry, I will not submit. You can write something else out later tonight, after you have had some sleep, but not a word about Meade. Your observations of how the change in order of battle affected the outcome will be removed. Just a straightforward narrative of your digging the tunnel is all that is needed."

Burnside paused and lowered his head, then looked up again with that curious smile.

"No recriminations about Meade's engineers saying it was impossible, about the lack of equipment, or the faulty fuses and the cutting of the powder charge down to forty percent of what we requested."

Burnside stood up, went to the coffee pot, poured more out, opened up the desk drawer and poured a fair amount of sour mash in, and returned to sit across from Pleasants.

"But, sir, I wrote the truth," the colonel protested.

Burnside smiled as he sipped his drink.

"The truth? What is the truth now? What you saw? Maybe, what I saw?" he hesitated. "God forgive me, but I should have gone forward and not allowed myself to be pinned down by that damn telegraph."

Pleasants did not reply.

"Did you know that Meade arrested my telegraphy operators today?"

"What?"

"Said they had been privy to private correspondence now related to the court of inquiry and therefore would be held incommunicado until after the trial."

"What correspondence, sir?"

"It will come out in the hearing," he paused. "I hope."

Burnside took another sip.

"And thus, to you, Colonel Henry Pleasants, the court of inquiry starts..." he paused, opening his pocket watch and then snapping it shut. "In one day and eight hours from now General Winfield Hancock will preside. Winfield is a fair man, but after what happened at Deep Bottom last week, I don't think he is quite the man I once knew."

Pleasants did not dare to reply. This was in the realm of one corps commander commenting on another. All in this army knew that Hancock was the most daring of all corps commanders, at least of those still alive after three years of war. His performance at Chancellorsville as a division commander, holding the rear while being attacked from three directions, and at Gettysburg confronting Pickett's Charge, was the stuff of legends. But he had taken a debilitating, near fatal wound back at Gettysburg and returned a shadow of the robust man he had once been.

Veterans often commented that even the bravest man, after being badly wounded, lost some of his innate courage and impulsiveness upon his return. It was rumored that when his command broke and ran the week before, Winfield had wept. That in the charges at Cold Harbor and Petersburg, he had stood silent, stunned by the slaughter of his gallant Second Corps. Was he still the same man all knew from a year before?

"The others on the board of inquiry, Generals Ayres and Miles, are fairly good men, but they are Army of the Potomac men."

Burnside fell silent and Pleasants knew the clear implication. They were Meade's men. The Ninth always had been something of a stepchild after falling under his command.

"But I never held much truck with Colonel Shriver as inspector general of the Army," Burnside continued. "Too much the lawyer."

He looked off, sipping his drink.

"And so, Colonel Henry Pleasants, I will not accept your after-action report."

"Sir, it is the truth."

Burnside just smiled.

"Rewrite it as ordered and make no reference to anything other than the digging of the tunnel and that you were in reserve when the attack went forward. That is it."

Pleasants started to protest.

"That is an order, Colonel."

"Why, sir?"

Burnside chuckled sadly.

"Because I do not like group hangings. You and your men came up with a plan—of course you wish to defend it—but it was not your plan that failed, it was the army . . ." he sighed. "And me."

Pleasants did not reply to that because there was indeed truth in what the man had said.

"Also, I have cut an order for you to go on furlough immediately, dated as of today. You are to take the morning packet out of City Point. Be there at dawn, so scribble out some quick report and one of your aides can deliver it to me, and then get the hell out of here. It is good for thirty days, and I am ordering you home—now."

"Sir?"

Burnside stood up, as if indicating the interview was at an end.

"Henry, if you're here you will be summoned to the court of inquiry. Knowing you, I know you will talk freely, too freely. Colonel, the decisions have already been made. I think that will become evident, and I refuse to see a good officer dragged down with me. And believe me, they will drag you down as well if you appear at the hearing."

Pleasants stood speechless. Part of him was just overwhelmed, stunned. *Home? My God—home, to my wife, my family, to my Pennsylvania mountains—away from this damned place with its heat, its stench, its death.* But everything inside him that had become a volunteer soldier across the last three years now rebelled.

"No, sir" was all he could say.

"What?"

"No, sir, I refuse."

"Henry, you can't argue with your corps commander."

"Oh, yes, I can, sir, and I will. I insist upon appearing before that damn court."

"For what?"

"To tell the truth of what I saw."

Burnside sighed, stepped forward, and put a fatherly hand on his shoulder.

"I forbid you to throw yourself on my funeral pyre."

"Sir?"

Burnside chuckled again.

"What about history, sir?"

Burnside actually threw his head back and laughed.

"History comes long after the war. For now let's focus on your survival, and the truth will not help you in that cause."

CITY POINT, VIRGINIA
6:00 A.M.

****

Henry Pleasants stood at the stern of the packet boat, foam churning up behind the boat, now clear of the dock as it began to race out into the broad James River on the journey back to Washington.

The river was alive with traffic this morning. Steamers were bringing in supplies, one hauling a barge loaded with lolling, terrified cattle that seemed to have sensed what their fate would be. By the end of that day they would feed the hungry maws of more than one hundred thousand men. A hospital steamer, a side-wheeler, the faded letters of Commodore Vanderbilt's line still faintly visible on its side, whitewashed over, green flags of the hospital corps snapping from its bow and stern, was just ahead of him. It was most likely loaded with the wounded from the crater, too gravely injured to be of further use to the army. Now they were going back to Washington, to the invalid hospitals, before being discharged and given a crutch or perhaps one of the new artificial arms made of gutta-percha.

Around him there was excited chatter of men going home on furlough or self-important talk about missions to Washington.

Few noticed him standing there, sipping brandy out of a flask, looking at the receding shore line.

"Say, you were with the Ninth, weren't you?"

He half turned and saw an officer, a one-star general, looking at him, gesturing to Pleasants's cap, adorned with the fouled anchor insignia of his corps.

He only nodded.

"Were you there at the big fight?"

Again, he nodded.

"Heard, if ever there was a botched affair, that was it. Bet you're glad to be getting out of here."

The man gazed at him with a strange smile.

"Heard the damn darkies really panicked and that's why we lost.

Whatever fool put them there should have been shot. What do you say?"

Pleasants simply gazed at him.

"Go to hell, you son of a bitch," he said ever so slowly, enunciating each word clearly.

The general blustered and puffed up.

"By God, I should bring you up on charges for that."

"Go ahead," Pleasants replied, voice again pitched cool, even gaze boring into the rotund general. "But it will be on charges of murder because in about ten seconds I am going to blow your damn brains out."

As he spoke, he let his hand drop to his holster and unsnapped the cover to his Remington revolver.

The general looked at him, stunned, and turned a bit to look to either side to see the reaction of others. Some had simply turned and walked away, not wanting to be dragged in as witnesses for a court-martial, which might ruin their furloughs. But at least a few, men obviously from combat commands, just stood there silent . . . none offering support.

With a foul curse the general turned and stalked off. Pleasants spared but a glance to the others. A few nodded approvingly and one half raised a hand in salute. He turned away, and they left him alone.

He gazed at the receding shoreline, but in his mind's eye he could not escape it, even as the miles separated him from his war. It would always be there, the dream, the hope, then the anguish, and the look in a young black soldier's eyes as he gasped out, "I ain't no coward, sir," closing those eyes, standing up to go back in—laden down with canteens of water for his wounded comrades—and dying but seconds later.

Colonel Henry Pleasants of the 48th Pennsylvania, who would miss the trial and thus return unscathed for promotion to brigade command, stood silent. At least for now, the war was over for him.

He lowered his head and silently wept.

CHAPTER FIFTEEN

CITY POINT, VIRGINIA
DAY TWO: COURT OF INQUIRY INTO THE
"INCIDENT" AT THE BATTLE OF THE MINE,
AUGUST 4, 1864

※※※※※※※※※※※※※※※※※※※※※※※※※

IT WAS HOT, BLASTED HOT. JAMES REILLY WIPED THE SWEAT from his face with his bandanna and tried to return to his sketching.

General George Gordon Meade was sitting before the tribunal; his hat was off and his face drenched in sweat like all the others, but his uniform was buttoned up as was proper.

Sitting opposite him was Winfield Scott Hancock, features pale, the heat obviously getting to him. To Hancock's left were Generals Miles and Ayres, to his right Colonel Shriver, inspector general of the Army, and then at the far end of the table a captain who knew this new thing called stenography and was furiously jotting down a word-by-word transcript. The windows were all closed to prevent eaves-dropping, and the audience was a select few of the more important officers of the Army of the Potomac, several others he could not iden-tify, and, finally, himself.

Gaining access had taken some rapid work on his part, a coded message to his friend in the White House that elicited an order sent back down to City Point the next day that an artist should be allowed to be present, as long as he took an oath not to write down any transcription of the session, to repeat not a word of what was being said, and that his drawings were to be released as an historical record only after the hearing had ended.

Meade was in his second and final day of testimony, the opening witness, which struck James as strange. An inquiry such as this should have started with the lowest ranks and then moved up the ladder of command. Any professional or volunteer army officer with a lick of sense knew to take his cues from the rank above if he wished to climb. If his testimony placed blame in the wrong direction, he could find himself stripped of a command and shipped to California to sit out the rest of the war.

Meade was finishing up. His report had been damning. He had adroitly avoided implicating General Grant in any of the decision making, stating that Grant, while in overall command, had seen to diversionary operations directly in front of Richmond to draw off Lee's reserves prior to the attack. He claimed that Grant had agreed with Meade's misgivings about the use of the colored troops for the first wave of the attack, but had, as per standard procedure, given him command of the assault. However, Meade stated that Burnside had tried to sidestep that chain of command with repeated inquiries directly to Grant. Finally, under pressure from Hancock, Meade had at least conceded that Grant had reviewed the plans, as submitted by Burnside, but Meade claimed that he had only given his grudging approval.

As for Grant, his testimony would never be heard; he was back in Washington on "official business."

Meade had testified that his own staff of engineers, all of them West Point men—unlike Burnside's engineers—had expressed misgivings about the amount of powder demanded, saying it was excessive and would have created vertical walls within the crater, making it unusable as a position to be held; that all adequate logistical support had been properly provided; and that it was his own decision to withdraw the black troops from the assault out of fear that fresh untrained men would panic in the opening minutes of the attack and create a debacle.

"Is there anything else that you should wish to add to your testimony?" Colonel Shriver asked, an obvious suggestion that the day's testimony was drawing to a conclusion.

Meade sighed.

"It turned into a tragic affair, we all know that. It could have been a *coup de main*, which might very well have succeeded if my orders had been properly carried out. I did see it as a forlorn hope and thus, as stated, felt that only veteran troops could see such a storming of a heavily entrenched enemy position through to a proper conclusion.

"To expect untried troops to achieve that end was a grave misjudgment on the part of the corps commander directly responsible for the assault."

"Why then did you delay until the last minute in changing the order of battle?" General Miles asked.

James could sense a stiffening on Meade's part, a glance at Miles that must have been chilling. Miles, across the two days, was the only member of the tribunal who had dared to ask pointed questions.

"Gentlemen, the press, as you know, is already commenting on that. I heard today that the *New York Herald*, no friend of the current administration, is declaring that the battle was lost because quote 'the darkies panicked and ran' and that in so doing, they sowed confusion and disorder among the white troops who had already successfully gained a lodgment in the Rebel lines.

"I think it obvious, gentlemen, that my decision was based upon sound military logic and my many years of service, dating clear back to Mexico and the campaigns in the West. If you wish a job done properly, you need professionals do to it, not amateurs, be they officers or enlisted men.

"I bear no prejudice against the colored troops. Their role in support positions for this army will free thousands of troops with experience for the front lines. Given seasoning on quieter fronts, I believe, over time, they can prove themselves. There was no time for that seasoning or for any gradual breaking in of those troops to a combat role. In their first action, to send them into that kind of frontal assault was a decision of utmost folly. If I failed, it was in deferring too long to one of my corps commanders."

As he said this Meade nodded to Winfield Scott Hancock, a man who, like him, had risen rapidly from brigade to division and then to corps command.

"But to answer your question: After a final reconnaissance of the Rebel position the day before the planned assault, and the analysis of how many reserves of the Confederates that General Grant had been able to draw off by diversionary actions north of the James River and around Richmond, it became clear to me that the decision to send untested troops into a frontal assault, against the flanks of the enemy line outside the perimeter of the explosion, would be a grave error. Their slaughter would have raised an even louder outcry with some in the press and general public. It would have sown panic among the follow-up divisions, and what little we did gain in this action would instead have been, far worse, a bloody repulse all along the entire front."

He fell silent.

James knew that he himself must remain silent, as it was only by covertly contacting Lincoln that he was even in this room, and to express anything, even a slight expression of disdain, might result in his ejection. He kept his eyes focused on his sketchpad, not even writing down a word or two of what had just been said. A provost guard had been ordered to inspect his sketches at the end of each day to insure no testimony had been jotted down.

Hancock leaned back in his chair.

"Gentlemen, are there any other questions?"

He looked to the other three on the board and there was a shaking of heads.

Winfield stood, in his role as head of the board of inquiry, for the moment at an end, and now rather than addressing a witness, he was again speaking to his commanding officer.

"General Meade, we thank you for your testimony, sir."

As Meade stood, Winfield saluted; Meade returned the salute, put on his hat, and walked out of the stifling room; all within breathed a sigh of relief. With the opening of the door, the heated air within could escape, a somewhat cooler breeze wafting in.

James looked down at his sketch. Drips of sweat had marred it, so he would have to redo it later. He waited until the others left, and then followed them out. A captain with the provost guard imperiously held out a hand for James to turn over his sketchbook, which the captain thumbed through, nodded, and handed back to him without a word.

James stood outside the doorway. The building they were in had been thrown up over the last month by the army. It was now part of a long array of clapboard and split-log structures lining the bluffs, which were quarters for staff supervising the rear area of the siege lines. The river was dotted with ships of every description, from tugs and side-wheelers to ironclad monitors and even one deepwater frigate. The quayside was lined with dozens of vessels, where supplies were being offloaded. An inclined rail powered by a steam engine mounted atop the bluff hoisted up the heavier loads.

The military railroad crews were even now laying out a narrow gauge–track line to run parallel to the siege line. Soon supplies could be raced within a matter of hours twenty miles off to the far western flank, which every day crept farther and farther out, drawing the Rebel forces ever thinner, like a taut bowstring that would eventually snap.

Hundreds of empty wagons, teams hitched, moved in an endless cycle, coming down one road and pulling into a field just behind the rows of cabins and warehouses to be loaded with rations, ammunition, medical supplies, tentage, boots, uniforms, and barrels of whiskey on consignment for sutlers. There was fine champagne and fresh Chesapeake oysters packed in ice for the officers. Only minutes later the wagons would be sent back up another road to their destinations in front of Petersburg.

He looked to the west, from which came a continual thumping, the siege guns at work. The horizon was cloaked in dust from the gunfire and bursting shells. And, as always, there was the relentless digging of over two hundred thousand men, men who, when not shooting, were digging trenches, and more trenches . . . but no more tunnels.

DAY FIVE: COURT OF INQUIRY INTO THE "INCIDENT" AT THE BATTLE OF THE MINE, AUGUST 7, 1864

✳✳✳✳✳✳✳✳✳✳✳✳✳✳✳✳✳✳✳✳✳✳✳✳✳✳

"General Burnside, I must return to a most fundamental question, which has disturbed me ever since first hearing of it."

James looked up from his sketchpad. It was obvious Colonel Shriver would not let go of this point, and it was indeed the weak link in Burnside's entire defense.

Burnside, towering in both bulk and height above all the others in this room, looked almost shrunken in the chair before the board. *At least he was not wearing his absurd hat*, James thought gratefully. He struggled in his drawings to make Burnside look as dignified as possible, deemphasizing his outlandish whiskers and bristling mustache, making his ill-fitting uniform look trim and proper, the way Hancock always looked, trying to give him a demeanor of dignity rather than, as he now looked, beaten and defensive, like a stock character in a bad melodrama being castigated in the final act.

Burnside merely nodded.

"This strange, must I say, outlandish decision of yours to select the lead division for the attack by the drawing of straws. What logic drove you to that decision?"

Burnside wearily shook his head. It made Reilly think of a cruelty he had seen more than once as a young man: the atrocity of bear baiting—where a chained bear would have a pack of dogs unleashed upon him, while a crowd, sick with bloodlust, circled about, cheering, placing bets as to which dog would finally deliver the fatal bite to the throat, or how many dogs would first be killed. The bear in its final moments often reared back, as if knowing its fate, ready to offer one more burst of defiance before finally collapsing.

"As I have explained," Burnside replied, his voice barely above a whisper, "the decision of the commander in the field, General Meade, was not finalized until less than eighteen hours before the assault was scheduled to begin."

"That is not the question," Shriver replied sharply, cutting him off.

"I know. I know that," Burnside replied, fixing the inspector general with what could be seen by all as a hateful gaze.

"But it is relevant to the question you have presented, yet again."

Hancock held his hand up in a gesture for silence.

"Please continue but contain your answer to the question at hand, General Burnside," Hancock interjected.

"As I have stated already," Burnside finally continued, "I sought from one of my three other division commanders a volunteer to lead the assault and none was forthcoming. All knew the unique . . ."

His voice trailed off for a moment.

With a stronger, more determined voice he continued, "They knew the desperate nature of the assault now that the plans had been changed by the general commanding."

Shriver slammed an open hand on the table.

"Please answer the question, sir."

"I am answering the question," Burnside snapped.

Shriver looked to the stenographer.

"Since this exchange is not relevant to the issue under investigation, I order you to strike this last exchange from the records."

The captain, not raising his head, simply nodded, his pencil moving to cross out the previous lines.

Burnside shook his head, again looking to James like a weary bear.

"None of my three other division commanders having volunteered, I felt that in all fairness, the only choice left was to leave it to fate, and thus my decision that they should draw straws."

"So you therefore failed to make a command decision?" Shriver asked, his voice tinged with sarcasm.

"I offered a fair chance," Burnside retorted.

"After General Ledlie drew the short straw, did you personally see to him, ensuring that proper orders as to what was expected of him and his command were conveyed, proper equipment issued, proper orders conveyed to his brigade and regimental commanders?"

"The plan, sir, had been a month in the making and in the training, and then the general in command, with only eighteen hours to go, changed everything. How, sir, was I to compensate for that in the time allotted?"

"That is enough, sir, answer the question, and refrain from answering a question with a question."

"I am answering the question, damn you," Burnside, snapped, as if rallying for one final act of defiance. "If he had ordered the change two days or, better yet, a week in advance, much would have been done differently."

"That is not my question."

"But it is my question!" Burnside shouted.

"Strike this from the record."

"Go ahead and strike it, but you all know it to be true."

Burnside, who was half standing as he exploded with rage, fell back into his chair.

Hancock leaned forward, looking at the stenographer.

"Please strike that last exchange."

"And cover it over," Burnside whispered.

"Sir?" For one of the few times in the inquiry so far, Hancock showed anger.

"I am in command of this hearing, sir," Hancock said, his voice pitched low and menacing.

Burnside glared at him but did not reply.

The stare down continued for a long moment, until Burnside finally lowered his gaze.

"Now, answer the question as presented by the inspector general as to whether you conveyed proper orders to General Ledlie in regard to the change in plans and what was expected of his command."

"Sir," Burnside sighed, "I placed my trust that General Ledlie would see to such details . . ." and again his voice trailed off.

"Why did you not accompany him and personally supervise the

briefings of his brigade and regimental commanders as many of those here have done?" Shriver paused, looking pointedly at Hancock. "It would follow as a normal part of your duties."

"I had not slept in two days, sir."

"What?"

"Just that. What with the change of . . ." he paused, looking over at the stenographer. "With all the duties to attend to prior to such a complex action, I had not slept in two days. For the sake of my ability to lead the action before dawn the following morning, I thought it important to at least try and get some rest."

James contained his sadness and frustration. He cared deeply for this man, who had shown such openness in how he had greeted the Fourth Division into his ranks, but here, indeed, he had utterly failed. An hour or two of work, of calling in the gallant Bartlett and his other brigade commanders to insure that the transfer of footbridges and axes from the men leading the two columns had been seen to, would perhaps have made all the difference.

"And when did you learn that such information and necessary equipment had not been conveyed?" Shriver pressed.

"Not until after the assault began."

"Did you not think it your duty to go forward and check prior to darkness and deployment of his division?"

"I trusted that General Ledlie would see to such issues. Beyond the extensive training given to the men of my Fourth Division, the other three division commanders had been briefed on their roles once the attack began."

"But those orders had been changed. Should you not have ensured your new orders were properly followed by those under you?"

"I trusted my division commanders," Burnside replied woodenly, and James sighed inwardly at the response.

"And when did you finally learn that General Ledlie had utterly failed to convey any information whatsoever to his brigade commanders; that they were tasked with seizing the Jerusalem Plank Road and the Blandford Church Cemetery, rather than simply charging into the crater left by the mine and hiding there? When did you learn that, in fact, General Ledlie was hiding drunk in a bunker behind the lines?"

Hancock cleared his throat and leaned forward.

"Strike that question please," he said softly, looking over at the stenographer, and he fixed Shriver with his gaze.

"Whether General Ledlie acted properly as an officer in command of a division or was in dereliction of duty has yet to be established, sir," Hancock announced. "Such a line of questioning of his character must wait until he himself is called before this board."

"My apologies, sir," Shriver replied but, as with any lawyer overruled, it was obvious he knew his point had been made.

Burnside blew out noisily, reaching into his breast pocket for another cigar, his eighth of the day, lit it, and leaned forward.

"As to the first part of your question: only after the assault had begun and I saw the men of the First Division go into the crater and not proceed on."

"Why did you not react, then?" Shriver pressed.

"I was at my headquarters and felt my responsibility was to be in communication with General Meade via telegraph at his headquarters, which were removed from my position by a distance of eight hundred yards."

No one spoke for a moment and finally it was Hancock who broke the silence.

"Sir, you and I have held the same position in the field as corps commander. Did the thought ever occur to ride forward and take direct command of the action and set things straight?"

James looked up from his pad. The question that zeroed in on the key point had at last been asked. Only Hancock, known as one of the bravest fighting commanders in the army, could ask it of another corps commander.

Burnside sat silent and then, with a gesture that James sensed was one of inner agony, answered the question that he had replayed in his soul a thousand times since that fight.

"Yes," he whispered. "I should have."

Shriver leaned forward as if to press a point home, but a gesture from Hancock, a rapping of his knuckles on the table, silenced him.

With those few words, Major General Ambrose Burnside had just professionally ruined himself. No matter his admiration for the man, James knew that without doubt he was now doomed. As Napoleon should have gone forward to join his Imperial Guard at Waterloo, and McClellan should have crossed Antietam Creek to press the final attack that could have ended the war nearly two years ago, Burnside's failure to act would haunt him to his dying day. He was not a coward, but he had become paralyzed. Tied to a telegraph, tied by a misplaced sense of loyalty to division commanders of either little competence or outright cowardice, he should have gone forward, the telegraph to Meade be damned.

Had Burnside ridden before the men of the Fourth Division, sword raised, calling upon them to stand up and follow him to glory, this tragic moment would never have occurred. There would have been either victory or a death befitting a corps commander, placing his memory alongside those of men like Reynolds at Gettysburg, Sedgwick at Spotsylvania, and even Stonewall Jackson at Chancellorsville. He would then have been forever spared the humiliation he was now going through.

Ambrose Burnside would be damned with the greatest burden that any man could ever carry, any man at least with a sense of duty, a sense of responsibility for the lives of others . . . He had failed the men who had entrusted their lives to him and now must live with that forever, because so many of them had died uselessly as a result of his personal failure.

Burnside lowered his head, unable to meet Hancock's gaze. The broader issue of Meade's obvious interference, and as James believed, his outright derailment of the battle plan from either jealousy or incompetence on his own part, had become moot.

The legend already building that, as the newspaper put it, the "darkies had panicked and ran," was now combined, as a means of shifting blame, with the failure of Burnside to ensure that proper orders had been given and followed. And if they had not been properly followed, his failure to have gone forward personally and, if need be, to die setting matters straight.

Burnside was doomed.

"It is the most unorthodox process of command decision I have encountered in this war," General Ayres sighed, shaking his head.

Burnside did not reply.

"Is there anything else before we conclude General Burnside's testimony?" Hancock asked.

He looked back and forth down the length of the table. No one spoke. It was evident that Shriver wished to press for more, but a cold glance from Hancock stilled his pursuit.

"General Burnside, you are excused and this inquiry is closed for the day."

Again the ritual of salutes, and the group left the room. James's sketches were again checked for notes before he was allowed to depart. The meeting had been convened late, this day, in a vain attempt to avoid the worst of the midday heat, so that the first stars of evening and a new moon shone overhead.

"Mr. Reilly?"

He turned; it was Captain Vincent, one of Burnside's staff. He went over to the man's side.

"How did it go in there?" Vincent asked, looking around conspiratorially.

"You must know I am pledged to silence. Ask General Burnside, instead of me."

Vincent put his hand on James's shoulder and led him a few dozen paces away from the others, who were calling for their mounts, and away from the usual press of correspondents hoping to get some indication of what was transpiring within.

"Can we take a walk for a few minutes?"

"Certainly."

Vincent made a point of offering a flask and then a cigar, both of which James gladly took.

"You are an unusual man, Reilly," Vincent said.

"How so?"

"You seem to have an uncanny knack for being at a crucial place at precisely the right time."

"It's my job," James replied cautiously. "Stay at the front long enough and you develop an instinct as to where things might get hot. If I'm to do my job, I have to be there."

"A lot of others though, Nast, for example, and most of the print correspondents, find it easy enough to sit back at some headquarters and report from there."

James did not reply, puffing on his cigar, stopping to look up at the emerging stars, breathing in the first hint of cool evening air.

"It is just that a few eyebrows were raised at the sudden order to allow you into the court of inquiry."

James blew out the cigar smoke, actually succeeding in making a ring, watching it float up.

"My editor with *Harper's* knows a few strings to pull."

"Spying works both ways, Reilly."

"Sir?"

"You spied on Colonel Pleasants, didn't you, when he was in Washington last month? Followed him to that instrument-maker's store."

"Just curious. Rumors were already flying that something was afoot with that regiment."

"Why were you in Washington that day?"

"To turn in my latest sketches to an assistant editor there. I don't trust them to the packets and couriers."

"Mind if I have my flask back?" Vincent asked, and James, realizing he had been hanging on to it, passed it over.

Vincent took a long gulp and handed it back.

"That's good single malt Scotch; I have a supplier in Washington, actually my brother, who takes care of me."

"It is good stuff," James replied, glad for another sip.

"As I was saying, Mr. Reilly, spying works both ways."

"I don't follow you."

"You were seen going to the White House a bit later that day, and you spent over an hour and a half there."

"What is this?" James snapped, stopping to look straight at Vincent.

"Yes, sir, exactly what is this?" Vincent replied.

There was a moment of silence.

"Colonel Pleasants had noticed you trailing him, and he decided to do a little stealth himself. Purely patriotic, I must add; he thought you might be covering as a Rebel spy. Otherwise, why your curiosity as to his business and what he was purchasing? Then he saw you go into the White House."

"And?"

"He reported that to me."

"But you still allowed me to observe the men of the Fourth Division and even to see the tunnel. Rather foolish if you thought I was a Rebel spy."

"But not if you were a spy for the White House."

"What?" James tried to put on his best acting ability to act surprised and outraged.

Vincent laughed softly.

"My brother was invalided out of the army after Antietam; a good old Hoosier boy, same as me. I was too young to know Mr. Lincoln well, other than to see him about Springfield at times, but my family knew Mr. Lincoln and my brother got a slot as an assistant secretary after he was discharged, working for an old friend of his, Mr. Hay. Ever hear of Hay?"

Reilly was silent. Of course he had; he was Lincoln's right-hand man.

"So I ran a little query up to him, described you, and my brother wrote back."

Vincent fished in his breast pocket and drew out a letter.

"Remembered you well. Says you have been in and out of Lincoln's personal quarters a number of times. Never listed on the official roster of visitors, which he was required to keep, but on occasion, after you left, the President would confer with Mr. Hay and some interesting orders might fly. Never once, though, was your name entered in any record of meetings with the President.

"My brother poked around a bit more and it turned out that years ago Mr. Lincoln took you in right after you came over from Ireland. You worked in his office for nearly two years as a janitor and then suddenly a 'benefactor' sent you off to a school to be trained as an artist. Then you crop up again with some most flattering sketches of Abe in the '58 and '60 campaigns."

"I admire the man, no sin in that."

He would not let it show that this man's depth of knowledge of his other life had shaken him a bit. Though he knew with almost complete certainty that Lincoln had helped with his education, it was still something of an embarrassment that he had relied on a charity of a friend to launch his life.

"And then the day this court convenes an order comes down through the war office granting you access?"

"Nothing unusual about that," James said, making a show of nonchalance while taking a long gulp of the single malt and handing it back.

"I think you have two jobs here, Mr. Reilly, and one of them is most definitely more important than *Harper's Weekly.*"

James tried to force a chuckle as he handed the flask back.

"And I think you are man enough, that even if cornered as you are now, you would not say a word."

James took the flask back, and in a display of Irish bravado drained the rest of it off before handing it back yet again.

"Anything else?" he asked, even as the Scotch hit his head, making him feel a bit light.

'Would you come with me?"

"Certainly. Am I under arrest or something?"

"No, not at all."

He led James down a row of rough-hewn cabins, stopping for a moment when they both saw General Ayres standing in the middle of the dusty street, talking with several others, waiting until that group had moved on.

Vincent opened the door of a cabin which was typical of field army construction; it was ten feet by twelve, with four bunks and no windows, and the air within was stuffy. By the light of a coal oil lamp a couple of officers, jackets off, sat around a small table, not much more than an oversized stool, playing cards. James recognized them as men of Burnside's staff.

"How'd it go?" one of them asked, looking up at Vincent.

"Would you gentlemen please excuse us for a few minutes?" Vincent asked.

Without comment, the two dropped their cards, had a bit of a squabble for a few seconds as to who owned the dimes and quarters in the middle of the table, and left.

Vincent watched them leave and then nodded for James to sit down on the far side of the low squat table. Going to his bunk he pulled out a haversack, sat down across from James, opened the canvas bag, which was waterproofed with black tar—standard army issue for an infantry man—reached inside, and pulled out a sheaf of papers and tossed them over.

"Go ahead, read them."

There were a couple of hundred pages and slips of paper. James picked one up, a slip of blue foolscap, the handwriting, in pencil, barely legible. He squinted and Vincent produced a second coal oil lamp, lit it, and set it on the table.

It was dated 2:00 P.M., July 30th from Headquarters, Army of the Potomac:

United States Military Telegraph.

The commanding general wishes to know if the crater is still in our hands and if so what actions you are now taking.

My God, that was when we were running for our lives, he thought, remembering how General Bartlett had shouted for them, especially the black soldiers, to flee while they still could. He recalled a staff officer with Bartlett taking out his pocket watch, only seconds before he would be killed, announcing the time.

And the commanding general was sending a telegram to Burnside asking if the position was still being held? Damn him, could he not see it with his own eyes?

"Look at this one," Vincent whispered, fishing out a sheet of paper and handing it over.

It was dated 8:00 P.M.; darkness would have already settled; another inquiry from Meade as to whether the crater was "still in our hands."

In our hands? If one could say it was filled with dead and wounded, perhaps, then.

"And here's another," Vincent said, handing a sheet over, dated 10:35 P.M., July 31st, with the same inquiry; Burnside had not replied to the telegram of 8:00 P.M.

"And now this one," Vincent said, and he all but threw the sheet at James.

It was dated August 1st, 10:00 A.M. and James felt even more rage. It was a query from Meade demanding to know who had authorized the raising of a flag of truce in front of Ninth Corps position. Meade wrote that requesting a truce rested solely with the commander on the field, that it was a mark of concession of defeat, and then ordered Burnside to immediately lower that flag and resume firing upon the enemy; all this while rescue parties from both sides were beginning to evacuate the wounded and clear the dead for burial.

James let the paper drop and just looked at Vincent.

"Why are you showing these to me, and where in hell did you get them?"

"The second question first," Vincent replied. He went back to his bunk, got out a half empty quart bottle of the single malt and set it down on the table; James gladly took a drink while sifting through the other papers. There were fragments of telegraphs, memos of requisitions for supplies for the construction of the tunnel and then the blasting of the mine, training orders for the Fourth Division, diagrams of the planned assault after the explosion to seize Blandford Church Hill and Petersburg beyond. Additionally, there were copies of the telegrams that had been fired back and forth between Meade and Burnside throughout that long bloody day and well into the next, while the two were in their individual bunkers less than eight hundred yards apart and both just eight hundred yards from the slaughter-ground of the crater.

Vincent took a long pull on the bottle, and it was obvious he was more than a little drunk.

"Where in hell did you get these?" James asked.

Vincent laughed and shook his head, offering the bottle. James was tempted but felt he needed to keep his head and refused.

"Did you know that Meade ordered the arrest of our telegraphy team at the end of the battle?"

"What?"

"Yup. Said they had been privy to private correspondence and were to be placed under arrest, with copies of all papers and notes to be confiscated.

"Of course, old Ambrose refused to comply, said the men were acting under his orders and merely doing their duty. A couple of provosts were sent down from Meade's headquarters to bring them in. Oh, that created a bit of a row there for a few minutes."

Vincent chuckled and took another sip.

"Our provosts refused to accept their provosts until they presented proper identification. Of course Ambrose was buying time, while several of us furiously wrote down copies of everything before we finally let those bastards into our command center to scoop everything up and to lead those poor damn telegraphers away. Chances are those lads will at least live out the war, most likely keying telegraphs up in Bangor, Maine.

"You saw them yesterday, when General Burnside finally went before the Board. He had a satchel full of these papers, which he asked to submit to the board and was refused. That damn weasel Shriver said that submissions of written documentation would take place at the appropriate time and place, and given what he called 'the sensitive nature' of personal correspondence involving General Meade which might have a bearing on current operations, copies from Meade would be sufficient after being properly vetted for reasons of military security."

Vincent, as if having exhausted himself by that statement, just sighed and sat back in his chair.

"Those are copies of copies by the way, but I swear to you they are all valid."

"Why give them to me?"

Vincent gave a strange conspiratorial wink.

"Someone outside the army needs to see them."

James looked back down at the papers, pushing them about, picking up one and then another to scan for a few lines, and he felt a rising anger.

"If you think I am going to hand them to my newspaper you can go to hell," James snapped. "The last thing we need is for the Rebels to see this."

Vincent chuckled softly.

"If you had said anything different I'd of taken them back by now or put a bullet through your head if you tried to walk out of here with them."

"Why not send them yourself to your brother?"

"A lot can happen to papers being shipped. Someone might get curious as to why a staff officer with Burnside is sending a package to the White House. My brother is only an assistant to an assistant. You know how that could go . . ."

His voice trailed off.

"But if someone was to hand them directly to the President . . ."

James reached over and took the bottle and allowed himself the indulgence.

He gazed straight at Vincent but did not offer a denial.

"So it is true, you do spy for Lincoln?"

James looked at him cold-eyed and said nothing.

"It's all finished here," Vincent said, voice slurring. "You saw it today. Oh, sure, the inquiry will go through the motions for the next few weeks, but Meade has spoken and Burnside has followed. Anyone with a lick of sense knows it should have started with the testimony of Colonel Pleasants."

"Where is he?"

Vincent smiled.

"Ambrose is loyal to his own. He got him the hell out of here, yesterday. The poor naïve fool wanted to tell the truth, and Ambrose knew the order of testimony already. Pleasants would have taken blame as well and the general would not allow that to happen.

Besides, what good would his testimony do before a board whose orders were already clearly laid out?

"It should have started from the bottom up. Regimental commanders like Pleasants, then those brigade commanders who went into the fight and got out of it, especially Siegfried and Thomas, who commanded the colored troops and in with them. Then those bastards Ledlie and Ferrero and that fool Potter, though I will say Wilcox is halfway decent. Then, only at the end of it all, to Burnside and Meade. Instead every single man will take his cue from the top down, the decision already obvious. Burnside, Ninth Corps, and the colored boys will take the blame and that will be the end of it."

"That's obvious, but why give these papers to me?"

"Let's stop the game playing, Reilly. I know, now even Burnside knows, who you are."

James took another look sip on the bottle.

"And even if that were true, what will you want of me in exchange?"

Vincent laughed softly.

"Nothing."

"What?"

"The outcome is obvious, isn't it? Ledlie will be drummed out and good riddance to him."

"Why did General Burnside ever place his trust in such a man to start with?" James asked. "I was in the crater and saw General Bartlett. By God, if that man had been in command of the division and properly briefed I daresay we could have still won the day. I met him as his brigade was going in, and he was in a fury; he had no idea whatsoever what his orders were, other than a vague notion to seize the crater.

"Burnside should have briefed him."

"Lord knows I love that rather strange man," Vincent sighed, taking the bottle back from James. "I've been with Burnside since New Bern. At times he's a bloody genius: New Bern, Knoxville, his original plan for this fight . . . but at other times . . ."

He sighed.

"He seems to become someone else. His mind becomes hesitating, slow, unable to make a decision, as if a fog has wrapped around his brain. You know, they said the same was true of Grant before he was weaned from the bottle, and of McClellan it was definitely true. I was with Burnside at Antietam and all of us were driven half crazy with his obsession to take that one damn bridge when, in fact, the entire creek could have been forded by waves of infantry and have turned Lee's flank by midday.

"But any who serve with that man will tell you this: that he is loyal to those who serve him. And maybe that is his curse. More than one of us tried to tell him Ledlie and even Ferrero were poor choices for division command, but he would just give that strange chuckle and say, 'Let 'em prove themselves first and then we shall see.'"

Vincent sighed.

"And he shall be destroyed and hanged."

"Oh, for God's sake, I keep hearing talk about hangings. We don't hang generals anymore," James said.

Vincent laughed.

"Rank does have its privileges, though in this case I think it will be more humane. Word is that a strong suggestion will be made that he agree to go home on personal leave. He will go back to Rhode Island, and then when enough time has passed and public attention focused elsewhere, he will be quietly told his services are no longer needed and that a resignation would be appreciated.

"Ledlie, maybe Ferrero, will be drummed out. There's no way in hell they can be let off without at least that," and Vincent's words were now bitter.

"And Meade?"

"Nothing. Of course nothing, though I daresay that henceforth he won't be able to sneeze without Grant standing over his shoulder with a handkerchief ready."

"But why, damn it?"

"Because we are losing this war," Vincent snapped. "Yes, things look promising with Sherman, but the election is only three months off. Unless someone pulls a miracle, and at this point it looks like it will have to be Sherman, Lincoln will lose and the opposition will end the conflict and all this sacrifice will be for naught. Drumming out Meade will only shake public confidence still more. Hanging Burnside and his division commanders with the blame will shift attention from where it belongs."

"And the men of the Fourth, what of them?" James asked bitterly. "I went in with them."

"I know."

"I saw their valor and by God above, if they had led the attack, we would be celebrating the end of the war in Richmond this day. We were so close, so damn close . . ."

His voice trailed off and he realized he had drunk too much and was on the point of tears of rage and frustration.

"I know," Vincent said softly. "And Burnside knows your feelings on that as well. Reilly, there were a couple of our staff watching you and how you handled their story. Burnside knows how you feel."

Reilly said nothing, a bit shamed that here he had thought himself so clever and yet these men had figured it all out.

"They will take the blame," Vincent sighed. "You saw the *New York Herald*. All the papers are trumpeting now that 'the darkies panicked,' that the battle was going apace until the 'colored division was pushed in and triggered a general rout.'"

"Damn whoever wrote that."

"It is now the convenient excuse. This was not a defeat of General Meade and the glorious Army of the Potomac, which, by God, really is a glorious army. Instead it was a defeat of outsiders, of our old Ninth Corps, wanderers from one front to the other, from Vicksburg and Louisiana to North Carolina and Tennessee and now here. Orphans, called in to fill out the ranks for awhile but never really belonging. And now the same is true of the colored. They weren't really 'one of us,' so who could expect anything different?"

"We could have expected so much more and seen so much more if they had been given their fair chance."

Vincent nodded, taking the bottle back from James.

"Take the papers and share them with that friend of yours. Maybe someday history will tell the truth."

"And you? What of you?"

"Oh, I'm one of the fallen," Vincent replied. "I've been in this war for three years and maybe I've seen enough. I'll go into exile with Burnside. Maybe it's time I go home, too . . ."

He looked down at the papers on the table, as if struggling for control.

"Maybe someday I'll feel that I did something right for my country after all."

He looked up at James, tears in his eyes.

"That's all I ever really wanted to do, Mr. Reilly: to serve my country. And giving these papers to you . . ."

His voice trailed off.

"Please just tell the truth to someone."

CHAPTER SIXTEEN

WASHINGTON, D.C.
SEPTEMBER 3, 1864

****

"MERCIFUL HEAVENS, JAMES, HOW ARE YOU?"

"Doing fairly, sir," he lied, as he stepped into the President's office. He had not slept in more than three days, and it had been weeks since he had shaved, let alone bathed or even changed his clothes. Ground into his trousers, duster jacket, broken-down slouch cap, and every pore of his body was the accumulation of two months of Virginia clay and sand and the stench of battle and trenches.

A more rational voice in his head had whispered that, before coming here, he should have gone straight to the Willard, ordered the best room in the house with the new-fangled plumbing—which included a tub that could actually be filled straight from a tap with hot water and an indoor toilet that flushed—and had someone sent down to the Brooks store with orders for a complete new set of clothes.

But, he decided, the hell with that; he'd do it later and charge the bill to *Harper's*. If they hollered, they could take it out of their payment for his sketches. That is, if they accepted any . . . and if they didn't, the hell with them, too.

Lincoln looked at him appraisingly and James felt a slight

embarrassment—coming to the White House like this, as if he had put on some sort of costume. Another part of him, however, no longer cared. Let this man, his old friend and benefactor, the man who commanded all the armies of the Republic, see what battlefield reality looked and smelled like.

"Sit down, son," Lincoln said softly, gesturing to a sofa of green velvet.

James hesitated; it looked far too clean.

"Oh, don't worry. Mary picked it out and personally, I think the thing is an overdone gewgaw. Mess it up all you wish, it'll be an excuse to get rid of it."

That simple gesture and comment disarmed him a bit, deflating some of the anger that had begun to smolder as he came up the walkway. He had reacted to the neatly trimmed guards blocking his way and a captain wrinkling his nose as if confronted by a beggar. He had wanted to ask the man if he had ever seen an actual Reb coming straight at him with bayonet leveled or if he had held a dying comrade—but he already knew the answer. The captain had gazed suspiciously at the precious pass he always kept concealed in his wallet, signed by Lincoln, to admit this bearer to his presence whenever and wherever presented.

The captain had made him stand outside in the evening drizzle for twenty minutes before returning, obviously a bit surprised by the order to escort him straight to the President's private office on the second floor.

"Coffee?" Lincoln asked as he came into the room, grabbing hold of James's hand as he guided him to the sofa.

"Yes, sir, thank you."

Lincoln pulled open the door to Hay's office and called for a fresh pot. Before Lincoln could close it, James walked over to stand by Lincoln and saw a clerk, crutches set to the side of his desk, left pant leg empty below the knee.

The resemblance was there.

"Mr. Vincent?" James asked.

A bit startled, the clerk looked up at him, gaze shifting from Lincoln and then to Hay, and he nodded.

"Your brother, Captain Vincent, sends his regards, though I've not seen him in a couple of weeks."

The clerk said nothing for a moment.

"He went back to Rhode Island with General Burnside," the clerk finally replied, "and from there back to our parents' home in Lafayette, Indiana."

"He's safely out of the war then, that's good."

Lincoln looked at the clerk and confusedly back to James.

"Mr. Vincent, there," James said, "is actually a rather good spy, sir."

Lincoln started to bristle and James shook his head.

"No, sir; no, don't blame him. He was curious about me and as the saying goes, 'tipped off' his brother on Burnside's staff that I might be more than just an artist. My compliments to him. It might actually have helped me . . . and you, sir."

There was an awkward moment until a colored servant came in, bearing a silver tray with a steaming pot of coffee, two delicate china cups, and silver bowls for cream and sugar. The servant edged his way into the office and set his burden down.

It was obvious that Vincent was nervous over the encounter, and James finally went over and shook his hand.

"You did the right thing, both as a man working for the President and for a brother in service to General Burnside. In the end it actually helped me with my own duties."

He looked back to Lincoln, who finally nodded an approval, and he followed the President back into his office, the tall gaunt man forcefully closing the door.

"Don't blame him; that was rude of me to bring him out like that. I guess I'm just tired."

"Frankly, James, you look like a cat that's been dragged through a gutter and then chewed on a bit for good measure."

James tried to smile, rubbing what was becoming a red beard flecked with streaks of gray and then looking down at his stained, grime-encrusted trousers—some of the stains from the blood of comrades.

"Face of war," James finally whispered.

"You wanted me to see you like this, didn't you?"

James suddenly felt embarrassed.

"I went to Antietam a couple of weeks after the fight there. I saw thousands of boys like you; smelled it, too, not just them but the graves washed out by the rains." Lincoln looked off. "You didn't need to try and show me something as though I am not already aware of it."

As he spoke the President played the proper host and poured a cup of coffee, motioned to the cream and sugar, which James refused, and handed the cup over. He was grateful for the hot brew; it was real coffee, damn good coffee, and he took a sip.

At that instant there was a brilliant flash of light outside the window, a split second later a window-shaking boom. Startled, James crouched down, as if ready to dive to the floor, dropping the cup and breaking it.

Another boom and then another and another . . .

Lincoln put a soothing hand on his shoulder.

"I should have thought of that and warned you. You must have heard the news by now, confirmed today that General Sherman has occupied Atlanta. The siege is over, an enormous victory won. A hundred-gun salute, along with fireworks, has been ordered for tonight in Lafayette Park."

Embarrassed, James looked down at the fine china, lying in fragments, the coffee soaking into the carpet.

Lincoln stood up, went to the door, cracked it open, and a moment later the servant returned bearing towels and another cup. James looked at the man closely. He was elderly, perhaps in his sixties, his white hair offsetting dark ebony features, which lent him a certain dignity.

"Sorry to trouble you with this, Quincy," Lincoln offered.

"Oh, no trouble at all, Mr. President, no trouble at all."

He was down on his knees, spreading out the towels, soaking up the coffee, and scrubbing hard. He glanced up at James and made eye contact, and then started to lower his eyes.

"Quincy, is it?" James asked.

A bit startled, the man looked at him and just nodded.

He thought of Garland, a few short years ago. That man, of such courage and dignity, would have been performing the same task at the Washington home of Senator Toombs, mopping up the spilled drink of a guest who was a bit too rattled, or more likely, a bit too drunk, and he would have done so with eyes averted.

"I'm sorry to have caused you trouble, Quincy," James offered.

"Oh, it's no trouble at all, sir."

"Quincy, do you have any sons?"

"Sir?"

"Do you have any sons?"

"Yes, sir."

"Where are they?"

"Why, in the army, of course," and there was a note of pride, but he could sense something else.

"Which regiments?"

"Both with the 32nd USCT."

"So they were in the battle at Petersburg a month ago?"

"Yes, sir," and the old man paused.

"Have you heard from them?"

Quincy hesitated.

"My oldest, yes. He got through fine, but my youngest . . ." and his voice trailed off.

James looked up at the President, who emphatically shook his head not to pursue the conversation further.

"I was with them in that fight," James said, ignoring Lincoln's warning. "I have never seen men go forward so gallantly."

"Perhaps, Lord willing, he is simply a prisoner and all will still be well," Lincoln whispered.

James knew it was most likely a lie, remembering the crater at night, the torches and the bodies being mined out to be thrown into unmarked graves behind Rebel lines.

Quincy could only nod. Finished with scrubbing up the spill, he stood and looked straight at James.

"You were there, sir?"

"Yes."

"I've been reading the papers, things people are saying, and . . ."

James stepped forward and put a hand on Quincy's shoulder.

"Believe not a word of it. I was there; I saw it all. Your sons went in like heroes, like men of war, and the truth will come out in the end."

Quincy lowered his head, and James felt a stab to the heart, for it was obvious the man was struggling not to cry.

Without a word, clutching the soiled towels, he left the room.

James looked back at Lincoln.

"Sorry, maybe I shouldn't have done that."

The booming outside continued and this time James only filled his cup halfway.

"The whole town is going wild with celebration tonight," Lincoln said, and James could detect a certain note of happiness in the man's voice, "more so than after news of Vicksburg."

"Makes it rather clear, doesn't it?" James replied.

"What?"

"You will win the election in November."

Lincoln sighed and looked at him, eyes a bit cold.

"You know how I would prefer to win, and that is without the blood of one more soldier being spilled."

"Sorry, sir," and James shook his head. "Maybe I should have waited till tomorrow to come here."

"No, James. I sent the order for you to report back immediately, before the trial was finished, and you did as ordered."

"At least changed, perhaps?"

Lincoln chuckled, "I've smelled worse . . ."

"So where do we start?" Lincoln finally asked, breaking a long silence while outside the window the guns continued to fire. A band struck up a series of jaunty patriotic airs, voices joined in . . . something he had not heard in a long time from the soldiers back at the front . . . Except for the day the men of the Fourth had crossed the bridge over the James.

"I don't know, sir," James whispered.

"The trial, it wraps up in a few days. What do you think will be the conclusions? What happened? I have time tonight; I was never one for impromptu speeches out there," and he gestured out the window toward the celebration.

"You should have the full printed transcript within a few days, sir."

"But it is your impressions I seek."

"A whitewash, a complete cover over."

"Go on."

James poured another cup, again only half full, and sipped it, glad for the warmth as he spoke. He described the impact of starting the testimony at the top ranks first, making clear to all subservient ranks the way events should be reported; how, halfway through the trial, one brave colonel of a Connecticut regiment dared to defy the entire process, denounced all the previous testimony, and announced that the black troops had fought with valor and if the plan had been left unhampered, victory would have been certain.

"And what happened to him?"

"Oh, he is still with the army of course; his regiment's enlistment is nearly up anyhow, and he'll go home and be forgotten in a few more weeks. Someone described it as the ill-judged observations of a volunteer without any professional skills."

"But Burnside?" Lincoln asked. "From what I heard the evidence is damning. Drawing straws, for heaven's sake, and then not personally following through to see that proper orders were followed?"

James nodded, sadly.

"An eccentric man."

"I don't need eccentric men in command," Lincoln said coldly. "I need fighting leaders if we are to finish this war."

"Please, sir, let me finish."

"Go ahead then."

"Eccentric, yes, but I think his plan was brilliant, and if properly followed, there would be a five-hundred-gun salute being fired tonight to celebrate the ending of this war. Richmond was in our grasp if Burnside's plan had been followed."

"But it wasn't."

"No, sir, it was not. I've seen it before with men who had been in one too many battles, sir. They get this strange look in their eyes, as if gazing off to some distant place others cannot see unless they themselves have endured the same nightmares. Too many scoff and say they are just cowards but they are not. They have seen one horror too many, seen one plan too many. So full of promise, they go astray for whatever reason, and then they just inwardly collapse. That is what happened to Burnside. When he was given that order to change the plan at the last second, he just inwardly collapsed, and then, without a leader, the battle went out of control."

"So, it is his fault."

"No, sir," James said and now his voice was cold. "Sir, I will make a recommendation, but before I do so, I want you to look at these."

He reached into his oversized haversack and drew out a bundle, sealed with waxed paper and bound tightly with a wrapping of twine. As he looked at it before handing it over, he thought it did look a bit absurd. He had compulsively spent an hour or more wrapping this package up, piling on the layers of wax paper to protect it from the elements, so that even if he should fall into the James River, the papers would remain untouched. He had showered greater care on it than on many of his drawings, the cords woven and tied in such a way that he could tell if someone had tried to tamper with them.

Lincoln looked at the heavy package dubiously, reached into his trouser pocket for a pen knife, pulled it out, and cut the cords. James watched a bit nervously as he carefully sliced open the side, reaching in and pulling out the sheaves of papers.

"What is this?"

"Sir, just take a few minutes to scan through them. They were handed to me by one of Burnside's staff, in fact the brother of that clerk in the next room. If he had not figured out who I was, I doubt if he ever would have entrusted them to me; he most certainly wanted them laid before you.

"They're primarily copies of records of orders and correspondence between Generals Meade and Burnside from just prior to the assault until the day after."

Lincoln picked up one sheet, a telegraph slip.

"No one is talking about it, but both generals refused to even stand together during the entire battle, remaining in separate bunkers just eight hundred yards apart, connected only by a telegraph wire. This is a record of what was being sent back and forth between them just before the battle and while it was under way."

Lincoln picked up a bundle of the telegraph sheets, which James had taken the time to sort out into proper sequence when possible and tied together separately. Lincoln cut the cord binding them together and began to read through them, one after another. After the fifth or sixth one, his features began to cloud.

From long ago James could remember that look. Many a case had come into his law office back in Springfield seeking counsel and, as a young lawyer hungry for business, Lincoln had taken on more than a few cases with little promise. But on occasion, while a potential client was pouring out his version of an event—making extravagant claims for compensation from whomever he wished to sue, which Lincoln would of course have had a fair share of upon winning—the prairie lawyer's face would darken. He would suddenly stand and, with voice strained, suggest that the man seek other representation. On the few times where words of defiance and even threats were fired back, his youthful reputation as the best wrestler in the county would all but come out, Lincoln stepping forward and making it clear that the man had but two choices as to how he would descend the flight of stairs to his office.

He saw that look now.

The President scanned a telegram, dropped it into a pile, went to the next one, and then, at times, went back and picked up a previous telegram to compare.

"Are you certain, James, that these are authentic?"

"Sir, some of them did get into the minutes of the court of inquiry, but some you are now reading did not. General Meade ordered the arrest of Burnside's telegraphers and confiscation of all records of communication. Several of Burnside's staff jotted down copies of these before the records were confiscated, and in turn, a copy was given to me."

"Could there have been more that you did not see?"

James shook his head.

"I can't promise on that one, sir. I was in and out of the headquarters for the first two hours or so of the battle until word was sent up that the colored troops were to go in. That's when I left the headquarters to go in with those men, so I overheard more than a few of these telegrams being discussed.

"I have no reason to believe Captain Vincent is deceiving me by passing along these records or has held some back because, as you can tell, more than a few do not cast his own superior in the best light. I've dealt with a lot of men during the years, sir, as you have. You can tell when a man is playing you square and when he is hiding an ace up his sleeve. I believe in what Captain Vincent gave me, but there might have been more that even he missed."

Lincoln continued to scan through the telegrams and then the various courier notes, orders, and counter orders.

"Tell me about the colored troops," Lincoln stated, even while continuing to look at the papers. "All reports are now saying they behaved poorly."

"That is a damn lie, sir," James snapped, embarrassed by his own flash of anger and heated response to his president.

Lincoln looked up at him with a bit of surprise.

"Calmly, James, calmly. You learn in court there are times to get excited and times to present your case softly; softness often carries more weight and truth."

"Sorry, sir." Unable to contain himself, James stood up and went to the window to look out over the park where the last of the guns had fired, the crowd still milling about. Some, seeing him in the window and hoping he was Abe, began to press toward the White House, held back by a cordon of guards, and shouted for a speech.

"Drop the curtain, come back, and sit next to me," Lincoln said quietly.

James did as ordered.

"Now tell me everything you observed."

The conversation went on for more than an hour: from first meeting Garland White and the men of the 28th at Arlington, observing them marching in to join the army before Petersburg, their enthusiastic and tireless weeks of training under the most relentless abuse; how at the end a veteran like Malady said it would be an honor to go in with them and die doing so. And from there to the final debacle and the madness within the crater.

It was a long talk, James emptying the silver coffee pot so often that he felt somewhat jittery by the end of it, heart racing.

"As for the overall battle itself, what did you see?"

As he spoke, James had opened his haversack and laid out the drawings, deliberately holding several back. The soundness of the initial plan for the tunnel and the soundness of Burnside's tactical and operational plan he went over in detail.

"If ever an opportunity for a war-ending battle was thrown away it was there, sir. It was thrown away on the morning the wrong load of explosives and fuses were delivered. If the original ten tons that Burnside had requested had been delivered, it would have torn a gap half again as big in the enemy line."

"And this report from Meade's staff that said it would have created vertical walls useless to our men?"

"That is precisely it," James retorted, voice a bit heated. "If the walls had been vertical and forty feet deep rather than as they were, would all those thousands of men have jumped in? Would they?"

Lincoln looked at him.

"Even without orders they would have fanned out to either flank to secure trenches that could have been used, creating a rupture in the enemy line a quarter mile wide, as Burnside had first planned, rather than a damn pit for thousands to just jump into and hide. I can't blame the veterans for doing that, after all they had been through . . ."

He paused.

"Especially after Cold Harbor and the bloody prior assaults, I can't blame them for wanting to go to ground, thinking that just seizing the next trench line was all they had to do. But, sir, just taking the trenches to either flank for a quarter mile, that alone would have placed Blandford Church Hill within easy artillery range and rendered the Jerusalem Plank Road all but useless. But that was not the final goal. It shows, nevertheless, the relentless series of mistakes and miscalculations," he hesitated again, "or outright willful obstruction of a plan that should have worked."

"And those final moments in the crater?" Lincoln asked, "when the black troops were sent in anyhow?"

"They went in like veterans; they did as much as was humanly possible. But by then, the Rebels had had four hours to draw a cordon and seal the perimeter off. It was futile, and they were slaughtered for no purpose."

Lincoln coughed a bit nervously.

"Is it true there were calls for no prisoners on both sides, and that in some cases our white troops murdered black troops within the crater?"

James could only nod.

Lincoln said nothing in reply, just leaned over, hands clasped, and wearily shook his head.

"You're holding something back," Lincoln finally said, motioning to one side of the table where James kept several drawings folded over.

"I'm not sure now, sir."

"Please, let me see them."

That was what he wanted to hear, and yet he questioned whether he should burden this man with even more. Then again, after all he had seen and endured, he wanted someone else to share this burden.

He pushed them over, and Lincoln opened the first one.

"Merciful God," he whispered.

"I call that one the *Depths of Hell,*" James whispered. "I went out with the stretcher bearers when a truce was finally called, thirty-six hours after the fighting ended."

He spat out the last words angrily. Thirty-six hours, when Burnside had wanted a truce that first evening, when hundreds still could have been saved, and the suffering of thousands of others alleviated . . . on both sides.

"That is what the crater looked like thirty-six hours after the battle, when General Meade finally allowed a truce so we could remove our wounded, the few that were left, and the dead."

Lincoln studied the drawing and then put it down, folding it over as if unable to bear gazing at it for another second.

The President finally motioned to the second drawing and opened it.

It was of Garland White cradling the wounded man pulled out of the crater, leg gone, stump swollen, Garland pressing a Bible into the wounded man's hands . . . but it was his eyes that James felt he had captured: hollow, wide-eyed, as if staring off into some distant void. Behind him, a line of dead was waiting to be borne away.

"I call that one the *Hundred Yard Stare*, sir."

"Why that?"

"It was only a hundred yards back to the safety of our lines, but for some, it was an eternity away. That man is a sergeant major I befriended; Garland White, a man of God, as much a minister as he is a damn good sergeant. His courage left me awed, but his compassion impressed me even more.

"I should add," and James was afraid his voice would break, "that a few minutes later a cry went up from the bottom of that hell pit that a wounded Rebel had been found still alive, and without hesitation Garland slid back down into that hole, stinking of death, to help. War is cruelty unimaginable, but it can also show a near Christlike compassion, and Garland White is one of those men."

James looked over sharply at Lincoln.

"Sir, he deserved better; he deserves better, this country owes him that."

Lincoln could only nod.

And, finally, the third one. It was two sketches on a single sheet of paper. To the left was a portrait of a young black soldier from the waist up, a dozen canteens strapped around his neck and shoulders, his face dripping with perspiration, eyes shut, and one could almost feel the paper trembling with the fear. Under it was printed "I ain't no coward, sir." The second was the boy lying dead at the lip of the crater, surrounded by a dozen or so others, all burdened down with canteens. It was titled *The Sacrifice for a Drop of Water.*

"I didn't see that myself, sir. One of the men, the coal miners with the 48th, described it to me, but valor like that was common that day. Apparently a watering party tried to break back to our lines to get water for the wounded. Of the twenty or so who set back out, maybe three or four made it back. Not one man would have condemned them if at that moment they had said they had done enough and stayed within the safety of our lines. Not a man would have condemned them. But all they could speak of was their comrades, their brothers, who needed water, and nearly all the rest died trying to get back to them.

"And, I say," and now his voice did choke, "may God damn to Hell any who ever dares to say they were cowards."

"Strong words, James, which I don't like hearing."

"Sorry, sir."

He lowered his head.

"So what do you think I should do?" Lincoln asked after several long minutes of silence, broken only by James's ragged breathing.

James looked over at him and stared straight into his eyes.

"Refuse to accept the court of inquiry. Demand a renewed investigation and make sure these papers," he pointed at the documents piled on the table, "are all entered into the record. Ensure that all the regimental commanders of the Fourth Division are given the chance to testify and be witnesses to the gallant behavior of their men."

He fell silent, Lincoln not replying.

"I will tell you one officer that you can count on for the truth, and that is Brigadier General William Bartlett. He lost a leg two years ago and then returned to service. He went in on the assault and commanded one of the brigades in the first division that went in."

"He was taken prisoner though? Is that why he did not testify?"

"Yes, because he refused to leave his men, and he couldn't move after his artificial leg was blown off. Think of that, sir: He lost a leg in the opening months of the war and then is taken prisoner because his leg, made of cork, is blown off in yet another battle."

James looked off, his own eyes filled with that "hundred yard stare," and shook his head.

"Surely an exchange could be arranged?" James asked, voice trembling. "For heaven's sake, why keep him a prisoner now?"

Lincoln nodded.

"We got a report that he is not doing well, having fallen ill, and that an exchange is being arranged even now. I promise to see to it personally. Rest assured, I will see to it personally."

"Put him on the stand, then. He'll tell the truth of it all."

Lincoln sighed and again there was silence. At last he stood up and went over to his desk. He picked up several newspapers and then returned to sit by James's side, passing the papers over.

"Look at the headlines of all of these . . ."

James did as requested, the bold type proclaiming: "Atlanta Is Ours!"; "Victory for Our Arms!"; "Sherman Triumphant!"; "End of War Now in Sight!"

Underneath were lurid details of the Rebels fleeing in panic, the city in flames, Atlanta, of course, fired by them before they ran, and the major rail junction of the South taken at last after a brutal campaign of over four months. The newspapers pronounced that the end of the war might be reached in weeks, and a pro-Republican paper already declared that this victory ensured the election of Lincoln and the utter rout of McClellan's party in the November elections.

Lincoln sat back on the sofa, stretching out his long legs, pant legs riding up to reveal his socks, which had slipped down around his bony ankles.

"Sherman succeeded where Meade failed," Lincoln finally said.

"Sir?"

"You can still hear the crowd out there, can't you?"

Lincoln fell silent and indeed James could hear their cheers, their chanting, snatches of songs, and now and then an occasional firework being lit off, bursting over the park in multicolored hues visible beyond the curtain.

"After word of Cold Harbor began to leak out, if I had gone out into that same park, I think they might have lynched me," he said with a cynical shake of his head. "Now they call for four more years, but has anything really changed?"

"Sir?"

"There will be a lot more suffering and dying before this tragedy is at an end, the worst of it perhaps still ahead. I pray never again, in centuries to come, that anything shall ever drive our country to such madness. If this suffering now is so seared into our souls that we recoil from ever repeating it, perhaps then it is worth the sacrifice of this generation to ensure that those who follow us make not the same mistake."

He gestured to the drawings.

"What are you saying, sir?" James asked.

There was a long moment of silence, of Lincoln just staring off. He sighed, forced a smile, and looked back at James.

"I will do nothing."

"Sir?"

And he could not keep the anger out of his voice.

"After all that? After such a chance thrown away?"

Lincoln nodded and leaned forward again, to his characteristic gesture of legs splayed wide, hands clasped.

"I've been thinking much of biblical verse of late," he said softly. "'Of woe unto thee that cometh with the sword,' and that perhaps each drop of blood drawn with a lash must somehow now be repaid with that sword.

"Perhaps in the end, it is all part of a greater plan. I can draw but two conclusions out of what you have shown me."

"And that is, sir?"

"I could take the political one and that will sound the more cynical of me, but yes, James, I must think politically. Let me take all of what you have shown me, go out to that jubilant crowd this evening—that crowd which sees an end to the war ahead now that Sherman has won such a victory at Atlanta. Let me then hold these documents up and demand another investigation into this tragedy. And what do you think would happen?"

James sighed and just nodded abjectly.

"Nothing, at best. At worst, it will give the opposition ammunition to negate Sherman's victory, divert opinion, drive more wedges, demand hearings, and yet more hearings, which will not change one iota the tragedy that you saw and endured.

"And perhaps even destroy what it was that these men died for, even if at this moment it seems like an act of futility."

James could not speak.

Lincoln put a hand on his shoulder.

"You know what I wish I could do, but, my friend, I cannot."

Lincoln sighed, his grasp on James's shoulder tightening.

"I must see this war through to a successful conclusion, no

matter what the cost. Too much has been sacrificed already. You were at Antietam; you saw the price paid and know as well as I do that it could have been ended that day. But McClellan lost his nerve; one man lost his nerve, while an entire army, in spite of their battering, was coiled to spring forward. The same at Gettysburg and now the same here."

He pointed to the drawings.

"And I find of late, I think of another side to it all."

"Which is what, sir?"

"Perhaps this must be endured, endured to such depths of sorrow that it is both atonement and a memory for generations yet to come. That in the end this war did not end by, as the soldiers call it, a *coup de main* or a 'forlorn hope.' Perhaps it means . . . what I suspect Sherman will do with torch in hand and Sheridan in the Valley—which he is preparing to do even now. And God forgive me if that is indeed something which will transpire, which I could somehow avoid. For, if that is the case, I shall surely answer for it. Perhaps, as to the cost of such a bloody conflict, not won easily by some sleight of hand, we need to frighten ourselves to forever change us. I do not want it ever to be whispered a generation later by some that they had been 'deceived into defeat,' and therefore teach their sons to try it again.

"No stab in the back, no 'next time we can do it.' I want both sides to finally lay down their arms and know that it will forever stand as the greatest tragedy in our history and now good men must strive together to ensure that it never happens again.

"Perhaps that is why this happened."

Though he did not fully agree, having felt and literally smelled and tasted the horror of it all, James could not offer a reply.

"But what of the men of the Fourth? It is a lie being told about them. Don't they deserve better?"

"Yes, they do," Lincoln sighed. "But I know no answer for the here and now. Perhaps, when the fighting stops and the hatred cools, all will see the folly of it. Two hundred thousand like them now serve and they at least, as Frederick Douglass has said, have shown to the world their right of citizenship and no one will ever dare to take it away from them.

"We all wish for change; I will be the first to admit that, but a short time past, I was willing to compromise their rights, their very souls, with a promise that slavery could continue so long as the Union stayed together. War brings changes that are unexpected, and that happened in my heart as well.

"We can never go back to what we were, ever again, but as for the future? You're telling me that some of these gallant men were shot in the back by their own comrades. That is as fearful as anything endured in the heat of battle. I pray that on the day the killing stops, we all look at each other and then ask God for forgiveness for all we have done.

"That is a shallow promise, James, but history, as we know, takes time; change takes time. It took more than four score years for us to come to the conclusion that when the Founders declared that all men are created equal, they did indeed mean all men."

He sighed again, and his voice was choked.

"I pray it takes less, far less time before we realize that, before God, we are all equal, that all should see that divine spark in the eyes of every man and honor them for that. If that comes to pass, please forgive me from quoting something I already said . . ."

He gestured to the drawing on the table.

"Then these dead shall not have died in vain."

He slowly stood, head bowed, and James rose.

"What's next for you, James?" Lincoln asked.

"I'm not sure."

"Back to the front?"

"I don't know. I want to say no, but I know it will finally draw me back until it is done. But for us, after this, I don't know how else I can serve you."

"I understand. But if you think you can, just bring that card to the gate as you always have."

James nodded.

He started for the door.

"Your drawings, James?"

James smiled and shook his head.

"Sir, there's not a one of them my publisher would ever touch.

Could you keep them, store them away some place? Maybe someday, if you see they are saved, someone will see them and understand the truth rather than the lies."

"You have my promise, James."

James stepped back and extended his hand.

"See you after the war ends, sir?"

"Yes, James, after the war I am certain we will meet again."

When the door closed, Abraham Lincoln picked up the drawings, sifting through them one by one. Alone, he allowed himself a luxury rarely seen by others—he wept.

Carefully, he bundled them up, putting them back into the waxed covering, along with the documents he knew would never be seen, at least while this war continued. He tied the shredded cord back in place, rose, and opened the door into Hay's office.

"I want these properly set aside in the archive."

"Sir?"

"You heard me."

"As your papers, sir?"

He hesitated.

"No, just general notes to be opened after I am gone."

Hay looked at him curiously, nodded, and said nothing. As the door closed he looked over at his assistant.

"Find some place to put these," he said.

ARLINGTON, VIRGINIA
SEPTEMBER 4, 1864
DAWN

✳✳✳✳✳✳✳✳✳✳✳✳✳✳✳✳✳✳✳✳✳✳✳✳✳

It was as he had last seen it: raining, a mist rising off the river, the burial details finishing out the graves, a line of ambulances rumbling across the bridge.

He had stumbled about the field for the last hour, ever since the first light of approaching dawn.

James was beyond exhaustion. He had gone to check in at Willard's after meeting with the President. He had taken the best room available, but he had skipped the bath and the buying of a change of clothes. Midnight was the deadline for this week's delivery of sketches to his publisher, and he had gone over to their Washington office. He turned the usual sketches in, the life of soldiers in the trenches playing cards, a grand review behind the lines, bedraggled Rebel prisoners being led to the rear. He had included several sketches of the court of inquiry with the absolutely clear understanding they were not to be released until after the official record was published.

He did share a couple of sketches of the digging of the mine, but his editor told him Frank Leslie had already beaten them to the punch on that, and Ward had turned in a magnificent drawing which had been featured as a two-page center spread the week before. It was old news now; too bad James didn't have something fresh from Atlanta. His editor strongly hinted that he could make something up and turn it in tomorrow, the usual stuff of a city burning and wrecked trains. He did however pay James five dollars extra for the mine drawings, which could be published in the back pages after the court of inquiry was made official.

They had gossiped a bit about the news. Burnside was indeed back in Rhode Island, supposedly on personal leave. All knew he would never return, Grant having already picked someone from outside the corps named Parker to command the Ninth. His editor said James stank like a dead hog, gave him a drink, and then actually offered him a good assignment, to go back to New York for a few weeks, get the war out of his system, perhaps turn in some drawings of political rallies. McClellan had already made it clear that he'd be delighted to sit for a portrait if *Harper's* would put it on their front page.

Reilly declined, took his pay in cash, drank five dollars of it back at Willard's, and then just went out. He just went walking, finally crossing the iron bridge over the Potomac to come here.

He had wandered in vain for the last hour; so much had changed since he was last here in June, just three short months ago. There were at least two thousand more graves, covering acres of ground.

Where his brother had been buried, he could no longer tell. The rains of summer had collapsed some graves. Some of the wooden planks that marked each grave had fallen over; some good soul apparently had tried to replace them, but doubtless the next storm would knock them over again. In many places it was just the sunken, muddy ground that marked where a body, or bodies, had moldered during the summer of this third year of war.

The gravediggers were more colored troops, men finishing their tasks and rising up out of the holes dug overnight, giving James a frightful chill as he remembered the bodies being hauled up out of the crater. Some were grumbling, and he wanted to go over and grab hold of them, scream that for heaven's sake they should thank God this was all that this war demanded of them. But, like all fresh fish that had yet to see the elephant, they would not have listened.

The ambulances drew closer, circled around, and stopped. The daily ritual was repeated. Bodies were pulled out, men who had died in the city hospitals during the night, now to be interred in a rain-soaked ceremony.

He drew back and stood to one side, saying nothing, head lowered. The first of the wagons set off, then the next. He heard the distant words of a minister, a ragged volley, then the sound of men shoveling the earth back in.

"Mr. Reilly?"

Startled, he looked up. Standing before him was Garland White.

Speechless, he could only stand there. Garland finally stepped forward and grasped his hand; a second later the two embraced and more than a few men, white and black, looked over at them with surprise, several muttering comments.

"What are you doing here?" both exclaimed and there were shy laughs in reply.

"You first, sir."

"Damn it, Garland, it is James. After all we been through together, it is James; it will be James forever with you."

"All right then, James. You first. Last I saw of you was the day after the crater," he paused, his eyes glazing over with that strange long-distant look, "out there at night."

James nodded.

"I went back to cover the court of inquiry."

Garland snorted with disdain but said nothing.

"Yes, my feelings as well" was all James could say.

"But here?"

"Came up to turn in my drawings, and," he hesitated, "to see an old friend and tell him about all that had happened."

Garland nodded sagely.

"Did he believe you?"

"Yes, he did. And I think it is all right to say he believed what you and your comrades did as well."

Garland looked at him quizzically but did not ask further.

"Heard a couple of rumors about who your friend is."

"What?"

Garland smiled.

"After it was all over. One of my men was an orderly for an aide to General Burnside after the battle; overheard a conversation or two."

He chuckled.

"Remember I once told you it is all rather amazing how often we, just standing in the corner, know far more than so many others realize."

James did not react, and Garland clapped him on the shoulder.

"Thank you, my friend."

James, with so many years of practice, did not react, even now before his friend.

"Why here, at this hour?" Garland pressed.

James gestured back to the acres of graves.

"I thought I might find my brother."

Garland sighed.

"I am so sorry, James. We did not have time that day. Perhaps we can try and find him now and make arrangements."

James suddenly felt tears welling up and could only nod in reply.

"Why are you here, though?"

"Two things. I was given a furlough to accompany some of our wounded back to a hospital for colored soldiers established here in

Washington. One of our boys died during the night, so of course I had to accompany him out here to see that all was fittingly done."

"So, at least we bury our dead side by side," James whispered.

"Yes, at least that is how it is done here."

"A good start."

"I think so."

"And what else?"

Garland tried to smile but the gesture was awkward.

"I was informed that I have to appear before a board. Apparently someone has decided to commission some colored officers."

"And you were nominated?" James asked, and now there was actually some delight in his voice.

Garland nodded shyly.

"Only as ministers for colored regiments; rank of major, but it is another step."

"I know you will make it, Garland. By God, if anyone can, it will be you."

"Thank you for that, James."

"I do have a few friends I could put a word in with . . ." James offered spontaneously.

Garland smiled but shook his head.

"Rather make it on my own merits, no matter who it is you know."

"You are naïve."

"Sometimes that's a blessing."

Garland took James by the elbow. The burial detail was finishing up its duty, the honor guard having already marched off through the mud.

"Let's see if we can find him."

The hour-long search proved to be a fruitless one. So much had changed in just a few months. Thousands of graves, the once immaculate lawn cut over, rutted, a sea of mud, fresher graves still mounded, older ones sunken in, the mud having run off in rivers from the driving summer rains.

The dead had not been buried by regiments, only by date of death. Though they found some plaques from around the time that

James's brother had died, it was impossible to pinpoint, out of a dozen or so in one line, exactly which one was his, shared with another comrade.

"I am so sorry, James," Garland whispered. "It bothered me deeply after we left for the front. I promised myself that someday I would come back here with some of the boys and set it right for you."

James could only shake his head.

"At least he's here."

Garland looked over at him as James's gaze swept across the lower field of Arlington.

"This will always be sacred ground. He sleeps with comrades, whether he has his own marker stone or not. I don't think it matters to him now. He is here, where he belongs, with comrades who understand what each other endured."

James did something that was now rare for him; he went down on his knees. He lowered his head, offered a Hail Mary for the repose of his brother, made the sign of the cross, and looked back up at Garland, who, with head bowed, had silently prayed alongside him and now helped him to stand back up.

He reached into his haversack and took out one drawing that he had purposely saved, with the hope of one day seeing his friend again.

"This is for you, Garland."

The sergeant major, soon to be a commissioned major, the first of eleven African American officers in the history of the United States Army, unfolded the sketch. It was of Garland, sitting by a campfire, comrades, many of them gone, perhaps some of them buried here, gathered around him.

"Thank you, my friend," Garland whispered. "My brother."

AFTERWORD

The USCT, the United States Colored Troops, were nearly two hundred regiments strong by the end of the war in the spring of 1865.

Troops of African descent had served in the Union cause as early as 1862, mobilizing in Louisiana, along the coast of South Carolina, and as far west as Kansas. The most famed of these early regiments, the 54th Massachusetts, immortalized in the movie *Glory*, saw combat service, but it was not until after the issuance of the Emancipation Proclamation, effective January 1, 1863, that the federal government undertook an active role in recruiting men of color to serve in the Union cause.

The effort could not have come a moment too soon. While, in the first eighteen months of the war, hundreds of thousands had flocked to volunteer, the relentlessly numbing casualty rolls appearing each day in newspapers across the North had stilled this early enthusiasm, and by late 1863, bounty payments of upward of a thousand dollars, the equal of nearly a hundred thousand dollars today, often failed to draw reliable recruits.

Compounding this was the fact that nearly all the regiments which had volunteered with such enthusiasm in 1861 had signed on for only three years of service, and by the middle of the summer of 1864, as their terms of enlistment ended, it was becoming increasingly evident that the armies in the field might very well collapse for lack of troops.

In addition, political will for this protracted and apparently endless war was waning in the North. If a modern Gallup Poll service had been around in that year, it might very well have found as few as one in three, or even one in four, in the North who still wished to see the fight pressed through to final and complete victory, thereby dooming the continent to more wars to come as both sides squabbled over what was to be done with territories to the west and even in other lands such as Mexico and Cuba.

It was at this exact moment that African Americans were at last given the chance to flock to the colors and join the cause. Contrary to popular myth, the vast majority of these men, at least in the early regiments recruited in late 1863 through early 1864, were not runaway slaves or "contraband," but instead were overwhelmingly freemen of color living in the North, many of them having lived there for generations, more than a few well educated. It is one of the few myths of the remarkable film *Glory* that nearly all the men of the 54th were "contraband," runaway slaves. Many of that famed regiment could trace lineages back to ancestors who had fought in the war of 1812 and even the War of Independence.

The story of Garland White is based on fact, and his story is intricately tied to the 28th USCT, recruited out of Indiana. He was indeed a slave of Senator Toombs of Georgia, who later briefly served as the Confederate Secretary of State and then as a general in the Confederate army. Doing what Frederick Douglass would have half jokingly described as "stealing himself," White left the "employment" of Toombs in Washington, D.C., and fled to Canada. If you study the still existing letters of Garland White, you will observe a remarkable transition in a period of but a few years from a man who could barely print and articulate a clear sentence to one writing with the classical flourish of an educated Victorian gentleman, and who penned letters of great eloquence, exhorting the governors of various states to begin the mobilization of their black citizens, if they could be called such, for the war effort.

Garland worked aggressively to recruit men for the 54th and

55th Massachusetts and was even offered the position of sergeant major with one of those regiments. He felt, however, a calling elsewhere, and focused his attention on the Midwest.

On December 24, 1863, Garland White was present at a black church in Indianapolis to begin the enrollment of men for the 28th USCT. By his side was one Doctor Revel, whose brother after the war would be a congressman representing North Carolina.

There is a terrible irony, worth considering even today, about the enlistment of this regiment. Every man who joined, and thereby helped Indiana to reach its quota of new recruits, was technically an illegal alien in that state. Although by the chartering of the Northwest Ordinance upon the creation of our Republic, this country forbade slavery in what would become Ohio, Indiana, Illinois, and other states, nothing was said of the nature of full citizenship. Blacks were forbidden to settle there, own property, attend public schools, sit on juries, vote, or even hold a public library card. And yet, nevertheless, the black men rallied, Garland promising them that by so doing they would affirm their rights of citizenship and return to a state grateful for their service.

When the regiment deployed out of Indianapolis, late in April 1864, Governor Morton formally reviewed the troops, his action seen by all as a significant symbolic gesture.

As described, the 28th did serve as gravediggers at Arlington, and were finally incorporated into the Fourth Division of the Ninth Corps, sustaining fearful casualties at the Battle of the Crater.

After the Crater, the division was held back from the front line for several months, though it did participate in limited actions along the western edge of the Petersburg front later that fall. When a corps made up solely of black troops was finally created, the two brigades of the Fourth Division were transferred to this new formation and positioned along the siege lines in front of Richmond.

During the night of April 2–3, 1865, troops in the trenches before Richmond saw fires glowing in the city and were finally ordered to go forward. What ensued was a remarkable footrace, as dozens of regiments, black and white, dashed ahead to claim that they were the first to enter the Rebel capital, which was being abandoned when, after more than nine months of deadly siege after the Battle of the Crater, Grant finally broke Lee's hold on Petersburg.

Nearly every one of those regiments tried to lay some claim to being the "first into Richmond," and perhaps history should award that title to all of them, for they were indeed there at the ending of the great siege.

What unfolded next is truly the stuff of novels and not just dry history. Garland described the utter jubilation of thousands of liberated slaves, pouring out to greet men of the "sable arm," pouring in disciplined ranks through the streets of the city. He wrote how, in all that confusion, he heard a familiar voice crying out his name and, turning, he saw his mother. His former master had brought her to Richmond as a house servant and, recognizing her beloved son in that surging column of troops, she pressed her way through the jubilant crowds to fling herself into his arms, a reunion after more than a decade of separation.

But the war was not yet over for Garland and the 28th; the actions of an emperor in France now kept them in service.

While our Civil War raged, Emperor Napoleon III launched a mad scheme to conquer Mexico as part of a French, Austrian, and Spanish alliance, and for a very brief time, with the connivance of England as well. Napoleon put an Austrian Hapsburg on the throne, the tragic Maximilian, who declared himself to be emperor of Mexico, backed up by the bayonets of the French Foreign Legion, Austrian, and even Belgian, troops.

With our fratricidal conflict at an end, it was clearly evident that the Monroe Doctrine would be back in play, and President Johnson ordered the deployment of over fifty thousand federal troops to the Texas border with Mexico. Yet while nearly all the volunteer regiments of white troops had signed on for durations of three years or "until the suppression of the rebellion," that was not so with the USCT. Consequently, the corps of over thirty thousand black troops, who had signed a slightly different contract, found that less than two months after the victory in Virginia they were on ships bound for Texas, led by General Phil Sheridan in a show of force, with the implied threat that unless the emperor of France backed off, our army, well seasoned in battle, would invade.

What they endured was six months of hell. Fresh water was so scarce that watering ships had to sail clear to the mouth of the Mississippi, there to fill up with "fresh" water flowing past New Orleans and into the Gulf of Mexico, to be rationed out in the Texas heat at little more than a quart or two a day. Scurvy was rampant and more men of the 28th USCT would die of disease or be debilitated by scurvy than those who were felled by combat at the Crater.

At home, the war was over, and Texas was now a forgotten front.

Finally, during the winter of 1865–66, the crisis defused; Napoleon III cut his losses, leaving Maximilian to dangle, and finally to be pulled down by Mexican freedom fighters led by Benito Juarez. Gradually the American troops on the Texas frontier were demobilized and sent home. It is interesting to note that more than a few black soldiers, upon being allowed to resign from the ranks while still in Texas, crossed the border to be offered commissions as officers with Juarez and gain distinction in that fight for freedom as well.

The survivors of the 28th, with Major Garland White helping to lead them, returned to Indianapolis early in 1866 and were demobilized.

The laws that they had endured prior to the war nevertheless greeted them upon their return, and it was not until the ratification of the Fourteenth and Fifteenth Amendments that some semblance of full rights were at last granted.

Pension records for some of the 28th can be found in the National Archives, dating well into the late 1920s. One man ventured as far as England to serve as a steward on a channel steamer; another became an "Exoduster," part of a movement of blacks to settle in Kansas claiming their "forty acres and a mule." Most settled back into life around the Indianapolis area, raising families, some well respected by friends and neighbors who realized all that they had given for their country.

As for Garland White? He crops up in a newspaper report out of

Toledo, Ohio, leading a fight to integrate the schools there. His efforts, sadly, failed.

The last record the authors can find of him dates from the mid-1890s. Impoverished, ill, and crippled from his years of service in the field and the lifelong effects of scurvy contracted in Texas, White, in the final entry in his pension records requested a meager increase of several dollars a month to help him in his final years with his medical bills. There is no further entry after that, though usually the pension records bear a stamped mark when the recipient is deceased. His date of death and final resting place remain a mystery.

If any who read this should know of Garland White's final resting place, the authors of this work would be deeply indebted, for surely his final resting place should be properly honored. We should all be indebted to men like him, the forgotten men of the Fourth Division of the Ninth Corps of the Army of the Potomac, who, on a terrible day in July 1864, did indeed offer up the "last full measure of devotion."

DURING THE AMERICAN CIVIL WAR 179,000 AFRICAN AMERIcans answered the call and served with the Union Army.

Over 4,000 United States Colored Troops participated in the Battle of the Crater on July 30, 1864. This number represents one of the largest concentrations of black soldiers on any field of battle during the American Civil War. Of that number 1,327 were killed, wounded, missing, or captured in the fighting.

Today as we approach the 150th anniversary of the battle, there is still no formal recognition of the role played by these soldiers in that fight.

Petersburg National Battlefield and American Enterprise Institute/ Newt.org are working together to memorialize and tell the story of the black soldiers during that chapter of the Siege of Petersburg.

To learn more about the United States Colored Troops during the Siege of Petersburg visit www.nps.gov/pete.